SONGBIRD

. Also by Josephine Cox

QUEENIE'S STORY
Her Father's Sins
Let Loose the Tigers

THE EMMA GRADY TRILOGY
Outcast
Alley Urchin
Vagabonds

Angels Cry Sometimes
Take This Woman
Whistledown Woman
Don't Cry Alone
Jessica's Girl
Nobody's Darling
Born to Serve
More than Riches
A Little Badness
Living a Lie
The Devil You Know
A Time for Us
Cradle of Thorns
Miss You Forever
Love Me or Leave Me
Tomorrow the World
The Gilded Cage
Somewhere, Someday
Rainbow Days
Looking Back
Let It Shine

The Woman Who Left
Jinnie

Bad Boy Jack
The Beachcomber
Lovers and Liars
Live the Dream

The Journey
Journey's End
The Loner

JOSEPHINE COX

~

Songbird

HarperCollins*Publishers*

HarperCollins*Publishers*

HarperCollins*Publishers*
77–85 Fulham Palace Road,
Hammersmith, London W6 8JB

www.harpercollins.co.uk

Published by HarperCollins*Publishers* 2008
1

A catalogue record for this book
is available from the British Library

ISBN: 978-0-00-722114-1

Set in New Baskerville by Palimpsest Book Production Limited,
Grangemouth, Stirlingshire

Printed and bound in Great Britain by
Clays Ltd, St Ives plc

This book is for my Ken, as always

Huge love and acknowledgement to Chloe and Milly.
Two very special little girls.

~

Also to our two fine sons,
Spencer and Wayne,
And Jane.

Thank you all, for the joy you give me.

CONTENTS

PART ONE
Bedford Town, 1996
A Caged Bird
1

~

PART TWO
London, 1978
In the Beginning
27

~

PART THREE
Blackpool, 1978
Lighter Hearts
145

~

PART FOUR
Bedfordshire, 1979
Hideaway
245

~

PART FIVE
Bedford Town, 1996
Sacrifices
341

~

PART ONE

~

Bedford Town, 1996

A Caged Bird

CHAPTER ONE

SOMETIMES, SHE COULD make herself believe that the bad things had never happened. And then there were the other times, when she could feel his breath against her face and his hands around her neck, squeezing, choking the life out of her. She could see the loathing in his eyes as the darkness enveloped her.

It was Alice – her dearest friend – who had saved her from the dark. Because of that fine, brave woman, her own life had been spared, albeit at a terrible cost.

Through the years that followed, the horror of that night had never left her. She remained ever-vigilant. The darkness kept her prisoner, and the daylight was her enemy. And on the rare occasions when she must go out during the daytime, with every step she was looking over her shoulder, anxious to get back and lock herself inside the house alone with her fears.

It was a lonely, forsaken existence. Her treasured collection of records and tapes, and the music she heard on the TV and radio, were her only consolation.

For Madeleine Delaney, once known as 'The Songbird', music was her life.

The beauty of nature also gave her immense pleasure. Come the dawn she would hear the birds welcome a new day, and when the sun lit the skies, she would sit at her open window and feel the gentle breeze on her face – until a passing stranger glanced up from the road outside and frightened her away.

In her isolation, Maddy had come to love the seasons like never before. Winter had its own special beauty, with snow-covered trees and laden boughs that hung their heads as though in shame. Her heart sang with the first appearance of the tiny robin redbreast that hopped about her front yard and peeped up at her with bright beady eyes. Below her window, the children threw snowballs in the street, laughing and screeching, wrapped in coats and scarves, oblivious to the driving chill of a winter's day.

Lighter of heart, she would sit and watch and imagine she was down there with them, a child again, with not a care in the world.

Inevitably, the same old question would burn its way into her brain: *How did you end up alone and unwanted like this, trapped in a self-imposed prison in a rundown house here in the town of Bedford, so very far from your roots?*

The answer was simple: she had fallen in love with the wrong man, and from the moment she met him, her hitherto contented life began to unravel.

Sometimes, she wondered if she would ever find the courage to venture out, live life to the full again, and face the consequences, whatever they might be. Oh, how wonderful, to love and to laugh – and not be afraid any more.

Many times she had promised herself she could do it, but seventeen years had come and gone, and now she felt more lonely than she could ever have imagined.

Yet in a strange kind of way, she felt safe in her solitude, because if she kept herself to herself, she could never be hurt again. *Not like before.*

'Who's that?' Curious at the sound of laughter from the street outside, she went across the room and peered out, hiding herself behind the curtain. A group of young people came jostling down the pavement, laughing and joking, full of life. She counted six of them; three boys and three girls. They were the students who lived next door. She had seen some of them come and go before.

Her attention was drawn to one particular young woman dressed in skin-tight jeans and a Levi's denim jacket. Elfin-like, with a cap of fair hair, she had an appealing smile, and when she laughed, it seemed to come from the heart.

Shifting the curtain to get a clearer look at this happy young thing, Maddy was shocked when suddenly, one of the boys said something and they all looked up. The fair-haired girl smiled right at her.

In the blink of an eye, something passed between the two of them; and Maddy felt a strong sense of kinship with her.

Maddy immediately dropped the curtain and backed away as the friends ran up the steps to the shabby student house next door.

The fair-haired girl was the last to go in. Lingering on the step she turned her head to glance back up at Maddy again, but seeing how the timid woman had disappeared, she went skipping up the step to join her pals, unaware of the trauma she had caused.

That was *me* once upon a time, Maddy mused. Young and pretty, full of confidence – with loyal friends and a song in my heart. She paused to remember. Oh, but we had such good times then, sharing our hopes for the future, our impossible dreams. She gave a half-smile, which lit up her sad face. Not a day went by when we didn't laugh out loud.

But those days and those people were long gone now. Her heart thickened with nostalgia as she thought, I don't suppose I will ever see any of them again.'

When she had started performing at the Soho cabaret club, all those years ago, she had fallen deeply in love with its owner, and her friends had drifted away, but not Alice. Alice was special

– always there, always watching over her, like the mother Maddy had lost in her teens. How terrible, then, that on that fateful night, darling Alice had paid the ultimate price for befriending her.

'May God forgive me,' Maddy murmured aloud, the tears threatening to fall. 'Why couldn't I see his badness? How could I have been so blind!'

But it was poor Alice who haunted her waking hours and tortured her sleep. Alice . . . *'Dear Alice.'* Her heart hardened. 'So many times you tried to warn me,' Maddy told the empty room, 'and I never listened.' A deep shivering sigh marbled her words. 'I know you forgave me, but as long as I live, I can never forgive myself.'

Closing her eyes, she thought of the lovers she had known before she met Steve – good and honest young men who had cherished her and wanted the best for her. And then she had become infatuated with that cruel, merciless man, who had used her and abused her for his own ends.

If it hadn't been for *him*, she might have found fame and fortune, travelled the world and made a decent life for herself. And through it all, Alice would have been right beside her.

That man had taken her confidence and her hopes, and left her in a dark place where there was no laughter, no love. She had fought him – and lost. Now, there was no fight left in her.

Like a wounded animal, she hid away, licking her wounds, afraid of the future and what it might bring.

Weary to her soul, Maddy went to the dresser and picked up the tiny mirror there, shocked by the image that looked back at her. Her long dark hair was carelessly scraped back with a rubber band. Her face was pale and dog-tired, and void of make-up: no lipstick to shape and warm the generous lips; no shadow to accentuate her once-sparkling dark eyes. 'I look like an old woman,' she sighed. 'I never realised there was so much grey in my hair.'

Desolate, she returned to sit in the chair. Through the bedroom wall, she could hear the low murmurings of conversation from next door. Maddy didn't mind the noise, or the occasional bursts of loud music. It was comforting to know that outside these walls, life still went on – for others if not for her.

She wondered about that pretty young girl and her friendly smile. Did she have a devoted family – a lover? A plan of sorts for the future? Maddy hoped so.

Most of all, she hoped that the young woman would be wise enough to avoid making the same mistakes that she herself had made . . .

CHAPTER TWO

UNAWARE THAT THEIR next-door neighbour had been so affected by their arrival, the students settled down to enjoy their supper, bought from the chippie on the corner. Dave Wright, who was studying Physics, called their attention to the new member of staff at the college. 'Hey, that new Maths lecturer is a bit of all right! Do you agree, lads?' With an appreciative eye for the women, Dave was a real Jack the Lad. 'Wouldn't mind a bit of private tuition from *her*.' He gave a long, exaggerated sigh.

'Behave yourself!' Betsy was the elfin-like creature with a soft heart and big smile. Thrusting his bag of saveloy, chips and two pickled onions into his hands, she asked, 'What on earth would Poppy say if she heard you talking like that?' Poppy was a Geography student at the college; she was also Dave's current girlfriend.

Taking a large bite out of his saveloy, Dave threw himself into the nearest armchair and mumbled, 'What she doesn't know won't hurt her.'

'Honestly, Dave, I don't know why you say those things, because you know you would never cheat on her.'

Dave nodded and grinned. 'You're right. By the way, have you got any tomato ketchup?'

'You're a prat, sticking to one woman. Play the field, that's what I say.' Hard-headed and self-opinionated, Darren Brown was a frequent visitor to the house. With his selfish manner and constant bickering, however, he was not always whole-heartedly welcomed.

'Treat 'em mean and keep 'em keen,' he went on, stabbing at the batter on his cod. 'There's hundreds of 'em out there, all gagging for it.' Good-looking and proud of it, Darren was never short of female company.

Used as she was to his callous remarks, Betsy now took stock of him. 'And what about Ruth?' she asked. 'I thought you said you two might get married after college? That's what *she* thinks, anyway.'

Darren waved a chip in the air in a dismissive gesture. 'They were just words . . . they meant nothing. Ruth is a passing fancy, that's all.'

'You don't deserve to have a decent girlfriend,' she told him bluntly. 'If Ruth knew what you were really like, she'd run a mile.'

All the same, Betsy could see how the girls might be drawn to Darren. Tall, with well-honed muscles and wild dark hair, he had an easy way with him, and when he turned those broody brown eyes on the girls, they simply fell at his feet. 'One of these days you'll come unstuck,' she warned him. 'I can see it coming a mile off.'

He shrugged. 'Sounds to me like you're jealous.'

At this, she burst out laughing. 'Huh! You should be so lucky.'

'Never mind the new Maths lecturer – you can give *me* tuition any time you like, Daz.' That was Abigail the dreamer, whose room they were in. Scatter-brained and vulnerable, she could see no harm in him.

'Sorry, sweetheart, you're not my type.' Sharp and to the point, he did not mince his words.

'So, who *is* your type?' That was Judith; hard-nosed and

ambitious, she had met Abigail in college and invited herself to the house on many occasions. Also, she had long fancied a relationship with Darren; though as yet he had not made a move.

'Well now, let me see.' Thrusting a chip into his mouth, the arrogant young man chewed and talked at the same time. 'Long shapely legs, big firm boobs and a small enough mind not to ask any questions. Oh, and she mustn't worry about being dumped the day after the night before, if you know what I mean?'

'Big boobs and a small mind, eh?' Judith gave a groan. 'That lets me out then.'

Darren surveyed her slim, boyish figure. 'Oh, I'm sure I could fit you in if you really wanted.'

'Are your fish cakes and chips all right, Rob?' Betsy turned her attention to the only one of them who had not joined in the banter. 'If they're cold, I can put them in the microwave to warm them up.'

'Thanks all the same, Betsy, but they're fine. Besides, I was that hungry I'd have eaten a scabby dog!' Not exceptionally good-looking like Daz, or the life and soul of any party like his best friend Dave, Robin was both studious and likeable. In his early twenties, he was a young man going places; studying medicine and working in a big London hospital. This evening, he had driven over in his elderly car to see Dave, whom he had known since their schooldays. From boyhood, nothing had swerved him from his goal to become a doctor, though his father was bitterly disappointed that his only son was not going to follow him into the established family business.

'Right then.' Scrambling out of his chair, Darren strode across the room to sort through the records. 'Jude, how about opening another bottle of wine and I'll put some good tunes on. There's a Smiths' LP in here somewhere, isn't there?'

Judith objected. 'Oh God, Morrissey is *so* depressing. Let's listen to the Police instead. Oh, and that reminds me. Susie borrowed my Alanis Morissette tape. I'll have to get it back before she lends it on, like she did with my Madonna one.'

'Hey! Don't start taking over,' Robin joked. 'Unless you fancy paying Abigail's rent between the two of you?'

'I wouldn't mind paying rent if I could live here,' Judith retaliated. 'It's got to be better than living in hall.'

'I second that!' Daz declared, lighting a roll-up. 'I can't see why you lot won't let us share with you. When all's said and done, there are four bedsits in this house. I could double up with you, Dave, and Judith could double up with one of you girls.'

'Not a snowdrop's chance in hell, mate.' In a light-hearted way, Dave made his feelings known. 'I'm not doubling up with anybody. I left four brothers behind at home, and I've got my own room at long last. And I am *not* giving it up for love nor money.'

Betsy and Abigail were of the same mind. 'At the moment, we can chuck you out when we've had enough of you,' they joked.

'Yeah,' Dave said, laughingly addressing himself to Darren. 'Gawd help us if we had to get up each morning and see your ugly mug.'

In no time at all, the Police were belting out their best, followed by some vintage Stones, and for a while, the friends drank the wine and chatted and smoked – until Darren decided to leap onto a chair and give a performance of his own, playing air guitar and screeching at the top of his voice along to 'Black Sugar'.

'Put a sock in it,' Dave begged him. 'You'll have all the cats round.'

Abigail threw a cushion at him and Robin threatened to douse him with cold water. But nothing stopped him, until Betsy pulled the plug from the wall.

'Party poopers!' Climbing down from the chair, Daz went storming off into the kitchen in search of more booze.

'Does anybody mind if *I* choose the next record?' That was Betsy.

'*I* mind!' Daz returned to his seat empty-handed. 'I'm not in the mood for listening to one of your soppy love-songs.'

'Too bad,' she told him, 'because whether you like it or not, we're *all* having a turn at choosing.'

She picked out a Nat King Cole ballad, 'When I Fall In love', and it came as no surprise when Darren immediately protested, 'Bloody hell! Do we have to listen to *that* rubbish?'

'Shut up, misery.' Judith was rapidly going off him. She gave him a shove. 'If that's what Betsy wants, that's fine by the rest of us, and if you don't like it, you can go home, you awkward sod.'

Folding his arms, Darren slouched deeper into his chair and pointedly started doing the crossword in the local free paper.

As the smooth silky tones of Nat King Cole flowed through the room, the girls sang along.

Unaware that Robin was watching her with fond eyes, Betsy let the song wash over her. She loved Nat King Cole's sensuous voice, and the words were so beautiful. Abigail had bought her the *Greatest Hits* CD last Christmas, and it was one of Betsy's prized possessions.

It was when Judith stopped singing to cadge a cigarette from Darren, that Betsy thought she heard something. 'Ssh!' Sitting bolt upright in her chair, she called for silence, and when everyone was attentive she said, 'Listen – can you hear that?'

Against all his instincts, Darren found himself listening too, 'Hey! There *is* somebody else singing . . .' He looked suspiciously from one to another. 'Come on . . . what are you lot playing at?'

The rich contralto voice of a woman sailed through the wall, as she sang the song again, to herself. Even muffled, like this, the voice was hauntingly beautiful.

'Who on earth *is* that?' Robin asked into the hush.

Dave voiced all their thoughts. 'It seems to be coming from next door,' he said.

Judith laughed, breaking the spell. 'What! You can't mean that strange old woman up at her window.'

'Never!' Darren was adamant. 'I should think the best she could manage would be a croak. She gives me the heebie-jeebies, she does, spying on us from behind her net curtains, and creeping about in the dark.' He gave an exaggerated shiver. 'There's something dead weird about her. The Shadow-Thing . . .' With an evil grin, he made moving gestures with the tips of his fingers.

Even Abigail had to agree. 'She is a bit frightening. I've never seen her out in daylight, yet as soon as it's dark she goes scurrying down the street, hiding in the corners like a little hobbit.'

Darren gave a snort of disgust. 'If you ask me, she's not all there. I reckon somebody should put her out of her misery.'

'You're a callous bastard,' Robin reprimanded him. 'The poor woman's obviously ill.'

'There you go then,' Daz insisted. 'Like I said . . . Loopy Lou! They should put her in a home, for all our sakes.'

'Ssh!' Betsy was still listening; the woman's voice was pure and powerful. 'It's *her*, I'm sure of it. It can't be anybody else.'

Judith was cynical. 'How could such a beautiful voice belong to such a strange-looking creature?'

Suddenly the singing came to an end and the silence was thick.

'I was in the paper-shop the other day,' Dave told them all, 'and she came in after me for some batteries and a box of matches. When she spoke to Mr Hassan, the shopkeeper, her voice was so low it was almost inaudible.' He shrugged, bemused. 'She seemed very nervous and a bit dithery. When she came rushing by me, she dropped her box of matches. Of course I stooped to pick it up.'

He could see her now. 'She seemed such a sorry little thing, all depressed-looking and dishevelled. But in that split second when she grabbed the matches from me, she looked up.' His voice sank to a whisper, as though talking to himself. 'She had the most *amazing* eyes . . . chestnut-brown they were, and yet against the paleness of her skin they seemed dark as night. It was strange. Even after she'd gone I couldn't get her out of my mind.'

He added thoughtfully, 'I swear, I've never seen anyone look so frightened.'

'Ooh, Dave!' Grinning spitefully, Darren sat bolt upright. 'You're done for now! She probably thought you were onto her. You'd best be careful, mate. Sounds to me like she's bewitched you already.'

'Oh, do shut up!' Like everyone else, Abigail had long been curious about the old woman, but she had no time for Darren's silliness. 'I can't help feeling sorry for her. I mean, what went wrong in her life, do you think?' She looked around at her friends. 'What could have happened to make her like she is, so terrified of people, and so paranoid about going out in daylight?'

For a while, they discussed their neighbour, until Robin suddenly remembered he had promised to call his father. 'I'd best get down to the phone in the hall and give my dad a quick ring.'

'Make him wait, why don't you?' Having fallen out with his own family long ago, Darren bitterly resented those who stayed together. 'He's always giving you grief over wanting to be a doctor, instead of going into his poxy veterinary business. He made his choice and it's time he let you make yours. For Chrissake, Rob! When will you stop running after him, like some frightened little kid!'

In the ensuing silence, all eyes were on Robin. A quiet guy, he was not easily roused into temper. But Darren's words were harsh, and the tension almost palpable.

Getting up, his face set like stone, Rob crossed to where Darren lay slouched in an armchair. 'You'd best explain what you meant by that,' he said, his voice low and trembling.

Shocked to see the dark anger in Rob's face, and like the coward he was, Darren swiftly withdrew his comment. 'I didn't mean anything,' he replied curtly. 'All I'm saying is, families aren't what they're cracked up to be. Look at me!' He held out his arms triumphantly. 'I had the good sense to dump my family long ago, and now I'm much better off without them.'

'Really?' Robin regarded him with contempt. 'Well, thankfully, you and I are very different. I would *never* turn my back on family. You see, the only family I have now is my father, and whatever the differences between us, I have no intention of ever dumping him. In fact, I love and respect him. Never a day goes by when I don't thank my lucky stars that he's around.'

His cold gaze was unswerving, 'So tell me, Darren, do you have a problem with that?'

The other boy shook his head. 'None whatsoever.'

'So, will we ever have this conversation again?'

'Not as far as I'm concerned, no.' Shaken by this unexpected confrontation, Darren the bully wanted the incident ended. 'You and your dad are none of my concern.'

'Glad to hear it. So now – if it's all right with you – I'll be about my business.'

Robin was almost out of the door when Betsy grabbed her denim jacket and went after him. 'I'll come with you,' she said. 'I could do with a change of scene myself.' Like the others, she had been appalled by Darren's spiteful remarks.

As always, Robin saw Betsy as a true friend. 'I'd like that, yes. Let's go down to the callbox on the corner. Get a breath of air.'

When the front door was shut behind them Betsy glanced

16

back to see their neighbour's curtains twitch. 'She's watching us again,' the girl whispered with a smile.

Deep in thought, they walked on.

'Rob?'

'Mmm?'

'How do you really think she came to end up here, all alone and scared to go out?'

'It could have been any number of things,' he mused. 'The loss of someone she loved, a disastrous business venture that left her short of money and friends, or it could have been a family fall-out. Who can tell? Life has a way of kicking you in the teeth when you least expect it.'

Betsy's curiosity was heightened. 'You sound very bitter.'

'That's because I am. But then I believe that whatever happens in life, and however devastated we are, we just have to make the best of what we've got and get on with it.'

Betsy sensed his sadness. 'You never mention your mother,' she ventured nervously.

Robin did not answer. Instead, he cast his gaze to the ground and quickened his step.

'I'm here if you want to talk about it,' Betsy went on.

He shook his head. 'Some things are best left unsaid.'

Affectionately squeezing his arm, Betsy apologised. 'Sorry. I didn't mean to pry.'

'I know that,' he replied. 'Thanks for caring anyway.'

They continued walking down the street until they reached a low wall by an area of wasteland.

'Let's sit down for a moment,' Robin said. A few moments later, much to Betsy's surprise, he began to confide in her.

'I was just a kid of six, when my mother was involved in a car accident.' He paused and took a breath. Even now it was hard to talk about it. 'It took them three hours to cut her out of the wreckage.'

He could recall every moment, of every tortuous day and

night. 'She was in a coma for weeks. In all that time, Dad and I never gave up hope, even though deep down, I think we knew she would never recover. One summer's morning, she just slipped away . . .' He cleared his throat. 'They said she didn't suffer, that she wouldn't have known anything.'

He took a moment to collect his thoughts. 'Afterwards, my dad changed beyond all recognition. He used to be always smiling and joking, the life and soul of the party. He adored my mother, and when she was gone, it was as if a big part of him went with her. He couldn't seem to function any more . . . couldn't work, didn't sleep. For days he just wandered round the house in a trance.'

He grimaced. 'Dad was well qualified. From an early age, he always loved animals; his one burning ambition was to have his own veterinary clinic. When he left college he became a junior assistant at the local vet's . . . worked his way up, and now he has four reputable clinics across Bedfordshire.'

Betsy was impressed. 'That's quite an achievement,' she said. 'And were you never interested in joining him?'

Robin shook his head. 'Before I started school, I'd go with him on his calls sometimes.' He gave a chuckle. 'It was all a bit scary and bloody.'

'But it didn't put you off wanting to be a doctor?'

'No, just the opposite. It made me want to help ease pain and suffering . . . but in people, not animals. So, in one way, I suppose my ambitions were much the same as my dad's. Although he can't seem to grasp it that way.'

Looking down on Betsy, he went on in quieter tones, 'At first – after the accident, I mean – the way it was, I began to think I'd lost *both* my parents.'

The girl was tempted to comment, to reassure him, but then she realised he needed to open the door which he had kept locked for too long, so she remained silent and let him speak.

'I was just six years old. He was my dad but he didn't even

seem to know I was there.' The boy's memory of it was still vivid.

'We never sat down to a meal any more. It was either curry or Chinese from the local take-aways, or beans on toast and Lyons individual fruit pies. He left me to my own devices for days on end. You see, he forgot that I, too, was desperately missing my mother.'

He still recalled the sense of helplessness and loss. The awful loneliness.

'After a while, Dad went back to work. It was as if he went from one extreme to another. This time, he drove himself like a mad thing – with extra clinics, longer hours, home visits . . . anything so's not to be in the house. I was only a kid, but I learned to fend for myself. I would get up, wash, dress and go off to school in the village, never knowing if he'd be there when I got back. Not knowing if he would *ever* come home!'

Robin gave a wry little smile. 'I never told anyone how things were at home, so nobody bothered. I went to school and all I could think of was my dad, and . . . everything. One afternoon, my teacher came round and told Dad how I was falling badly behind in class; it made him realise how much he'd neglected me. After that, things were better. He talked to me, about my mother, and how much he missed her. He would hug me and cry, and tell me how sorry he was that he hadn't been look-ing after me. But he never once asked me how *I* felt. Inside, I was crying too, but he couldn't see that. He couldn't see past his own grief.'

Betsy gently urged him on. 'What was she like, your mother?'

He smiled, a soft, loving smile. 'Best mother ever. She was caring and understanding. And small, much like you. She always knew what to say and when to say it. Oh, and she could be so funny. She made us all laugh with her silly jokes and made-up stories.' His voice caught with emotion. 'She was more than my mother. She was a special friend. I never felt lonely when she was around.'

When the emotion threatened to overwhelm him, he took a moment to compose himself before going on. 'After my teacher came round to see him, Dad worried they might send social services to check up on us. So, eventually he found a married couple to come and stay. Joan and Tom were lovely – they were a great help to Dad on the farm, and Joan used to make me all my favourite puddings. I was so upset when they went to live at the seaside. Dad was, too.'

An enormous grin suddenly spread over his face. 'After that, we had Sheelagh. I'll never forget her, Betsy. She made our house really happy again ... But I'll tell you all about her some other time. Still miss her, all these years later, you know. She was like a second mother, for the short time she was with us. As for Dad, looking back, I think he fell in love with her, only to be left alone again.'

Restless, Robin got up. 'For a while when Sheelagh left us, he seemed hellbent on destroying himself again. He turned his back on his business ... leaving things to his accountant. It was another really bad period for us – one minute up, the next down. The turning-point came when two of Dad's best vets left the practice and he had to close down one of his clinics. Then he discovered that his accountant had been stealing huge amounts of money from him. He finally came to his senses, got himself together and picked up the reins. He built on what he had, and now he has those four clinics within a twenty-mile radius. Somehow I got through school without making too much of a mess at it, thanks to Dave, whose mum was a friend of our family.'

Like the others, apart from Dave, Betsy had known nothing of Robin's background. Now she asked: 'Do you think you'll ever meet up with Sheelagh again one day?'

Robin shook his head. 'Dad did try to find her, but nothing

came of it. He stopped looking . . . said she deserved to have her own life back, if that was why she had gone missing.

'And has your Dad come to terms with losing your mother and . . . everything?'

'He still lives on his own and works far too hard. I'm his only child, and that's why he was so disappointed when I wouldn't join him in the family business.'

'He sounds like a determined bloke.'

'He is. But so am I, and he won't change my mind.' Robin grinned down at her.

'Do you look like your dad?' she asked.

'Hmm . . . not much. I've been told I take after my grandad on my mother's side.'

'So, what did *he* look like?'

Smiling broadly, Rob gave Betsy a little playful shove. 'Oh, you know – handsome, well-built, and with this animal magnetism that women couldn't resist . . .' They were still chuckling as, arm-in-arm, they arrived at the phone box.

Robin asked if she wanted to come inside with him, out of the cold.

Betsy graciously refused. 'I don't want to eavesdrop on your conversation,' she said, stepping back. 'I'll wait out here.'

As it was, she couldn't help but pick up some of the conversation, because the evening was unusually clear, and Robin's voice could be easily heard.

'Yes, Dad, everything's fine. Yes, I would tell you if it wasn't. No, I don't need any money – I already told you, I'm getting my accommodation and meals free at the hospital.'

There followed a short pause during which Robin turned and rolled his eyes at Betsy through the glass. 'No, I haven't reconsidered,' she heard him say patiently '. . . and I wish you'd stop asking me, because it only causes friction.'

Another pause. 'I'm in the booth at the bottom of North Park Street. No, I'm not on my own. My friend Betsy's waiting outside.' Another slight pause before he chuckled and said, 'I don't think she'd appreciate you saying that.'

The conversation was ended with Robin assuring his father, 'You know I will. I've said before many times, I don't mind helping out with the animals when I'm home. I just don't want to do it for a living.' He nodded. 'Okay, Dad. Take care of yourself. Talk again soon.'

When he emerged from the booth, Betsy asked him, 'What did you mean when you said I wouldn't appreciate that?'

The boy grinned. 'Oh, nothing.'

'Tell me!'

'Well, for some reason, he thinks you're my girlfriend.'

'I see. And that worries you, does it?'

Concerned that she might have been offended, Robin changed the subject. 'He should not assume things. He has a way of doing that – like thinking I would naturally follow him into veterinary medicine, without ever actually talking to me about it.'

'I suppose he just wants what's best for you.' Disappointed that he had chosen to shift the conversation on to a less personal level, Betsy nevertheless played along. But all the time she wanted to shout out, 'I'd love to be your girlfriend! The first day I met you, I knew I wanted to be part of your life!'

But she made no mention of her feelings, and neither did Robin. Instead, they walked on together, chatting of other things. There was to be a student fashion show soon, and one of the models would be wearing a dress designed by Betsy herself.

'I can see you being one of the best designers in the country,' Robin told her proudly.

'Oh, I don't know about that.' Betsy was not one to brag. But in truth, she had already set her heart on establishing her own label one day.

~

They were almost home, when Betsy whispered, 'She's there again . . . look.'

Against the soft background lighting of the next-door front bedroom was the silhouette of a woman.

'Sometimes I want to knock on her door and make friends with her,' Betsy told Robin. 'She must be so lonely.'

The boy looked down on this lovely young woman beside him, and his heart was warmed. 'You know your trouble?' he said tenderly.

She looked up. 'No. But I'm sure you'll tell me.'

He took a moment to regard her, that small uplifted face and those appealing dark eyes, and he felt the urge to kiss her right there and then. Not wishing to frighten her away, he answered, 'You're far too nice for your own good.'

He desperately wanted to tell her how he felt, but some instinct held him back. Besides, if she'd wanted to be his woman, she had had her chance to say something back there when he told her what his dad had said, about her being his girlfriend. Anyway, a girl like Betsy, talented and pretty with an exciting future before her – why would she be interested in a humble young doctor like him? Though there was a fleeting moment when he was tempted to convey his true feelings. Twice he opened his mouth to speak, and twice he could not bring himself to say anything.

So, the moment passed, and with it his opportunity to tell her how he felt.

As they went up the steps and into the house, Betsy never knew how close he had come to sharing this last secret with her. From the relative safety of her hiding place, the woman watched them disappear into the house. 'So young,' she sighed. 'Such a lovely couple.' She drew away. 'My life is over now, but they've got all their lives in front of them. Don't be like me . . . so much heartache,' she muttered brokenly. 'Don't waste your chances of happiness.'

Turning from the window, she drew the curtains together and ambled across the room to the sideboard. In the light from the small lamp, she opened the drawer and took out a bundle of papers tied with string.

Taking them with her to the chair, she sat down and for a moment made no move to open the bundle. Instead she laid herself back in the chair, and allowed the anger to envelop her. 'I stood up to him once,' she murmured proudly, 'Oh, but he was such an evil man . . . *an evil, evil man!*'

Taking a moment to compose herself, she then untied the string and laid it carefully across her lap, then the same with the bulk of the parcel. Rummaging through the photographs, she found the one she was looking for. It was a photograph of herself many years ago. She gazed down on it with fondness. 'That was me!' she whispered incredulously. 'I may be haggard and worn now, but there was a time when I could hold my head high.'

Clothed in a clinging dress that drew in at the waist and fell naturally over her young figure, and with her long dark hair caught in a black bandana about her head, she looked amazing. 'I remember that dress as it was yesterday,' she chuckled joyfully. 'Purest ivory it was, with a sweetheart neckline, and a teasing split at the hem . . .' She laughed out loud. 'Cost me a week's wages it did!'

Her mood sobered. 'That was the night it all started to go wrong,' she whispered, laying the photograph on her lap.

Having taken a few minutes to reminisce, she glanced again at the photograph and a whimsical expression crept over her features. 'Was that really me,' she asked wonderingly, 'with a figure like that . . . up there on the stage with everyone looking at me, listening to me sing . . .' She tried to recall the feelings, but like so much of her past, they were pushed to the depths of her mind.

She looked again at herself as a young woman with the world at her feet, and a sense of desolation took hold of her. 'Come on now!' she reprimanded herself. 'It won't hurt to remember the way it was . . . the laughter, the songs. You did nothing wrong, you have to remember that.'

Shyly glancing down to study the photograph once more, she gave a hearty laugh. 'What a dress! And look at the black patent-leather high heels, oh, and the silk-stockings. It's all coming back . . . and how it riled him, when the men couldn't take their eyes off me.' She groaned. 'Hmh! If they could see me now, they wouldn't even help me across the road, and who could blame them, eh?'

Standing the photograph on the mantelpiece, she began gently swirling and dancing around, losing herself in the joy of yesteryear. In her head she could hear the soft music of her favourite song, 'I Believe'. Twirling and swaying, she began to sing . . .

One of her all time favourite songs was 'I Believe'. As she sang it how her heart was filled with joy as the poignant words took her back over the years . . .

All alone now, with no audience and no wickedness waiting for her, she danced in the twilight, lost herself in the song, and for a while she felt incredibly free. It was easy to imagine herself back there, in the night club, with the people looking up, their hearts and minds tuned into the song and the music.

But always in the wings or leaning on the bar . . . he was there watching . . . waiting.

She could see him now, dark and menacing in her mind's eye. It was a bad feeling.

PART TWO

~

London, 1978

In the Beginning

CHAPTER THREE

H E HAD ALWAYS been confident that Madeleine would return to him. But on this particular night, he had no inkling that she was about to make a surprise entrance.

Alice Mulligan knew though, and she had done everything in her power to dissuade the girl from coming back to a man who had proved time and time again that he could make her life a misery. But her young friend was utterly besotted with their boss.

Steve Drayton had never accepted any of the blame for the couple's rows. And this time, as usual, he believed himself to be the injured party.

Turning to Alice, the manageress of his club, the Pink Lady Cabaret Bar off Soho Square, he murmured, 'If I find out she's left me for another bloke, I swear to God . . . she'll live to regret it.' He stared at the little Irishwoman suspiciously. 'You know something about this, don't you? Thick as thieves, you two are. As a matter of fact, I wouldn't be at all surprised if you'd known where she was all along. All right – out with it! Where is she? *Is* she with another man? Is that why you're afraid to tell me?'

When Alice chose not to answer, but merely carried on removing notes from the cash register to transfer to the office safe, he grabbed her by the shoulders and almost lifted her off her feet. 'Answer me, woman!' he hissed. 'Where is she?'

'Well now, you'd best ask her that yourself, hadn't you? You being the big boss-man an' all.' Small in stature but big in courage, Alice had been around the block a few times and was not one to be intimidated by the likes of Steve Drayton.

'Don't you get clever with me,' he growled. 'No one's indispensable, lady!'

With a flick of her head, Alice gestured to the door. 'Like I said, she's here now, so you can ask her yourself, can't you?'

The open street-door sent a rush of cool air through the smoke-filled haze of the nightclub. Curious, he glanced up, and there she was: the Songbird, star of the show – his woman.

Though secretly relieved to see her, Steve was inwardly seething with anger, vowing that he would make the bitch pay for humiliating him. But he was cunning enough not to show his feelings here, in front of all these adoring people. Madeleine was a valuable asset, the reason why his club had flourished. In the early days, when he had let his gambling habits get the better of him, her charismatic appeal and popularity as a singer had brought him back from the brink of financial ruin. He still owed money to some undesirable types, but was reluctant to settle his debts. Steve Drayton never liked to pay what he owed. Arrogant and selfish, he played on his sexual appeal to get what he wanted – from women – and sometimes from men, too.

In the three weeks or so since Maddy had gone on the trot, his takings had dipped to an uncomfortable level. Deeply concerned, Steve had searched high and low, had even put the word out on the streets, but to no avail. The girl had simply disappeared.

Meanwhile, Steve had recruited other entertainers but they were no substitute for Madeleine. She had a certain special something – the punters came back to hear her time and again. 'Songbird' was what all the regulars called her. Or, 'our own Pink Lady' when she wore one of her glamorous pink stage dresses. Her accompanying musicians, pianist and bass-player Dave and Dino, were very grumpy without her. In desperation, with clients and money rapidly dwindling, Steve had been forced to sack the odd cleaner and even one of his two chefs but that was merely throwing out ballast to keep the ship afloat.

The truth was, only the loyal and the believers had continued to frequent his bar, in the hope that she would be back.

Well, here she was, and now the atmosphere was charged with excitement. But for all that, he was determined to teach her a lesson.

Shoving Alice aside, he gave a cynical smile. 'Here she comes, strolling in as though she hasn't a care in the world.'

For what seemed an age, Madeleine paused to glance across the club, her dark eyes seeking him out. And then she was moving towards him, and despite himself, he felt his pulse quicken.

In that darkened room with the soft music playing in the background, all eyes were turned on the woman.

Of petite build and with a certain quiet beauty, she wended her way between the clients, acknowledging their greetings with a ready smile and a friendly word and, much to the annoyance of the man who laid claim to her affections, occasionally accepting a kiss on the cheek.

Steve Drayton's hungry eyes followed her every step of the way. In spite of his violent temper and his liking for anything in a skirt, the sight of Madeleine could still thrill him like no other. With her mass of rich chestnut hair tumbling to her shoulders, and that lazy, swaying walk which had first attracted him to her, she could turn any man's head.

She was uniquely talented, yet even now, when she could see how much they thought of her, Madeleine did not seem to realise just *how* good she was. In truth, she possessed a kind of childish innocence that shone from within. Up there on the stage, when the music filled the room and her voice cut to their hearts, she was magnificent. When the music had died down and her voice was still, she became shy and hesitant, almost naïve in her trust of others. She had fallen under Steve's spell after auditioning for the club two years ago. Between boyfriends, and feeling lonely, she had found herself in her new employer's bed by that first nightfall.

Now, as she stopped to chat with a regular, Steve stared at her and felt the familiar arousal, though it still rankled, the fact that she had walked out on him – without even a phone call to let him know what was going on. No woman had ever done that to him before.

He turned to Alice. 'I knew she wouldn't be able to stay away for long. Didn't I tell you she'd be back?'

'Mebbe so, but she's a damned fool, so she is!' As Irish as the Blarney Stone and wick as a leprechaun, Alice Mulligan was herself a force to be reckoned with. 'It's a mystery to me how she ever puts up with you.'

'Women are no mystery to me,' Steve boasted. 'I've always been able to twist 'em round my little finger.'

'You're too clever for your own good, that's your problem, mister.' Being a woman of some fifty years, Alice had lovely skin and a slim figure that looked good in her smart business suit. Her blue eyes were alive with vitality. 'When you said she'd be back, I hoped you might be wrong,' she sighed. 'But here she is, an' may God and all His Saints help her.'

In truth, Alice was not at all surprised to see the younger woman here tonight, because it was not the first time today that Maddy had walked through these doors, though Steve Drayton didn't know that.

'She must have lost her mind, to make her way back here,' Alice said, closing the till and putting a rubber band round the notes. Earlier on, she had said the very same thing to Maddy. 'It just goes to show what bloody fools we women can be!' she added cynically. If only Maddy could see through this bully.

'My girl is nobody's fool,' Steve argued. 'She knows which side her bread is buttered, and come to think of it, so do you. But I can see it's put your nose right out of joint, now she's done the sensible thing and come home to me.' His mood darkened. 'The truth is, you never thought I was good enough for her.'

Undeterred, Alice ignored his last remark and looked him in the eye. 'That's because you're *not* good enough for her! And ye never will be.'

Steve helped himself to a large Scotch from the bar, and added a handful of ice. 'I don't give a sod what you think.' He glanced over at Maddy. '*She* thinks differently, and that's enough for me.' He preened himself. 'Besides, she won't get better than me, however hard she tries.' . . . Steve didn't believe in God, but he did believe in 'An eye for an eye'. Two could play at that game of 'now you see me, now you don't'.

'Well, all I can say is, she must be a divil for punishment. Gawd! When I think of the way you treat her . . .' Alice tossed her head.

'She can't do without me,' he declared smugly. 'In fact, I haven't yet decided whether I'll have her back or not.'

'Oh, but you will, me boyo.' Alice had no doubts about that.

'Really, and why is that then, eh?'

'Because without her, the punters would soon stop coming and you'd be broken like a twig underfoot. Besides, one time when you were drunk out of your skull, you actually spoke a few home truths, so ye did.'

'Is that so? And what might *they* have been, then?'

'You said she was a feather in your cap, for all the other men to envy.' Alice had no liking for this self-centred man. 'Deep down you don't love her at all,' she scoffed. 'That poor girl is just another acquisition for you to show off.'

'Hmh!' Swigging down his Scotch, Steve pressed his glass

against the optic for another shot. He searched Madeleine out, to smile lovingly on her. 'Since she walked out on me . . .' his voice grew softer 'I . . . might tell you, I've really missed her.' It was the truth. The man sometimes wondered if he had foolishly fallen in love with Maddy; it scared him, brought out the violence in him.

'Missed the money she brings in, more like!' Alice snapped, completely unsympathetic. 'Deep down, yer a bad bugger, only she can't see it. You don't deserve a woman like that, kind and giving; the loveliest thing who ever walked onto a stage. There's not a man in the crowd who wouldn't give his right arm for a woman of her calibre.'

Alice threw Steve a contemptuous glance. 'And then there's you – a bully and a womaniser – treating her like the dirt under your feet.' She was angry with Madeleine for coming back, and proving him right. She had no liking for this man who provided her wages; though she earned every penny twice over.

Since the nightclub had opened eight years ago, Alice had worked tirelessly, shown her true worth and earned her boss's trust. As a result, her wages had increased in line with her responsibilities.

To her credit, Alice had fought her way up from the bottom; in turn she had cleaned the toilets, scrubbed the floors, worked as a cloakroom attendant and then behind the bar, had also served at tables and run errands. Eventually she had risen from taking money as the clients arrived, to being entrusted to bank the takings. And now she was a fully-fledged manageress.

From the start, she was honest, reliable and knew how to keep her mouth shut when necessary, as long as there was nothing criminal or harmful involved. Though when she heard how a certain client had been beaten so badly he ended up in hospital, that was a turning-point in her loyalty. From that moment she kept herself to herself and never showed interest in any of Steve's shadier activities.

While Steve Drayton valued and respected her, she could never respect him; he reminded her too much of her own cheating husband, Eamon. It was five years now since she'd walked out on him, and good riddance to the man! Childless, she had taken young Maddy to her heart and loved the girl as her own blood. After seeing how badly Steve treated every woman who took a shine to him – and there were many – Alice had grown to dislike and distrust him; especially these past two years, since Madeleine caught his eye.

Steve might love her and he might not. Alice could not be sure. But it was a strange, destructive love, for he seemed determined to make the young woman's life a misery.

Steve interrupted her reverie. 'I *do* love her,' he said, answering her unspoken question. 'The trouble is, when I get drunk and senseless, I find myself agreeing with you, that she's too good for me – and then I get insanely jealous. Like you said, any man would want her, and maybe even give her a better life than I do.'

He dropped his gaze to the floor. 'The thought of losing her sends me wild,' he said hoarsely. 'Then I hit out and hurt her.' He swished the ice cubes in his glass, and she could barely catch his last few words as he whispered, 'I swear I don't mean to.'

He watched as Madeleine lingered to chat with another one of the customers. There was no denying, she was a special woman, and Alice was right . . . he did not deserve her.

'I'm not surprised she cleared off,' he conceded regretfully. 'The last time we had a set-to, she took a terrible beating – and all for something and nothing. A fella at the club put his arm round her as she walked out and as usual, I laid the blame on her.' He shrugged. 'Yeah, that's what it was all right – something and nothing.'

He sighed self-indulgently and took another measure of whisky. 'Mind you, we were busy making up till the early hours, and I can tell you here and now, your precious Maddy didn't have no complaints about my performance *that* night!'

'You're an arrogant divil.'

'Yes, so you keep saying.'

Straightening his shoulders beneath the beautiful cloth of his Jermyn Street suit, Steve drew himself up to his considerable height. 'She always comes running back. It only goes to prove how bad she wants me.' He flicked open a box of Dunhill cigarettes and lit one with a gold lighter. 'Want one?' He offered the box to Alice, who ignored it.

'Why don't you marry her?' Alice was known to come straight to the point.

He laughed. 'I *never* marry my women. Can't trust a single one of 'em. My old mother taught me that, the poxy tart. God knows who my father was – she had more men than you've got spuds in Ireland, love. No, there's no woman alive who'll get me shackled to her.'

'Have you told her that?'

'I don't have to, she already knows my opinion – that women are good for one thing only.' Swinging round to face Alice, his mood suddenly darkened, as it so often did. 'I think it's time you got back to work,' he hissed. 'Before I get to thinking I might be better off with somebody who doesn't ask so many questions! Bloody women, it's nothing but yap, yap, yap.'

Despite her recent vanishing act, Steve was satisfied that he had his Maddy exactly where he wanted her; his little songbird on a string. And it didn't matter what he did to her, because she always ended up singing along to his tune.

Still weaving a path through the dining-tables, Madeleine was stopped many times by clubbers who were delighted to see her back, from what they had been told was a well-deserved holiday away from the hustle and bustle of Soho.

With a sweet smile, she thanked them and moved on towards her tormentor; the man she could neither live with, nor without. She loved him, she hated him, and now as she glanced at him across the room, she wanted him as much as ever.

Not overly handsome, Steve Drayton was a big man. Fit and toned, with a quick mind and an instinct for making money, he had built the Pink Lady up from nothing. There was an aura of power about him that was very sexy, and a certain kind of look from his narrow hazel-coloured eyes that could turn Maddy's blood to water. Sometimes he was so good to her; at other times, he became a devil.

Though apprehensive, she was glad to be back, to realise that he still wanted her. And yet there was always that niggling doubt that he might throw her aside; that he would find some-one else, younger than her thirty years, and she would have no part in his life. In her heart she knew that might well be for the best, but she hoped it would never happen.

Now though, she had something to tell him. Something that might seal their future together, once and for all.

As she drew nearer, the doubts set in. He was such a volatile man, so unpredictable. How would he react? The moment she was standing before him, her courage began to waver.

'So! Here you are at last, eh? Took you long enough to make your way back, didn't it?' he said smoothly, in the soft-est tone that made her shudder. 'You needed to punish me, was that it?' He traced her jawline with his finger and she felt hypnotised by his touch.

'That's not true, Steve, and you know it,' she whispered.

'So why don't you tell me what the truth *is*, then.' He stepped closer, his eyes boring into hers. 'You've not been singing else-where, or I would have heard. So where have you been hiding? Got a bit on the side, is that it?'

'Will ye leave her be!' Sensing trouble, Alice quickly intervened. 'Go easy on her, for heaven's sakes,' she urged in a low voice. 'There's a million an' one eyes trained on the pair of youse.'

Steve's display of temper had not gone unnoticed by the regulars, some of whom did not believe the holiday story. They had seen the way he acted with her, controlling and possessive. So who could blame them for hoping she might have escaped, found a new life, a new man, one who might cherish her the way she deserved.

Impatient, they called out to her now. 'Come on Madeleine, we've missed you! Get up there and strut your stuff!'

The clapping rose to a deafening crescendo. *'We want Songbird! We want Songbird!'*

'All right, all right!' Laughing, she gestured towards the stage. 'I'm on my way.'

As she turned from him, Steve caught her by the arm. 'What do you mean?' he demanded. 'Surely you're not thinking of performing *tonight*?'

'Why shouldn't I?'

'Because you've only just walked in, dammit! We need to go somewhere quiet, somewhere we can . . . talk.' Although he had other things on his mind than talk. 'You'll want to rehearse – decide the songs, organise the musicians. It all takes time.' He gave a lazy smile. 'Besides, we've already booked a comedian for tonight.'

'He's been cancelled,' Alice interrupted.

'Cancelled!' Steve swung round to face her. 'What the hell are you talking about, woman? Who cancelled him?'

'*I* did. And if ye want to make something of it, I'm ready.' The little woman had a look in her eye that Steve knew all too well. If it wasn't for the fact that Alice ran the club in his absence, was totally trustworthy and knew how to keep her mouth shut about his business deals, he would have thrown her feet first out the door long ago.

Instead he issued a stark warning. 'Be careful, lady. You don't want to overstep the mark.'

There were many ways of being rid of people like Alice, and he knew them all.

Defusing the situation, Madeleine told him hastily, 'It's not Alice's fault. It was *me* – I arranged it all. And now the boys are backstage, ready when I am.' She smiled, pleased with herself. 'You see, I haven't just walked in,' she admitted. 'I was here this afternoon while you were at the races. Me, Dave and Dino rehearsed all afternoon.

'You did what! And why the devil wasn't I told?'

She shrugged her shoulders. 'I asked them not to let on,' she replied boldly. 'We timed it for when you wouldn't be here. I'm sorry, but, well . . . we all thought it would be a nice surprise for you.' She peeped at him from her soft dark eyes. 'But it's all right, isn't it, Steve?' Most times she could wheedle her way round him, and thankfully this proved to be one of those times.

He studied her a moment, wanting to hit her, aching to love her. 'You're a witch!' His desperation to have her was all he could think of. 'Well, all right. But I won't pretend I'm not rattled at being hoodwinked.' The sound of hand-clapping and foot-stamping was deafening. 'Your fans are getting restless. You'd best go.' He took another moment to study those mesmerising dark eyes, then warned her, 'Don't think you've got the better of me. I can take you or break you.' But his cutting remark was a lie, and they all knew it.

Without a word and giving him no time to change his mind, Madeleine hurried away to the dressing-room,

∼

Steve took his drink to the small table at the side of the stage which was reserved for him. On the way, he paused to exchange a word or two with his clients.

'She's back then?' The well-dressed man who spoke was a known thug. 'If she were my woman, I'd never have let her get away in the first place. Not losing your touch, are you?'

'You'd best mind your tongue.' After Madeleine's sudden disappearance, Steve Drayton had been made to suffer many such comments. 'You'll never see the day when I lose my touch,' he retaliated. 'Keep them on a string but cut them a bit of slack now and then . . . they'll always come running back. Steve Drayton will never be short of women. What's more, I'll still be making money, long after you and your kind are finished so you'd do well to remember that!'

Moving away, he placed his drink on the table, lit up a Dunhill and settled back in his chair, the beginnings of a smile crossing his face as he swept his gaze over the many customers, so flush with money he could almost smell it.

He was no fool. Since Madeleine had been gone and the clients had begun to drift away, the vultures were circling, biding their time in the hope that he might be forced to sell. The club was in a prime location, and in excellent nick. There were many competitors who would just love to walk in and take over.

Yes, it was true, Madeleine was the star attraction and there was no one else like her; she was the one who drew people from every corner. He had been in business long enough to know she was the magic money-spinner who kept him at the top. But he mustn't let *her* know that. Nor must he let her forget that it was *he* who had given her the chance to show what she could do.

Over the past two years he had built her up. *And if she didn't play his game,* he thought fiercely, *he could so easily knock her down again.*

He would too. Without a second thought.

Looking about, Steve was pleased with what he saw. Every manjack here was thrilled that Madeleine Delaney was back in town!

Like himself, they were settling down, confident that they were about to enjoy a very special performance.

And as usual, they were not disappointed.

~

It was twenty minutes before Madeleine appeared onstage. Prior to that it was organised chaos behind the scenes, with Alice helping her choose from the three dresses she had brought earlier. 'You'll be wanting to knock 'em dead tonight.' Alice was beside herself with excitement. 'Ooh now! This is the one to send 'em wild!' Whipping the shocking pink dress from its hanger, she held it against the girl. 'What d'ye think, me darling?'

Madeleine thought Alice had chosen well. 'OK, let's go for that one,' she agreed. 'Pink dress, black belt and shoes . . .'

'And that sparkly diamond clip in your hair?' Alice suggested.

The two women worked methodically in front of the big illuminated mirror, with make-up, perfume and hairspray until finally, Maddy Delaney – the Songbird – was ready to face her public.

~

When she emerged onstage, the punters went wild, and who could blame them? In the sexy knee-length gown with its sweetheart neckline, long skinny sleeves and back kick-pleat, she was both classy and glamorous.

Her long thick locks were swept off-centre to the top of her head, so as to cascade naturally down one side; the diamond clip accentuated the depth and sparkle of her eyes, and the stiletto heels gave her legs a long, slender appearance.

When the music started up and her pure, powerful voice rose to the rafters, the crowd fell silent. Maddy had chosen to sing The Beatles' new hit, 'Yesterday' – a song which the public all over the world had taken to their hearts. The hush was complete as she sang to a sea of upturned faces about the sorrow of lost love and loneliness.

Each haunting song that followed was a story, and when finally she bowed and thanked them, the audience gave her and the musicians the rapturous applause they deserved.

And so, the evening was finally over. As Steve Drayton watched the punters go, a celebratory cigar drooping from his mouth, his hands were itching to count the takings. 'I reckon we've done all right,' he boasted, as Alice closed the outer door. 'Now that Madeleine's back, there'll be no holding us.'

'If you want her to stay, you'd best mend your ways,' Alice declared. 'You almost lost her because of your bullying. Next time, it might well be permanent.'

None too pleased at her unwelcome advice, he bit back, 'When I need your opinion, I'll ask for it. And if I find you've been trying to turn her against me, well now . . .' He nodded affirmatively. 'I'll have no choice but to deal with it . . . if you know what I mean?'

Alice knew well enough what he meant, but she played him at his own game. 'Whatever makes you think I might try and turn Madeleine against you?' she asked sarcastically. 'When you're doing a perfectly good job of it yourself!'

'This is the last warning, Alice. Just keep your nose out of my business.' He caught the defiant look in her eye and shook his head. 'You need to listen to what I'm saying! Oh, I won't deny you're worth your weight in gold here. But like I said before, you are *not* indispensable.'

'I never thought I was,' Alice said, beginning to empty the till. 'Though you won't find better than me.'

'Maybe I would, maybe I wouldn't. We'll just have to see,

won't we? So now, if it doesn't go against your high principles, d'you think you could close up and see yourself off these premises? I'll cash up tonight. Tell everyone they can go home – you've all done very well tonight.'

Steve sank into a reflective mood as he mechanically counted the takings. The sight of Madeleine on stage, her slim curves draped in silk, had reminded him of what he had been missing; twice he'd been to the flat he'd bought for her in Battersea, but there was no sign of her, and so he began wondering where she was, and who with. And yes, there had been others to satisfy him in Madeleine's absence, but they were just filling in, until she came back . . . as he knew she would.

Hearing a noise behind him, he swung round. 'What! Are you *still* here?' Alice had become a thorn in his side, and if he had his way, it would be a mere matter of time before she was permanently removed.

On his words, Alice picked up her handbag which she'd left by the till and hurried away. There was no need to antagonise him further, she wisely decided. But she vowed to make Madeleine see sense; if not today, then soon.

Before something really bad happened.

With that in mind, she set off in search of Raymond, a shy, bumbling giant of a man who worked like a dog, and was solely responsible these days for keeping the club clean and shipshape.

Being another fortunate 'find' for Drayton, Raymond kept himself to himself, avoiding company and speaking only when spoken to. An orphan raised in a strict children's home, he had been a wanderer sweeping the streets when Drayton came across him. Within a week, he had him working at the club.

Poor Raymond was forever grateful to his new boss. Given a windowless room where he could lay his head, free food from the club and a measly wage on a Friday, he thought himself a fortunate man.

'Ray, where are you?' Alice looked about, but could see no

sign of him. Going to the bar, she asked one of the barmen there, 'Jack, have you seen Raymond anywhere?'

Jack was genuinely friendly, honest as the day was long, and deeply fond of Madeleine – not in any sexual way, he was not that way intended – but he was prepared to stand up and defend her. Alice had seen the way his boyish features tightened whenever he saw Drayton bullying her. Hard-working and ambitious, Jack nevertheless remained untainted by the world of Soho; in fact, he wanted to run his own club one day.

In answer to Alice's question, Jack gestured to the far side of the room. 'Last time I saw him, he was clearing the back tables.'

Alice thanked him. 'The boss is especially keen to have the club emptied and locked for the night.'

'Why? What's got into him? Most nights he's here till all hours, him and his cronies, gambling and drinking. What's so different about tonight?'

'Sure, it's no good asking me!' Alice rolled her eyes to the heavens. 'Best do as he says though. Ye know what a vile bugger he can be.'

'Alice . . .' Jack lowered his voice to a whisper. 'He doesn't know, does he?'

'If you mean, does he know Madeleine was with you all that time, the answer is no – at least I don't think so. He hasn't said anything.'

Jack was concerned all the same, 'You and I both know, he'd go mental if he found out. Not because anything would have happened between me and Madeleine.' He smiled a sad little smile. 'He knows the way things are with me. It's just that I care about her! When I caught her crying in the back alley that night, I knew she needed to get away from him . . . if only to send him the message that she's not his sole property to do with as he pleases!'

Alice understood his frustration. 'The trouble is, she loves him – though God only knows why.'

'I'm well aware of that,' Jack sighed. 'It was plain enough – the way she kept mentioning his name, even wanting to get back to him from the minute she came in through the door.'

'Well, it was Drayton who put her up there in front of the crowds,' Alice conceded. 'Unfortunately, she seems to think she owes him for that for all eternity, when all the time any self-respecting club-owner would have cut his arm off for the chance. Anyways, all we can do is hope she comes to her senses, sooner rather than later.'

'I did right, didn't I?' Jack asked worriedly. 'I mean, offering her my spare room for a while?'

'Of course you did the right thing,' Alice assured him. 'No way should we have let her come to me because, as we suspected, it was the first place *he* came looking.'

Jack pursed his lips, folded a bar-towel and placed it over the pumps. 'For her own sake, I wish she could see him for what he really is. A complete bastard!

He knew how fond Alice was of her. 'She's too trusting, and he knows it.' The anger trembled in his voice, 'I tell you, Alice, if it wasn't for her asking me not to, I'd have tackled him long before now. But she won't have it. As it was I pleaded with her to stay on at my place – even offered to move out for as long as she wanted. I tried all ways to stop her from coming back here to him, but she wouldn't be told.'

Alice chuckled. 'That's the way she is – headstrong and independent. But I'm keeping an eye on things, don't you worry.'

'Alice, promise me. If he hurts her, you will tell me, won't you? I can't abide bullies.' Jack's face darkened. 'I swear to God I'll swing for him if he touches her again.'

'I will.' Alice could lie convincingly when necessary.

And she was lying now.

The last thing she wanted was to involve Jack any deeper. He was a sensitive young man, albeit strong and able, and no doubt in a fair fight he could easily take on a man like Drayton.

45

But there were others – ruthless criminals and villains who, if paid enough, would snuff his life out like a candle.

Alice could never risk that happening.

Losing no time, Jack went away to instruct the others, 'The boss wants us off the premises – like now.'

'Why the hurry?' The old barman had been with Drayton these past four years.

Jack shrugged. 'Who knows?'

'Another closed game with his mates, is it . . . losing their ill-gotten gains at the table.' The man gave a snort of disgust, 'Bloody fools. More money than they know what to do with.'

∼

Having located Raymond, Alice asked, 'How long before you're done?'

Six foot tall, with shoulders wide and strong as an oak door, Raymond often doubled as a bouncer, evicting the undesirables. 'Half an hour tonight,' he answered shyly, avoiding Alice's eye. 'Back at eight in the morning to finish off.'

Alice nodded, and then gave a stifled yawn. 'It's been a long tiring day, and I need my sleep.' Bidding him farewell, she hurried away to get her coat.

Before leaving, she intended to have a quiet word with Madeleine. She was deeply suspicious. Steve Drayton was acting out of character and it worried her. What with Maddy taking off the way she did, without so much as a word, and then turning up out of the blue like that . . . and all he had done was give her a gentle chiding. It was not like Drayton to suffer public humiliation quietly. There would inevitably be some kind of retribution.

∼

In her dressing-room, Madeleine had changed into a robe and was seated before the mirror, removing the make-up from her face.

Engrossed in what she was doing, she did not hear him come in. It was only when he stepped forward that she saw his image in the mirror.

'God Almighty, Steve!' she exclaimed. 'You scared the daylights out of me.'

Before she could turn round, he was on her, his long lean fingers toying with her hair, caressing her slender shoulders, then sliding down towards her breasts. When she raised her head, he leaned forward to kiss her on the neck.

Suddenly, without warning, he clenched his fingers about her throat and squeezed.

When she began to struggle, he increased the pressure until she could barely breathe.

Then, just when it seemed she might pass out, he released her.

'You've been a bad girl,' he murmured. 'You walked out on me without a word.' He tutted. 'That was so cruel.'

Cursing her to hell and back, he began to pace the floor, madly ranting on about what she had done to him. 'Weeks you've been gone, and not one word! I went to the flat twice, and it was empty, so I knew you hadn't been staying there. Then you just walk back in, as though nothing has happened. Did you never think how *I* felt? Christ! I was almost out of my mind, not knowing what was going on, not to mention being slagged off by the regulars with their smartarse remarks. "Where's your woman? Frightened her off, have you?" Laughing at me behind my back!' His face looked wild.

'I'm not your woman,' Maddy said hoarsely. Shaken by the brutal way he had gone for her throat, she recalled Alice's warning that, 'One of these days he'll lose control, and Lord only knows what he might do!'

Her open defiance stopped him in his tracks. 'What – did – you – say?' he whispered.

Holding her head high, she shakily repeated the words. 'I said, I'm not your woman.'

'Is that so?' Throwing his head back, he startled her by laughing out loud. In an instant, the laughing stopped. 'So, if you're not *my* woman,' he demanded, 'whose woman *are* you?'

'I'm my own woman,' she answered. 'That's who I am.'

'What's that supposed to mean?' he sneered. Dropping into the nearest chair, he regarded her with suspicion. 'Explain!'

Sensing the onset of a fierce argument, Madeleine chose not to answer. Instead, she put her hands up to her neck, remembering what he had done; remembering what Alice had warned so many times.

'I'm talking to you, bitch!' He was out of the chair and standing before her. 'Answer me!'

Ignoring him, she hurried to the door. 'I had something important to tell you,' she confided angrily, 'but I can see you're not in the mood for talking. Not to worry. It can wait till tomorrow – if I can still speak, that is, let alone sing.'

'Where the hell do you think you're going?' In two strides, he was across the room, where he slammed shut the door and thrust her against the wall. 'Don't fight me, sweetheart,' he murmured. 'You know I don't like you to fight me.' His tongue was rough against her skin as he licked the length of her neck, where the marks of his fingers still showed, and downwards, towards the rise of her breast.

Against all her instincts, Madeleine felt herself succumbing to his touch. 'No! Let me go,' she whispered. 'I don't want . . .' But her words fell on deaf ears.

Even as she protested, she could not help but love him. Yet it was an uncomfortable love, a love that she knew deep down was not returned in the way she needed it to be, and never could be. Steve Drayton was too damaged a person to know what love meant.

Yet she would have given anything for him to love her completely, to care for her as a woman. And especially now, when she desperately needed him to see her as a future wife.

'Don't ever tell me you're not my woman.' The tip of his tongue encircled her ear. 'You will *always* be my woman,' he murmured passionately. 'And God help anyone who tries to come between us.'

'Steve?' His nearness was intoxicating.

He stroked her breast, curving it into the palm of his hand. 'Ssh.'

She stiffened against him, making him draw back slightly. 'Do you love me? I mean, *really* love me?'

'You know I do, otherwise why would I go crazy when I see other men ogling you?' Cupping her face in his hands, he kissed her full on the mouth. 'I'd kill anyone who tried to take you away from me.'

'But are you *in* love with me?'

He laughed. 'Haven't I just said I love you?'

'Yes, but there is a difference. I mean, you can love a mother or a sister, but being *in love* is something else.'

'You're talking in riddles.'

When he began peeling off her robe, she held him away. 'No, Steve. I really need you to listen to what I have to say.' The time was right and she had to tell him now – while she had the courage.

'What the hell's wrong with you?' His need of her was driving him crazy. 'I know you want it as much as me, I can feel it.' He slid his open palms over her buttocks. 'Come on, stop teasing.'

Maddy laid her hands over his. '*No*, Steve! Not until you've heard what I've got to say.'

Inching away, he looked at her for a moment, at the tears

in her eyes, and the nervous way she was fidgeting with her fingers. It puzzled him; a wave of paranoia swept over him. What was she hiding? Why did she look so guilty? 'What's going on?'

For weeks, she had dreaded this moment, but it had to be faced – and so had the consequences.

'I'm pregnant,' she confessed. 'That's why I went away – I needed time to think.' At the look of horror on his face, she began to gabble, 'I thought you might be angry. I was planning to get rid of it . . . I even went to see somebody – an abortion clinic in Harley Street. In the end though, I couldn't go through with it! I couldn't kill an innocent baby . . . *our* baby.'

Seeing the look of astonishment on his face, she took hold of him, pleading, 'It'll be all right, Steve. You said you loved me. We can get married and be a family.' She giggled nervously. 'It's what I've always wanted.'

For what seemed an age he stared at her in disbelief then, with one mighty swipe of his fist, he sent her flying across the room.

'You're nothing but a slut!' he shouted. Grabbing her arm, he yanked her to her feet, twice slapping her hard across the mouth. 'A filthy little slut! What d'you take me for, eh? I'm no fool, I know why you went away. You've got yourself a new man, haven't you, eh? And now he's got you knocked up and the pair of you think you can offload his bastard onto me?'

'No!' Taken aback by his violent reaction, Maddy tried to explain. 'There is no other man . . . there's only ever been you. I swear to God, Steve, it's *your* baby. Yours and mine.'

Picking up her hair-drier, he sent it crashing into the mirror, shattering it into a million airborne fragments. Some of the glass splinters cut her face and arms, sending sprays of blood across the wall.

Turning to her, Steve spat out, 'It sickens me to touch you! You dirty little cow, shaming me in front of everyone. I expect they all knew what was going on – and all the time they were laughing at me behind my back. Bastards, all of you!'

He was like a madman. 'GET OUT OF HERE – OUT OF MY SIGHT, AND OUT OF MY CLUB! GO ON – CLEAR OFF OUT OF IT!' As he slung her out the door, his voice was raised to the rafters. '*He* can have you. Who'd want to touch you now? And when I find out who he is, that bastard you're carrying won't have a father. Make no mistake, I'll find out who you've been with if it's the last thing I do. D'YOU HEAR WHAT I'M SAYING! Nobody makes a fool out of Steve Drayton and gets away with it!' He stormed off into his office, trampling on the broken glass, and kicking it across the room.

From the cloakroom, Alice heard the commotion and came running. Horrified at the sight of Madeleine spattered in blood, she took her by the arm, and led her away. 'I knew this would happen, I could see it coming,' she muttered to herself. Glancing up, she saw Drayton peering at them through his office window. 'Look what you've done to her, you lunatic!' she cried. 'You should be ashamed! Only a coward would hurt a woman like this!'

Afraid that Alice might enrage him further, Madeleine stopped her. 'Alice, don't! He's gone crazy.'

'He's always been crazy,' Alice said loudly. 'It's just that you've never believed it.' Taking her behind the bar, she ran the cold tap and with a clean bar-towel, dabbed at the cuts until they were cleaned, then she went to the first-aid box and smeared them with antiseptic ointment. 'Thank goodness they are only superficial,' she consoled her friend. 'But they'll take a while to heal, nevertheless. In a minute or two, we'll get a taxi and go to University College Hospital, to get them seen to properly.'

Out of the corner of her eye, she saw Drayton in his office, pacing up and down like a wild animal. 'Whatever sent him off on the rampage like that?' she asked worriedly.

Maddy blamed herself. 'I should never have gone away for all those weeks. I thought it might make him value me more; instead, it made him think I had a lover.' She was shivering with shock, she was grateful when Alice took off her coat and wrapped it round her.

'But that's ridiculous! You've always worshipped the ground he walks on – though *why*, I'll never know. Look! I'll tell him how it was, that after the big row you had, it was me who persuaded you to put some distance between you for a time. I'll tell him there was never any other fella, that there was nothing underhand going on.'

Jerking away, Madeleine shook her head, and the pain made her cry out. 'I don't want you to go anywhere near him,' she said. 'He wouldn't listen anyway.'

'Oh, he'll listen to me. We've clashed many times, and he's threatened to be rid of me – but I'm still here. That's because I keep this club operating smoothly where previous people have almost run it into the ground, robbing him blind in the process.' She squeezed Maddy's hand gently. 'Unlike you, my girl, I've learned to stand up to him.' She dialled the local taxi firm. 'A cab will be here in a minute.'

Madeleine kept a hold on her. 'No, Alice. Leave him be for now. It was my fault for telling him tonight, after me just turning up without warning. I should have told him tomorrow morning in the light of day maybe, when he might have been more rational.'

Alice's curiosity was growing. 'Told him what? It must have touched a nerve, whatever it was, for him to blow up like that.'

Madeleine was still dwelling on Steve Drayton's reaction. 'I hoped he might be pleased,' she said, and began to sob.

Exasperated, Alice tried again. 'So, what was it you told him?' Then the truth hit her like a ton of bricks. *'My God! You're pregnant!'* She understood it all now. 'I should have known, what with you refusing food and cutting out the alcohol. Yes, and the other week, Jack told me you'd been sick all morning.' She recalled the moment. 'You'd been looking peaky of late, so I did wonder.'

Sobbing, Maddy admitted that yes, she was pregnant, but, 'Steve refuses to accept that he's the father. He's convinced I've been with somebody else . . . called me a dirty little slut.'

'You're well shot of him,' Alice said gently. 'And don't you worry, everything's going to be all right.' Her face was wreathed in the widest smile. 'Oh Madeleine, you're going to have a baby – isn't that wonderful?'

~

At the Emergency department of the local hospital, a nurse cleaned the cuts again and removed a tiny sliver of glass from the biggest one. She warned Maddy to only wear her stage make-up for the shortest time – to take it off as soon as possible, to allow the skin to breathe and to heal.

After a cup of tea and some biscuits, Maddy was feeling a lot better. Alice's excitement was infectious, and by the time they'd taken another taxi to Whitechapel, where Alice lived, Maddy had promised herself that everything was going to be all right.

Alice herself was not so sure. In spite of promising Maddy that things would sort themselves out, she had a murmuring dread that more trouble was bound to come out of all this.

Yet, even now, after witnessing the violence he was capable of, neither Alice nor Madeleine fully realised the true evil that was Steve Drayton.

CHAPTER FOUR

Alice had always been a light sleeper. She couldn't tell whether it was the sound of Maddy crying that had woken her, or whether she had just woken like she normally did, after a few short hours of sleep. Either way, she was now wide awake and concerned about the younger woman. 'Poor little devil,' she yawned. 'What's to become of her?'

Taking her robe from the bedside chair, she slung it on and crept into the kitchen of her two-bedroomed flat to make a cup of tea. It was a bright summer morning, and even in this busy area of London, near the big roundabout at Aldgate East, she could hear the blackbirds calling to each other.

Coming into the kitchen, she found Maddy hunched across the table. Red-eyed and sorry-looking, the girl immediately apologised. 'I didn't wake you, did I?'

Alice laughed and filled the kettle. 'Away with you! Sure, the walls are so thin, I can hear the man next door pulling on his trousers,' she joked. Looking to see if there was an empty cup on the table, she gently chided her young friend, 'I see you've not yet made yerself a cup o' tea then?'

Maddy shook her head.

'Hmh! Well, let's have one together now – you're bound to be thirsty, all the tears you've cried. Then I'll make us a good breakfast. Remember that you're eating for two now.' She bent

55

to look at Maddy's face. 'Ye look awful, so ye do. There's not a man this side of the Irish Sea who would want to kiss that sorry little face, and who could blame them, eh?'

Her cheeky words had the intended effect, for they made Maddy laugh out loud, even though it hurt to do so. 'Well, that's not very nice, is it?' she chuckled.

Alice gave her a hug. 'Tea then, is it . . . with a dash of milk and one sugar?'

'Thank you – yes, I'd like that.' Heartened by this darling woman who always seemed to say the right thing, Maddy drew the dressing-gown Alice had lent her tighter about her. 'I really am sorry if I woke you,' she murmured.

Alice prepared two cups and opened the biscuit tin. 'The thing is,' she answered cheerfully, 'I'd have woken up sooner or later, and if I didn't wake up it wouldn't matter, would it, because I'd be dead and gone, so I would.'

'Don't say that!' Maddy didn't believe in joshing about such things.

It was like tempting Fate.

Having made the tea, Alice brought the tray to the table. 'And I'll thank ye kindly not to eat all them custard creams,' she warned drily. 'There's two for you, an' two for me. And I won't be pleased if there's crumbs all over the table neither.'

Her banter had done the trick, and soon Maddy was brighter. 'You're such a good friend to me,' she told the older woman, 'letting me stay with you like this.'

Alice brushed away her comments, saying, 'What are we going to do with you, that's what I'm wondering. You can't possibly go back to him – not after what he did. Like as not, if he takes another bad mood, he could finish you off. Think of the baby, my love.'

Maddy took a sip of her tea and sighed. 'I'm sure he'll be in a better frame of mind today,' she said hopefully. 'When he's had time to think, he might realise what he's done.'

'Don't you believe it, me darling! That'll be the day, when Steve Drayton admits to being in the wrong. No.' Alice was emphatic. 'I can't let you go back to him, at least not until we're certain he really wants to take care of you and the child.'

'Oh, if only he would . . .' Maddy said wistfully. 'Tell me the truth, Alice. Do you think there's a real chance he might come to terms with the idea of a baby?'

Alice was silent for a moment, chewing on her biscuit and washing it down with another swig of her tea. 'D'ye want the truth?'

Maddy nodded. 'Please.'

Leaning forward, the older woman secured the girl's full attention before saying bluntly, 'I don't think there's a cat in hell's chance of him accepting the baby.'

'But he *is* the father!'

'Oh yes, he may be the father, but he will *never* admit that the child is his. And I can't see a child playing any part in his life. You know as well as I do, he's a bad lot – along with the other villains he keeps company with. And not a single one of them has any scruples or conscience whatsoever.'

She paused, all manner of images going through her mind; of late-night visitors to the club, shady deals and vicious arguments, often ending in violence. Steve Drayton lived in a dark world, one in which she feared Maddy might get swallowed up.

'We both know the rumours that circulate about him and his cronies, and you know what they say – there's no smoke without fire. That's no environment in which to bring up a child.'

'I know all that,' Maddy admitted soberly. 'And I still can't help but love him.' She was well aware of all the warnings that Alice was sending out. 'I wish I *didn't* love him, but I do. I want to live with him and for us to bring our child up together.'

Dear God in heaven! What would it take for the girl to see the truth about Drayton? Alice insisted, 'You must stay here with me for a while, until we know for sure he wants the two of you. Will you do that for me, if only for *my* peace of mind?'

For what seemed an age, the air was thick with silence.

Maddy had never seen Alice so agitated and, to tell the truth, she was beginning to wonder if her friend could see more badness in Steve than she could see herself. Oh, she knew he had a shady reputation, and she had witnessed at first hand how cruel he could be. But how could he not love her, when she loved him so much? She wanted to understand him, to heal his unhappy past, to restore his faith in womankind.

Her first impulse was to tell Alice that she was going back that very day. She had to reason with Steve, and the sooner the better. But something in Alice's warning made her cautious. 'Very well, I'll promise not to come back with you today.'

'And what about tonight? You've got to teach him a lesson! Don't turn up. Hit him in his pocket – where it hurts most.'

'I don't know if I can let him down again.' Maddy was in turmoil. 'I've only just got back onstage. Me being away has already cost him money. Besides, it's Saturday – his best night. The place will be full to bursting. I need to think on it.'

'Well, while you're thinking on it,' Alice said, 'think about the way he attacked you. Think how he beat you up, even after you told him you were carrying his child. And even though you might by some miracle talk him into family life, just think what the future would be like – never knowing when he might turn on you or the child. God knows, he's capable of it.'

'I know he'll probably turn his back on me,' Maddy answered quietly, 'but I still have to try and win him round, for the baby's sake, if not for mine.'

'Then I'm not going to work.'

'Why not?'

'Sure, if I can't make you see sense, and you insist on going in tonight, so soon after he's done this to you, then you give me no choice. I'll write my letter of notice and send it in. I can't stand back and see him play you for a fool any longer.'

Maddy was horrified. 'You can't send in your notice! You love your work. Besides, it's not so easy to find a job in the clubs. You know how they are a closed shop.'

'Don't you worry, me darlin'.' Alice could see her little ploy beginning to work. 'I'll find a job, even if I have to move away.'

'I can't let you do it,' Maddy said. 'Promise me you won't send in your notice?'

'I've made my decision,' Alice answered.

'No!' Maddy knew from experience that when Alice said something, she meant it. 'I can't let you lose your work and possibly your home, on account of me.' She bit her lip. 'I'll do what you ask, then. I'll stay here tonight and make him sweat.'

'Well, all right then,' Alice said, after a pause. 'And I'm not saying you shouldn't go back at all, because clearly you still have things to decide between the pair of youse. But not tonight. Let the bugger calm down and think it through.'

Maddy threw her arms round the little woman's shoulders. 'I'm sorry,' she said. 'But I may go in tomorrow. You do know I can't stay away too long?'

'I understand that, so I do. But if you were to go in tonight, he'll think he can do whatever he likes and you'll always be there at his beck and call. And when you *do* get to talk it out with him, be prepared for him to give you an ultimatum.'

'What kind of ultimatum?'

Alice did not mince her words. 'He could ask you to get rid of the baby.'

'NO! I would *never* do that! I tried – and I just couldn't do it.' The idea went against every instinct in her body.

It was the answer Alice had expected. 'Good girl.' Reaching across, she took hold of Maddy's hand. 'Listen to me,' she urged. 'London is full of unsavoury characters and Steve Drayton knows each and every one of them; no doubt they're all on his payroll. What I'm saying is . . . be on your guard. You've already seen a glimpse of what he's capable of.'

'I know.'

Sensing her hesitation, Alice assured her, 'If you're worried he might bring somebody else to take your place on stage tonight, I can tell you now, that won't happen. While you were away, he trawled the clubs and agents, looking for a replacement. He managed to find two girls, but neither of them could hold a candle to you. In fact, they were so bad, Dave and Dino threatened to leave. Sure, there are talented girls about, but they're all tied up in secure contracts.'

Up until then, it had not crossed Maddy's mind that she might be so quickly replaced. Instead, she still harboured the illusion that Steve might yet feel proud at having fathered a child, and that in time he might even put a ring on her finger.

She relayed all this to Alice, but as ever Alice was non-committal. 'Let's wait and see, me darlin',' she said encouragingly, 'Who knows? Possibly you and the wee one can make him change his ways, after all.'

Deep down though, she knew it would never happen.

~

When Alice left for her duties at the club after lunch, Maddy reflected on their conversation. This time, she was less optimistic. 'What if she's right and I can't talk him round?' she asked herself. 'What if he throws me out? What if he changes the locks on the flat and turns his back on me altogether?'

It was a frightening thought. She couldn't put all her troubles on Alice, and she couldn't afford a place of her own, as Steve only paid her a pittance, so where would they go, and the baby? How would they live?

A shocking thought rippled across her mind, and it brought her up sharp. Whatever happened, she would *not* have a termination. If Steve didn't want her, she'd find a way to manage without him.

Yet the thought of making it on her own, with a baby in tow, was a terrifying thing. She was a singer; since the age of sixteen, when she was orphaned, she had always been a singer, scratching a living in shabby pubs and clubs until Steve had discovered and promoted her. It would be hard to sing in the clubs, as a single parent, impossible almost.

A sense of outrage coursed through her. 'This is his baby, and he can damned well face his responsibilities!'

Determined either to win him over, or fight him tooth and nail, Maddy found herself regretting her promise not to go in tonight. What if 'making Steve sweat' just got him in such an awful rage that he went and did get himself another singer – and then she would never be able to talk him round!

Pacing the floor, she could not rid herself of all these doubts and fears, until eventually, her instincts decided for her. Making herself believe that Alice would understand, she came to a decision. 'I'll play him at his own game,' she decided. 'I'll turn up tonight as usual, wear a gown to knock him out, and go onstage as though nothing has happened. Steve will come round to my way of thinking. I know he will.'

Her spirits uplifted, Maddy ran a hot bath and soaked in it for a time, until her thoughts were formulated and her wounds soothed.

After towel-drying her long hair, she then let it fall into its natural wave. She applied more antiseptic cream to her cuts, wincing as she rubbed it in, then quickly dressed in the clothes she had worn the previous day.

After making sure everything was secure, she put on her coat and left, deciding to catch a tube down to Clapham

Common station and walk the rest of the way to the Battersea flat to get some fresh air.

If all goes well, I should be travelling back to the flat with Steve tonight, she thought, but she remained apprehensive. After all, she had learned the hard way how easily he could lose control.

~

The journey across town seemed to take forever. She felt oddly isolated and unsure of herself, and wondered if the confrontation with Steve had affected her more than she realised. Thankfully, by the time she had walked to the flat from the tube station, her confidence had grown.

Her key went into the lock easily, much to her relief. At least he hadn't had the locks changed. That must mean something. Perhaps he had had time to think, and was regretting what he had done. The thought of making up brought a smile to her face.

The flat was a credit to her – though, as he enjoyed reminding her, the money she'd spent on making it both smart and cosy had been Steve Drayton's, not hers.

The cream-coloured carpet was of finest wool, as were the many different-coloured rugs laid throughout. The elegant navy and cream colour scheme varied from room to room; creating an effect that was unifying yet individual.

The leather settee and chairs set around a large fireplace in the lounge were warm and squashy, with a scattering of over-size cushions. The whole place was stamped with Maddy's friendly and open personality, though with a discreet dash of elegance.

Encouraged by the fact that Steve had not changed the locks or thrown out her things, Maddy made her way to the bedroom and went straight to his wardrobe. Throwing open the doors, she stood a moment observing the expensive tailored suits hanging there. She roved her hands over them. 'Are you really as bad as Alice says?' she murmured. 'Would you really turn your back on your own flesh and blood?' She persuaded herself that somehow, she would make him love the child she carried inside her.

For herself, she laid out fresh lingerie, along with a smart cream-coloured shirt with stand-up collar; then a short brown skirt and matching fitted jacket. Next she fished out her silk stockings and high-heeled cream-coloured shoes. Although the skirt was rather tight, since her tummy was acquiring a rounded shape, she looked very fresh and pretty in the outfit.

Almost ready, she sat at the dressing-table and skilfully applied foundation to her face, hiding the scratches. Eyeshadow and mascara followed, then a touch of coffee-coloured lipstick and a generous spray of lightly scented perfume.

She gave her hair a final brushing, then checked herself in the full-length mirror. 'Right, my girl!' The merest smile lit her face. 'You're about as ready as you'll ever be.'

For the first time today, she felt good. It was off to the shops now, to find the ultimate glamorous outfit, with maybe an extra-long split to show off her legs and avert people's eyes from her midriff. Or a low top to show off the bits of herself that he hadn't marked. The smile fell from her face as she recalled his vicious attack on her. How could she risk her safety, and that of their child, with such an unpredictable man? When he fell into one of his rages, Steve Drayton became a monster.

~

Being Saturday, the Underground was busier than usual, the pavements heavy with people, and the Oxford Street shops full to bursting. At every pedestrian-crossing, there was a long wait before the road was clear.

'I hate coming into London on a Saturday,' said a grey-haired woman, who was almost lifted off her feet when a gaggle of girls came rushing past. 'I can't stand all this pushing and shoving!'

Taking the pensioner by the arm, Maddy helped her across the road, to receive the loveliest smile for her trouble. 'I'm glad not all young people are loud and selfish,' the woman said, ambling away with a tut and a grumble.

Maddy headed straight for Liberty's on Regent Street. They had such fabulous evening wear there, suitable for showbiz.

'I want to open Steve's eyes and make him see what he might be losing,' she told herself. 'No more pink ladies. I'm going to get a fiery red dress! Yes, that's it – I'll go for red and be a scarlet woman instead.'

The saleslady looked at Maddy, at her voluminous golden-brown hair and her striking dark eyes, and said, 'Oh no, my dear! Not red. With your colouring, you should wear the palest ivory.'

Maddy was amazed. 'I've never even considered wearing ivory,' she confessed. 'I've always thought that it would make me look washed out.'

The woman persuaded her to give it a try.

The first dress she put on was nipped in at the waist and full-skirted. 'No, it's definitely not me.' Maddy was unhappy with the style, but amazed by how flattering the colour was.

The second one was straight-skirted and fitting, but the neck was high and the sleeves too full.

The third was stunning – low-cut at the top, but with straps instead of sleeves. 'Good heavens, what on earth did you do to your arms?' The woman was shocked by the bruises.

Maddy stammered an excuse, and returned to the cubicle where, both disappointed and embarrassed, she began quickly dressing to cover up the bruises where Steve had gripped her last night.

She was reaching for her blouse when there came a knock on the cubicle door. 'My dear, I've found a dress I think you really should try.' The door inched open and an arm reached through, over which hung the loveliest-looking gown. 'You looked wonderful in the ivory,' the saleslady explained, 'so I went away and searched through another batch of stock that's just arrived from Italy. This one is absolutely right for you . . . trust me.'

Suspecting the woman was trying hard to make a sale, Maddy agreed to try it anyway.

Five minutes later, she emerged from the cubicle, looking a million dollars.

'Oh my dear!' The woman's mouth fell open. 'I knew it was the one for you!'

The ivory-coloured dress was plain and elegant; with long, slim sleeves, small silk-covered buttons at the cuffs, it hung exquisitely. In fact, it could have been made for her.

'It simply flows over you!' The attendant was delighted. 'And the ivory . . . so beautiful.'

Maddy was pleased to note the discreet split in the skirt, running down the left side from thigh to hem, which opened only when she stepped one leg forward. The punters at the Pink Lady adored it when she wore something a little bit sexy but still ladylike.

Wondering what Steve might say, she looked at herself in the long mirror. Against the ivory, her eyes and hair seemed richer, deeper in colour, and more importantly, the long slim sleeves hid the marks he had made on her arms.

And so she bought it, though it was more than she could easily afford. Steve liked her to have decent stage outfits, but the money he gave her for them was on the mean side. But this was a special dress. A dress on which her whole future depended. Thanking the woman, she left with her precious cargo, and went home to Alice's flat.

She could hardly wait for the evening, when she would walk out on that Soho stage with her head held high.

Seeing her in that dress must surely melt her lover's heart? Even a hard man like Steve could not turn away the woman who loved him; the singer who brought in the bulk of his money. And the fact that she was carrying his child must surely mean the world to him. Shouldn't it?

She was both nervous and excited. Was she taking a chance too far? Was Alice right . . . would he still reject her, and his child?

There was only one way to find out.

CHAPTER FIVE

IN THE EVENING, dressed in her new finery, Maddy took a taxi to the club. She was desperately nervous about Steve's reaction, but was hoping that tonight she could make him see sense.

She felt ashamed and worried at having broken her promise to Alice, even if it *was* for all the right reasons. Later, she would explain it all to her friend, convinced that she would understand.

Her heart beating fifteen to the dozen, she carefully inched open the door and peeped inside. As usual, the club was busy, with Jack and the others rushing about behind the bar. It was difficult to see clearly across the room because of Raymond's sizeable frame as he meandered about, clearing tables and shyly answering the occasional remark from a client. She smiled. No wonder they all love him, she thought. He's a real gentleman.

In that moment when Raymond stooped to collect something from the floor, she saw Dino and Dave sitting having a quiet drink at the side of the stage. Steve was standing at the far end of the bar, leaning forward, glass in hand, the usual Dunhill cigarette drooping from his lips.

At the sight of him, her heart leaped, and all kinds of bitter-sweet memories flashed through her mind: of the wonderful times they had shared – the many occasions when she was made to feel like the most beautiful woman in the world, and other times when he was so tender and loving, she thought it would never end. But then there was his explosive jealousy, the inquisitions, and the recent beatings she had suffered at his hands, with Alice's premonition of worse to come. Steve was like Dr Jekyll and Mr Hyde, and Maddy wondered if she could really face a future with this constant battle on her hands.

For a moment, she was deeply troubled; unsure of whether she should go inside, or turn about and never come back. It was a strange, unnerving sensation.

Needing to think clearly, she closed the door and stood on the pavement, her back against the wall and her thoughts in turmoil. She felt incredibly sad, and lost – and for a moment, all the belief she had in him and their life together seemed to ebb away.

'Pull yourself together, my girl,' she reprimanded herself sternly. 'You can't turn back now – not when you've come this far.'

As always, the pull of her feelings for Steve proved to be stronger than her fears, and as she swung round to enter the building, a mischievous smile lit her eyes. 'I'll sneak in the back way,' she murmured, 'have a quick check of my make-up, and then I'll let him know I'm here.' The idea of taking him by surprise was thrilling.

Hurrying down the alleyway, she hoped the back door was not locked.

Good. The door pushed open at the touch of her hand. Excited and hopeful, she slipped into the building and made her way through the corridors which led directly to her dressing-room.

As she neared it, she heard a door slam, and then footsteps hurrying away. Not wanting to be seen, she pressed herself into the doorway of the store-room, emerging only when the footsteps had died away.

With the coast clear, she hurried on, agitating over who those footsteps might have belonged to. She knew it wasn't Alice, because that dear woman's light steps were as familiar to her as her own. She was equally certain it wasn't the man who looked after the stage-lighting because he had a distinctive limp. Nor could they have belonged to Raymond, whose lumbering tread rocked the building. And as far as she was aware, the barmen hardly ever came back here.

Of course, it could have been someone looking for the loos and taking a wrong turn. Yes, that must be it! Someone had taken a wrong turn and got lost.

Nonetheless, for some strange reason, Maddy was filled with a sense of foreboding.

'You're beginning to imagine things,' she told herself, and gave a harsh little laugh. 'It's Alice's fault, for putting the fear of God into you.'

Having reached the dressing-room, she went quickly inside, instantly taken aback by the odour of a heady perfume, quite different from her own. 'Raymond's been at it with a new cleaning wax, she thought. He's always trying some new product or another.

She glanced about. There were no signs of the struggle from last night, she observed wrily. All had been neatly swept aside . . . like herself!

Going straightway to the new mirror that had been secured to the wall, she stared at herself, feeling like a kid on her first date.

He won't be able to resist me, she beamed. Then, reaching for her lipliner, she was amazed to see that her own hairbrush and cosmetics were gone, and in their place was an expensive range of powders and lipsticks, together with a beautiful silver-backed hairbrush.

While her mind was reeling with the shock, she heard the musicians strike up and then the sweet uplifted voice of a woman in song. It was a voice she had not heard before, and it was really good.

At first she would not let herself believe the obvious, but when she was made to accept the truth, her hopes of a reunion with Steve were cruelly dashed. He's found another singer to take my place, she thought, and her heart lurched. It seemed that Alice was right, after all. Steve really did want to get rid of her. She had let herself believe that her love was strong enough to bring him round to the idea of family and commitment. But now, she realised that it was never meant to be.

Not only had he beaten and humiliated her by throwing her out onto the streets, but hardly was her back turned than he had brought in another singer to take her place.

That was the final turning-point.

If there had been the slightest hope that he might come round to wanting her and the baby, that hope was gone; she had no illusions now. It was over. Steve Drayton had wiped her out of his life, as though she never existed.

Slumped in the chair, she let the emotions flow, and when sorrow flared to anger, she picked up the silver-backed hairbrush. For what seemed an age she examined the beauty of it; with the fine, curved handle, it was a magnificent thing.

The sight of a few delicate strands of blonde hair caught in the bristles was like salt in the wound. *He* gave her this, Maddy thought – and no doubt he told her the same wicked lies he told me. It wasn't all that long ago since he gave *me* a hairbrush not too different from the one I am holding. The man is a liar and a cheat. No good to anyone.

Gripping the hairbrush so hard it hurt, with one vicious swipe Maddy sent the entire collection of cosmetics crashing to the floor. She glanced at the wreckage and thought how like her own life it was.

Taking a moment to compose herself, she reached into the bottom drawer, took out a box of her own make-up, and dabbed a shower of cream-powder over her cheekbones. She then tidied her crumpled dress, and fluffed her thick, dark hair. 'You don't need him.' She spoke to her reflection in the mirror. 'But you can't let him get away with it so easily. Don't let him think he's broken you.'

Striding from the dressing-room, she made her way to the top of the stairs; from here she could view both the stage and the bar area.

She saw him straightaway. Leaning against the bottom of the stage, he was looking up at the singer. Long-limbed and youthful, her slim figure draped in darkest silk, she made a striking image.

From below, his eyes ogling her every move, Steve Drayton was like a dog drooling over a juicy steak. With every wink and 'come-on' gesture, he was not ashamed to let her know he wanted her . . . in the same way he had once wanted Maddy.

When all of a sudden he straightened up and turned towards the stairs, Maddy fled to the safety of the alcove, where she remained until he walked by, blissfully unaware of her presence.

She knew exactly what he had in mind, because of the countless times he used to give her the 'come-on' from the foot of that very stage – and hadn't she always answered his call by making straight for his office after finishing her set? The minute she was in the door he would draw the blinds and they would make love.

She recalled these times with a surge of pleasure, because she had believed in him, believed every lie he uttered. But now, after learning the truth, these times would be shut out of her mind forever. They meant nothing to her now, just as they had meant nothing to him then.

As she made her way to his office, the rage she had felt

dissipated, meeting under a rush of fear. What would he do when he saw her? How would he try and explain himself away? Or would he throw her out as before . . . treating her with the contempt she now knew he felt for her?

As she approached the office door, her fears deepened and for a moment she hesitated. She could see him closing the blinds in anticipation of his new woman's arrival. She heard the telephone and watched as he answered it, and all the time he remained unaware that she was just outside.

He seemed agitated by the conversation. Pacing up and down beside the desk, he was threatening the person at the other end of the line. 'You heard what I said, and let that be an end to it. Now, I suggest you make other arrangements. In fact, from where I'm standing, you don't have any alternative!' With that he slammed the phone back into its cradle, at the same time thumping his other fist against the desk. 'Bastards! If they think they can get the better of me, they'd best think again!'

It was then she made her move. As she flung the door wide open, he glanced up, astonished to see her there. 'What the devil do *you* want?' Crudely staring her up and down, he laughed out loud. 'All glammed up and nowhere to go, eh?'

Closing the door behind her, she boldly approached him, determination etched in the set of her features. 'I want to know why you took on another singer.'

'Because I'm done with you, isn't that reason enough?' His spite was cutting. 'I needed a new face, a younger woman who would know better than to come crying to me, after she's been knocked up by some other bloke who's cleared off and left her in the lurch.'

'I was never with any other bloke, and you know it.' It was time to speak her mind and to hell with it. 'It's *your* child, Steve. The reason you won't admit to it, is because it might hamper your precious lifestyle with a woman and child in tow.'

'You've said enough. Now get out!' Taking a step towards

her, he gestured to the door. 'You're a dirty little tart, and everyone will know it soon enough. And even if this . . . *thing* . . .' repulsed, he prodded her in the stomach, 'even if it is mine, which it most definitely is not, you and I both know I would never admit to it.'

'Tell me why not.' Hurt and angry, she stood up to him. 'I need an explanation. You owe me that much.'

'I don't owe you anything! The hard truth is, you've had your fun and now it's over. It wouldn't bother me if I never clapped eyes on you again. What would I want with you anyway? Like I said – you've had your day. It's time to move over for someone more talented.'

Maddy understood his thinking. By 'talented', he meant young and pliable.

She stood her ground. 'You can try every which way you like to get out of it, but in the end I promise, you'll be made to face the consequences. You know as well as I do, I never loved anyone but you. And now, you want rid of me. All right, that's your choice.'

Looking him straight in the eye, she calmly warned him, 'I also have a choice, so understand this: whatever happens between the two of us, I will not let our child grow up without knowing who their father is.'

The smile slid from his face. 'Are you threatening me?'

Unflinching beneath his hostile gaze, she promised, 'I'll do whatever it takes, to give our child a name. I'll make sure it's common knowledge that you're the father, and that through no fault of ours, you've washed your hands of us.'

She smiled at the look of disbelief on his face. 'You wouldn't like that, would you, eh? The great Steve Drayton – no one ever got one over on him, did they? But I give you my word, I'll fight tooth and nail, until you're made to admit that you're our baby's father. I'll make you take your responsibilities seriously, you see if I don't!'

No sooner had she finished issuing the warning than she felt the full force of his fist, and when her lip split open and the blood spattered over his hands, he was like a madman.

'Bitch!' Ripping at her new dress, he tore it from neck to waist, leaving her desperately clutching the remnants with both hands. 'I've seen off more threats and danger than you could ever imagine. So don't make the mistake of thinking you'll come out on top, lady, because you won't.'

Holding her trapped with one hand, he fished into her evening bag, drew out the keys to the flat and thrust them into his pocket. 'You won't be needing these again.'

When she struggled to get away, he held her there. 'I swear to God, if you show your face here again, or try to get in touch with me, I'll have you done away with. Make no mistake, I will do it!' Taking her by the arm, he dragged her through the door and down the back stairway; halfway down, with one great heave, he sent her careering down the remaining steps.

Then, coming down the steps two at a time, he went after her, grabbed her by the neck and threw her out onto the back alley, tossing her handbag after her. Wiping his hands together as though ridding himself of something dirty, he warned her, 'If you bother me again, I won't hesitate to have you and the kid set in concrete. Do you hear what I'm saying?' When she didn't answer, he raised his foot and kicked her in the groin. 'DID YOU HEAR WHAT I SAID!'

With her lip swelling, and her body bruised and battered, she could only nod, which thankfully was enough to appease him.

And then he was gone; only at the top of the stairs did he momentarily turn, to look down on the fallen woman with contempt.

Through tears of shame, Maddy watched him go, and for a moment she felt nothing, no hatred or desire for revenge; all the love she once felt for him was as though it had never been.

~

After a while, she levered herself up and felt her way along the wall, managing to stumble a short distance. Just when she was beginning to believe she might make it to safety, the wall caved into a doorway; she fell inside, and for a moment she feared as though she might never be able to get up. Faintly, she could hear the sound of a Latin beat coming through the wall, as the club carried on with its usual Saturday-night party mood. But for Madeleine Delaney, the party was well and truly over.

When she made an effort to stand, her legs crumpled beneath her. '*Alice!*' Twice she sobbed out her friend's name, before her senses began to fade.

Yet somewhere in the dark recesses of her mind, she drew strength from the knowledge that Alice was never far away.

CHAPTER SIX

T HOUGH IT WAS only minutes, it seemed an age before she opened her eyes. She must have passed out, she thought. The cold was numbing; and even when she drew the fragments of her dress about her, she could not stop trembling.

With determination, she took stock of the damage Steve had done to her. She had taken a hard beating, yet she was relieved to find she could move her arms and legs, and thankfully, she still had her wits about her.

She slid the tips of her fingers over her face; it was bruised, and the cuts from yesterday had reopened, but as far as she could tell, nothing was broken.

Her fears were for the child inside her. Was it harmed in any way? Had he hurt the baby when he had kicked her in the groin? How could she tell? She needed help . . . she *had* to get away from here.

Thankfully, her legs took the weight when she uprighted herself. It was then that she heard a flurry of girlish giggling, and a voice asking, 'Why are we out here? It's so much cosier in your office, Stevie.'

Steve Drayton's low, thick voice was unmistakable. 'Too many interruptions,' he said huskily, 'but you needn't worry about the cold.' There was a sexy chuckle. 'I'll keep you warm enough, I can promise you that.'

There was a moment of silence, then another burst of giggling and the man's voice urging her to, 'Keep quiet, eh? We don't want them coming out to see what's going on, do we?'

'Was it true, what you said earlier?'

'You'd best remind me.' His voice was soft and persuasive, and then there was the wet, smacking sound of a long kiss. 'What was it I said?'

'That you'd never seen anyone as beautiful as me, and that you would always look after me – even when I'm older and not so pretty.'

'Hmh!' His laughter echoed through the alley. 'You really are a little worrier, aren't you? Well, you can stop worrying, because I meant every word.' Steve Drayton had enough experience to know that a little flattery and a few cleverly placed lies would melt any young fool like her.

'And what about . . .' the girl hesitated, 'the singer before me – the one they called Songbird.' She paused again. 'Did you say all these things to *her*?'

'*Never!*' Maddy heard him light a cigarette, the soft glow from the lighter flickering through the darkness. 'Why would I say those things to her? She meant nothing to me.'

'I was told she was a wonderful singer.'

'Were you now?'

'Was she? A good singer, I mean?'

'She may have had a passable voice, but she could never hold a candle to you. Besides, she was a slut – a cheap tramp who would go with anybody.' Disgust trembled in his voice.

'I've made you angry now, haven't I?'

He laughed – an angry sound, and then his voice thickened as he said, 'You'd best make it up to me then, hadn't you?' Tossing his cigarette butt to the cobbles, he ground it out with the toe of his shoe.

A long silence followed, during which Maddy eventually

managed to manoeuvre herself into a position from where she could see them. And what she saw only deepened her shame, because hadn't she been equally besotted with this vicious man, who had turned his back on her when she needed him most? She thanked her lucky stars that at long last, she could see the badness in him.

Out there, in the darker shadows of the alleyway, Steve Drayton had the girl pressed against the wall, his trousers round his ankles as he pushed into her. The girl was wrapped round him, her skirt above her waist and her shrill voice emitting little gasps of pleasure.

Maddy wanted to look away, yet somehow, finally seeing him for what he was, the sight of his fornicating had a mesmerising effect on her. She needed to keep the moment, so never again would she be deceived by him, or any other man. She stood, hurt and bleeding, agonising with herself as to whether she ought to tell the girl what she was letting herself in for, or whether to stay quiet, out of sight, and make a hasty retreat once they were gone.

In that moment, after a final surge, Drayton thrust the girl from him. 'Get back inside before they miss you.' He hastily pulled up his trousers. 'If they ask where you've been, tell them you had to get out for a breath of air.'

'I'd rather stay out here with you.' Hopelessly infatuated, she clung to him. 'I've never loved anyone like I love you.'

Impatient, though clever enough to keep her sweet, he replied teasingly, 'You don't know me enough to love me.'

While they dressed, they talked, she offering herself again and he trying to worm himself out of a difficult situation; though mindful of the fact that if he intended using her, he'd have to play it smart.

Maddy was sickened at how easily he manipulated the girl, and was torn two ways. She wanted to warn the girl as to the monster Steve Drayton really was. On the other hand, if she took another beating, it could well be her baby who paid the price this time.

So, she waited for her chance to escape, hoping that even now, the girl might see the wrong side of him; though from the way she continued to throw herself at him, it did not seem likely.

~

While Steve Drayton had been satisfying his lust outside in the alley, something more sinister was unfurling inside the club.

The four men were eager to find him. Having barged in through the front door, ignoring the ticket desk and cloak-room counter, they made straight for the bar, where Raymond was dumping a crate of bottles. 'You! Drayton – where is he?' Smartly dressed in an expensive dark suit and overcoat, the leader had an air of authority.

Raymond placed the crate on the bar and glanced around, searching for someone else who might deal with the situation. However, the older barman was pulling a pint at the far end of the bar, and there was no sign of Jack.

'Look, sunshine,' prodding his finger into Raymond's chest, the man leaned forward. 'You deaf or what? I'll ask you again. *Where can I find that thieving bastard Drayton?*' He had the look and manner of a man who always got what he wanted.

'I've n-no idea where he is,' Raymond answered nervously. 'M-matter of fact, I don't think he's been about this p-past hour or m-more.'

'Think again.' This time, the man took Raymond by the throat and drew him close until their faces were almost touch-ing. Raymond was more than capable of teaching this nasty piece of work a lesson, but he doubted he could take on the other three as well. Fearing he might be blamed if the club was trashed, Raymond thought twice.

'Give me a minute,' he said gruffly. 'I'll find out where he is. What name is it, please?'

With one of the men keeping a wary eye on him, he repeated the gang boss's name, to make sure he'd got it correctly. 'Den Carter. Right you are, mister.' And he went away to the office, to find Steve.

Unaware of what was happening upstairs, Jack was down in the cellar, changing barrels.

He was surprised and pleased to see Alice. 'Raymond said you were looking for me earlier,' she told him.

'That's right.' Straightening from his task, he conveyed his concern over Maddy. 'What's been going on?'

'What do you mean?'

'Aw, come on, Alice. Don't shut me out. If Maddy's in trouble, I need to know.'

'What makes you think she's in trouble?' Her calm expression gave nothing away.

Jack was incredulous. 'You mean you don't know?'

Alice tried to put his mind at rest. 'If you're talking about what happened last night, there was no real harm done.'

'How can you be so sure? Raymond found broken glass, and things scattered everywhere . . . there was blood on the walls and over the floor.' Coming to stand before her, he pleaded, 'For God's sake, Alice, what went down? Was it Maddy – did they have a row?' His face darkened with rage. 'If that twisted bastard has hurt her, I swear I'll cut his hands off.' Jack had been bullied by his stepfather as a child, and could not tolerate it. 'Where is she now? I need to know she's safe.' Jack was beside himself. 'Does she know he's taken on a new singer?'

Alice gave him as straight an answer as she could, without betraying Maddy's secret about the child. 'You're not to worry. Yes, they had a set-to, but Maddy is fine. I took her home with me, and as far as I know, she has no idea he has taken on a new singer. Even *I* didn't know, until I saw her up there on

81

the stage tonight. Look, Jack, with any luck it'll make Maddy finally see the light where Drayton is concerned.'

'What about the blood?'

Alice chose not to answer this, merely repeating, 'I can assure you, Maddy is fine. She's keeping her distance for a while – trying to teach him that he can't just take her for granted.' She had seen how her words were calming him. 'Look, Jack, she intends coming in tomorrow. You can talk to her then.'

'I'd rather come round to your place tomorrow morning before work and see her there, if that's all right with you?'

'Yes, I don't see why not. You'll be very welcome.'

'I'll tell her about this new girl, if you like. She's bound to be upset,' Jack said protectively.

Alice nodded; she too had concerns as to how Maddy might react to the news of another singer taking her place. It was a cruel thing to do.

But then Steve Drayton had always been a law unto himself.

~

In the alley, the girl was proving difficult to appease.

'Move yourself, Ellen.' Taking her by the arm, Steve Drayton drew her towards the back door. 'They'll be wondering where you've gone. Besides, I'm paying you good money to entertain the clients.'

She giggled. 'I'd rather entertain *you*.'

He sighed, bored. 'And you shall. But there'll be time for all that later, when I get you home.'

An idea struck him as being profitable. He had seen the way his clients had drooled over his new singer. She was pliable enough; she was also besotted with him, so if he played his hand right, there was money to be made. No doubt his rough and ready counterparts would give a handsome sum for a few hours' playtime with her.

The idea grew. I can't see her refusing, the insatiable little slapper, he thought greedily, especially when she's so keen to please me. Oh, yes! Putty in his hands, that's what she was.

Her voice startled him. 'Tell me you love me, Stevie, and I'll go back inside.'

Irritated, he studied her for a minute, wanting to give her a slap and shut the bitch up, but controlling himself with an effort. He'd had as much woman trouble as he could take. 'Of course I love you,' he lied. 'Why do you think I brought you out here?'

Her resolve melting, she looked up at him. 'You're not just making a fool of me . . . playing me along to get your own way?'

'I would never do that!' He cupped her small features and kissed her soundly on the mouth. When he released her, the smile on her face told him she was his for the taking.

'So, we're a couple then?' She wanted so much to believe that.

'Oh, absolutely.' He had her right where he wanted her. 'But we have to be discreet.'

'Why's that?'

While he fought to find an answer that would satisfy her without compromising himself, Maddy realised the girl was falling into his cleverly woven trap. She had seen how easily he had twisted her words. Morever, she could almost read his mind with his ideas of how he might eventually make money from this innocent.

With that in mind, she knew that even if it meant getting another beating, she could not keep quiet.

Taking a few deep breaths, she gathered her strength and began walking towards them, slowly at first, but then with purpose.

When Drayton glanced up and saw her, his face opened in astonishment. Pushing the girl aside, he turned, legs astride in that antagonistic stance she had come to know so well. 'What the devil are you playing at? I thought I told you to sod off.' His mean eyes boring into hers, he took a step forward. 'Get the hell out of here before I lose my temper!'

'That's *her*, isn't it – Songbird – the singer whose job I took?' The girl's cry pierced the tension. Curiosity turned to anger. 'You said she'd left for foreign parts! You told me she would never come back – that she didn't want the work. So, what's going on? Look at the state of her – she needs an ambulance! Jesus, Steve, what have I got myself into here?'

'Shut your trap!' Turning on her, he issued a warning. 'Do what you're paid to do – get back inside and entertain the clients. *I'll* deal with this.'

Unsettled, the girl looked from Steve to Maddy and back again. 'So, you and me, Steve – *are* we a couple, or not?'

The sight of Maddy had been a shock. Why was she here, and why was her dress torn like that? She looked like a tramp off the streets. Was she ill, or drunk maybe?

Either way, there was something going on here that made her deeply uneasy.

Maddy turned her gaze on the girl and for a moment their eyes met. Recognising herself when she was younger and more foolish, Maddy offered her a warning. 'Don't trust him,' she urged quietly. 'He's a liar and a thug. He'll hurt you, just like he hurt me.' She patted her stomach. 'I'm carrying his child, but that didn't stop him from beating me. Listen to what I'm saying – I've no reason to lie. He'll promise you the world, but he'll use you in every way imaginable. If you have any self-worth at all, you must get away from him – *now*. While you still can.'

Suddenly, he was on her. With the back of his hand he lashed out, knocking Maddy hard against the wall.

What he didn't expect was the girl's reaction. 'LEAVE HER BE!' she shouted, and clawed at his face. Steve was like a wild animal. Spinning round, he took Ellen by the shoulders and threw her towards Maddy.

With murder in his heart, he hissed, 'You're welcome to each other,' and took a step towards them; but then was made to stop when a man's voice called out to him.

'You can deal with your women later, Drayton. For now, you and I have more important business to attend to.'

Swinging round, Drayton found himself confronted by four thugs. The big one, Den Carter, addressed himself to Ellen. 'Get away from here, slag. And keep your trap shut if you know what's good for you!'

Recognising her former boss, the girl didn't need another warning. With Maddy leaning on her, she led her away. 'I worked for him before,' she whispered as they stumbled down the alley. 'He's a bad lot. He'll make that scum Steve pay for enticing me away.'

At the top of the alley, they paused, long enough to see two of the minders pounce on Drayton and twist his arms up behind his back. Then as the big man approached, Drayton began blustering and threatening all manner of retribution. Suddenly, he broke free.

There was a lot of shouting and scuffling, followed by the unmistakable sound of gunshot; the big man stumbled backwards while the others fought with Drayton to secure the gun.

Seconds later, the club doors were thrown open and the alley was alive with people; some keeping a sensible distance and others too curious to stand off. 'He's got a gun!' Trying to herd them away, Raymond yelled a warning. 'Keep back, all of you!' But it was like trying to hold back a burst dam, as with morbid curiosity and a lot of drink inside some of them, the people surged forward to get a better look at the drama that was taking place.

Jack was up at the front, with Alice not far behind, though he urged her to keep her distance. 'I don't want you getting hurt,' he said. Concerned for her safety and increasingly worried that Maddy might somehow be caught up in this too, Jack was taking no chances.

The whole terrible event seemed to happen in slow motion, and yet it was over in seconds. Mortally wounded, the big man was lying groaning on the ground, with Steve Drayton locked in fierce combat with his henchmen. When Alice and Jack came running forwards, Drayton was like a madman as he struggled to free himself. In the mayhem, two more shots rang out. Jack was the first to go down. Then Alice.

With no thought for his own life, Raymond ran to Jack, who appeared lifeless. Desolate, he turned his attention on Alice, taking her in his arms and comforting her as best he could until the older barman, Ted, tried to drag him away. 'You can't help her now, mate,' he said kindly, and glanced down at Alice; bathed in her own blood and lying so still, she seemed beyond earthly help.

At first Raymond resisted Ted's attempts to take him from her. But then, in tears and deeply saddened, he let himself be led away.

From the first day he had spoken with Alice, something had taken hold of his lonely heart. He had loved her from afar, waiting for his chance, hoping that one day she might see him in the same light. And now, because of a man who did not deserve to wipe her shoes, his dream of taking care of Alice, and hoping she might come to love him, were ended.

At that moment, all hell was let loose as the shrill scream of sirens heralded the arrival of speeding police cars. People were running all over the place – it was chaos. And Steve still had the gun.

From a doorway at the top of the alley, the two women had seen it all. 'My God!' Shocked to the core, Maddy could think only of Jack and Alice. 'They've been shot! I've got to go to them!'

Holding onto her, the girl kept her safe. 'There's nothing you can do now. Come away, there's bad stuff going down. The police are everywhere. We'll be interrogated. They won't give us a minute's peace.' Desperate to put a distance between themselves and the authorities, she kept a tight hold on her new friend. 'We need to get away before they see us. If we go now, they'll never know we were here!'

But Maddy wasn't listening to reason. All she could think of was her injured friends. 'Let me go!' Frantic, she tore herself away. 'I need to go to them.' And no matter how hard she tried, the girl could no longer restrain her.

As Maddy rushed down the alley, total confusion was unfolding all about her. Police were everywhere; some grappling with the thugs, others handcuffing Drayton, and people were being ordered to get inside, where they should remain for questioning.

The first ambulance drove in and attendants tumbled out, armed with all manner of equipment. Maddy saw how one of them went straight to the big man, now lying silent in a pool of blood, looking up and shaking her head to indicate there was nothing to be done for him. And then they moved on to Jack, who was crumpled against the far wall.

Maddy got to Alice first. 'Alice . . . it's me, Maddy.' Tenderly holding her hand, she looked down on that dear, still face and her heart broke. 'You'll be all right,' she promised brokenly. 'They're here to help you.'

Turning, she shouted over the chaos, 'OVER HERE – please hurry!' But her cries fell away in the wake of all the confusion. Through the hordes of people being herded back to the club, she could see ambulancemen tending to Jack, and others bringing out more equipment and stretchers.

Terrified that assistance might come too late, Maddy sobbed, 'Alice, please don't leave me,' devastated when it seemed that the injured woman was beyond hearing her. 'We need you,' she pleaded. 'Me and the baby.' Giving the limp hand a little shake, she said, 'Alice, wake up. *Please!* You can't leave us now. What will we do without you?'

When Alice grabbed her hand in reply, Maddy thought her heart would stop. For a moment she couldn't speak. Then she quietly thanked the Almighty for sparing her friend, and carried on gently patting her hand, like a mother soothes her child; and now she was telling her softly, 'You'll be allright . . . you'll see. Help is on its way . . . you'll be allright my darling.' Turning her head she gave another frantic shout, 'OVER HERE . . . SHE'S HURT . . . HURRY . . . PLEASE HURRY!!'

'Go from here.' Alice's voice was almost inaudible, gasping. 'No more contact with *him* . . .' Slipping fast away, she could hardly make herself heard. '*Promise me.*' When she now took a breath, it was a rasping, frightening thing for Maddy to hear.

'Be still,' the younger woman pleaded. 'Be still, be still.'

But Alice would not be still. With a huge surge of strength, she had slightly raised her head and was looking the girl straight in the eye.

'*Promise*,' she said, then fell back again.

Desperate, Maddy shouted again, this time her voice charged with anger. 'Hurry! For God's sake, hurry!'

In that moment, one of the ambulancemen looked up from treating Jack and spoke to his colleague before making his way over to them.

With Alice's flickering gaze trained on her, Maddy gave her her word. 'I promise,' she whispered, holding her close. 'I'll never come back . . . I swear it. Just hold on, please, Alice. Help is on its way. Don't die, please don't leave me all on my own. I can't bear it.'

As the medics took over, Maddy clambered up on shaky legs, and looked *straight into the face of the devil himself.*

Two policemen had arrested Drayton. Handcuffed, he was

being marched towards the waiting squad car. Before they managed to get him inside, however, he turned and spat a message at Maddy, the words of which would haunt her for the rest of her days. *'Your card is marked, you bitch. Keep looking over your shoulder. Day and night, wherever you try to hide, I'll find you.'*

When the officer yanked him forward to stuff him into the vehicle, the dark and sinister smile he gave Maddy was a testament to his evil – and it flooded her bruised and battered heart with fear.

~

While Alice was being tended to, Maddy stated to walk over to the place where Jack was being cared for.

Her heart sank when the medic there prevented her approaching, and informed her that his patient was beyond help.

Maddy began to sob again, but then Ellen appeared out of nowhere, swooped on her and stole her away. 'There's nothing you or anyone can do for him now,' she said. 'As for your other friend, she's in good hands. They said they are taking her to UCH,' she told Maddy.

University College Hospital, where she had been only last night. Maddy was stunned – she could barely take it all in.

Eager to get herself and Maddy as far away as possible, Ellen took charge, sneaking them through the kitchens of the Chinese restaurant next door. 'Luckily, the police are all so busy dealing with everyone else, they haven't had time to catch up with us,' she said.'

And so, the two of them made their escape from this nightmare scene, their ears ringing with the sounds of gunshots, screams, sirens and loudhailers, their minds grappling with the dreadful sights they had witnessed.

CHAPTER SEVEN

E LLEN HUSTLED MADDY along the pavement. 'Let's get a cab and go back to my place.'

'What did you say your name was?' Maddy had taken a liking to this young woman. She seemed strong and sensible.

'Ellen Drew.'

'All right then, Ellen – where are you taking me?' Maddy limped along beside her, cold, bedraggled and bleeding.

'I live in Bethnal Green – in the East End. It's not too far.' The younger girl flagged down a taxi. 'Once we get home, we'll have a cup of tea, fix you up, and sort out what to do.' As the cab drew to a halt, she helped Maddy in before climbing in beside her. 'Bethnal Green please, mate' she instructed the cabbie. 'Drop us off at the corner of Wilmot Street.'

Safely installed in the cab, Maddy took a sideways glance at her companion. She had been wrong about her, she thought. When she overheard her and Drayton talking in the alley, Maddy had believed the girl to be naïve and innocent. Now, having seen how she took charge of the situation, she realised that there was more to the girl than she had previously thought.

A few minutes later, on arriving at their destination, the cabbie stopped exactly where Ellen had instructed. 'That'll be three pounds, if you please.'

JOSEPHINE COX

'I'll have to give you an IOU,' Ellen admitted. 'Neither of us have got a penny to our names. You see, we had to leave in a hurry and all our stuff is back in Soho.'

Realising the awkward situation they were in, Maddy slipped off her watch, and handed it to the driver. 'This will more than cover the fare,' she said.

'Look, lady, the fare is three pounds – hard cash and no messing.' From the tone of his voice, the man was ready for trouble. 'I don't work for trinkets.'

Leaning forward so as to see his face, Ellen put on her sweetest smile. 'Like I said, we got caught up in a brawl, and left our purses behind. It happens, as I'm sure you understand.'

Straining his neck, he looked from her to Maddy. 'Working girls, are you?' He winked.

'If you like,' Ellen enticed him.

Maddy was shocked. 'NO!' Tugging at Ellen to come away, she told the cabbie, 'We're not prostitutes! It's just like she said – we got caught up in a fight, and now we just want to get home.'

He glared at them through the mirror. 'You must think I was born yesterday,' he said, and gave a snort. 'You've only got to look at the state of you to know you're lying.' Gesturing at Maddy's torn dress, and Ellen's tousled hair, he sneered, 'Picked up a dodgy punter, did you, girls?'

Maddy touched him on the shoulder. 'Please, just look at the watch. It's worth a lot more than three pounds.'

Something in the timbre of her voice made him examine the watch under the light. He was pleasantly surprised. With a gold and silver plaited strap, it boasted the prettiest diamond in the centre of the dial. 'Stolen, is it?' He knew enough to realise that the watch was good.

'No way! It's my own watch.' In a softer voice, Maddy entreated him to look on the back.

He scanned the engraving. *To Maddy. Happy sixteenth birthday from Daddy.*

The driver chuckled nastily. 'Sugar daddy, was it?'

'If you don't want it,' Maddy said angrily, 'just give it back!'

'Whoa! Whoa! Take it easy.' He began to believe her story. 'What's your name?

'Maddy . . . Maddy for short.'

'So what's the inscription on the back?'

Realising he was testing her, Maddy correctly repeated it.

'Mmm. I still can't be sure if it's stolen. I mean, you could have just memorised it.'

'Like I said, it's my watch, given to me by my father on my sixteenth birthday.' Choked with memories, she could say no more.

'Okay. But if your father gave it to you, why would you want to let it go?'

'Because I pay my debts, that's why.'

Maddy recalled the very day her father gave her that watch. Less than a year later, he was taken ill and died soon after; the shock of which killed her mother. Being an only child, Maddy had been left to fend for herself.

Unable to afford the rent on their two-bedroomed flat in Kilburn, North London, she had sold the bits of furniture for knockdown prices to a local secondhand shop, and started a series of live-in jobs at West End pubs, clubs and hotels. Her musical career had started very slowly in just these places. She'd be washing up one minute, and performing the next. It had been a long and often lonely journey through life, until she met Alice and fell in love with the monster she had now left behind.

'Get out, the pair of you!' the driver said resignedly.

As they climbed out, so did he. Seeking Maddy's attention, he handed her the watch. 'Here you are, love. I can see this watch means a lot to you.' He had noticed how tearful she was when handing it over. 'We'll forget the fare. You keep the watch, and don't go offering it to strangers.'

Taken aback when she flung her arms round him and kissed him on the cheek, he simply nodded and hurried back round to the driver's door. 'Silly girls!' He watched the two of them go arm-in-arm down the street. 'Let's hope they learn how to keep out of trouble.'

As he drove past them, he opened his window to offer a few words of advice. 'I don't know what you've been up to, the pair of you, but you need to keep your guard up. There are some real bad buggers out there!'

Having sowed his seed of wisdom he moved on to his next fare, leaving Maddy and Ellen to head for the end terrace house, where they climbed the steps, waited while Ellen found the spare key in a secret place on a ledge by the front door, and went inside.

'It's nothing grand,' Ellen apologised, putting on the lights and setting a match to a gas fire in the cosy back room. 'It was my Aunt Dora's house. She wasn't short of money, so when she moved abroad, she signed the deeds over to me.'

While she flung off her jacket she explained, 'I haven't seen my dad for three years. He and my mum and I had a falling-out and somehow none of us ever had the guts to apologise. You know how it is ... things get twisted and nasty, and everybody digs their heels in. But I'm past worrying about it. The sad thing is that Mum died of liver cancer a year or so ago, before we'd made it up. But, you know what, Maddy, I didn't cry. She and I never saw eye to eye, and Dad always took her side, even when he knew she was in the wrong – which was most of the time.'

'Have you any brothers or sisters?'

'A sister, Sally.'

'Is she younger or older than you?'

'She's twenty-six – four years older and a great deal wiser than me.' Ellen gave a knowing smile. 'A bit selfish too, as I recall.'

'In what way?'

'Well, for a start she never let the arguments upset her, the way I did. Instead she always managed to blame everybody else for her own shortcomings. Rather than try and make things better at home, she began making plans to get away from there. Eventually she went to Spain to live with my aunt. Last I heard, the two of them had gone into the hotel business and were doing very nicely, thank you. Mind you, I think she was jealous of me. I went to stage school and had extra music lessons while she had to go out to work in a boring office.' Ellen gave a chuckle. 'I daresay I was a spoiled brat, and if I'd been her, I would have hated me too!'

Maddy grinned, but then asked, 'Don't you miss them?' She would have given anything to have her parents back.

Kicking off her shoes, Ellen fell into the big squashy armchair. 'Oh, Sally always kept herself to herself, and Aunt Dora never had much to do with me. In fact, I reckon she only signed this place over to me because she felt guilty, seeing as she had already taken Sally under her wing.'

She fell silent as she thought of it all. 'I didn't know Aunt Dora as well as Sally did, so I don't really miss her. But if I'm honest, I do miss Sally. I reckon her and me could be friends, now that I've grown up a bit. No way do I miss my parents though. My mother was a secret drinker, you see, and as for Dad . . . well, he'd always idolised her. In his eyes, she could do no wrong. He was either too stupid or too besotted to stand up for himself. And now I gather he's got himself into a similar situation with a new woman. No. I'm well out of it. I'm lucky enough to have the best grandad in the world, though. He's my mum's dad, but I wish in a way *he'd* been my father.'

Clambering out of the chair, she gave vent to her curiosity. 'What about you, Maddy? Are you still in touch with your family?'

Maddy took a moment to answer; it was still painful to talk

about it, especially with a virtual stranger. 'My dad got ill when I was seventeen,' she answered softly. 'It turned to pneumonia, and he went downhill so fast, it was frightening. He never recovered, and from then on, it was as if Mum had gone with him.'

'In what way?'

Maddy shook her head. 'She just never got over it. It was as if her world had come to an end. She gave up her job, hardly ate or slept.'

She remembered it as if it was only yesterday. 'Sometimes early in the morning, I would hear her go out of the door, then hours later I'd find her up the churchyard, kneeling on his grave. It was awful, like she was a different person – someone I didn't know any more.'

Her voice broke. 'I tried so hard to help her, stopped going to school and stayed at home to keep her company, but she didn't want to be helped. She wanted my dad back, nothing else . . . just my dad.' She paused. 'I miss her so much. I miss them both, every day, every minute. It's like an ache that won't go away, so if *I* feel like that, how must *she* have felt?'

'Did you talk to her – about your dad, I mean?'

'Time and again I tried, I really did! Sometimes when I heard her sobbing in her bedroom, I'd knock on her door and beg to be let in. But she wouldn't open the door. In the end, there was nothing anyone could do for her.' She shrugged. 'Less than a year later, she followed him. And left me behind.'

'Oh, Maddy . . . I'm so very sorry.'

Maddy didn't hear her. She was back there, living it all over again. 'The doctors said it was a massive heart-attack that killed her, but others said she died of a broken heart. And the more I think about it, the more I believe they were right. It wasn't her fault – she just couldn't live without him.'

'Have you any brothers or sisters?'

Maddy wearily shook her head. 'My parents married late in life. I was an only child.'

'Are there any aunts and uncles?'

'There's nobody. For a time I really thought there might be a future and a family with – that man – but I was stupid even to entertain the idea. I should have seen through him a long time ago, but I didn't, and now I'm carrying his child.' She looked up with soulful eyes. 'Oh Ellen, I've been such a fool.'

There was a timeless span of silence while Ellen and Maddy reflected on the evening and all its consequences, and possibly came to terms with some of what had happened.

A moment later, without saying a word, Ellen crossed the room, wrapped her arms round Maddy, and held her for what seemed an age.

To Maddy, already grieving for Jack and fearing for her darling Alice, that warm and sincere embrace meant more to her than Ellen could ever realise.

～

A short time later, Ellen gave Maddy a quick tour of her two-up, two-down home. 'This used to be my aunt's bedroom.' She led Maddy into a surprisingly large room, with deep windows and homely décor. There were seascapes hanging on the walls, and a deep fluffy rug either side of the bed. 'You should have seen it before,' Ellen revealed. 'It was stuffed with all manner of old relics – and I'm not just talking about my aunt either!' When she laughed, it was a bright, infectious sound that set Maddy off.

'That's better,' Ellen told her. 'A laugh is as good as a tonic. Now – how about a pot of tea and some beans on toast with a poached egg on top, eh? We'll feel better when we've had some grab, and that nipper of your's probably needs feeding!'

Before they went back downstairs, Ellen showed Maddy her huge collection of shoes and clothes hanging in the alcove-cupboards. 'There's never enough room up in the wardrobes,' she explained with a grin. 'So if you need to move in with me, I'll have to sort myself out.'

'Thanks, Ellen.' Though they had only just met, Maddy felt as if she had known the other girl all her life. 'The thing is, I'm not sure what to do. I can't go back to the flat, as it belongs to *him*, and the police are bound to be all over the place, they'll probably be searching it before long.'

Only now did she truly accept the enormity of her own situation. 'For all we know, the police could be looking for us right now, wanting to question us. Then there's *him* – he blames me for what happened, I know he does. He said so, and he's a vindictive man. I know what he's capable of, and I can't put my baby in danger. So you see, I think it might be for the best if I heed Alice's advice and get away from London altogether, at least until it all blows over. But I can't – *won't* – go, until I find out how she is.'

Ellen understood her concerns. 'What makes you think Steve Drayton would want to harm you?'

Maddy described what had taken place earlier. 'When they were taking him away in handcuffs, he said something to me. I can't get it out of my mind. It wasn't just empty words. It was a real threat, which I have to take seriously.'

His words were emblazoned on Maddy's mind. 'He said I should look over my shoulder, because wherever I went, he would find me.' Her flesh crawled as she recalled the demonic look on Drayton's face. 'We both know what he meant by that,' she murmured. 'He means to kill me, if he can. I'm what he would call "unfinished business".'

Ellen did her best to comfort her newfound friend. 'He can't hurt you if he's locked up. And he will be – for a very long time, I reckon.'

Maddy gave a sad smile. 'You don't know him like I do.' Many times she had overheard his conversations on the phone, and because she was so infatuated with him, had chosen not to believe what she was hearing. She knew now what an evil creature he was. 'It won't make any difference if they lock him up and throw away the key, he'll still get to me,' she assured Ellen. 'He's pally with every lowlife in London. And because he knows their every secret, they owe him favours.'

She let that piece of news sink in before she went on, 'So you see, he only has to click his fingers and they'll do whatever he tells them. One thing I know for sure is that one way or another, he *will* get to me. The word will go out, a contract will be made, and I'll be as good as dead; and the baby with me.'

Her voice shivered with fear. 'The fact that I'm carrying his own flesh and blood will make no difference to a man like Steve Drayton.'

Ellen too, was fearful, not so much for herself but for Maddy and the baby. 'I don't know him like you do,' she agreed, 'but from what I've seen and heard tonight, I realise that you're right. One thing though – I don't believe the police will be looking for us, tonight at least.' She was convinced of that. 'I reckon we managed to get clean away. Nobody took any notice of us; the ambulancemen were too intent on treating the injured, and when the police weren't busy rounding up the mob, they had their hands full, keeping everyone back.'

After a time, they made their way back down to the kitchen, where Ellen cooked them a delicious supper. 'I know how concerned you are about your friend Alice,' she told Maddy, pouring out a second cup of tea, 'but you can't go to the hospital – it will be too dangerous. The police are bound to be crawling all over the place.'

'I have to make sure she's all right.' Maddy was desperately worried.

'I can see how anxious you are, but you can't risk it. Look don't worry,' she urged, 'leave it to me. I'll find a way.' Ellen had an idea, though until she had thought it through, she wasn't going to mention it.

Maddy's thoughts now turned to Jack – kind, loyal Jack, who had helped her out time and again and was more of a man than his macho boss could ever be. 'I can't believe Jack was killed,' she said shakily. 'It all seems so . . . unreal.'

Haunted by images of him lying there in that filthy alley, his life ebbing away, and Alice – so frail yet desperate to know that Maddy and the baby would be safe – was all too much for her. Shock set in. Her body suddenly grew icy cold and she couldn't stop shivering. Then she was sobbing, deep wrenching sobs that tore her apart.

As the sadness overwhelmed her, she felt Ellen's arms slide about her shoulders again, holding her, allowing her to cry it out until, after a while, she was quiet.

'I'm sorry.' Her sore red eyes swept Ellen's kind face. Maddy could never recall a time when she had not faced life and its troubles head on, alone and strong, with no one to share her burden; but now, she felt ashamed. 'I never meant for that to happen.'

Ellen shook her head. 'You've been through a lot,' she told Maddy bluntly. 'You've seen one friend killed, and another hanging on to her life by a thread. You're worried for your baby, and in fear for your life.' She gave a wry little smile. 'Lesser women than you would have broken down, long before now.'

She regarded Maddy with admiration. Eight years older than herself, Maddy had a warm, kindly face with regular features and wide, honest eyes. Ellen took her hat off to her, for the way she had stood up to both the trials of that night and the bad times before, when Drayton had taken away her home, her livelihood, and cruelly dismissed his child as 'somebody's else's bastard'.

On top of all that were the beatings, still evident on Maddy's arms and face. And now the threat to take the lives of both her and her child.

From what she had learned about the man, Ellen had no doubts whatsoever that he would carry out his dark threat. It was a sobering thought. She could scarcely believe that, a few short hours before, she had been having passionate sex with him in a stinking alley: a murderer and a bully. There and then, Ellen promised herself, she would never sink so low again.

Maddy's voice interrupted her reverie. 'What can I do? How can I find out if Alice is all right?' Try as she might, she could not get her dear friend out of her mind.

'Well,' Ellen said sensibly, 'we're neither use nor ornament as we are, so why don't we just try and get some sleep. Come the morning, we'll have a clearer head. Then we'll decide what's best to do. And look – I'm certain that your pal is being well taken care of.'

'But we don't know that.' Maddy so much wanted to see Alice, to hold her and tell her that she wasn't alone; that everything would work out all right. She began to cry again.

'Maddy? What's up? Is there something else on your mind?' Ellen asked, worriedly.

A brief pause, before Maddy nodded. 'Yes.'

Paramount on her mind was the promise that had passed between her and Alice, in those few frightening moments when she held the wounded woman in her arms. Thinking back on it now, Maddy found it profoundly humbling, to realise that Alice's own dire situation was secondary to her love and concern for Maddy and the unborn child.

Needing to share her anxiety with someone, Maddy told Ellen everything.

'She was desperate to know that I would be out of danger, so she made me promise to go away from London and never come back or make contact with her ever again. I expect she thought it was the safest and best thing to do.'

'Don't forget she was badly wounded when she took that promise from you,' Ellen reminded her. 'She would never hold you to it, I'm sure.'

'I gave my word,' Maddy sighed, 'so until Alice tells me otherwise, I have to keep it.'

'Do you always keep your promises?'

Maddy shook her head. 'I broke my promise to Alice only last night, and look where that has led us all.'

'Did Alice hear Steve's threat to you?' Ellen asked suddenly.

'I don't know. She may have.'

'If she did, that explains it. She needed you to get away from him, to go somewhere you could never be found.' The more she thought about it, the more convinced Ellen became. 'From what he told me, she's been with Drayton for a long time. More than anyone else, she would know what he's capable of . . . wouldn't she?'

Maddy agreed. 'Yes. Alice was closer to him than anyone else. She virtually ran the club; she did his accounts and kept his address book. He was always suspicious of everyone, but not Alice. He trusted her implicitly. He told her secret things – sometimes they were bad things that she didn't want to know, and which she never spoke about.'

'Why did she stay with him?' Ellen asked curiously.

'I'm not sure. Maybe because he paid her well and she'd been there a long time, I don't know.'

'Was she a part of the bad things?'

'Never!' Maddy was horrified. 'She kept as far away from his shady doings as possible.'

In her mind, Maddy went over all their conversations. 'Alice is a good woman – the best friend I have ever had, more like a mother than a friend. In fact, just lately I don't know what I would have done without her. She knew how *he* went off his head, claimed that I'd been with some other man and the two of us were trying to land him with a brat that was none of his making. She found out he beat me up badly, and she was always there for me. So how can I desert her now, tell me that? I can't . . . I won't!'

'I understand what you're saying,' Ellen assured her, 'but you're up against a madman, and it seems that Alice knows that, better than anybody.' Ellen herself had not realised the mark of the man she had almost tied herself up with. In fact, if it hadn't been for Maddy's intervention, she might well have been caught up in that fateful shoot-out.

Personally, Ellen thought that both she and Maddy were lucky to have got away so easily.

Maddy had been thinking along the same lines. She accepted that the police would question the staff at the club, and though Raymond would not willingly give anything away, the others might not be so cautious. Unfortunately, it was common knowledge that she and the boss were lovers who had been going through a bad patch. It must also be common knowledge that he had boldly poached the new singer from under the nose of his arch-rival; the man he later shot dead in the alley.

So, all was not cut and dried. Ellen was right: if she were to go to the hospital, she might well put herself and the child in jeopardy.

'I'm glad he didn't get his claws into you,' she told Ellen now. 'He might well have ruined you, like he's ruined me. But I have to be honest with you: I nearly didn't tell you about him. It was only when I heard him weaving the same evil spell on you that he did with me, that I just knew I had to make you see what he was really like.'

Though she accepted it would have been safer for her to have walked away, Maddy was glad she had done the right thing.

Ellen thanked her yet again. 'Even after the way he treated you, you still put yourself at risk for me.' She could only imagine how much raw courage that must have taken. 'I want you to know,' she said, taking hold of Maddy's hand and giving it a squeeze, 'I'll be forever grateful to you for that. And now, I want you to have a few minutes' rest while I get the spare room ready.' She switched the radio on low, to keep Maddy company while she was gone. 'I reckon I'll put a hot water-bottle in the bed, to warm you and the baby up, and you can chuck that dress away tomorrow. It's ruined – what a pity. I'll put a nightie and a clean towel by the bed. You can have a nice bath to soothe your aches and pains as the water stays hot till late because of my working hours.'

Grateful for the few minutes alone, Maddy watched her go. 'I've found a new friend there,' she yawned. 'And if I need anything at all just now, it's someone to talk with.'

Laying the palm of her hand across her tummy, she felt the slight baby-bulge. 'We've a long way to go yet, you and me,' she sighed, looking down at it with a weary smile. 'It's not much of a start to your existence, what with your daddy arrested for murder, and us running for our lives. He wanted nothing to do with us, but d'you know what? We don't need him. You and me, my darling, we'll manage well enough. I'll take care of you, and things will work out, you'll see.'

Then she thought of Alice, and of how ill she was. Clasping her hands together, she bowed her head, closed her eyes and prayed like she had never prayed before. 'Please, Lord, don't let her die. Help her, if You can.'

Upstairs, Ellen went to the landing cupboard from where she took a pair of sheets and a pillow case. She found the duvet cover still in the wash-bin. 'Dammit!' Returning to the cupboard, she collected a bedspread, blue and yellow and festooned with flowers; it was one of those things bought in a rush and forever regretted. But it would do for now.

Going into the bedroom, she made the bed, turned back the covers and lit the bedside lamp. 'There!' Pleased with herself, she ran down the stairs two at a time. 'All ready!' she called as she went into the sitting-room. 'Oh, and you'll find pyjamas in the top drawer of the . . .' She came to a skidding halt. 'Aw, Maddy, just look at you!'

Maddy had obviously not been able to keep herself awake. Squashed into the cushions, she was sleeping soundly, and lying on her side in an awkward fashion.

Trying not to wake her, Ellen made her comfortable, before returning upstairs to retrieve the bedspread, which she then carried back downstairs. Here, she tenderly wrapped it around Maddy's slim figure, making certain the baby-bulge was well covered and warm. 'Night, God bless.' She gave Maddy a fleeting kiss.

Switching off the overhead light, and leaving only the dresser lamp burning, she tiptoed out of the room, making sure the door was left open, just in case Maddy called out in the night.

But it was Ellen who woke several times and crept quietly downstairs to check on Maddy.

Her heart went out to this lovely young woman who had done nothing wrong, except to fall for the wrong man. Now she was caught up in a nightmare, homeless and abandoned, with a child growing inside her, and her dearest and closest friend lying badly injured in a hospital somewhere.

For a long moment, Ellen looked on Maddy's tear-stained face. 'You don't deserve any of this,' she whispered, 'but you're strong and determined. You'll come through it. And just like Alice, I'll always be here for you, Maddy. That's my promise to you.'

Several times she glanced back as she made for the stairs, and even when lying in her bed, she strained her neck to listen for the slightest sound. But all remained quiet.

~

It was gone three o'clock in the morning when she was startled by the sound of Maddy's frantic screams.

Running down the stairs she found Maddy on the floor, her arms flailing and her eyes wide open with terror, as though fighting off some unseen attacker . . . 'It's allright, Maddy!' Rushing to calm her, Ellen found it difficult to make her realise she was not in any danger. 'Ssh. Be still, Maddy.'

There was no calming Maddy; terror-stricken she hit out, her fearful screams subsiding into deep heart-rending sobs.

In her deepest mind Maddy and the baby were in grave danger. The alley was dark and the bad ones had seen her. They wanted to kill her baby . . . and her.

'Ssh now.' Folding Maddy into her arms, Ellen soothed her, 'It's allright. You're both safe, here with me.'

She held her until the sobs subsided.

When she sensed Maddy was looking up at her, Ellen gazed down, only to be transfixed with shock, as she regarded Maddy's ashen face. There was such crippling pain in those dark, stricken eyes. So much anguish. And as she rocked her back and forth, never in her short life had Ellen been so deeply touched by another human being, 'No one's going to hurt you or the baby,' she murmured, her voice soothing as Maddy clung to her. 'We'll be away from here soon enough . . . somewhere they'll never find us.'

Calmed by Ellen's assurances, Maddy fought to shut out the darkness that threatened to overwhelm her.

Quieter now, the girl looked up, smiling through her tears. She felt the strength of Ellen's arms about her, and she was safe.

For now.

Ellen made no attempt to go back to her own bed.

Instead, she got Maddy comfortable, drew the big armchair to the side of the sofa, and snuggling up in it, she watched her new friend sink into a restless sleep.

Each drawing strength from the other, the two young women spent their first night together.

~

That first night in Bethnal Green, the two young women dozed lightly, listening for any unusual sounds and intermittently watching for the dawn; each of them deeply troubled by recent events, and haunted by what the future might hold.

Ellen woke first. She was drawing back the curtains when Maddy opened her eyes, yawned and asked, 'Is it morning already?' Sitting upright, she blinked at the inrush of light.

'How are you feeling?' Ellen wanted to know.

Maddy looked down. 'I feel ashamed.'

'What do you mean?' Ellen crossed the room to her and sat on the sofa. 'Why would *you* be ashamed?'

'Because of last night – all that crying on your shoulder. I've always been strong, you see, able to cope with anything life throws at me. From when I lost my parents, I've had to deal with everything myself. But last night . . .' She thrust away the images. 'I'm sorry, Ellen. It won't happen again.'

Ellen paused, regarding Maddy with respect. 'Shall I tell you something?'

Curious, the other girl nodded.

'Out of the two of us, *you* are by far the bravest.'

'No.' Maddy smiled. 'I don't think so.'

'I mean it,' Ellen said. 'I made a bad choice that could have had dire consequences. But you stepped forward and made me see what Steve was really like.' Her affection for Maddy shone in her eyes. 'I've always missed never having a sister I could talk to, but it looks like I might have found one.'

'And me.' Maddy had no doubts. Almost from the first, she had seen Ellen as being much like herself, and the more they got to know each other, the closer they grew. Maddy believed that their friendship could only get stronger with the coming years. 'We'll look after each other, you and me,' she told Ellen. 'We have so far, haven't we?'

Chuckling, Ellen gave Maddy a playful shove. 'Hey! We could be like the Beverley Sisters – you know that song they sing, about being sisters!'

Maddy laughed, and they sang along together, harmonising really nicely. 'We could band together and call ourselves The

Songbirds,' she joked. 'I think we sound a bit like Dusty Springfield and Debbie Harry rolled into one.'

'Not half!' Ellen quipped. 'We'd be up in the Top Ten before you could say Bay City Rollers!' Then she went on more seriously, 'I know you need to find out how Alice is, and I've been thinking about that. I may have found a way that will keep you out of danger. First though, we should get some breakfast.'

She gave a kind of snort. 'Mind you, having said that, I reckon all I can rustle up is toast and marmalade.'

'That sounds great.' Maddy's hungry tummy was playing a tune. Looking wild and wanton with her hair massed about her face and her eyes raw and bleary, she asked, 'Shall I get washed and tidied up first?'

Ellen nodded. 'Good idea. Now don't hog the bathroom,' she warned light-heartedly. 'You're not the only one who looks like something the cat brought in.'

'Oh, thanks,' Maddy bridled. She thought it wonderful, how she and Ellen had quickly formed such a warm and natural friendship.

In the tiny, well-kept bathroom on the first floor, Maddy squeezed the tiniest measure out of Ellen's tube of Freshmint toothpaste and, wetting her finger under the tap, scrubbed away at her teeth until they felt clean.

She twice rinsed out her mouth, then washed her face with warm soap and water. 'My God!' Staring into the mirror, she could hardly believe it was herself looking back. Her hair was a tangled mess, her eyes swollen and sore-looking. If only she had her comb and make-up with her.

When she emerged, wrapped in her towel and feeling much fresher, Ellen lent her a hairbrush and chucked a big bag of cosmetics at her, saying, 'Here, help yourself. I've put some clothes on your bed – choose what you want.'

Then she went back downstairs. 'The kettle's on,' she called back. 'And the bread's already sliced for toasting. I'll wait till you're ready before putting it on.'

~

Later, over tea and toast, the two young women discussed the aftermath of the previous evening. 'Do you think the police will be looking for us by now?' Maddy wondered. Dressed in a pair of Ellen's jeans and a skinny-rib sweater, with her long hair combed back into a high ponytail and the make-up concealing her battered face, she looked about the same age as her new found friend.

Ellen didn't know the answer to that. 'I hope they're not,' she replied. 'They will have already worked out that Steve and my boss Den Carter were arch rivals in the club business. Plus Steve owed him money and then had the front to trick me away from him. It was a mad thing to do. Den would never have let him get away with it. Anyway, the cops will have questioned every member of staff by now – for witnesses and all that. So I expect they already know about me and you.'

Maddy agreed, but, 'As far as anyone knew, we weren't even there in the alley when it happened. Besides, there were more than enough witnesses who saw everything – the guests who ran out to see what was going on, and the staff from our club and other businesses down the alley. They couldn't see me, but I could see them. So, if there were all those witnesses, why would they need to bother about us?'

'They may not,' Ellen said, 'but I wouldn't count on it. Think about it, Maddy. Steve Drayton murdered two people and badly wounded another. It's major stuff. It won't matter that they already have him in custody. They'll want to make the case absolutely watertight. They'll question everybody. To be on the safe side, we'd best make tracks, and the sooner the better! The police will find this address in Den's staff records. And if Drayton *is* hellbent on putting out a contract on you, that's all the more reason for keeping our heads down.'

Maddy told her she was going nowhere, until she knew that Alice was safe.

Ellen conveyed her plan. 'Look, I did a lot of thinking last night, and I may have come up with something. You see, I know someone who might be able to help. Her name is Connie; she's been kind to me in the past, and she knows how to keep her mouth shut when needs be. She was a cleaner at Carter's club when I first went there, but he sacked her after accusing her of being a thief. I stood up for her, and got a black eye for my pains, but I also bunged her a few quid to keep her going until she found a new job. We've kept in touch, Connie and me, and guess what? She's only working as a ward-cleaner at the hospital, so she might be able to find out what's happening with Alice.'

'Do you think there will be police at the hospital?'

'You can bet on it! But it's far easier for a cleaner to get places where we can't. Besides, there'll be all kinds of gossip going on amongst the nurses, and though I say it myself, Connie was always a bit of a Nosy Parker.'

Maddy thought it was a good plan and anyway, what alternative did they have? 'Great! Alice's surname is Mulligan, by the way. So, when can you get in touch with this Connie?'

'Right now.' Glancing up at the clock. Ellen saw that it was not yet eight-thirty. 'Depends which shift she's on, but I should be able to get hold of her.'

While she rummaged for the phone number she murmured, 'Connie's a good sort. We can trust her, and I'll make sure she gets a drink out of this. Oh, here it is!'

She dialled and waited, for what seemed an age. 'I hope we haven't missed her,' she was saying, when suddenly she cried out, 'Connie? It's me, Ellen. Yes, fine thank you, and how are you?' There was a moment while Connie answered, then, 'So, you're still working at University College Hospital, are you?'

Another pause, then, 'Connie, I wonder if you could do me

a huge favour – it's really important. What? No, I haven't seen the news, but I already knew about the shooting. Yes, I know that Den is dead – can't say I will shed any tears for him. But that's a part of the reason I'm calling you now.'

There was a brief exchange, before Ellen fully explained that Alice Mulligan, the injured woman, was a friend of a friend, who needed to know what was happening with her.

Another short pause while she listened to what the other woman had to say, then: 'Yes, I fully expected the police might be there, that's why I'm asking this favour. No, Connie, I'm not involved – well, not in the way you might think. Let's just say, I've got nothing to hide.'

She cut short the conversation. 'Listen, Connie, there isn't much time. I'm about to tell you something that I know you won't ever repeat to a living soul.'

She quickly outlined how, though they were not directly involved, she and Maddy had been in the alley when the shootings took place, and now they were afraid the police might want to talk with them. Moreover, when Carter turned up looking for blood, Steve Drayton laid the blame firmly at Maddy's door. Just before the police took him away, he had threatened Maddy's life, vowing to find her wherever she might go.

'He means to have her done away with,' Ellen told Connie bluntly. 'That's why she can't show her face at the hospital. But Alice is her closest friend and she's desperately worried about her, won't go anywhere until she knows what the score is. Please, Connie, we need you to find out anything you can. We thought, what with you being a cleaner and probably having access to the staff-room, you might be well-placed to hear things . . . nurses' gossip, police talking to each other and all that.'

While she listened to Connie's reply, Ellen glanced at Maddy, who was feverishly pacing the floor.

Another minute, and then a great sigh of relief. 'Oh Connie, love, I knew I could count on you!' Swinging round, Ellen made a thumbs-up sign at Maddy. 'Thank you so much. Listen, when can you call me back? Midday? Right, we'll be waiting. Bye, now – and good luck.'

Replacing the handset, she crossed the room to where Maddy was now seated in the chair, looking pale and drawn. 'It's as we thought,' she told her. 'There's a police guard outside Alice's door. But Connie is due to wash down that corridor this morning, so she's hoping to pick up some news or actually get inside the room.'

'Has she seen Alice?'

'No, but she has overheard conversations. Apparently, when Alice was admitted, she'd already lost a lot of blood, and there was internal damage. They had no choice but to operate. She came out of that . . . had a blood transfusion, but although the doctors thought she was too badly hurt to survive, your Alice proved them wrong, and seems to be doing okay. Though she's still under intensive care.'

Maddy wiped away a tear. 'She's a fighter. She'll win through, I know she will.'

'We'll know more by midday, when Connie rings,' Ellen said. 'Meanwhile, I've another call to make. Because, once we've had news of Alice, we will need to get going on our own course of action.'

~

As she put the kettle on for another pot of tea, Maddy was too engrossed in thoughts of Alice to ask what call Ellen was about to make.

But she wasn't too concerned; whatever it was, and whoever she was about to call, Maddy had no doubts about Ellen's good intentions.

Because, against all her earlier instincts, she had come to trust the girl. With not only her own life, but also that of her unborn child.

CHAPTER EIGHT

A SMALL, ROUND woman of ample proportions, Connie had been surprised to hear from Ellen. 'Time and again I told her never to get tangled up with Den Carter,' she muttered as she walked the hospital corridors. 'I said he was a bad lot, and I was right. But would she listen? No, she would not!'

'Morning, Connie.' That was Molly, who helped to run the staff canteen. 'Have you heard about the shootings?'

'I have, yes.'

'And that poor woman . . . they say she's on her last legs.'

'Who says?'

'The porters and suchlike. They're all talking about it.'

'Well, they're talking out of their backsides, then, 'cos I've heard from the nurses that she's pulling through all right.'

'Guarded night and day, isn't she?' Molly sighed. 'Fancy guarding somebody who's been at death's door. I mean, it's not as if she's gonna run off, is it, eh? And she's a victim, not a culprit. Them Soho nightclubs . . . vice rings . . . it'll all be in the *News of the World,* come Sunday.' She beamed excitedly.

'You're right, gel.' Connie nodded sagely. 'But I'd best get on. The police have given me clearance to go up there and do what I'm paid for.'

'Hmh! About time too, if you ask me. Germs will still gather in dirt and dust, whether there's a guard outside the door or not. If you find out any extra details, don't forget pass them on, eh?'

'Will do. See you then, Molly.'

'See you, Connie. Take care now.'

~

Just a few more yards and Connie was outside the staff-room. Pausing for a second, she leaned her ear to the door and listened, falling in with a shock when the door quickly opened and there was the Ward Sister. Thankfully, being in full conversation with the nurse inside, she did not realise that Connie had been earwigging.

'So, I'll leave you to it then. After the doctor's been, she'll be scheduled to come off the drip. Make sure she has a regular supply of fluids. She's still very weak, so you'll need to keep an eye; make sure she's able to manage.'

As the Sister turned to leave, she almost fell over Connie, who had quickly stepped back. 'Ah!' Pinning the cleaner with her beady eyes, the big woman instructed, 'You know you've been cleared to enter the side-ward up on Corridor Nine today?'

'Yes, Sister.'

'Do your usual rounds first. Doctor Myers will be with the patient from eleven o'clock. Then you must be in and out quickly. We don't want to disturb her unnecessarily.'

'No, Sister. I mean, yes, Sister!' The big woman always managed to unnerve her.

'And do a proper, thorough job. I expect that room to be spotless. I shall be making my round later, and I intend examining every nook and cranny, you can depend on it.'

'Yes, Sister.'

Never sure whether Connie was sending her up, or being

114

unduly servile, the big woman took a long moment to scrutinise her. 'Go on, then. Get on with it!' With that she was away
down the corridor, heels thumping and arms swinging.

'She should have been a sergeant in the Army,' the nurse
told Connie, coming out of the office.

'Not bloody likely!' Connie retorted. 'Then no one would
ever enlist.'

~

It was eleven-thirty by the time Connie made her way towards
Alice's room.

Having done her usual round, she paused at the top of
Corridor Nine, leaning on her broom and stretching her back.
'I'm done in!' she grunted. 'Rushing about, bending down,
reaching up, fetching and carrying. Is it any wonder I ache
from top to toe?' One of these fine days she would search out
a man with means and grab him quick. But she'd been saying
that ever since her old man deserted her six years back, and
it hadn't happened yet.

Pushing her trolley, with its fresh bucket of hot soapy water
and clean mop, to where a portly policeman stood sentry
outside Alice's door, she asked, 'Aren't you allowed to sit down?'
She noted how he was switching from one foot to the other,
and rubbing his back as though in pain.

'Nobody ever said I couldn't,' he answered thoughtfully, 'so
I don't see why not.'

'Shall I get you a chair then?'

He glanced up and down the corridor, as though looking
for his superior. 'Sounds like magic to my ears,' he confessed.

'Mmm.' Exchanging smiles, she asked him to keep an eye
on her trolley while she nipped into the empty sluice-room
opposite and brought out a small plastic chair. 'There you go,'
she said, beaming from ear to ear. 'It's not exactly an armchair,

but the seat's just about big enough for your bum.' She slid the chair towards him. 'There you go.'

Another anxious glance up and down the corridor. 'I'd best wait until the nurse comes out, eh?'

'Oh, so the nurse is inside, is she?' Connie's first thought was how that made it impossible for her to talk with Alice.

The officer nodded. 'The doctor's been and gone, but the nurse has been in there a while,' he nodded. 'Just doing her job, I expect.'

'Well, in that case, I'd best go in and do my job, hadn't I?'

Leaving her trolley outside, she collected only the items she would need – cleaning cloths and such, and the mop and bucket.

The nurse was the same one the Sister had instructed earlier. 'Oh Connie, I'm so glad you're here,' she said, when the cleaner popped her head around the door. Seated by the bed, she was holding Alice's hand steady while she drank from a cup. 'I need to check another patient, and I'm already running late. Would you mind just helping Mrs Mulligan finish this tea?'

Connie wasn't surprised. The nurses were in such short supply that they were doing the work of ten. 'I don't mind at all,' she offered. In fact, it was the ideal opportunity to talk to Alice. 'I'll just give my hands a quick wash.'

'Don't tip the cup up too far,' the nurse told her. 'Let the patient take the liquid in her own time.'

After promising she would be no longer than ten minutes at the most, the woman was quickly away, hurrying to her next patient.

Helping Alice to drink was a slow and painstaking task, and while Alice drank, Connie spoke to her. 'You're a lucky woman,' she said warmly. 'They tell me you're on the mend.'

Alice concentrated on her drink.

'Just a little more, then you're all done.' Connie hoped the nurse would stay away until she'd had a chance to talk with

Alice. At the moment though, the injured woman was finding it difficult to swallow, let alone get into a conversation.

A moment later, Alice pushed the cup away. 'Enough.' She gave a weary sigh. 'No more, thank you.' Lying back on the pillow, she asked Connie, 'Could you close the curtains, please?'

As the cleaner pulled the curtains against the bright morning light, Alice spoke in little breathless snatches. 'I know I am lucky. I should . . . be dead!' She momentarily closed her eyes; when she opened them again, they were immensely sad. 'They told me . . . about Jack.'

Connie wasn't sure what to say, so she simply answered, 'I'm sorry. A friend, was he?' She had not heard the name Jack when listening to the news, but she assumed it must be one of the men who were shot dead.

Alice gave a sad little smile. 'A good man, so he was. A kind friend.' The events of the night rode through her mind. Where was Maddy now? Was she safe? She hoped the girl had kept her promise and got as far away as she could, or *he* would track her down, sure as day followed night. Please God! Let her be safe.

'Mr Mulligan? 'Alice, are you all right?' Fearing she had tired the sick woman, Connie made to stand up. 'I'm sorry, I'd best go now.'

Alice reached out. 'No! Please . . . I need you to stay.'

'Now don't be wearing yourself out,' Connie said with a kind smile. 'Or Sister will have my guts for garters.'

'I have to . . . to . . . get out of here.'

'Oh, you can't do that!' Connie was horrified. 'You're nowhere near ready to go home. They've only just taken the drip, and who knows? They might have to put it back if you can't take your nourishment.' She saw how pale and ill the other woman looked. 'I should not be here, talking to you like this. Whatever would Maddy say?'

Alice gave her a strange look. 'How do you know about Maddy?'

'I saw it all, on the news,' Connie answered carefully.

Sensing that something was not right here, Alice asked her straight out, 'What do you want from me? Why are you really here?' She began to shake. 'Did Steve Drayton send you? Are you here to find out where Maddy is?' She was beginning to falter. 'Please, tell me the truth.'

Seeing the frantic look in Alice's eyes, Connie attempted to soothe her fears. It was time to come clean and explain her mission.

'Look, I had a phone call this morning. It was from my friend Ellen Drew – the new singer at Drayton's club.'

Alice bristled. 'The one who took Maddy's job?'

'Yes, but she's a really nice girl.' Increasingly concerned for the other woman's well-being, Connie suggested, 'Maybe we should talk later. Right now, I think you need to rest.'

'No! Please – tell me now.'

And so Connie told her everything – how Ellen was a long-time friend, and that she had spoken about Maddy. 'Apparently, Maddy is staying with her. She's very worried about you. She just needs to know you're all right, that's all. Then she'll leave London. She wanted to come to the hospital but Ellen said it was too risky. That's why she asked me to find out if you were okay.'

Relief echoed in her voice as she patted Alice's hand and said, 'So now I can call her back and tell her that you're on the mend, and that with any luck, you'll be out of here before too long. She'll probably pop in to visit you . . . '

'No!' Grabbing the cleaner's hand, Alice gabbled, 'She can't come here! You mustn't tell her that I'm on the mend. He threatened her, you see – I heard him!' She shuddered. 'He said, wherever she went, he would find her. And he will! He will!' She began coughing and weeping, clutching at Connie's hands.

'Hush now, hush now. Be calm.' Alarmed by the sick woman's

outburst, Connie asked, 'So, if you don't want me to tell her you're on the mend, what *do* you want me to say?'

'Tell her I didn't make it.' Alice gulped. 'Tell her . . . they did their best, but they couldn't save me.'

Connie was astounded. 'I can't say that!' she protested. 'It would be an outright lie; it would tempt Providence. No, I can't do it – I'm sorry.'

Desperate, Alice tried another tactic. 'Are you fond of your friend Ellen?'

'Of course. When we worked together she was more like a daughter than a friend. Lately though, we've both been working so hard it's been difficult to keep tabs. But now she's contacted me, we'll soon make up for lost time.'

'And how would you feel, if she got killed, *because of you?*'

'What are you getting at? How could Ellen get killed because of me?'

'Listen to me – *please*. You don't know who you're dealing with. Den Carter might be a wrong 'un, but Steve Drayton is worse! He's a monster. Life means nothing to him. Maddy's carrying his child, but he'll snuff them both out . . . without a second . . .' Falling back into the pillow, Alice lay still, her breathing laboured and her skin grey and moist.

'Hey!' Panicking, Connie was all for calling the nurse back. 'Don't you die on me!'

Drained by the whole encounter, Alice's voice was barely a whisper. 'Please. *He'll kill them all.*' She took a laboured breath. 'Promise me. Tell them . . . I didn't make it. Tell them . . . *Promise!*' She closed her eyes, leaving Connie to decide on her course of action.

She was already out the door and about to speak with the officer, when the nurse arrived. 'She got a bit agitated,' Connie hurriedly explained. 'But she seems quieter now.'

Blaming herself, the nurse pulled a screen around the patient and quickly checked that everything was in order. 'It's all right,' she told Connie quietly. 'She'll be fine now. I'll stay with her. Finish up in here now and be as quick and as quiet as you can.'

For the next few minutes, Connie did exactly that. On her way out, she glanced back at Alice, who was looking at her with her heart in her eyes, as if to say, *Don't let me down.* Her unspoken plea only made Connie all the more nervous.

What Alice had asked her to do went totally against her moral code. Connie had been many things in her life, but never a deliberate, outright liar. How, in God's name, could she tell Ellen such a terrible untruth? And what would it do to Maddy, poor girl, if she was told that her friend had not survived?

Dreading her return call to Ellen, she arrived at her own little headquarters three floors down, where she emptied the bucket down the drainhole, before rinsing it out and spraying it with disinfectant. Then she washed her cleaning cloths and soaked them in the sink.

That done, she hurried the short distance to the kitchen and made herself a cup of tea, which she took to the farthest corner and sat down with a cigarette to reflect on what Alice had said.

So Drayton would kill them all. Those were Alice's exact words. In her mind, Connie went over the entire conversation again and the more she thought on it, the more she knew that whatever the consequences, she could not go against her own values. But if she didn't do what Alice had asked, what would happen to Maddy and her unborn child – and what about Ellen? Would they really be murdered, or had Alice exaggerated the situation for her own ends?

Torn every which way, Connie tried to get it all into perspective. But the look in Alice's eyes burned in her memory like a beacon.

Connie had to ask herself, 'If I was to go against my conscience and lie, could I live with it for the rest of my life?'

To deliberately claim that someone was dead when you knew they were not, was a huge burden on the conscience. Moeover, it was akin to opening Pandora's Box . . . letting loose all the bad things along with the good. At best, lives might be saved, yet she only had a stranger's word for that. At worst, somewhere down the years, such a deliberate deceit could have dire consequences, for all concerned.

In all her life, the plump little woman had never been in such a dilemma.

~

Pacing up and down the small front room of the house in Bethnal Green, Maddy was beginning to jump at every sound.

'Sit down, Maddy. You're wearing the carpet out.' Ellen was also anxious.

'She's not going to ring, is she?' Maddy began to bite her nails; an old habit that she had been rid of these past two years, and now with all the troubles, it was back again. 'What's happening? Why hasn't she got back to you?'

'The phone won't ring any sooner with you looking at it every two seconds,' Ellen said quietly.

Maddy had a bad feeling about this. Her heart told her to get to the hospital as quickly as possible; her head urged caution. Either way, all this waiting was unbearable. She glanced at the mantelpiece clock. 'Look at that. It's already midday.'

Ellen shook her head. 'That clock is always five minutes fast. Look – how about making a pot of tea? Oh, and don't forget – I have two sugars.'

Realising it would drive her crazy if she didn't busy herself, Maddy went into the kitchen. No sooner had she put the kettle on than the shrill sound of the telephone ringing made her almost leap out of her skin.

Rushing back into the sitting room, she anxiously waited,

121

watching Ellen's every expression, every sign, with her heart in her mouth.

'Oh Connie, thank goodness.' Having picked up the receiver, Ellen listened with interest to what her friend had to say.

'She's conscious and stable.' Connie had searched her mind and soul and had not been able to tell the lie Alice wanted. 'They say she'll be well enough to go home within a matter of weeks. But listen to me, Ellen. There's something else . . .'

Before Ellen could question her she went quickly on. 'Alice was on to me fairly quickly,' she admitted. 'She knew I wasn't just there to do my job. In the end I told her the truth – that I was there on an errand for you and Maddy – that Maddy was desperate to know how she was. That got her all agitated; she started panicking when she knew Maddy was with you. She said she had hoped Maddy would be long gone from London by now.'

The words tumbled out in haste. 'She asked me to do something that went right against my nature. I can't do it, Connie, I just can't. It was awful. She begged me to let Maddy believe that she was dead! Oh Ellen, you should have seen her. She was really worked up. At one point I was worried she might have a fit and die on me there and then.'

'What's she saying?' Anxious, Maddy moved forward. 'Is Alice all right? Ask Connie to tell her, if she's worrying about me, I'll go in and see her. I know I promised not to, but she'll understand, I'm sure.'

Fearful that Maddy might hear what Connie was saying, Ellen put her hand over the mouthpiece, 'Be patient.' Her mind was racing. 'It's a bad line – I can't hear what she's saying.'

'Sorry, Connie.' Returning her attention to the phone call, Ellen lied, 'I didn't quite catch that last bit, can you repeat it?' She had heard clearly enough, but she couldn't believe it.

Connie repeated it – how Alice had begged her to tell Maddy that she had not survived, because she knew that the girl would come to the hospital to see her. '. . . She said that if Maddy didn't soon get away, you would all be killed, that's what she said. Oh Ellen, I'm so afraid for you both. And the baby . . . I didn't know. I'm sorry, but I couldn't bring myself to fool Maddy into believing her friend was dead! How could I say a thing like that? It doesn't bear thinking about, does it?'

Ellen could not disguise her shock at Connie's unforeseen news. 'Thank you, Connie,' she answered softly. 'I'll tell her. I'll do what's right, don't you worry. I'll see to it.'

Maddy had seen the look of shock on Ellen's face. 'Is something wrong? Alice is all right, isn't she?' Her heart trembled. 'What did Connie say?' More afraid than she had ever been in her whole life, Maddy's heart turned over. 'Tell me, Ellen. I need to know.'

In those few anguished seconds, Ellen had to make the most difficult decision of her life. Tears of regret flowed down her face as she spoke the treacherous words. 'I'm sorry, Maddy . . .' She slowly shook her head. 'I'm so sorry.'

For a long, shocking moment while she struggled to take in the enormity of Ellen's words, Maddy was unable to speak. She stood transfixed, the colour draining from her face as she saw the pain in Ellen's face.

Alice was dead.

Pounding her fists against her temples, she crumpled into the sofa.

'It's all my fault,' she wept. 'If I hadn't fought with *him* – if I'd stayed on at the club, he would never have poached you from Carter, and none of this would have happened. Oh Ellen, . . . Alice . . . what have I done?'

Just minutes ago, Ellen had believed that she was doing the right thing, but seeing her friend like this was so hard, she almost confessed to the deceit. But she didn't, because after all was said and done, Alice was right. She truly believed that with every bone in her body; and her respect for Alice was tenfold.

'None of it was your fault,' she told Maddy. 'You went away because he was giving you a difficult time and you needed to think. And I accepted his offer because I was not told what had happened between the two of you. I don't believe we had any part in what happened between those two. It was always on the cards that at some time or another, they would face each other; two bad people wanting what the other had.'

But Maddy seemed not to have heard. With wide, shocked eyes she stared straight ahead, unseeing, her mind shattered with the terrible news.

Mortified at having deceived Maddy in such a cruel way, Ellen had to remind herself of how Alice had known Maddy far better and longer than she had. And if Alice was so desperate for Maddy to be told this untruth, it must be for the girl's safety, and that of her unborn child.

And so, Ellen consoled herself with the belief that she had done this for the best reasons. Maddy was beside herself with grief at the moment, but in time she would get through it and survive. For survival was what all this was about.

Either way, it was done, and there was no going back.

And with that thought in mind, Ellen felt oddly comforted.

~

It was a long, lonely night for Maddy, and even though Ellen was in the room next door, waking at Maddy's every move, the knowledge that Alice and Jack were both gone had left the young woman distraught beyond belief.

Hour after unquiet hour, the questions rampaged through Maddy's tortured mind. Was it somehow her fault? Or was Ellen right, when she had said that none of us have any control over what happens?

Yes, that was it. And hadn't she seen it in her own life so

far – that no matter how much we fight and struggle, life sweeps us along, whether we like it or not?

But what about the new life inside her – a life for which she alone was now responsible? How could she ever take care of that tiny mite, without work, or even a place to call her own?

Placing the palm of her hand on her abdomen, she murmured, 'I'll take care of you, my baby. Whatever happens, your mammy will always put you first; always keep you safe.'

It was a daunting prospect, but Maddy had been through many trials in her thirty years. This was simply one more.

The most important one of all.

CHAPTER NINE

As MORNING BROKE the skies, Maddy remained resolute. There were urgent matters to be attended to, and decisions to be made. None of them easy, but all necessary.

Hearing Ellen moving about downstairs, and smelling the delicous aroma of bacon she quickly washed and dressed, and made her way down to the kitchen. It seemed odd, being here in a strange house, with someone she had known for such a short time yet with whom she had so quickly bonded.

For now though, all she could think of was Alice . . . and Jack; both kind and good, both murdered, simply because they were in the wrong place at the wrong time.

As she entered the kitchen, Ellen was there, looking tired and worried. 'Maddy!' Rushing forward, she wrapped her arms about her. 'How are you feeling? Did you manage to get some sleep?'

'Sort of . . .' Maddy gave a half-smile. With Alice gone, she wondered if she would ever sleep contentedly again.

Ellen walked with her to the table; she had seen the dark circles under Maddy's eyes and she noticed how Maddy occasionally clenched her fists, as though warding off an attacker. There was no doubt in Ellen's mind that the news she had so cruelly imparted to Maddy, had scarred her deeply.

'Look, come and sit down and have some breakfast,' she urged her friend. 'I can see that you haven't had much sleep. I daresay you're still in a state of shock. Food and drink should help.'

'Thank you.' Maddy needed to talk with her, 'Afterwards, there's something I have to tell you.' She knew Ellen would be appalled at what she was about to say. But she had a debt to pay. She owed Alice that much.

Ellen told her that she had been out to the corner shop to buy in some food. She had fried up some bacon and mushrooms, and there was a pile of hot buttered toast and a freshly brewed pot of tea. When they were each seated and were tucking into their meal, Maddy explained what was playing on her mind.

'Alice was divorced, and there are no children or close relatives, except for an elderly half-sister who passed on some two years back.'

'What are you getting at?' Ellen asked, pouring them both a second cuppa.

Maddy hesitated; it all seemed so unreal. 'What I'm saying is, someone . . .' When her voice began shaking with emotion, she composed herself before going on. 'Someone has to make sure Alice is put to rest.' She stopped to wipe the tears from her eyes.

Realising that Maddy must have thought long and hard about this, Ellen simply listened and made no comment. Outwardly calm, inwardly her brain was working overtime as she wondered frantically how to cope with this new challenge. It was understandable that Maddy felt the need to take on such a responsibility. Alice had been her closest and dearest friend, and because Maddy was a warm and loving human being, she would see organising the funeral as her bounden duty.

'Someone has to take care of everything,' Maddy insisted, 'and if I don't do it, who will?'

'So, you're doing it because you believe there is no one else, is that it?' Ellen asked, seizing on this.

'That's part of it, yes.' Then there was that deep-down need, to gaze at Alice's face, in the undertaker's parlour, for the very last time.

'Maddy?'

'Yes?'

'If you thought there was someone else who would make the arrangements, would you think again?'

'I might – I don't know. But there isn't anyone.'

'What about Raymond?' Before Maddy could say anything, Ellen went on, 'From what I saw in the short time I was at the Pink Lady, it was obvious that Raymond adored her. Alice knew it too. In fact, I got the feeling that she was learning to love him back. Jack said, they were always chatting and laughing, and you know how shy Ray is. He was confident with her. They were two old friends who were getting closer with every day that passed. I bet the poor man is gutted.'

Maddy too had witnessed the growing affection between Alice and Raymond; though whenever she mentioned it to Alice, the woman would laugh it off. But Alice's denials had only served to make Maddy more curious.

'You're right about Raymond,' she admitted to Ellen. 'I've always known he was besotted with her. But I was never sure about her feelings.'

'But you did have suspicions, didn't you?'

Maddy nodded slowly. 'Yes, that's true, I did.'

'So, given another few months or so, Raymond might well have taken Alice for his wife?'

'It's possible.' Maddy found the idea both comforting and sad.

'So, why don't you give Raymond the choice?' Ellen gently persisted. 'Why don't we ask him if he would like to take on this final duty?'

'I don't know, Ellen. I'm not sure if it's the right thing to do.'

'Look, Maddy, I know you and Alice were close friends, and you loved her fondly,' Ellen acknowledged. 'But Raymond seems to have loved her in a different way, not so much as a friend but a sweetheart. And I believe, if he'd had the courage to ask her to be his wife, Alice would probably have said yes.'

Maddy smiled at that. 'Yes, all right, I know what you're saying,' she conceded. 'But I feel I owe it to her to make sure she's laid to her rest with dignity.'

'So, you don't feel that Raymond would want the same?'

'I didn't say that.'

Taking a deep breath, Ellen played her last trump card. 'Don't you think Alice would rather you kept your promise to her?'

Struggling with her conscience, Maddy remained silent.

'You don't always keep your promises, Maddy – that's what you told me. So, when Alice begged you to save yourself and the baby, and you gave her your word, did you never mean to keep that promise either?'

Mortified when she saw the tears flowing down Maddy's face, she almost relented. Instead, she deliberately hardened herself against weakening, because this was a fight she had to win. For all their sakes.

'I intend keeping my promise,' Maddy said brokenly, 'but not until she's properly laid to rest.'

'That's not good enough.' Ellen was dogged. 'It's not what Alice would have wanted, and you know it! She wanted you and the baby to be miles away from here, out of harm's reach. Don't fool yourself that Drayton will wait for Alice to be laid to rest before he sets the hounds on you!' She leaned forward, her voice softening, 'Listen to me, Maddy, if you were to go against what she wanted, the promise you gave would be empty and cruel. And you might as well never have made it.'

There followed a long intense moment, during which Maddy searched her soul. She still found it hard to believe that Alice was gone, that never again would she and Alice sit and plan, and grumble about everything and nothing, and when one of them needed a friend, the other would always be there, helping and supporting.

And it wasn't simply the hard facts of arranging a funeral. No, it was more than that. She longed to look at Alice's face one more time, to hold the moment in her heart and take it with her wherever she went.

She told Ellen as much now.

Ellen understood and was gentle. 'I can understand how much you want to see her . . . to keep her image in your heart and mind. But oh Maddy, wouldn't it be better if your lasting memories were of the two of you together, chatting over a drink and putting the world to rights, and looking out for each other, like friends do. Wouldn't they be far lovelier memories to keep?'

Another long span of silence, while Maddy contemplated Ellen's wise words. Maybe she was right, after all. 'What if Raymond doesn't want to do it?'

'We won't know if we don't ask him.' Ellen was relieved. 'Let me contact him. See what he says.'

'And if he says yes, he'll need money. I have some rainy-day savings put away – not a fortune, but it's his if he needs it.'

Ellen nodded. 'I also have rainy-day savings,' she offered, 'but first, we need to know what Raymond has to say.'

With all that in mind and for obvious reasons, Ellen knew she had to approach Raymond *before* Maddy got to him. Although it did make her anxious, because she knew he would be shocked at what she had to tell him.

An hour later, after going through their plan, Maddy gave Ellen the phone number that would take her straight to the desk at the Pink Lady.

Ellen had suggested she should be the one to speak with him first. 'It might be best if *I* was to ring the club,' she said.

'Whoever answers the phone would recognise your voice far easier than they would mine,' and Maddy had to agree.

~

It was early afternoon at the Pink Lady. The club had been closed for twenty-four hours after the shootings, but then the police had given permission for it to be reopened. From prison, Steve Drayton had instructed his accountants to take temporary management of the place.

Raymond sat against the bar, talking with Ted, the older barman. 'They still won't let me see her at the hospital,' he said gloomily. 'They say she's doing well, but that she can't have visitors just yet.'

'And are the police still guarding her?' The older man had been rocked to his roots by what had happened the other night. He still couldn't get used to Jack not being there.

Raymond nodded. 'It would seem so.'

'So, d'you know when she'll be allowed home?'

'Nope!' Raising his head, Raymond looked straight at the other man. 'I'm just so glad that she's alive. But I'll tell you this, Ted. When Alice does come out, I'll be there for her, every minute of the day. She'll not have to lift a finger, I'll see to that.'

The other man smiled. 'You've been sweet on her a long time, ain't you, matey?'

Raymond nodded affirmatively. 'Longer than that,' he said proudly.

'And who can blame you,' Ted kindly remarked. 'She's a good woman.' He dared to speak further. 'Why have you never asked her out?'

'Hmh.' Lately, Raymond had suffered regrets over that very thing. 'Somehow there was never the right time,' he answered regretfully. 'But then I never could tell if she liked me enough.

I was scared that if I *did* ask her and she turned me down, my chance would be gone for good.'

Ted knew different. 'If you'd asked her, she would never have turned you down, take it from me.'

Raymond's face lit up. 'D'you reckon?'

'I *know* it.'

How d'you know it?'

With a teasing grin on his face, the barman tapped his nose. 'That's for me to know, and you to find out.'

Raymond would not let it go. 'I promised I'd swap tomorrow's late shift with you,' he said, 'but I don't think I can do it now. Sorry, Ted.'

'You can't do that to me!' Ted protested. 'I've promised the wife I'd take her somewhere special. It's our anniversary, you can't let me down now. Oh, come on, Ray! I've booked a room at that hotel she likes, the one up near Marble Arch.'

Raymond waved a hand. 'Sorry. No can do.'

Ted groaned. 'All right, all right.' He scratched his head. 'Alice asked me never to tell you, but . . .' He paused, thinking how she would tear him off a strip, if ever she found out he'd betrayed her confidence.

Raymond grew impatient. 'Well?'

'All right! Alice always had the idea that you fancied her, and—'

'For God's sake, man! Spit it out, will you?'

'Well, she said that she fancied you an' all. Only she was too shy to tell you. D'you remember when we had the last Christmas do here?'

'Yes.' Raymond was almost hopping with excitement.

'Alice had a sprig of mistletoe in her pocket all night . . . said she was waiting for the right opportunity. There! You know now, don't you? But you must never let on that it was me who told you.'

'What! Alice fancies me? Oh Ted!' As Raymond grabbed

him by the shoulders and was about to hug him, the sound of the telephone ringing in the background caused him to let go.

'I'll answer that.' Having feared that Raymond was about to leap over the bar at him, Ted felt the need to escape.

'No, it's all right.' Raymond rushed to the desk. 'It might be news of my Alice,' he said, with a grin on his face a mile wide. 'Leave it to me.'

Stifling his excitement, he picked up the receiver. 'Pink Lady Cabaret Bar. Can I help you?'

'I'd like to speak with Raymond Baker, please.'

'This is Raymond Baker.' His heart dropped a mile as he feared the news might be bad.

Having deluded Maddy into believing that it might be safer if she was to go outside and use a public phone-booth, in case Steve had somehow got her phone tapped, Ellen said hurriedly 'Raymond, it's me – Ellen. You remember? I was the new singer at the club.'

When he acknowledged her, she asked, 'Can you talk? Is there anyone within hearing distance?'

She waited a moment before Raymond checked. 'No. But what's wrong?' Horror shook his voice. 'It's not Alice, is it? Please God . . . tell me it's not Alice.' ·

'No, she is doing all right. We've seen her and she is on the road to recovery. Just listen to me, Raymond, and don't be too upset by what I'm about to say.' Ellen took a deep breath, then went on: 'Like I said, Alice is going to be okay. Drayton puts the blame down to Maddy for what happened. I have her here with me and she's in fear for her life. I'm not sure if you know, but she's carrying his child, which he refuses to accept. He thinks she and some bloke are trying to stitch him up. He's made a threat, to track her down and kill her.'

'The man's mad!' Raymond had assumed that Maddy was miles away from the alley when it all sparked off. Now though, he was worried. 'If Drayton has his sights set on her, she's as good as finished. There'll be no escape; it won't matter that he's up for murder, he'll find a way. His sort always do.' He lowered his voice. 'Where is she now?'

'She's with me.'

'Get her away then . . . somewhere safe. As soon as you can.' He sounded frantic.

'I mean to.'

'Alice doesn't know about any of this, does she?'

'Yes. You see, Maddy was there, in the alley holding Alice after she was wounded. They both heard Drayton issue the threat.' She wondered how to tell him. 'Raymond, there's something else – something Alice said. It's the real reason I rang you.'

'You mean you've spoken with Alice?' The big man became excited. 'They wouldn't let me near her. No visitors yet, they said.'

'No, we haven't been able to speak with her either. Maddy was all for going to the hospital, but I thought it was too dangerous, so I got an old friend of mine to talk with Alice.'

As Ray listened carefully to what she had to say, Ellen explained, 'Her name is Connie. She cleans the wards there, in the post-surgical part, and by sheer luck, she managed to see Alice, just for a matter of minutes, that's all. No, listen – please. Oh, damn!' Quickly dropping another coin into the slot, she told him everything.

'Alice is beside herself with worry. She told my friend that Maddy must be deceived into believing she had not survived, that they had not been able to save her. It must have been a hard thing for her to ask, but as I've already had the devil of a job trying to dissuade Maddy from going to the hospital, I'm sure Alice did the right thing. She obviously knows her better than anyone so, may God forgive me, I told Maddy what Alice wanted her to believe.'

For a while, Raymond made no response. And then, in a quiet voice he told Ellen that yes, Alice *did* know Maddy better than anyone, and yes, to his mind also, she had done the right thing. 'Alice loves her like a daughter, and however much she might want her near, her only concern would have been for Maddy, and the child.'

Greatly relieved, Ellen explained how Maddy nonetheless was insisting on staying in the area to oversee 'official' things with regard to Alice. 'You know what I mean?' she said in a whisper. 'She means to stay until Alice has been properly laid to rest.'

Raymond did not hesitate. 'Please, go back and tell Maddy that she's to leave everything to me; and that I would be *honoured* to take care of Alice.' In truth, to love and honour Alice was the uppermost thing on his mind, so he wasn't really lying.

Thanking him, Ellen assured Raymond that she would contact him later, when they were more settled.

For now though, she had yet another call to make, which was short and to the point. And she made it immediately.

'Hi, Grandad, it's me – Ellen.'

The old man was delighted to hear from her. He was even more delighted when she told him she was on her way to see him, and that she was bringing a friend to stay for a while.

~

Maddy was already at the door when Ellen returned. 'What did Raymond say?' she entreated Ellen. 'Will he take care of her?'

Seeing how pale and drawn she was, Ellen thought it best to make their move within the hour. 'Everything is organised.' She slid an arm round Maddy's shoulders. 'Raymond said he would be honoured to take care of Alice, and that I should get you to safety as soon as possible. Oh, and you mustn't worry about money.'

Her mind was made up. 'We'd best be away, Maddy . . . the sooner the better, like *now!*' Holding Maddy's shivering body, and looking into those bloodshot and sorry dark eyes, Ellen feared for the other girl's state of mind.

All Maddy could think of was Alice. 'Dear Raymond, he'll look after Alice, I know he will. And when this is all over, I'll maybe see where she . . . where . . .'

She could not bring herself to say it, because the idea of looking down at a headstone with Alice's name on it, was more than she could bear.

~

The girls spent a couple of hours packing and tidying up the house, making all safe and secure. Ellen took all her important documents with her, not knowing when she would be back. Fortunately, Maddy had her cheque book and her handbag, with a few momentoes in the bottom, but that was all.

In no time at all, they were on their way to Euston station.

Deep in thought, Maddy had little to say during the journey. The London traffic was thickening by the minute, as rush-hour approached. Their cab frequently stopped and started, heading down the City Road towards the Angel and Pentonville Road, then on to King's Cross and Euston. Maddy observed the office workers, errand boys and deliverymen, and wondered how it was that something so bad could have happened such a short time ago, and all those people could just go about their normal lives, unaffected, unaware.

The world kept turning, she thought sorrowfully. Day followed night, and life went on as usual.

As they drew up at the lights opposite Eversholt Street, her quiet gaze strayed to the large, handsome church which stood like a sentry guarding the corner of Upper Woburn Place.

Maddy was deeply drawn to it. 'I'll catch you up in the fore-court – near platform thirteen,' she cried, grabbing her bag and coat. In a moment she was hurriedly climbing out of the taxi. 'Don't worry. I'll find you. I just need a minute, okay?'

Afraid that her friend had a mind to run away, Ellen tried to take hold of her and pull her back inside, but she was too late. Then, as the lights changed and the traffic began to hoot behind them, she realised she'd have to get out too.

Frantically fishing through her bag, she gave the driver a five-pound note, then heaved herself and the big suitcase out on to the pavement. And then she was hurrying after her friend, who was dodging round the corner and up the steps of St Pancras Church.

'Maddy . . . wait!' Ellen panted, but the other girl had already disappeared.

Lugging the suitcase after her, Ellen puffed around the corner, to the huge, imposing double doors of St Pancras Church, and went inside. It was only a minute or so before she spied Maddy. Kneeling in the front pew, her head was bowed and hands clasped in prayer, the soft sound of her crying echoing eerily from the walls.

Quietly, so as not to disturb her, Ellen slid into the back pew, and sat on the hard wooden seat, her eyes on Maddy, and her heart sore.

She herself had only known Alice for five minutes, but she had recognised a good woman when she saw one. Alice had been Maddy's confidante, and it was common knowledge that in the absence of any family of her own, she had loved and cared for The Songbird as a mother would.

That love had been proven in Alice's selfless act when, at a time when she needed her most, she had sent Maddy away.

Ellen could only imagine Maddy's pain right now. And so

she waited, and watched, until Maddy was able to continue the journey that would take her further away from everything she knew and loved.

~

Unaware that Ellen was just a few steps behind her, Maddy prayed through her pain. Gazing up at the statue of Jesus on the cross, she was deeply moved by the loving eyes that seemed to look right into her soul. She observed the wounds on His hands and feet, and a sense of wonder flowed through her.

She sighed, a deeply felt sigh that drained her emotions. 'You took so much away from me, Lord – my family, my place in this world of Yours. Everything I knew . . . it's all gone.' She paused awhile, to think of Alice; the comfort she had brought and the wisdom she shared. 'You gave me Alice, and oh, I loved her so much. And now, for some reason I don't understand, You've taken her away from me.'

Passing her hand over the place where her baby lay, she whispered, 'But You've given me Ellen, and You've given me something else, too, something so very precious.'

She pressed the palm of her hand over the tiny shape. 'This baby is a new life, a new start. Someone of my own, who I can love and cherish, and take care of, for the rest of my life. And I thank You for that, Lord.'

Standing up, she walked towards the altar, beside which the arc of candles burned like a beacon. Taking one out of the box, she lit it from another, before pressing it into the holder, where the flame flickered and grew, until the brightness hurt her eyes. 'This is for you, Alice,' she murmured. 'To light your way to heaven.'

She knelt on the footboard. 'Goodbye, my Alice. I'll never forget you, as long as I live.'

Making the sign of the cross, she prayed, 'Keep her safe, Lord. She is one of Your special people.'

When a gentle hand reached over her to light a second candle, she saw that it was Ellen, and she was not surprised. 'I'm sorry I ran away,' she told her. 'I just felt I had to come in here.'

Ellen knelt beside her in the empty, echoing church, and together they prayed.

Maddy prayed for Alice's soul.

Ellen asked forgivenes for the cruel deception she had played on Maddy.

~

A while later, the two girls crossed the busy main road into Euston station, where Ellen studied the noticeboard. 'We'll need to make two changes,' she told Maddy, 'but we should be there in three hours or less.' She glanced at her watch. 'We've got forty minutes before the next train arrives . . . time for food and drink.'

Starting at every sound, Maddy was visibly on edge. 'You still haven't said where we're going.' She felt out of her depth. The past forty-eight hours had been like living through a nightmare. Back there in the alley and later at Ellen's house, events had swept her along. Now that she was really on her way out of London, destined for unfamiliar places and people she knew nothing about, the reality of it all was unsettling.

'We're going to my grandad's house, in Blackpool,' Ellen explained. 'I've already spoken to him, and he's looking forward to seeing us.'

Maddy felt somewhat easier. Now that she had a name and a place, it didn't seem such a frightening prospect.

Moreover, with Raymond having put her mind at rest with regard to Alice, she felt more able to focus on what lay ahead of them. She had lost Alice, but she had found a friend in

Ellen, and she still had her baby. That much at least, she was deeply thankful for.

The old saying was right, she thought solemnly. A life out, and a life in. Poor Alice had been so excited about the baby, and now she would never see it. That was a desperately sad thing.

As they walked towards the café, Maddy swallowed another rush of tears, but just then, just for a split second, she felt the life within her quicken. 'It's moving!' she exclaimed. The tiny flutter in her belly came again, and she beamed. 'He's anxious to be out in the big wide world.'

Ellen took her by the arm. 'That baby has a long way to go yet.' Because Maddy was still surprisingly slender, Ellen assumed there must be at least another six months of waiting. 'You never said when the baby is due.'

Maddy made a mental calculation. 'By my reckoning, I'm almost four months gone.'

'By your reckoning?' Ellen was slightly disturbed by Maddy's comment. 'Do you mean you haven't been to the doctor's yet?'

Maddy shook her head. 'Not yet, no. I wanted Steve to know first.' Her heart sank. 'Like a fool, I had an idea that he might want to come with me.'

Ellen groaned. 'It's not you that's the fool,' she said grimly, 'it's *him*! But if there's any justice, he'll get his comeuppance and, if you ask me, it won't be before time, neither.'

Maddy thought of Steve Drayton, and all those hopeless dreams, and was amazed at herself for being taken in by him. 'Why did I let him get me pregnant?' she sighed. 'I should have had more sense.'

'These things happen.' Ellen screwed up her face in concentration. 'I'm on the pill, thank heavens! Anyway it's late July now, so if, as you say, you're coming up to four months, the baby should arrive about . . .' She gave a whoop and a holler. 'Christmas! Think of that – a baby for Christmas!' she laughed out loud.

Maddy laughed with her. 'Oh Ellen, that would be the best Christmas present in the whole wide world.' Then her smile faded. 'He or she won't have a daddy though, and what will I say, when the baby grows old enough to ask after him?'

Ellen thought it a very difficult thing, but, 'All you can do is love and protect the baby – be the best mother you can,' she said wisely. 'And maybe, when all's said and done, that will be enough.'

Maddy hugged her impulsively for those beautiful words.

One thing she knew for certain.

For as long as she lived, whatever sacrifice was required of her along the way, or whatever danger might threaten, she would move heaven and earth, to keep her child safe.

That much she knew.

From this day on, it was her goal in life.

~

Back at Scotland Yard, the activity following the shooting had been intense. With yet another briefing over, about twenty officers tumbled out of the incident room and hurried away to their desks; all but two – Detective Inspector Warren, and his colleague Sergeant Edwards.

Continuing on down the stairs to the pavement outside, the stockily-built Sergeant commented, 'That Superintendent Bates is a miserable bugger! Does he show any gratitude for us having nabbed some of the biggest villains in London? Oh no! And already we've had two press conferences, going over the same scenario. I tell you, not only is he milking this for all he's worth, he's running the rest of us into the ground. What the hell does he want – blood?'

'It's no good complaining,' came the fed-up reply. 'You should know what he's like by now. He wants every loose end tied up in a pretty pink bow, which he can then present to the prosecution, so he can claim credit for doing his bit.'

'But we've already established what happened. It's gang-warfare, pure and simple. Two low-lifes face each other down: one gets shot and killed; a man gets caught in the crossfire and a woman gets wounded. Moreover, there were enough witnesses to fill a courtroom; even Carter's men spilled their guts to save their own necks. So, as far as I'm concerned, we've already tied up all the loose ends. *I* reckon it's time to concentrate on other matters, such as keeping a wary eye on the villains who are already straining at the leash to rule the roost, especially now that Carter will be pushing up the daisies and Drayton is locked up.'

'You've learned nothing then.'

'What's that supposed to mean?'

'All I'm saying is, you must never underestimate men like that.' DI Warren knew from experience that there was always more going on than met the eye. 'Being locked in a prison cell won't stop a low life like Drayton from keeping his thumb on the pulse. He's still in control, don't you worry about that. And it won't matter how many smalltime thugs are straining at the leash, they've got no chance, because locked up, or loose on the streets, a man like Drayton is still top dog. Take my word for it. Nothing goes down without his say-so.'

The younger man glanced at him. 'So, we'd best keep our wits sharp then, eh?'

'That's about the size of it. As for the two singers who worked at the club, I for one wouldn't mind clearing that one up. According to one of the regular clubgoers, Drayton got rid of his regular artist, in favour of a bright young thing who just happened to be working for Carter.' Pausing to light up his cigarette, he continued, 'I'd like to meet up with these two girls and hear their side of it. We're still trying to get an address for Ellen Drew. Delaney is missing from the Battersea flat – no one there has seen her for a good while.'

'Okay. But you're surely not suggesting they had anything to do with what happened? I mean, it's common knowledge that Carter and Drayton have been at each other's throats for years.'

'I know all that. From the clubbers who witnessed the incident, we know enough of what went down in that alley, anyway. All the same, I'd still like to take their statements.'

The younger man dismissed the idea of even more work. 'If you ask me, we don't need to hear what they have to say. We've got Drayton bang to rights and I reckon there's little point in wasting valuable resources in tracking the women down. If you ask *me*, that is.'

'Well, nobody *is* asking you!'

'Maybe not. But I'll say it anyway. Moreover, we should not be engaging time and manpower in an operation that would add little or nothing to what we already know. I say we'd be best employed in consolidating what we've got. We need to keep a sharp eye on Drayton's contacts, and make damned sure the bastard never again sets foot in the free world. Or at least, not until he's old and grey.'

The DI gave his Sergeant a shove towards the car. 'I think we've heard enough of your opinions. Now get in and drive!'

'Where to?'

'University College Hospital.'

'You'll not get much joy there,' the Sergeant predicted. 'That woman doesn't have a clue what went down. If you ask me, the poor cow just happened to be in the wrong place at the wrong time.'

DI Warren lit a cigarette and took a deep, calming breath. 'Like I said, nobody's asking you. So, until somebody tells me otherwise, *I'm* giving the orders around here, and *I* say it's time we paid another visit, to see how the patient is getting on. Put your foot down, Sergeant, and we might get there before the canteen closes. I'd swap my old granny for a nice cup of tea and a Garibaldi biscuit . . .'

PART THREE

~

Blackpool, 1978

Lighter Hearts

CHAPTER TEN

WHEN MADDY AND Ellen clambered off the train at Blackpool North station, it was still light, a beautiful warm summer's evening. 'I hadn't realised how much I enjoy train rides,' Maddy said as they strolled up the platform. 'It's been years since I went on one.'

Ellen couldn't help but wonder about her – what kind of childhood she had endured; where she hailed from, and what her life had been like, up to Drayton taking her on.

Drawing on what she had learned so far, Ellen surmised that Maddy had been a bit of a loner, an orphan without other relatives to fall back on. But then she had met up with a man like Drayton who earned her trust and her love, before using and abusing her. That was the worst kind of blow.

Maddy's saviour had been Alice, who gave her love and friendship and asked for nothing in return. And now, because of what had occurred back in Soho, and the deceit in which Ellen herself had played a large part, Maddy was made to believe she had lost the only real friend she had ever known.

Shivering suddenly, Ellen wondered whether she had done wrong, taking it on herself to carry out Alice's wishes. But the more she had thought on it, the more she realised that if Maddy were to be brought to safety, there really was no alternative.

JOSEPHINE COX

She had noticed how, several times on the train, Maddy had sat and gazed out the window, watching the miles speed her away from everything familiar. Occasionally, she made an excuse to go to the toilet, and when she came back, her eyes were red raw from crying. And when Ellen asked if she was all right, she would smile and nod, and say not a word.

'I'm sorry,' Maddy apologised. 'I wasn't much company on the train, was I?'

'No problem,' Ellen answered. 'You had things on your mind, and who could blame you for that?'

'I owe you a lot,' Maddy said. 'I don't know what I'd have done without you.' She threaded her arm through Ellen's. 'Besides, we're here now, and we have to make the most of it – isn't that right?'

'And are you okay with that, Maddy? I mean, you've gone along with all my suggestions, because you have no one else and nowhere to go. You're in a vulnerable position, what with the baby and everything. You must be so nervous, coming here with me.'

'What makes you say that?' Maddy thought she had managed to keep her anxiety to herself. Certainly that had been her intention.

Now that the subject was breached, Ellen answered honestly. 'I was just thinking, how it must all be so strange to you – leaving familiar surroundings on my say-so; travelling hundreds of miles to a strange place you've never even seen.'

'I trust you, don't I?'

'Obviously. But as far as you know, it could be yet another catastrophe. And while I've known and loved my grandad all my life, to you he's just a stranger.'

Ellen couldn't help but wonder how she herself might cope: having no family whatsoever, meeting up with a man like Drayton, being beaten and abused and made with child, then have him reject you both so callously. Then there was the ordeal of watching her two dearest friends shot down in cold blood. And now, being torn away to travel miles from her home, with practically only the clothes she stood up in.

Laying it bare like that, Ellen truly believed that if it was her in Maddy's shoes, she might well have cracked up before now. But who could tell? Who could predict what Fate has in store, and whether or not we will have the strength of mind to cope with it all?

As Maddy had not yet answered her question, Ellen put it again. '*Are* you okay with us coming up here, Maddy?'

Maddy took a second to think, then said, 'Yes, I'm okay, and I'm very grateful to you for taking me under your wing.' She had never leaned on anyone in her life – not even on Alice. But the recent sequence of events had taken a terrible toll on her. She felt isolated and lonely. Moreover, try as she might, she could see no real future. Today was a hurried and temporary measure. But where she might go from here and what lay ahead, she had no idea.

On the train she had tried to get her thoughts together, to make some kind of plan. But by the time they reached Blackpool, she was as unsure as ever. Heartsore and deeply shaken at losing both Jack and Alice, there was little else she could think of right now and, in her heart of hearts, she knew it would take a long time to come to terms with everything.

On the other hand, sitting quiet on the train, steeped in thought and with the rhythmic throb of the engine lulling her fears, she was made to think about her child. And as the miles had sped away, the burden of what she had left behind seemed to somehow lift from her shoulders.

At first, when she absentmindedly gazed out of the window, nothing interested her. It was just a journey, a strange and frightening journey she had never wanted to make. Then, so slowly she had hardly noticed, she found herself soaking in the landscape and appreciating the beauty of God's world all about her. With appreciation came a deep sense of calm, and a quiet murmur of hope. It was a small, but comforting thing.

Interrupting her thoughts, Ellen now told Maddy, 'Who knows? Coming away from the nightclub scene could be the best thing in the world, for both of us. As long as we can keep singing, that is! I hope you like Blackpool, Maddy. It's so different from London.'

'It's always been on my mind to come up here and see the sights, but somehow I never did,' Maddy replied. 'So, what can I expect?'

Ellen chuckled. 'When it's cold, you'll shiver to your roots, and when it's windy, you can hardly stand up straight. If it's cold *and* windy, you'll likely be picked up and frozen in mid-air.'

Maddy laughed out loud. 'It's not that bad, surely?'

'Can be, yes. That's why it's almost deserted in the winter, save for a few brave souls, come to see our famous Illuminations.'

'And in the summer?'

'Ah, now that's different.' Ellen loved Blackpool, whatever the season. 'In the summer it's noisy and you can barely find a table in the cafés. There are groups of bare-chested blokes strutting down the street, fancying their chances with every girl that comes along. You'll find an ice-cream parlour and a pub round every corner, with theatres and amusement arcades everywhere you look. And I'm going to leave you to discover the amazing Tower for yourself: I won't say a word!'

Seeing the line of cabs waiting, she ushered Maddy towards the queue. 'There's nowhere else like Blackpool in the whole wide world,' she sighed happily. 'Whenever you're feeling low, all you have to do is take a ride in a horse-carriage and clip-clop along the front to the Pleasure Beach, or climb onto a tram and let yourself be taken back in time . . .' Then, realising she had gone all sentimental, she swiftly changed her tone. 'Honestly, Maddy, it really is so amazing! And oh, how I've missed it while I've been away.'

'If you love it so much, why did you ever leave?' Maddy asked. She had seen the look on Ellen's face, and heard the love in her voice as she talked of her beloved Blackpool, and it made her curious.

Ellen explained, 'Like many another starry-eyed girl, I left it because I wanted to see the world and make a career in showbusiness. Sometimes though, the world is right there on your doorstep, and you don't even realise.'

Maddy leaned forward. 'You had a special boyfriend here, didn't you?'

Ellen looked at her in surprise. 'How did you know?'

'Because I saw the expression on your face just now.' Maddy did not want to pry, but had to ask all the same. 'What happened to him?'

Ellen gave a wry little laugh. 'Oh, he went off with the boss's daughter. You see, he was always ambitious, and her father owned half the rides on the Pleasure Beach. Naturally, he saw himself as the future owner. So, you see, she had more to offer than me.'

'Do you miss him?'

'Not likely!' But that was a white lie, spoken in defence. The real truth was, even now, Ellen still cherished the memories the two of them had shared together.

A few moments later, it was their turn to get inside a taxi and, at Ellen's request, the driver took them along the promenade. 'It's too early in the year for the lights to be switched on,' he told them, 'but even when they're not lit, they make a splendid sight. The normal period for them to be switched on is the end of August until the first week in November. Will you ladies still be here then?'

'We might be,' Ellen answered cautiously.

Maddy was thrilled to see every street-lamp along the four or five miles, beautifully decorated with shapes of Disney characters, each and every one peppered with coloured bulbs. 'How wonderful!' she kept saying. 'How amazing!'

'Hah! I can tell you're a newcomer to Blackpool, young lady!' Born and bred in this fun town, the driver was proud to call it home. 'But I promise you this, if you've never seen Blackpool Illuminations all lit up at night, you've never seen anything! There's nowhere else like it in the whole wide world.'

When, a few minutes later, they turned away from the seafront and into Ackerman Street, the driver asked for the door number. 'It's number eight – the fourth house after the icecream parlour.' While Ellen directed him, Maddy dug into her purse for the fare.

'And don't forget to go on the Big Dipper,' the driver said as he waited for them to disembark. 'It's one hell of a ride, and I should know, because I've been on it more times than I've had hot dinners.' He gave a gruff laugh. 'Not willingly, I might add. The thing is, I've got four kids; they're all mad for the funfair, and they won't go on without me.'

'I've been on it just the once,' Ellen admitted, 'and that was more than enough, thank you very much!'

'Yes? Well, I've told my missus, *she* can go on with the kids next time. I mean, it's not safe for a man with a dicky heart!'

'Oh dear!' Maddy said sincerely. 'So you've got a dicky heart, have you?'

'Not yet. But if I have to go on that thing once more, I'm sure I *will* have!' With a cheeky grin and a wink, he was away full throttle, accelerating onto the Promenade so fast, there erupted a volley of car-horns. 'AND THE SAME TO YOU . . . BLOODY LUNATICS!' he bawled. Though he was plainly in the wrong, their driver gave as good as he got, adding a shake of the fist for good measure.

'There goes a character,' Ellen chuckled.

'Not much of a driver though, is he?' Maddy giggled. 'I'm glad he got us here safely, before deciding to take on the world.'

Pausing outside her grandfather's house, Ellen asked of Maddy, 'Well, what d'you think?'

Maddy observed the house. Small and smart, it was part of a terrace of similar houses, though it was the only one with a blue door and window-sills. The cream-coloured net curtains were pretty, the lion-head doorknocker was handsome, and in general the house looked much loved and well cared for. It's a fine house, Maddy thought, and said so aloud.

'Grandad has a thing about bold colours,' Ellen explained. 'When Grandma was alive, he would never have dared to paint the door blue. But nowadays he does pretty much as he likes.'

'Ellen!' A woman spilled out of next door. 'Ellen? Is that really you?' Small and squat with a red face and a wide, tooth-less mouth, she was just like one of the characters on a bawdy seaside postcard.

Calling as she went, she hobbled down her path and up to Ellen, flung her arms round the girl's neck and kissed her with the exuberance of a dog finding its master. 'I were looking out the window and I saw you, and I thought, No, it can't be. Oh, lass! You've been gone for so long, I couldn't be sure it were you, d'you see? But then you turned and I knew straight off, and there you were . . . walking up the street as though you'd never been away!'

She was so excited, Maddy feared she might have a fit. 'Oh, Ellen lass, it's so good to see you back home . . . and will yer be staying this time, d'you think?'

Feeling like she'd been in a rugby tackle, Ellen tactfully released herself from the woman's hold. 'I'm not sure,' she replied. 'I hope so.'

'And who's this?' Swinging round to scrutinise Maddy, she gave her a wide cavernous grin. 'Well, you're a pretty thing and no mistake!' Her eyes cottoned onto Maddy's little bump.

'When's it due? Oh, and don't tell me you're not expecting, because I've had six of my own, more's the pity, and I can tell just by looking. There's summat in a woman's face that gives it away, a kinda glow, if yer know what I mean.'

She gave a heavy sigh. 'Sadly, my lot 'ave all flown the nest. Since the last one took off, I've not seen hide nor hair of any o' the buggers!' Visibly bristling, she snorted, 'All I can say is good shuts to 'em. If they think I've outlived my usefulness, they can think again. I'll tell you what though – the buggers'll need me afore I need them, yer can count on that!'

Overwhelmed by this lively little person, Maddy sensed that she did not mean one word of what she'd just said.

'This is Maddy,' Ellen intervened. 'And Maddy, this is Mrs Winterhouse from next door.'

'It's Nora!' the woman chided. 'We don't stand on ceremony in these parts. So, don't you forget,' she addressed Maddy, 'the name is Nora.'

Maddy held out her hand in polite greeting, but was astonished when the litle woman threw herself into a rough embrace. 'You're very welcome, pet,' she said, eventually letting her go. 'Have yer been to Blackpool afore?'

Maddy shook her head. 'No, but I hope I might get to know it.'

'Oh, but yer will,' the little woman assured her. 'The noise and bustle in summer and the quiet in winter – then the sea air and the sound of gulls overhead . . . Like a poor man's paradise, it is. I would never want to be anywhere else, I can tell yer that.'

She might have gone on for longer, but Ellen had seen how pale and tired Maddy looked. 'It's really lovely to see you, Nora but we'd best go now. We've travelled a long way, and I can't wait to see my grandad. But we'll drop by tomorrow, if you like. We can talk then, eh?'

'All right, if you say so. Honestly, you young 'uns are all the same – allus in a rush, no time for anything. Seems yer can't wait to be somewhere's else. Well, go on then.' She gave Ellen another bear-hug. 'Oh, and tell your grandad hello. Let him know, he mustn't be a stranger.' She hobbled back inside her own house.

Having given up her front door key long since, Ellen raised the lionhead knocker and letting it go with a clang, was taken aback when the door was flung open and there stood her grandad, a look of impatience on his face and the fire-poker in his hand. 'Yer little bugg—. Well, I never! If it isn't our Ellen!' Hugging her hard, he laughed out loud. 'I thought it were them damned kids from Fitzroy Street. They've tekken to knocking on doors and running off.'

Thinking how wonderful it must be to have someone like him in your life, Maddy stood back and watched them. Ellen's grandad was nothing like she'd expected. While Ellen was small and perfect, this man was the size of a mountain, though obviously fit and strong. And with his red hair and sporty beard brightly speckled with grey, he was a sight to behold. Still striking in look and manner, Maddy suspected he must have been extremely handsome in his youth.

Now, as he peered at her over Ellen's shoulders, Maddy was very taken by the bright sparkle in his smiling green eyes. 'Hello, and who have we here then? Is this the young lady you told me about?' His warm, resonant voice seemed to shake the ground beneath them.

Drawing her friend forward, Ellen explained, 'This is my friend Maddy . . . Maddy Delaney.'

Reaching down, he placed two huge hands on her shoulders and gave Maddy a kiss. 'I'm Bob, and you are very welcome in my home, lass,' he told her affectionately. 'This is your home for as long as you see fit. You and Ellen both.'

Maddy felt uneasy. 'I'm pregnant,' she blurted out. 'Did you know that?'

'No matter. You are still welcome to make this your home,' he affirmed. 'All three of you.'

Leading them inside, he gave them a quick tour, starting with the sitting room. 'I've changed a few things since you've been gone,' he told Ellen. 'This room's had a coat of paint and a few new pieces of furniture.' Then, ushering them inside the front parlour, he explained, 'You might recall this front room was never hardly used. Well, now it's my workshop. See?' He pointed proudly across the room. 'What do you think?'

Beautifully arranged on the brand-new shelves was a fine collection of wooden sculptures. Painstakingly fashioned and polished, there were fiery prancing horses, pretty girls on swings, and all manner of animals and birds in every pose imaginable.

'Oh, they're beautiful!' Maddy was amazed. 'Did *you* do all these?'

'I did, yes.' The pride shone from his face. 'And there are more out in the shed, ready to be sold at market.'

Ellen had always known her grandad was talented, but she had never realised just how much so, until now. 'You used to say you would never sell your pieces,' she reminded him.

'Ah, yes . . . well, that was when your grandma Kitty was here. Everything I ever made was for her alone. After she'd gone, I got to be a bit sad, hour after hour working on these lovely pieces, with no one but me to see them. Then, some time ago, when I had this room done up, the young man who decorated the walls saw the sculptures in the hallway. He begged me to sell him one, for his wife's birthday.' He scratched his head as he tried to remember. 'As I recall, the particular one he fancied was a little lad, holding a butterfly in the palm of his hand.'

Maddy told him she thought it sounded wonderful.

'Mmm. I have to say, I always thought it was one of my best,' he answered thoughtfully. 'The idea came after walking through the park and seeing this lad. Running around for ages

156

he was, trying to catch a butterfly. But he never did manage it.'

Maddy could see the boy in her mind. 'So, you thought you would let him actually catch the butterfly, is that it?'

He smiled down on her. 'Something like that, yes,' he answered, 'seems to me that you've the heart of a fine artist.'

~

After lingering in that amazing workshop, and viewing the tiny but serviceable scullery, they were now seated in comfortable armchairs in the homely sitting room, while Grandad Bob insisted on preparing a meal. 'Did Nora from next door catch you out?' he asked.

'You could say that,' Ellen replied.

'I hope she didn't worry you too much?' he called back, going into the scullery.

'No, Grandad. She was just pleased to see us.'

'She's got a new boyfriend – did she tell you that?'

'What! Are you serious?' Somehow it was not easy to imagine Nora Winterhouse with a man.

'Oh, aye. He's the third one this month. Gone a bit mad of late, she has. To my reckoning, there's been men at the house most every week.'

'So, is she looking to marry this latest one, or what?'

'She'll not marry any of 'em, I can tell you that, lass.'

'Why not?'

''Cause she's already said – it's *me* she's after. In fact, she's been after me ever since poor Kit went to meet her Maker. I might be wrong, and may the Lord forgive me if I am, but I've an idea she fetches these men home, just to make me jealous. Huh! She should be so lucky.'

Winking at Maddy, Ellen asked in serious voice, 'Poor Nora. So you don't fancy her then?'

'What! I'd rather be tipped upside-down in a tub o' wet spinach!'

Both Ellen and Maddy laughed out loud. 'I'll be through in a minute,' he called. 'The kettle's on the boil.'

Still smiling, Maddy felt as though she had known him all her life. 'You're so lucky,' she told Ellen now. 'Your Grandad Bob is so nice and kind, and it's plain to see how much he loves you.'

Ellen nodded. 'I know I'm lucky,' she said, 'but I'm stupid too – going away from him, from everything I know, when all the time my happiness was right here, under my nose.'

'So, will you never go back down South?'

'Never!'

'And what will you do for money?'

'Well, I shall let out my aunt's house – I might get Connie to organise all that for me, and pay her. Or I could sell it, I suppose, and buy a little house here for us. Eventually, I'd like to get back to singing – find work on the Northern club circuit. Showbiz is in our blood, isn't it, Maddy?'

She got up and went over to her friend. 'We'll be all right. Don't you worry now. You, me and the babe – we're going to be just fine. I've been sensible. I've got a deal of money stashed away, so we won't be desperate for a while yet.' She chuckled. 'Who knows? When the money runs out, we could buy an ice-cream van and go up and down the front.'

Maddy didn't think that was such a bad idea. 'Sounds like a fun way to earn money. Meanwhile, *I've* got money put away too,' she said, 'and I insist on paying my way. Thank God I kept my handbag with me. So, when your grandad comes back in, we'll have to talk about that side of it.'

'All in good time,' Ellen assured her. 'For now though, let's just be content to be safe.'

~

For one magic moment, Maddy had almost forgotten about London, and the turmoil they had left behind.

Now, however, it all came flooding back.

And even though they were some two hundred miles distant, the reality of that night was like a living thing in her mind.

CHAPTER ELEVEN

O<small>N THEIR FIRST</small> morning in Blackpool, Bob Maitland insisted on accompanying Maddy and his grandaughter on a walk along the promenade. 'Now that I've got you back,' he told Ellen, 'I'm not having some handsome cockney fella snatch you away again.'

'That's not likely to happen,' Ellen assured him. 'I've seen enough of the bright lights of London to last me a lifetime. I prefer the bright lights here, Grandad.' In fact, if she never left Lancashire again, it would not be a hardship.

'And how do *you* feel about that, love?' Addressing himself to Maddy, he saw how preoccupied and nervous she seemed. 'Are you ready to swap the sophistication of London for cheap and cheerful Blackpool?'

Maddy answered truthfully. 'I hope so,' she said. 'I just need to find my way around, and get a feel for the place.'

Everything was so strange though. Where London was her familiar stamping ground, Blackpool was a completely different environment. It was exactly as Ellen described; at times noisy, other times quiet. Outside the pubs, there were waste-bins spilling over with squashed beer cans and crisp packets. Ice-cream cornets had been dropped on the ground and trodden into the pavement cracks, and there were people everywhere, laughing, arguing, taking up the entire promenade with their playful antics.

The atmosphere was so different from the hubbub of Central London. Having seen only part of this renowned seaside resort, Maddy thought it was far from being the most beautiful place in the world. There were areas that came across as bawdy and tatty, and sometimes when a group of exuberant, well-oiled, bare-chested young men started chasing each other, you had to stand your ground or be accidentally knocked flying.

Yet for all that, there was a sense of fun and excitement, with holidaymakers wearing kiss-me-quick hats and colourful wigs, while most children and some adults merrily buried their faces in whirls of pink candy-floss. Uplifted voices of the bingo callers echoed through the air, and like a fantasy army on the march, the rhythmic clip-clop of horse and carriage-wheels played a tune over the ground.

As they neared the Pleasure Beach, a portly, smiley-faced woman tapped Maddy on the arm. 'Can yer hear *that* lot, screaming like banshees?' She gestured towards the Big Dipper ride. 'You'd never get *me* on that – not for a million dollars. I've nowt against showing me knickers,' she winked knowingly, 'Lord knows, I've already done that a few times in my heyday, but when it comes to having me stomach turned upside down, no thank you very much!'

With that, she gave Maddy a surprisingly gleaming smile, before chasing after her young son, who had run off to feed a carrot to the carriage-horse. 'Yer little sod!' she bawled. 'Come away afore he bites yer bloody fingers off!'

Smilingly averting her eyes, Maddy glanced across the pier and on towards the beach. It was an awesome sight: little girls in pretty sun-hats, boys playing with frisbees, young people lying on towels beneath the wonderful sunshine, and the old ones sprawled in bright stripey deckchairs, wearing big-rimmed hats and sucking on ice creams.

The scene evoked other memories. There was a time, eons ago, when she too had enjoyed days out at the seaside with her parents. She had visited Brighton, Clacton and Southend, but she had never seen anything quite like Blackpool, with its trams and horse-drawn carriages, and endlessly long, wide promenade.

'Well then, Maddy?' Grandad Bob interrupted her reverie. 'So, d'you think you might settle here, or what?'

Maddy looked up at him, shading her eyes with the palm of her hand when the sun half-blinded her. 'I do like what I've seen so far. The people are really friendly, and there seems to be so much going on.'

'So?' he persisted. 'You still haven't given me a proper answer.'

She laughed. 'You're worse than Ellen,' she chided. 'And yes, I think I'd like very much to settle here . . . if you'll have me?'

'What! I wouldn't have you going anywhere else,' he declared. 'As far as I'm concerned, you're part of our family now.'

Choked with emotion, Maddy could only nod. It had been so long since she was part of a family, she had made herself believe it would never happen again.

Seeing the glint of tears in Maddy's eyes, Bob quickly rescued her by putting on his best Sergeant-Major voice. 'Right, that's settled then.' Content with his lot, he wrapped one arm round Ellen and the other round Maddy. 'I bet I'm the envy of every manjack here,' he declared proudly, as he marched them along the promenade, his face uplifted in the happiest of grins, and his step more brisk than it had been in a long, lonely time.

'I might be old and ugly, but there can't be a luckier fella anywhere, to have two darling little females hanging on his arm.'

'You're not ugly!' Maddy thought him to be 'a fine-looking man, for your age' and said so; much to his delight.

He laughed, that deep-throated laugh that seemed to shake the ground beneath. 'That's a back-handed compliment if ever I heard one!'

'You want to be careful, Grandad.' Ellen whispered a warning.

'Oh? And why's that then?'

'Because we might run across Nora from next door, and *then* what would you do?'

'What would I do?' He winked from one to the other. 'I think I would wish her good day, and let it be known that I'm already spoken for – *twice over.*'

Maddy's heart was warmed by her two delightful companions. As they now cut across the wooden ramp to chase recklessly along the sands, she made a secret wish. '*Please God, let this be a brand new start for all of us.*'

There was so much to think about. Firstly, she would need to make sure she did not become a burden on Ellen and Bob – financially or otherwise. She must pay her way and pull her weight and with that in mind she must be quick to locate the bank. Later, when the baby was born, she might have to think about a place of her own or going halves with Ellen. Oh, and just thinking about the baby made her heart leap with joy.

'Look, Maddy.' Jumping up and down with excitement, Ellen was pointing to a red and yellow striped balloon hovering above their heads. 'Look what it says – three pounds a go, from the top end of the pier. D'you fancy a trip on it?'

Grandad Bob was quick to tell her she need not include him, because there was no way he would ever let himself be taken up in an oversized toy balloon '. . . with a flimsy wicker-basket dangling on the end of it. I'd like to think I'd got more sense than to trust meself to such a dangerous article. You two can do what you like, I can't stop you. But you won't get *me* in no blown-up balloon, flying on the wrong end of a rope, no siree.'

But in no time at all, all three of them were up, up and away, soaring into the skies and loving every minute of it. 'Trouble with me is, I let meself be talked into anything!' Grandad yelled from the other end of the basket. 'I must want my head tested!'

Maddy thought it was the most exhilarating thing she had ever experienced; even more than her very first night on stage at the tender age of fifteen. The breeze whipped against her face and the feeling of weightlessness set her heart pounding. 'I can't believe how fast it's going!' Silent as a ghost, the balloon whistled along, until they were so far out to sea, the landline looked like a thin, hazy shadow in the distance. 'Oh, look! You can almost see the curve of the earth!'

Ellen laughed. 'I knew you'd both love it,' she said. 'All that arguing and moaning, and now look at us – like birds in flight, we are.'

Soon, the balloon was brought gently to earth on the pier, with only the slightest of bumps; the passengers all fell out, breathless and laughing, thrilled by the experience but immensely relieved to feel the pier beneath their feet once more. 'Come on!' Ellen was the first away. 'I want the biggest, most chocolatey milk-shake in Blackpool.'

In the open café at the top of the beach, that is exactly what she had. In fact, they ordered one each, and devoured every last drop.

As they strolled home to Ackerman Street, Maddy thought it had been the most wonderful day. 'I've laughed so much I ache,' she told them.

Ellen said she'd like to do it all over again, while Grandad Bob had turned an interesting shade of green. 'I'd best get home a bit quick,' he warned. 'I reckon that milk-shake is churning to get out.'

While Grandad had a lie-down to settle his stomach, Maddy and Ellen sat downstairs, talking about the future. 'I reckon you and me will be fine here,' Ellen told Maddy. 'We're far enough away from the bad stuff not to worry. It's best if we just go from day to day, then by the time your baby comes, we'll have decided what to do, long-term.'

'I think that's a good idea.' Maddy was content with that. 'But I can't stop thinking about Alice. You said Raymond would let you know about . . . ', she gave her a knowing look.

'I did. And he will.' Ellen tried not to show her guilt. The less Maddy knew about the truth of it all, the sooner she could let her mind rest and concentrate on the future.

'Thank you so much, Ellen.' Reaching out, Maddy took hold of her hand. 'You're such a good friend. I don't know what I would have done without you.'

Coming here with Ellen had given her an opportunity to start again. And yet, she still had not found peace of heart. She knew, more than most, how vengeful a man Steve Drayton could be; he did not forgive his enemies; especially one who he believed to have brought the authorities down on him.

Like Ellen, she felt safer having put the miles between herself and Soho though her deeper instincts warned her to remain ever-vigilant.

It was as Drayton had promised. No matter how far she might run, or wherever she might hide, one day, somehow, he was bound to track her down.

And when it happened, she must be ready; for *all* their sakes.

~

During that first week in Blackpoool, Maddy felt more loved and wanted than at any time she could recall.

Every day she made a new discovery as she explored the town; her friendship with Ellen deepened and blossomed, and Grandad Bob was so loving and attentive, she almost began to believe he really was her very own grandfather. And, most glorious of all, she and Ellen were practising daily at the piano, keeping their voices exercised, learning new songs together.

Now today was Friday, and it was Maddy's first appointment at the hospital. Her new GP, round the corner from Ackerman Street, had taken her on and booked her an early appointment for a full pregnancy check-up.

She and Ellen had already been waiting for an hour, and Ellen was growing increasingly impatient. 'What time did you say your appointment was?'

'Two o'clock, I think.' Opening her handbag, Maddy checked her appointment card. 'Yes, that's right.'

'Hmh!' Ellen glanced up at the wall clock. 'And here it is, already five past three. I think it's time to have a word with the receptionist.'

'No, Ellen.' Maddy was nervous enough without antagonising anybody. 'I'm sure they'll call me soon.'

Another five minutes passed, then ten, and Ellen was about to storm the desk when a brisk, official voice called out, 'Maddy Delaney?'

Flustered and anxious, Maddy leaped out of her chair and rushed across the room.

'Right!' Turning on her heel, the floppy-faced woman instructed Maddy to follow her. 'Your first check-up, isn't it?'

'Yes, er . . . yes.' She wasn't sure whether to call her Sister or Nurse, so she decided not to address her as anything.

When the woman marched into a little white room, Maddy obediently followed. 'Sit down there.' She gestured to an upright chair beside the desk. 'I need to ask you a few questions.'

Clutching her bag and biting her lip, Maddy did as she was told, though mentally wishing herself anywhere but here.

Thankfully it did not take long to establish her name, age, address and situation. 'So, you've only recently moved here then?'

'That's right, yes.'

The woman looked at her. 'Are you nervous?'

'Yes, I am a bit.'

'No need to be. I don't bite.'

Wishing it was all over, Maddy managed a half-smile.

'I'm here to help – to make certain that you and the baby are healthy and fit for the birth. Now, how far along do you think you are?'

'Well, I've missed three periods.' Maddy did a mental calculation. 'So I thought I might be about four months, or maybe more – I'm not really sure.' She could not quite pinpoint the exact moment when she began to suspect she might be pregnant. 'You see, I had a little show, but then nothing, so it was confusing.'

'Right. Well, let me asssure you, even if you did have a little show, it doesn't mean to say there is anything wrong.'

Realising that, unlike her previous expectant mother that afternoon, Maddy was not about to give her any trouble, the woman smiled warmly. 'So relax, stop worrying; everything will be checked thoroughly. And before you leave here, we'll know within a fortnight of when the baby might be due. All right?' Another, even warmer smile.

'Yes, thank you.' Maddy was beginning to relax.

'Off you go then.' She pointed to the cubicle. 'Strip to your bra and knickers, then step on the scales.' While Maddy did that, the midwife dug in her desk-drawer for the tape-measure. 'How tall are you?'

'About five foot two, I think.' Dreading the examination, Maddy draped her skirt over the back of the chair, and waited.

To Maddy, the next half-hour seemed more like three hours. Until at last she came back into the waiting room, flushed and breathless. 'Ooh, let's get out of here,' she said in a low voice. 'I need a decent cuppa tea.'

At the café, Maddy relayed the news. 'The midwife said that

everything seems to be going to plan. She reckons, give a week either way, the baby should arrive late December.'

Ellen was thrilled. 'Oh Maddy, that's great! You never know, it could be born on Christmas Day – wouldn't that be amazing?'

Maddy went on excitedly, 'She said if I seemed to be carrying it more back than front, that can often mean it might be a girl, but then she said she'd been fooled a couple of times, so I wasn't to take that as gospel.'

'So, how would you feel about it being a girl?' Ellen asked.

Maddy shrugged. 'I'm not sure,' she said. 'At first I thought I would love it to be a girl. But now, I'm not so sure.' She grinned at Ellen. 'Twins would have been nice, because then I might have got one of each.'

'So, are you saying you really want a boy?'

'No, I'm not saying anything, either way.' Her face lit with the softest of smiles, as she told Ellen, 'You see, this baby already has my love, and that will never change.' She tenderly laid her hand across herself. 'Boy or girl, it won't matter one way or the other.'

Just now, as she looked into Maddy's face, Ellen suddenly understood the depth of her friend's love for that tiny new life inside her. It was a humbling thing; one of those magic moments when you feel as though you have been given an insight into someone else's soul.

Right from the start, Ellen felt that she had known Maddy forever, and that their deepening friendship would overcome every bad thing that life could throw at them.

Reaching out, Maddy took Ellen's hand into her own. 'I promise you something,' she said. 'This baby will know and love you . . . just like I do.' She had seen Ellen studying her face, and she felt the kindred spirit. In this life, you meet many people, she told herself – fleeting acquaintances, neighbours, and sometimes a passing friend or two. But you only ever get that one very special friend. For Maddy, that friend was Ellen.

And as long as she drew breath, Ellen would be in her life. Maddy believed that, without any shadow of doubt.

~

On the way home, Ellen took Maddy on a route where they were less likely to see a newspaper. So far, she had managed to prevent her reading the ongoing reports of the Soho slayings or hearing about them on Grandad Bob's TV. Surely the media would get fed up with the story soon. Thakfully most of the headlines were about the birth of Louise Brown, the first IVF baby in the UK.

Ellen had learned a lot about Maddy in the short time she had known her. She knew that Maddy was not one to burden others with her worries. Instead, she was kind and thoughtful, and never took it on herself to judge anyone.

Many times of late, she had caught Maddy quietly crying alone; when Ellen came along, Maddy would quickly wipe away the tears and try to smile.

Ellen worried that, sooner rather than later, Maddy was bound to read a big article about the London killings. When that happened, the best Ellen could hope for was that more would be said of Drayton, and less about Alice. If Maddy found out that the latter was still alive, who knew what would happen then? One thing was for sure: their friendship would probably not survive.

~

On the following Saturday morning, Grandad Bob was coming down the stairs when a clutch of mail fell through the letter-box.

Carrying it to the kitchen table, he saw how Maddy and Ellen were already there, so he momentarily set the letters aside. 'Morning, you two. Been up all night, have you?'

Glancing up from her cornflakes, Ellen gave a grunt. 'Nope.'

'Still, it's nice to see you up bright and early. What are your plans for the day then?'

'Not much,' Ellen informed him. 'Maybe we'll catch up with the washing and ironing. Oh, and Grandad, I notice you've already filled the linen-tub in the bathroom with shirts and such. I'll have them washed and hung out before you can say Jack Robinson.'

'You will not!' Horrified, he explained, 'I've always washed my own things, and I see no reason to change now that you're here. I'll have you know I'm more than capable of doing my own laundry. Besides, when have I ever suggested that you and Maddy should take on the task of being servants?'

Ellen groaned. 'That's silly, and you know it,' she gently chided. 'I just thought that, being as I'm already doing a wash, I might as well throw your stuff in at the same time. It cuts down your electricity bill.'

'Listen to yourselves,' Maddy light-heartedly intervened. 'Anyone would think you were having a barney.' She liked the banter, and normally, would have joined in. But her stomach was churning and she felt very queasy.

Nevertheless, she found a smile for the big man. 'You have to admit it, Bob. Ellen is right in what she says.'

Grandad Bob looked from one woman to the other, knowing that whichever way he turned, the argument was already lost to him. 'Oh, very well then,' he told Ellen. 'Whatever you say. It does make sense, I suppose.' He glanced again at Maddy, who was sitting quietly. 'Here, are you all right, lass?'

'Yes, thank you,' she answered. 'I'm just not quite my usual self today, that's all.' Feeling sick and exhausted, she gave him another smile. 'Ellen and I do want to be useful though. You've been so kind, taking us in like you did. The least we can do is throw your washing in the tub when we're doing ours.'

'I see that now,' he assured them, 'and it's fine by me. But

I have to say, lass, you don't look none too chirpy this morning.' Clambering out of his chair, he went round to Maddy and hugged her. 'Why don't you go back to bed, sweetheart? Have another hour's sleep. It'll do you good.'

'That's what I told her,' Ellen chipped in, buttering a slice of toast.

'Stop fussing, the pair of you. I'm not ill,' Maddy protested. 'I'm just a bit washed out, that's all.' In truth, she felt like something the cat had dragged in. 'The midwife described morning sickness as like having a tooth out; you feel really uncomfortable for a while, and then it's over.'

Bob chuckled. 'So, that's what she said, is it? Okay, I'll tek your word on it, though I'm just a cowardly man, so I'd rather have a tooth out any day.'

He turned his attention to the mail.

'Nothing but rubbish!' he kept saying as he slung it aside. 'Look at that! Why would I want a big expensive kitchen when all I've got is a tiny scullery that takes a cooker, two cupboards and a fridge. Oh, and look, I've won a new car – I don't think.'

He continued to tear the paperwork up and throw it aside, until he came across a postcard. 'It's from Peter, landlord of the Cart and Wheel in town, enjoying a break in Spain, lucky devil.'

He gave a grunt. 'I've just realised, he owes me six pounds from that bet he did for me. The bugger's spending it in Spain, I expect, sitting at the bar watching the pretty girls go by and supping his pint of golden ale. Whoa! Just wait till he gets back – I'll have him. Six pounds with interest, that'll tek the smile off his hairy face!'

The next was a large brown envelope, addressed to Ellen Drew and postmarked London. 'I reckon this is yours, lass.' With Maddy running the taps at the sink, ready for the washing up, Ellen was collecting the crockery.

Both women looked up. Maddy remained at the sink, visibly

anxious as Ellen tore open the envelope, then giving a sigh of relief when Ellen told her, 'It's all right, Maddy. It's just that letter we've been expecting.' She knew Maddy would realise that she was referring to Raymond.

Bob tactfully excused himself. 'I'll best get out early,' he teased, 'in case randy Nora from next door is peering through her net curtains, ready to pounce on me.' He paused, scratching his head as he asked, 'Has anyone seen my newspaper?'

Maddy said no, while Ellen told him, 'I'll pop into the paper-shop later and get you another one, shall I?'

'Okay, and while you're at it, ask Mrs Patel why my paper was not delivered . . . again! It's happening too regular for my liking. Make sure you tell her that, will you? I'm sure she'll sort it out.'

'I'll do that, and I'll bring you a paper home, don't worry.' Ellen was not about to tell him how she had been scanning the papers first and if there was even the slightest mention of the London killings, she quickly got rid of it.

'I like my newspaper. I like to know what's going on in the world. Even the radio seems to have given up the ghost.' Stony-faced, Bob blew out a long, slow sigh of exasperation. 'I must put my mind to taking that thing apart and finding out what's wrong with it.' He groaned. 'Mind you, I suppose it must be going on fifteen years old by now. Happen it's time I bought myself a new one.'

He was not to know how Ellen had also nobbled his radio.

As yet, Ellen had thought it best to keep secret the real reason why she and Maddy had turned up on his doorstep; though she knew her grandad was nobody's fool. It was only a matter of time before he started asking questions, and then she would have to tell him at least some of the truth – though she would certainly leave out the part where she and Raymond had deceived Maddy so cruelly.

Now, with Grandad out of the way, Ellen quickly took out the letter; with it came another large envelope, sealed and marked *For Maddy*.

Ellen handed it to her.

Though curious, Maddy placed it on the table. 'Read the letter first,' she asked of Ellen.

Equally eager to know what Raymond might have to say, Ellen flicked through the contents of the letter.

'So, what does he say?' Maddy was by her side as she finished reading.

'There you go, Maddy.' Having satisfied herself that Raymond had not said anything untoward, Ellen handed over the letter. 'It might be best if you read it yourself.'

Taking the letter, Maddy walked to the chair and sat down, already concentrating on what Raymond had written:

Dear Maddy and Ellen,

First of all, I hope the both of you are well, and that you are all right in your new surroundings.

The word here is that Drayton will shortly be brought before judge and jury. The police have been busy questioning everyone who saw what happened, and now it seems they have more than enough evidence to put Drayton away for life.

They were keen to talk with you both, but nobody knew where you were, though everyone was certain you were not in the alley when the shootings took place. Carter's henchmen argued that you were there – but as they were in Carter's pay and already lying to guard their own backs, it seems their evidence was not taken too seriously.

The Pink Lady is now fully open again, and we've got a new manager. Drayton's accountant and solicitor have been in and out, and now everything's beginning to settle down again, though the clients are not coming in like they used to.

Everyone asks after you, Maddy. Some of them have known you for as long as I have. And we all miss you, very much.

But you need to stay away. A man like Drayton has longer arms than the law. Please remember that, my dear.

As far as young Jack and darling Alice are concerned, I can only imagine how much pain you must be feeling. But you must take heart, Maddy, for in time, it will ease.

I can tell you that, as soon as the police allowed it, Jack's family took him home to Suffolk. As for Alice, I did everything that was asked of me. I took care of her, like I promised. She's safe now, and you have my word, hand on heart, that for as long as I live, I will always take care of her.

One day some time in the future, I know we will meet up again. Until then, you and Ellen must keep yourselves safe. You know that's what Alice would have wanted.

Please, do not contact me, or anyone at the club. It's best if you keep your heads down for now.

I'll keep in touch. Meantime, look after yourselves.

God bless, and lots of love,

Raymond
XX

'Has that eased your mind a little?' Ellen knew better than anyone how Maddy had been punishing herself for 'deserting' Alice.

'Yes, I think so.' Maddy had been both saddened and uplifted by what Raymond had written. 'I will never be able to thank Raymond enough,' she said, 'but I won't rest easy until I go to where she is, and tell her what's in my heart.'

Ellen understood, and her guilt was tenfold.

Shifting her attention onto the large envelope as yet unopened, Maddy carefully tore it open, and as she tipped it upside down, an amazing array of photographs and folded posters tumbled onto the table. 'Oh, my God!' Clasping her two hands over her mouth, Maddy was laughing and tearful all at the same time.

She couldn't believe what she was looking at – photographs of herself in full evening wear, singing into the mike onstage. Some were of her performing with a visiting artiste, both of them smartly dressed in Fred Astaire top-hat and tails, and brandishing a walking cane. And there were others, of her and Alice laughing at the camera, and fooling around in the club, and another one of her seated at the piano, next to a renowned jazz pianist. And oh, so many more, some she had completely forgotten about.

'Ellen – look what Raymond has sent me,' she cried. 'They're all the photos and posters from the Pink Lady!' She was thrilled. 'I never imagined they'd taken this many photographs . . . ooh, they bring back so many memories. And look!' She pointed to a particularly beautiful one of herself. 'Some of them have never even seen daylight. Oh, Ellen!'

These things were such a powerful part of her life. 'All my dreams and ambitions are written here,' she said now. 'And this is what it's amounted to – a collection of paper images.'

One minute she was laughing and excited, and the next, a great tidal wave of pain and rage swept through her as she swiped them all from the table. 'They don't mean anything any more!' Running from the room, she fled up the stairs, crashed into her bedroom, and flung herself on the bed, where she sobbed helplessly.

Ellen found Maddy lying across the bed, face down and breaking her heart. 'I've made such a mess of my life,' she wept. 'I've lost everyone I love, apart from you, Ellen – and I miss Alice so very much. She should be here,' she kept saying. 'Poor Alice should be here.'

Sitting down beside her, Ellen gathered her into her arms.

'It's good if you cry,' she said earnestly. 'Seeing those pictures of yourself and Alice, and of the life you shared . . . well, it's hurtful. You need to let it out, Maddy.'

Not for the first time, Ellen wondered about her decision regarding Alice. But it was done now and could not be undone.

They sat for a while until Maddy – still shaken by the photographs and the memories they evoked – silently vowed to stay strong for Ellen's sake. 'I'm all right now,' she sighed, getting off the bed. 'I'm sorry for that performance. I'll go down and clear the photos away.'

Ellen followed her downstairs, and the two of them collected the discarded memories. 'I'll put them away and keep them safe,' Maddy decided. 'Alice would want me to.'

~

The evening was spent quietly, with Ellen stitching new buttons onto her best jacket, and Maddy curled up on the sofa, reading a library book and enjoying the series of LPs playing in the background. Grandad Bob made background music of his own, when his whooshing, rhythmic snoring rippled through the room.

When the snoring grew louder, Maddy and Ellen would giggle, and Grandad would shift and grumble, and then snore all the louder.

All in all, it was a cosy scene.

CHAPTER TWELVE

R EADY AT LAST to leave the hospital, Alice had been looking forward to this day for weeks. 'All packed, are you?'
Nurse Jackie was a trim, pretty young thing with a heart of
gold.

Alice thanked her for everything. 'I've already seen Sister
and the other day nurse,' she said in her soft Irish lilt. 'And
I've left a note for the night staff.' Pointing to the white envelope on the bedside cabinet, she said, 'Oh, and there are two
boxes of chocolates in the cupboard. They're good ones – I
know that for sure, because Raymond chose them, and he likes
to show off, so he does. Anyway, there's one for you nurses
and one for Connie, the cleaner.'

'Well, thank you, Alice.' The nurse was appreciative. 'That's
a lovely gesture.'

'Ah well, I'm really grateful to all of you. But I'm *so* glad to
be going home at long last, as you can imagine.'

'I'm sure you are. Even so, you must remember to follow
the doctor's instructions. Rest easy and try not to walk about
too much. You've still got that weakness in your chest wall,
which will take a while to heal completely, so keep away from
anyone with a cold. You don't want to be coughing and putting
your muscles under any strain. Keep the corset on as instructed,
and make sure you take the prescribed medication.'

Alice made a face. 'All right, all right. I get the message. I'm an old crock who can't do anything for herself.'

Nurse Jackie chuckled at that. 'Oh, I don't think that's what you are,' she teased. 'I'd say you were more like an impatient woman who hates people fussing round you. Isn't that so?'

Alice laughed until her chest hurt, when she took a deep, invigorating breath. 'You could be right.' Very carefully, she stretched her back, until she felt more comfortable. 'I can't deny it. I'm impatient, stubborn, fussy, bossy and aggravating.' She gave a mischievous wink. 'But don't tell anyone else, will you?'

The two of them were still chatting when Raymond arrived.

Guided by Alice's gentle suggestions, he looked smart and presentable in grey trousers, a navy jacket and cream-coloured shirt. His hair was newly cut and falling smartly about his ears, and as he approached them, his face was wreathed in a happy smile. Today, he was taking Alice home.

'My, but he's a fine fella.' The nurse was first to see him enter the ward. 'If I wasn't already married, I could fancy him myself.'

'Ah, don't give me that,' Alice protested. 'Sure, haven't I seen your husband – got the dreamy look of a film star, so he has.' She glanced at Raymond, big and bumbling, very slightly knock-kneed, and not one 'film-star' feature on his lolloping square face.

Tongue in cheek, she asked the nurse, 'I bet you wouldn't swap your fella for mine, would you?' There was a twinkle in her eye. 'I mean, why would you want to swap a rose for a cabbage, eh?'

The two of them chuckled at that.

In truth though, Alice had come to love Raymond as much as he had always loved her. It was not the kind of love where the world turns upside down at the touch of someone's hand. Instead it was a warm and wonderful experience, and now, as he walked her gently through the ward, she felt that no one in the world could ever hurt her again.

~

Safe in the car and headed home, Alice asked him, 'Have the police been to see you?'

'Not since last week, no.'

'So do you reckon they've given up on finding Maddy?'

'I hope so. But who knows?'

'So, what did you tell them? Did you remember what I said?'

'I just told them what I'd said before, time and again, that Maddy no longer worked for Drayton, and that she had *not* been in the club at all that night.'

'And did they ask about Ellen?'

'Yes, and I explained that, as far as I could recall, Ellen had been feeling unwell after she came offstage, and so probably went straight home. I said there had been talk of her going on holiday for a week or so. I told them, I knew nothing more than that.'

'Did you send the letter?'

Raymond nodded. 'I did.'

'You didn't change anything, did you?' she asked. 'You copied it down exactly as I said?'

Raymond fell silent.

'Ray?' Alice gave him a tap. 'I'm still waiting for an answer.'

Looking sheepish, he apologised. 'I copied down everything you'd written, word for word,' he confirmed, 'except I told them not to contact me or anyone else at the club; I said the police were still about, so Maddy and Ellen needed to keep their heads down.' He paused. 'I hope I did right?'

Alice could tell he had more to say. 'What else did you write?'

When the traffic-lights changed, he quickly swung the wheel

to the left. 'I'm sorry, love. Don't be cross. I just . . . kinda mentioned that we'd meet up again one day – me, her, and Ellen. That's all.'

When Alice made no response, he glanced down at her. Alarmed to see her crying, he drew the car over to the kerb. 'I did wrong, didn't I? Oh look, I'm sorry. Please . . .'

But as she answered him, he was amazed to see her smiling through the tears. 'Oh Raymond, aren't you the lovely man? As for what you wrote, as long as you didn't give Maddy any idea that I'm still alive, it was not wrong to tell her that we might meet up one day. In time, she will have to know the truth, but only when I'm satisfied that she's safe from harm. Meanwhile, you've given her a glimmer of security, letting her know that she hasn't been altogether abandoned. And I truly thank you for that.'

With her two hands she drew his face down to hers, and kissed him with all the affection she felt.

'I do love you, Alice,' he murmured. 'You know that, don't you?'

'I love you too,' she said. And meant it.

~

As they drove on, she wagged a finger at him. 'Next time I ask you to copy something I've written, don't take it upon your-self to add a whole new letter of your own.'

'I won't.'

'Ah sure, I can't abide folks who think they know better than anybody else.'

'I know you can't,' Raymond agreed stolidly. 'As for me, I can't abide folks who are argumentative, frustrating, and diffi-cult to please.'

'Oh! Would that be *me* you're talking about, by any chance?'

'Well, if the cap fits . . . ?' He gave her a sideways glance.

Alice had to laugh. 'Will ye listen to the two of us,' she croaked. 'Going at each other like an old married couple, so we are.'

'That's exactly what I want,' he answered softly.

'What ... the two of us fighting and feuding?' As if she didn't know what he was getting at.

'Me and you – "an old married couple".' Another sideways glance. 'So, what do you think?'

'Glory be! Are you asking me to marry you?'

'I might be.'

'Then I might think about it,' she replied teasingly. She pointed to the cyclist wobbling alongside them. 'Watch out for the old fella. And for goodness sake, keep your mind on the road!'

He smiled to himself. Alice had said she might think about them getting wed. That meant there was a chance.

His smile grew broader.

'And what the divil are you grinning at, like some Cheshire Cat, might I ask?'

'Just thinking.'

'Well, stop thinking and do like I said – keep your eyes on the road!'

Though, as he came onto the straight, her heart couldn't help but smile too.

CHAPTER THIRTEEN

B Y THE END of November, winter had really begun to settle in. Blue skies had fallen to grey, the wind was bitter and for three days now, the driving rain had been relentless. But as always, inside Bob Maitland's house, at number 8, Ackerman Street, it was cosy and warm.

'Look at me! I'm so big and heavy, my legs are going bandy.' Having negotiated the narrow stairway, Maddy ambled into the kitchen for breakfast. Patting her swollen belly, she eased herself into a chair. 'I'll be glad when the baby's born,' she groaned.

'I'm not surprised.' Grandad wagged a finger. 'You're never still – making beds, sweeping the yard like somebody possessed, and insisting on your turn to do the washing and cooking. In your condition, you need to take things easy, lass, not drive yourself into the ground.'

Like any woeful man with misguided intentions he hoped to make her see sense by pointing out how, 'It's obvious you're dog-tired, and I can't help but notice how lately, you seem to be covered in spots.'

Oblivious to the fact that his kindly-meant comments were not helping to restore Maddy's confidence, he went blithely on, 'All the upheaval of moving here, and the burden of carry-ing a child – well, it's plainly telling on you, lass. It stands to reason, you can't push yourself to the limits and still look bright and lively. So will you listen to me, pet, and be kind to yourself. Ease up a bit, eh?'

Feeling more self-conscious than ever, Maddy gingerly stroked her puffy face. 'Where are they, these spots that I'm supposed to have?' She felt miserable now. 'I haven't seen any.'

At that moment Ellen arrived from the front room, where she had been hanging her smalls on the clothes-horse. 'Ellen? Have I got spots all over my face?' Maddy asked.

'I can't see any,' Ellen said, peering at her. 'What makes you think you've got spots anyway?'

'Grandad Bob said I had some.' Getting out of the chair, Maddy went to the fireplace, where she stretched up to look in the overhead mirror. 'Where are they?'

'I'm surprised at you, Grandad,' Ellen gently chided. 'I would have thought you knew better than to tell a woman she's look-ing at her worst, especially when she's eight months' pregnant and already feeling self-conscious.'

'I'm very sorry, lass.' It came as no surprise to the old gent, that he had put his foot in it, because women had always been a mystery to him.

'I know you are.' And to prove it, his granddaughter gave him a huge cuddle. 'You're just a bit dippy at times.'

At which both he and Maddy smiled at each other, and when he gave her a reassuring wink, she gave one right back.

～

Later that day, Grandad popped down the road to the bookies. 'I'll not be long,' he announced. 'If you two want to go into town, I'll run you there one day this week.'

'We might take you up on that,' Ellen replied.

When he was out the door, she checked in the cupboards and fridge. 'We're short on bread and sugar,' she told Maddy, 'and there's only half a pint of milk left. If you really want to make that rice pudding tonight, we'll need another couple of pints.'

'And I desperately need some bigger knickers,' Maddy groaned. 'My belly's hanging over these ones – look!' Dropping the waist of her elasticated skirt she displayed the pink mound of flesh that was her baby. The knickers were all bunched up underneath. 'Every time I stand up, I'm frightened in case my pants end up round my ankles!'

Laughing, she rolled her eyes. 'Honestly, Ellen, I feel like a walrus out of water. I long for the day when I'm normal again, and I can throw out all this baggy underwear.'

'Oh no, you mustn't throw them out.' Ellen acted horrified. 'Best to burn them in the grate.'

Maddy was puzzled. 'Why?'

'Because it makes sense,' Ellen replied with a twinkle in her eye, 'Why spend good money on expensive coal, when your big knickers will keep us warm for a week?'

When Grandad opened the front door, he could hear the two of them helpless with laughter. 'Tell me the joke then,' he asked, and they did. 'I had thought about having radiators put in,' he confessed, 'but I can hang on a bit, if you like.'

When the laughter subsided, he thought how wonderful it was having them here. 'You're a pair of terrors,' he chuckled. 'One thing's for sure, this house is more alive since you've been here, and so am I. God only knows what I'd do if you ever upped sticks and left.'

With that he collected his pipe and baccy and retired to the front room, to check on his cherished sculptures.

Grandad's innocent remarks had set Maddy and Ellen to thinking, and when he was out of hearing distance, Ellen reminded Maddy, 'I would hate to hurt him, but you and I both know, we can't stay here for ever. When the baby's born, we said we'd find a place of our own. But if we move out, he'll be heartbroken.'

'Maybe not.' Maddy had seen for herself how strong-minded and independent Grandad Bob could be, and after all, he had been content enough, before they arrived on the scene.

'We owe him a lot,' she told Ellen now, 'but if we don't find a place of our own soon, he might begin to think we're taking advantage, and that wouldn't be fair on him, or us. So, maybe the sooner we do get a place the better; as long as it's not too far for us to visit each other, I'm sure he'll be fine.'

'You could be right,' Ellen conceded. 'We can't put on him for ever, and with a baby, it's bound to be a bit squashed here.'

'So we're agreed then,' Maddy asked. 'We'll get a place of our own, yes?'

'Hopefully, yes. We'll stick to our original plan, and like you said, Grandad will still be a big part of our lives. He can visit any time he likes, and when he's had enough of us, he can always come home for some peace and quiet.'

Maddy said she thought that would be kinder to him than having his sleep and his life disturbed by a new member of the household. 'Babies are small and wonderful, but we all know, they can make their presence felt.'

Maddy was ready to go along with whatever Ellen and her grandfather decided, but, 'The baby isn't due for nearly a month, so we don't need to fret about it just now, do we? I mean, there's still plenty of time for us to talk it all through if needed.'

One thing she was sure of. 'It would only be fair to let your grandad know what's on our mind. He might even have some good advice for us, especially if we let him have a say in where we choose to live.'

'Of course!' Ellen clapped her hands. 'We'll let him feel as though he's in charge – well, to a certain extent,' she added with a wry little grin. 'I know from old that Grandad Bob likes nothing better than to be at the helm.'

SONGBIRD

~

The truth was, neither Ellen nor Maddy could have known how events were already out of their hands.

Very soon, the decision as to whether they might stay or go, would be decided for them.

~

The next day was like a mini summer. The skies cleared and the wind dropped, and even the sun showed its face. 'Why don't we take a run out to the Ribble Valley?' Grandad asked, his nose pressed to the window. 'We should take advantage of this fine weather, in case it turns cold and wet again tomorrow.'

Both Maddy and Ellen thought that was a brilliant idea. 'We've been cooped up long enough,' Ellen declared lightheartedly. 'Let's go where the road takes us.'

Maddy was excited about taking a drive out to the countryside. 'It's just what we need, a change of scene.'

Ellen recalled a place from her childhood. 'Can we stop for lunch at that lovely old inn on the moors – Whitely Inn, Whalley ... oh.' Screwing her face up in frustration, she admitted, 'I can't recall the name now, or even where it was exactly.'

'I reckon you had it right the first time, lass.' Grandad Bob scratched his head in that comical way he had when thinking hard. 'Whitely Inn, that's the one. I think!' He also was uncertain.

An hour later, they were making their way along the Preston New Road. 'This is the best car I've ever had.' Grandad Bob loved his second-hand Rover, though it was a little car and he was a big man, and sometimes he got a crick in his neck. However, the freedom of driving more than compensated for any niggling discomfort. 'I'd forgotten what joy it was to get wherever you want, without waiting for a bus or a train. I got rid of my Escort after your nan died, and missed it ever since.'

'I remember that Escort,' Ellen said, and she giggled. 'Always breaking down.'

'Aye well, I'll admit that, but when it were gone, I missed it all the same. Many was the time when I thought of getting another, but I never did. Then you and Maddy came along, and that was the excuse I'd been waiting for. I'm not short of money, because I've been prudent over the years. And anyway, like I said, I'd been thinking of getting a car for some time. Oh, and I've already altered the insurance to accommodate you girls, so you can take it out whenever you like.

'You do have a licence, don't you, lass?' He looked at Maddy through his driving mirror. 'If not, we can soon teach you the ins and outs, once the baby is born.'

'I do have a licence,' Maddy informed him, 'but I haven't driven a car for a long time now. The traffic is so awful in London and parking is always a problem.'

'Aye well, it's like riding a bike. Once you've been there you never forget.' He discreetly made reference to Maddy's grow-ing proportions. 'Travelling about on trams can't be very pleas-ant, when you're eight months' pregnant and—' he was about to say, 'with a belly the size of Blackburn Gasworks.' Instead, he tailed off and gave a sheepish grin. 'So, you're all right, are you?' he asked lamely.

'Fine and dandy, thank you, Grandad Bob,' she replied with a knowing smile. 'And you're right, it's *not* easy getting on and off buses and trams when you're as big as an elephant.'

'I never said that!'

Maddy laughed. 'Ah, but you were *thinking* it, I could tell.'

'But it were *you* that said it, an' if it had been *me*, the two of you would have been down my throat like a ferret down a rabbit-hole!'

'You're a loose cannon, Grandad,' Ellen grinned, 'but we love you all the same.'

Bob Maitland smiled to himself.

He had family about him, and though he was prone to making the odd gaffe, he knew he was loved. There was laughter in his house, and a new baby on the way.

What man could be happier, he thought contentedly.

Maddy thought it was wonderful, seated here in the back of the car with two lovely, caring people up front. Sometimes in the house she had little time to think, but now, with the drum of the engine and the swish of tyre against tarmac, she felt relaxed and at ease. But it wasn't long before the doubts came flooding in. What future had they, she and the baby? She wondered how it would all end, and whether she would ever have the peace of mind she craved.

When the fears threatened to overwhelm her, she thrust them to the back of her mind, and now, as Grandad and Ellen got caught up in sharing old memories, she turned her attention on the unfamiliar landscape.

~

Preston New Road watched out over Blackburn Town from a great height. Flanked by handsome Victorian houses with deep bay windows and tall roofs, it was a main artery out of town; the roadway echoed to the rumble of vehicles, and the pavements were worn down by the dogged rhythm of passers-by.

Nearby, Corporation Park, where the three travellers stopped to stretch their legs, was a haven amidst the hustle and bustle. With its impressive entrance and colourful flowerbeds, it was a treasured and well-used place. Along its many paths and deeper into the woodland areas, there were ancient trees older than the town itself. Excited children could slide down manmade cliffs, play in sandpits and run about to their hearts' content.

There were swings, and a lake, where the ducks and other birds played and chased, to create delight for the onlookers.

Maddy was already thinking how, in just a few short weeks, she could walk the baby in its pram, and show him or her the ducks in the lake, and when the child was a little older, the two of them could swing together and play in the sand, and create that special bond that united mother and child forever.

Like every other visitor, Maddy was amazed and delighted to see such a beautiful place set right there, so close to traffic and houses, creating a special world all of its own. Everything appeared so neat and precise, yet there was a savage wildness about it that drew you in, deeper and deeper, until your soul mingled with the primitive, and your senses were brought alive by all manner of sights and smells, and all the while you were made aware of the tiny creatures which foraged about in the trees and shrubs.

From one end of the park to the other, you would find any number of benches and alcoves, where you could hide from the world, or just sit and watch, and sometimes when you strayed from the main path you would stumble on secret, tree-lined walkways where you could wander at will and lose yourself for hours on end.

Maddy was thrilled at the thought of showing all that magic to her baby one day.

Soon they were back in the car and heading towards the moors. 'Can you recall exactly where the inn was?' Grandad asked Ellen. 'Because I'm buggered if I can.'

'It was too long ago,' she told him. 'We'll just have to try every which way and all keep a look-out.'

For the next hour or so, they enjoyed the beauty all around. They stopped at a babbling brook and paddled in the freezing cold water, afterwards wiping their feet on Grandad's old coat from the boot.

They lingered in the heart of the moors and looked out across a bleak and magnificent landscape. As they were watching the deer, timid and wary as they flitted across the horizon, on the skyline a rider and horse leisurely hacked along, and there in the trees a magnificent falcon stared down on them with bright, fierce eyes.

Enthralled and as wide-eyed as a child, Maddy thought she had never seen anything so extraordinarily beautiful.

After a while, when they grew hungry and in need of refreshment, they got back in the car again and meandered on. 'Turn right,' Ellen suggested as they came to a fork in the road. 'I've a feeling the inn is down this way somewhere.'

They had gone about half a mile, when Maddy shouted for them to stop. 'Look – there it is! *Whitely Inn!*'

The sign on the tree was weathered and barely legible, but close up, you could just about read the writing.

'Good girl.' Grandad was aching for a long glass of something cool.

Another quarter of a mile and there it was.

'That's it!' Ellen was amazed. 'It must have been ten or eleven years since I was here, and it hasn't changed a bit.'

'That's not surprising,' Grandad quipped, 'when it probably hasn't changed much in hundreds of years.'

After parking the car, they walked the short distance on foot. Maddy took stock of the fine old building; with its tall windows and thick, impressive doorway, it resembled an old-time castle.

The interior carried the same style and atmosphere, with stone floors and dark narrow doorways, and all around, the wood-panelled walls were hung with gilt-framed images. Some of them depicted huntsmen seated by a fireplace, with their faithful hounds at their feet; others portrayed noblemen sitting around a table, their hounds in full sweat, with merry maids bringing them jugs of ale and tending to their every need.

Grandad caught the eye of a waitress. 'Do you have a table for three?' he asked.

'For lunch, or a snack, sir?'

'Lunch, if you will.' He bestowed one of his beguiling smiles on her. 'We're all a bit famished.'

Ushering them to a table by the window, she then brought three beautiful menus which, being designed in brown and gold with a coat of armour at the head, were works of art in themselves.

She took their drinks order. 'Let me make sure I've got it right,' she said as she read it back. 'One large strong coffee, a glass of sarsaparilla, and two pots of tea, one with milk and one without?'

Satisfied, she moved away, leaving them to study the menus.

By the time their drinks arrived, the choices were made. Grandad was having steak and chips, with peas on the side; Ellen opted for fish-pie and mash, and Maddy fancied Lancashire hotpot. 'I haven't tried it yet.' she told the others.

~

The meals were delicious.

Having downed his cool drink, strong coffee and cleared his plate in record time, Grandad patted his full belly. 'By! That were good,' he declared. 'Just enough, and not too much.'

Ellen agreed. 'I couldn't eat another thing,' she said, niosily blowing out her cheeks.

Maddy ate less than the others. 'It's so filling,' she apologised. 'Tastiest meal I've ever had, but half that portion would have been enough.' She groaned. 'I feel as if I've eaten a whole cow.'

Ellen said she was not surprised that Maddy could only manage half. 'I bet that poor little baby is feeling all squashed up,' she chuckled, 'under that mountain of Lancashire hotpot.'

None of them had room for a pudding. But they each ordered another drink.

They enjoyed the banter a while longer, and then the girls decided they must 'pay a visit to the lavvie' before they set off again.

Having got directions from the waitress, they made their way through the next room and down the long hallway; Ellen up front and Maddy waddling in the rear.

The Ladies Room was a revelation. The deep, wide window was set above a curved seat upholstered in plush red velvet. Each of the toilet cubicles boasted pretty oak shelves carrying dishes of dried and perfumed autumn leaves, and spare toilet-rolls clad in pink fabric bags. There were old-fashioned brass knobs on the door, and a sample of embroidery depicting two lines from a Wordsworth poem, hanging on the wall.

'Wow!' Ellen emerged to find Maddy waiting for her. 'It's even nicer than I remember,' she said.

The two of them were still deep in discussion as they approached the kitchen. 'Phew!' Heavy with child and having eaten too heartily, Maddy paused for a breather and remarked on how the heat from the kitchen had made the corridor uncomfortably warm.

'I expect they leave the door open to let the heat out of the kitchen,' Ellen assumed, while looking anxiously at her friend.

As they drew nearer to the kitchen, they overheard a conversation between two men – presumably employees. 'He got what he deserved,' one commented. 'Pity they ever did away with hanging, that's what I say.'

'You're right. If any man needs a rope round his neck, it's that Steve Drayton and all his kind. Scum of the earth, that's what they are. But at least that one won't be walking the streets again till he's old and grey.'

'Hmh!' His colleague was not so sure. 'I wouldn't count on him being old and grey,' he snorted. 'He'll probably be out in less than ten years, and that's no justice at all. A life-sentence should *mean* life.'

The conversation brought Maddy and Ellen to a halt. 'Oh, Maddy! Did you hear that?' Ellen saw how pale her friend had become. 'We can breathe easier now. Did you hear? They've put Steve away for life.'

Maddy felt as though a band of iron had been clamped to her chest, and she could hardly breathe. *That man*, put away for the rest of his life? She hardly dared let herself believe it.

'Look there!' Ellen pointed to the nearby windowsill, where a newspaper had been discarded. Its glaring headline straddled the top half of the page:

KILLER GETS LIFE
No Mercy For Drayton

Having settled the bill, Grandad came looking, concerned that the girls had been gone such an age. He found them slowly walking down the corridor, heads bent and immersed in earnest conversation.

He instantly noticed Maddy's pallid complexion, and in a minute was at her side. 'What's happened, lass? Have you had a bad turn? What is it?' His kindly old face was wreathed in anxiety.

Maddy did not hear him. She was still thinking of those glaring headlines and the horrendous thing Steve Drayton had done. Alice was uppermost in her mind, and Jack, and the way she and Ellen had been forced to leave everything and flee for their lives. And even with Drayton put away, the danger would always be there, she thought dully. For as long as she lived, she would never again feel safe.

Ellen was quick to allay Grandad's fears. 'Maddy felt unwell,' she said, 'but she's feeling better now. All the same, we'd best get her back to the car, eh, Grandad?'

Maddy forced a smile. 'I'm sorry.' She felt sickened to her

stomach. The only thought in her head now, was to get as far away from here as she could. 'It was just a twinge, that's all,' she assured them. 'Nothing to worry about. Oh look, I know we planned to make a day of it, but I need to get home, if that's all right with you?'

'O' course, lass, and don't you worry. There'll be plenty of days out that the three – no, *four* of us – can enjoy together.' Grandad Bob was very excited about the new baby coming. At his time of life, joys of that kind were few and far between.

Leaving Ellen and Maddy waiting in the foyer, he hurried to the car park to fetch the car. A few minutes later, they were all settled into the Rover and were headed for home.

While Ellen chatted away to her grandfather, Maddy remained quiet. She felt strange. Yes, she was elated to know that her ex-lover had got his just deserts, and she hoped he would be made to serve out the full length of his sentence. But, like the kitchen-hand said, he should have been hanged for what he did; not least because he had taken the lives of two good people, but also because in his warped, crazy mind he saw *her* as being the means of his downfall. And there was no doubt in Maddy's mind that, while there was breath in his body, he would spend every waking minute of his time inside, planning his vengeance on her.

For months now, she had been haunted by images of her fallen friends Jack and Alice, and the monster who had run rampage that night in the alley. Yet somehow, she had coped. She had begun to sleep more soundly; the nightmares had eased, and life had eventually settled into some kind of pattern. Now though, she could not stop trembling. She was hot, then she was cold, and now something was happening that she could not explain. 'I need to get out of here,' she said suddenly. Frantic, she scrabbled at the door handle. 'Stop – please, stop!'

Seeing how flushed and ill Maddy looked, Ellen said, 'Pull over, Grandad . . . quick.'

With traffic front and back, and no obvious lay-bys, it was not an easy thing to do, but he managed it. When they got Maddy out of the car, she stumbled on her feet and looked about to pass out.

'Easy now, lass.' Grandad slipped his arm round her waist, while Ellen supported her from the other side.

'Maddy, what is it?' Ellen cried. 'Are you in pain?' Like Grandad, she was deeply alarmed.

Maddy's first thought was for the baby. Every instinct told her there was something wrong, and though she had a tight, strangling feeling across her chest, she was in no real pain. 'I can't breathe.' It was as though her throat was closing up. 'What's wrong with me?'

She gulped the fresh air, and then she was talking to herself. 'Come on, Maddy, breathe easy. Don't let *him* win.' Seeing that headline had been a shock, yes, but this was something else. Something was not right.

A short, sharp pain almost brought her to her knees. 'Oh, God! I think the baby's coming. I can't ...' As she turned towards them, she felt the darkness envelop her.

As Maddy slumped forward, Grandad and Ellen caught her in their arms, and half-carried her back to the car, step by gentle step.

'The Infirmary's nearest.' Having settled her in the back seat with Ellen holding onto her, Grandad lost no time. Shifting the car into gear, he put his foot down and made for Blackburn Infirmary.

In the back, Ellen was praying that all would be well. If, as Maddy suspected, the baby *was* on its way, that could not be good. The poor little thing wasn't even due for another month.

~

On arrival at the Infirmary, Maddy was rushed straight to the maternity ward.

'The baby is in difficulties.' The consultant was specific. 'We have to perform an emergency caesarean.'

The next three hours were a nightmare for Ellen and Grandad. 'I blame myself,' Grandad said as he relentlessly strode up and down. 'Only a madman would take a woman across bumpy lanes in an old bone-shaker when she's eight months' pregnant.' Raising his arms in frustration, he ran his two hands through his red hair. 'I'll never forgive myself if anything goes wrong with her and the child.'

'Don't blame yourself,' Ellen entreated. 'It was nobody's fault. Maddy is a strong, determined girl. They'll be fine, you'll see.' She could not bring herself to tell him the truth – how she and Maddy had escaped London in fear for their lives, and now it was all brought back by what they had seen and heard.

It was a ghost from the past which had obviously caused Maddy to go into premature labour.

Certainly, none of this was Grandad's fault, and Ellen could not let him believe that. Yet he must not know the truth, in case he reacted in a way that would put *his* life in danger as well as Maddy's.

~

Everything had happened too quickly for Maddy to be afraid. But now, as they wheeled her to theatre, the fear was like a tangible thing. Though it was not for herself, because as things were now, if there was no baby, there would be little reason to live. 'The baby . . . will it be all right?' she mumbled. Already the pre-med was beginning to take effect. 'Please . . . Don't let my baby die.'

As the anaesthetic took hold and her senses fell away, she

heard the doctor assuring her, 'Relax now. We haven't lost one yet.'

~

Having been informed of the situation, Ellen and Grandad were directed to the small waiting room beside the maternity ward, where they waited nervously.

After what seemed a lifetime, the doors swung open and the doctor arrived to tell them the news.

'Just to let you know, Mother will be fine. As for the baby, he's in an incubator; it's too early to say whether there will be any long-term problems. We just need to keep a wary eye on him.'

'So, it's a little lad then, is it?' Grandad asked shakily.

'Six pounds four ounces,' the doctor informed them cheerily. 'And look, try not to worry. He managed to fight his way into this world, so now, all we can do is hope he can overcome anything untoward. He's a strong little fella, don't forget that.'

Ellen had a question. 'Does Maddy know about the baby being in an incubator?'

'Not yet. She will be told though, as soon as she wakes.'

'So, she doesn't even know that she has a son?'

'No.'

'When can we see her?'

'Soon.' The doctor was non-committal. 'Give it a few hours, then we'll see.' He urged them to go home and come back later. 'You might want to bring her toiletries and such?' he suggested.

'There'll be time enough for all that.' Grandad was adamant. 'But for now, it might be better if we're here when she wakes. If that's all right?'

'Of course. In that case, I'll see if we can rustle you up a cup of tea. Try not to worry too much,' he repeated. 'The incubator is merely a precaution, but you must understand, we do need to be prepared for all eventualities.'

With that sobering remark he went on his way, leaving Elllen and her grandfather to reflect on all that had occurred.

A short time later, they were brought a tray of piping hot tea and a plate of biscuits. 'You ought to consider yourselves lucky.' In her early twenties and dressed in a kitchen pinny and floppy net-hat, the nursing auxiliary had a distinctive Scottish accent. 'Not everybody gets tea brought to them. Still, I'm told you've been here a long time, and things haven't gone too well.' She regretted saying that, so, attempting to rectify her gaffe, she declared brightly, 'But you know, things are never as bad as they might seem.'

Placing the tray on the side table, she went on, 'Nobody told me if you needed sugar or milk, so I've brought both.'

She left with a sound piece of advice in Ellen's ear. 'I've known babies be put in an incubator, and in a matter of days they're right as rain, and back with their mammy.'

While Grandad poured the tea, Ellen fretted. 'I can't bear to think how Maddy would take it, if her baby was damaged in some way.'

That would be a blow too far, she thought. Even for Maddy.

~

It was growing dark when a nurse came to fetch them. 'Mrs Delaney is awake. You can go in now, but try not to stay too long. She's very tired.'

Looking pale and gaunt, Maddy's face lit up when she saw her friends coming towards her bed, and when they each gave her a hug, the bittersweet tears ran down her face. 'I knew you wouldn't leave me,' she said, 'but they won't let me see my baby. They say the doctor will be round soon. What's wrong? Why won't they let me see my baby?' She began to sob.

'Ssh!' Seeing how distressed she was, Ellen feared for her well-being. 'Have they told you anything yet?' she enquired.

'Nothing.' Maddy shook her head forlornly. 'The orderly said there would be someone along to talk to me, but I haven't seen anyone yet. Oh Ellen, what's happened? Is my baby alright? Is it . . . oh, please Ellen, you have to tell me!'

Ellen relayed as much as she had been told. 'Firstly, the baby was having problems, so they had to do a caesarean.' She gave Maddy another hug. 'Oh, Maddy! You have a son – six pounds four ounces. A fine boy – what do you think of that, eh?'

Maddy's heart leaped with joy, but then she cried, 'But where is he? Why haven't they brought him to me?'

Ellen allayed her fears. 'Don't be afraid, Maddy. He's being well looked after. They had to put him in an incubator – as a precaution, that's what they said. Just because he was a little bit early.'

Maddy was fearful. 'Tell me everything you know.'

She listened intently while Ellen repeated what the doctor had said. 'The doctor assured us it was necessary to monitor him, simply because he came along a little early, that's all.'

Grandad confirmed Ellen's explanation. 'The doctor said he was a strong little fella to have fought his way into the world,' he told her 'All we can do now is wait for him to prove that he's made of the same stuff as his mammy – strong as they come.' He held Maddy for a long, emotional moment. '*Will* him to come through for us. Can you do that, lass?'

~

And that was exactly what Maddy did. When later, the nurse wheeled her away to see that small measure of life, she reached down and touched the tiny fingers, and with all her heart she prayed to the Lord that her baby would survive.

'You're some kind of a miracle,' she whispered to her newborn child. 'The two of us have been rejected, chased and hounded – and look, here we are now, you and me together.' She gazed on that small face and was filled with such love it hurt.

'I shall call you Michael Robert Delaney,' she told him. 'Michael after your grandfather who died, and also after the Archangel Michael, who protects us all – and Robert after Ellen's Grandad Bob, who rescued us and saved our lives.'

She bent and kissed his hand. 'I'll always be here for you,' she whispered. 'You're my special little gift, and you will never truly know how much I love you.'

She gave thanks for being blessed in so many ways; she had such wonderful friends, and now a son. And though she was still fearful for her child, in her heart she had the warmest feeling that the Lord had heard her prayers, and that in His wisdom He would help her.

~

On the way home to Blackpool, to collect night-clothes and toiletries for Maddy, Ellen told her grandad how moved she had been by his kind words to Maddy. 'You took us in when we needed a friend,' she murmured, 'and we love you for that, and for being the warm, caring person you are.'

'And why wouldn't I take you in?' he demanded. 'You're both lovely lasses.' He paused meaningfully. 'Being there when you're needed – that's what families are for.'

There was a brief silence between them, before he gave her a sideways glance. 'I'm not an old fool though.'

Ellen was taken aback. 'What makes you say that?'

'Happen it's because I know you're running from something,' he confided quietly. 'But I won't pry, you know that. All I will say is this: just remember, I'm here for you and Maddy, if you need to talk. A trouble shared is a trouble halved, isn't that what they say?'

He looked away, and concentrated his attention on the road ahead; while Ellen quietly came to terms with the stark realisation that he had known all along how she and Maddy had fled London, looking for sanctuary. And, yet again, she had been made to recognise what a wily and wonderful old fox her grandfather was.

CHAPTER FOURTEEN

RAYMOND WAS DELIGHTED. 'It's taken a long time – a good four months – and a lot of work and worry, but look at you now,' he told Alice as they strolled round the Cambridgeshire village where Raymond had rented a house for her to recuperate in. With their savings, and the wages he got from pulling pints in the Wagon and Horses pub four nights a week, things were going pretty well. He observed how confident she was, and how sprightly, as she walked alongside him. 'You've mended well, my darling. It's so good to see you back to your old self again.'

He took hold of her hand and squeezed it fondly. 'Maybe now, you can start thinking about . . . well, you know?'

Alice knew exactly what he meant, because hadn't he inundated her with his idea for weeks now 'About getting wed, you mean?' she asked with a twinkle in her eye.

'That's it.' Relieved, he pursued it, 'So, what do you reckon?'

Alice took a moment to answer. 'Well, I don't think we need to rush. I've agreed to be your wife and we will get wed. But not just yet.'

'When, then?' He had to know. 'A month, a year . . . give me an idea, that's all I'm asking.'

'Don't push me, Ray,' she entreated. 'I've got too many other things on my mind to be planning a wedding.'

Realising what she was referring to, he said, 'Aw, Alice, I'm sorry. I know how upset you've been, about deceiving Maddy. But, you know what I think? Even with Drayton under lock and key, the danger is still there.'

Alice readily acknowledged it. 'I also know it would be a terrible hurtful thing for Maddy to find out how she was lied to, in such a terrible way,' she sighed. 'Day and night, she's never far from my mind. I desperately needed to be with her when the baby came!'

'Alice, listen to me. What good will come of tormenting yourself? What you did, you did for Maddy's sake, not your own. And if there ever comes a day when she finds out, Maddy will know that, and she'll understand.'

Alice wasn't so sure. 'Think of the pain I must have caused her,' she sorrowed. 'Think of how my poor girl was sent on her way, pregnant and frightened, with the belief that I . . . her only close friend . . . was dead and gone. How could she ever forgive me for that?'

Raymond would have spoken again, but she stopped him. 'No, Ray. Whatever you say, you can't ever ease my conscience.'

'But we have to move on,' he argued. 'Punishing yourself won't help anybody – not you, and certainly not Maddy.'

When they arrived at the garage, Alice stood aside while Raymond handed over a small sum of money. 'Another three months payment for storage,' he told the clerk.

'I could have sold that Mini a dozen times over.' The clerk rang the amount up on a greasy cash-register and handed over a receipt with a large black thumbprint on it.

'Well, I don't want it sold,' Raymond replied, pocketing the receipt. 'I've already told you my daughter has gone abroad for a year or two, and she doesn't want to part with her car. She asked me to look after it until she gets back, and that's what I'm doing.'

Afterwards, Alice said, 'We daren't sell it, and we can't use it. Cars and their details are traceable to the owner, and Steve Drayton is nobody's fool. He's bound to put two and two together and surmise that where Ellen is, you'll find Maddy. I reckon the best place for that blessed car, is at the bottom of a deep lake, miles from anywhere.'

Raymond said nothing, but he thought that Alice was right. Moreover, paying storage was becoming a burden on his modest finances. So, at some time in the future, running it into some deep dark lake, might be just the thing.

~

It was visiting time in Brixton Prison, and Steve Drayton had been brought down to meet his visitor. 'Hands flat on the table, Drayton. You know the rules!'

The hard-faced prison officer had already experienced numerous confrontations with this 'cock of the roost'. And knowing how Drayton manipulated everyone around him, it was his avowed aim in life to watch him like a hawk.

'What's his problem?' The visitor was a little man who had been a friend to Drayton in their younger days. Now older and wiser, wizened and sharp as a shrew, he had bright eyes that darted left and right, seemingly to cover every corner and exit, as though looking to escape.

'Take no notice of him,' Drayton snarled. 'He'll get his come-uppance soon enough. What I need to know is, why are *you* here, Danny Boy?'

'Hmh! Charming way to greet an old friend,'

'Old friend, be damned! It's been nigh on fifteen years since we've set eyes on each other, and as I recall we did not part on good terms. You and I might have started out on the same side, but you managed to change all that, with your ideas of taking over my patch.' He grinned wickedly. 'You should have known you'd be the one to come off worse.'

'Okay! You did me good and proper, I'll give you that. But you went too far. You not only humiliated me in front of my men, you broke me into the bargain, and I've never been able to get back up. Dammit, Drayton, you owe me.'

'I owe you *nothing*!'

When he leaned forward, looking as though he might go for the other man, the warden was quick to step in. 'You've got a few more minutes yet, Drayton, and the choice is this: you can keep the temper in check, or we can take you back to your cell right now.'

'Sorry, guv.' Drayton was wily enough to know that giving out trouble brought trouble in return, and if he was set to be the number one here, he had no choice but to toe the line with the screws, however much it rankled.

Returning his attention to the little man, he showed his impatience. 'Well? I'm waiting for an answer.'

'What was it you wanted to know?' Unnerved by the screw coming too close, the little fellow had forgotten what it was that Drayton had said.

'I'll say it again – what's brought you here? What is it you're after?' The prisoner lowered his voice until it was almost inaudible. 'And don't fob me off with your lies, because I know you from old.'

'It's simple.' The little man's confidence was growing. 'I'm here to do you a favour.'

Drayton gave a low, strangled laugh. '*You* . . . do *me* a favour? Huh! You will never see the day.'

'It's a small favour, but I'll want paying.'

'Haven't I just said, I want no favours from you.' Although in truth, he was intrigued.

'It'll cost you nothing to listen.' The little man went on quickly, 'I hear you're keen to find a certain little bird . . . I'm told she used to sing for you, until you replaced her with another little chirper. That put the first one's nose out of joint

208

– quite rightly, as I see it – but then she dropped you in it good and proper, and you want her taught a lesson. At least, that's what I was told.'

'Then you were told wrong!'

When Drayton began to move away, the little man persisted. 'Listen to me, Steve. You've said yourself that I had a nose for "sniffin' the buggers out". Well, I still have the nose, and I can find her for you – at half the price you're paying the other geezer. He hasn't found her yet, has he, eh? Give me a chance, that's all I want.'

'Why should I?' Drayton had a long memory. 'You tried to stitch me up once. What's to say you won't try it again?'

'Because while you've gone on the up and up, my fortunes have changed for the worse.'

Drayton laughed in his face. 'Still the hapless gambler, eh? You'll never learn, will you?'

'Look, I need the money. I'll do you a deal, Drayton. I'll find her, or you don't pay me, apart from expenses. Now I can't say fairer than that. So, what do you say?'

Leaning back in his chair, Drayton regarded the other man closely. He saw Danny Boy's worn jacket and the clutch of grey hair that was once black and thick; he noticed how the little man's hands were nervously fidgeting, showing that he could well be using drugs, and he realised that his old enemy, Danny Boy Maguire, really had fallen on hard times.

He also recalled how good a 'sniffer' he was, and that where many others failed to track down a certain person, Danny always came up trumps. Moreover, it was true what Danny had heard, that Steve was running out of patience with his own man.

'Well?' Maguire had waited patiently while Drayton digested the proposed deal. 'Do you want me to find her or not?'

Drayton looked him straight in the eye. 'One month,' he said. 'You don't succeed, you don't get paid – that's the deal.'

'*Six* months,' the little man returned, 'and I'll deliver her, like a hamburger on a plate.'

Another minute, while Drayton considered, then, 'What makes you think you can find her, when my man can't?'

The little man smiled proudly. 'Have you forgotten my nickname? "Bloodhound", that's what they call me.'

Drayton grinned. He *had* forgotten the nickname. '"Call the Bloodhound", that's what they'd say,' he chuckled. 'Yeah, I remember.'

'So, is it a deal then?'

'Not on your terms, no.'

'What then?'

'Three months, and that's it. And if my man finds her first, the deal is off. No money, no nothing. That's it. Take it or leave it!'

Because of his dire circumstances, the little man had no option. 'I'll take it,' he agreed, 'but I'll need you to organise expenses. I mean, she won't still be hanging about these parts, now will she, eh? And I've got no money to play with, or I wouldn't be here with a begging bowl.'

Drayton slowly nodded; there was a ring of truth in everything that Danny was telling him. And in any case, it could all be checked out if necessary, and Maguire knew that all too well.

'Okay,' he said. '*Find the bitch!*'

Money was discussed.

And the deal was done.

CHAPTER FIFTEEN

'Amazing, isn't it, lass? I can't recall a January like this one.' Hair standing on end and wobbling dangerously on a rickety chair, Nora Winterhouse peered over the adjoining fence between numbers 8 and 10 Ackerman Street. 'Last year it were cold enough to freeze the balls off a pawnshop sign, and here we are, the first of January, 1979, and it's like a September day. I'm sure I don't know what to make of it.'

Making a wide gesture to the skies, she almost fell off her perch. 'Them crazy prophets down at the market-hall might be right after all,' she spluttered as she struggled to retain her balance. 'Happen the end of the world really *is* nigh.' And judging by her precarious stance, she could well be right.

Having already startled Maddy with her sudden appearance, she then proceeded to give her a lecture on childcare in her usual tactless way. 'I heard the babby crying last night,' she informed her with a tut. 'I've had six childer, so I think I can tell a hungry babby when I hear one. I expect you're breast-feeding him, aren't you? Well, hope they told you at the hospital, you need to sit him up and burp him every so often. I don't mean to tell you how to bring up your child' (although she did), 'heaven only knows. But it's just commonsense, when all's said an' done. Y'see, sometimes the wind gets caught in their little gullet, and they need to let it out, one end or t'other.'

'Really?' Maddy decided the best way to deal with this was to humour her. 'I'll remember that. Thank you.'

'Eeee!' Nora declared sadly. 'I used to baby-sit for a lass on her own, like you are. Gave her a chance to get out now and then, it did. Poor little soul.'

The 'poor little soul' apparently went by the name of Sarah, and was taken advantage of '. . . by a local troublemaker. There were those who said he made her believe they'd get wed one day, and there were others who said he'd never even been out with her, but that one night he followed her home from the pictures and trapped her against the wall in Montague Street.'

She bristled with indignation. 'I reckon men who take advantage of an innocent lass – well, they want shooting, don't they? Or at best, they deserve their cobbles chopping off. Don't you agree, lass?'

Having come to realise how Nora often let her tongue run away with her, Maddy didn't know whether to believe a word of it. 'So, what happened to the girl and her baby?' she asked, curiously.

'That bugger drowned them in the canal, that's what!' Taking both hands off the wall to shake her fists in anger, the plump little woman lost her balance and went clattering down in a hail of arms and legs, at the same time emitting a long, woeful scream. There was a second or two of silence, and then: 'Ooh! Me back . . . me back! Bloody chair . . . I've allus said it were neither use nor ornament!'

'Nora!' With nothing to stand on, Maddy gripped the top of the wall and jumped up and down. 'Are you all right?' She could see their neighbour upended on the ground, showing her bloomers to all and sundry. 'Nora – are you hurt?'

'Oooh! I think I've done meself a damage.' There came a stream of cusses and the sound of something being flung across the yard.

When the groaning subsided and she couldn't see her any more, Maddy grew anxious. 'Stay where you are, Nora. I'm coming round.'

'Nay, lass!' Nora was back on form. 'I'm all right – it's only me pride that's hurt, and me backside.' She hoisted herself onto her perch. 'Bloody chair.' She peered down on Maddy. 'Damned thing nearly did for me.' Making the sign of the cross on her forehead, she looked upwards with penitent eyes. 'Sorry lord, I didn't mean to cuss,' she mumbled.

Now she was looking down on Maddy. 'I lied,' she confessed. 'It weren't the lad who threw them in the canal – it were the lass herself. Some fella passing saw her jump from the bridge and called the police . . . but it were too late.'

Maddy was deeply shocked. 'Oh Nora, that's terrible.'

'Aye, well. I know *she* threw herself in, but if you ask me, it might as well have been him that pushed her. She used to tell me, "He's ruined me, Nora," she'd say. "No man will ever marry me now, not with a little one in tow".'

Being in that same situation and often wondering how her own future would pan out, Maddy made no comment.

In her darkest moments, she too had thought about finishing it all. But then little Michael arrived, and her life was changed for ever. She would hold him in her arms and experience such love and tenderness, it took her breath away.

And where that other poor girl was taken and violated against her will, Maddy had freely and foolishly given herself to a known gangster with a streak of madness in him. God forbid that her lovely son Michael should ever know who or where his father was. Or take after him.

After chatting a while with Nora, Maddy pegged out the last item of clothing, and was securing the line with the long prop, when she heard the baby cry out. 'All right, Michael . . . I'm coming!' Grabbing the clothes basket, she hurried into the kitchen, where Michael was kicking his legs in the pram and howling for all he was worth. 'Hey now . . . ssh!' Taking him in her arms, she carried him into the sitting room by the cosy fire, and pressing him close to her, she began to softly sing:

> 'Go to sleep, my baby, close your pretty eyes
> Angels watch above you, from the deep blue skies
> Great big moon is shining, stars begin to peep
> Time for little Michael, to go back to sleep.'

Outside in the street, Ellen and Grandad had climbed out of the car and were at the door, when they heard the sweet sound of Maddy singing.

'By, that lass has such a beautiful voice.' Bob Maitland did not spare his praise. 'The pair of you should be earning a fortune on the stage.'

Ellen thanked him for saying so, but added, 'I can sing, yes. But Maddy has a magical way with a song. She lifts the soul in a way I could never do. I reach the notes and I entertain. People *listen* to me,' she smiled wistfully, 'but our Maddy takes them with her, into the song . . . into her world.'

Curling his arm round her thin shoulders, her grandfather looked down on her. 'I'm so proud of you,' he told her. 'When you were no higher than the table, you could always entertain . . . singing away to your heart's content. You have a lovely voice, my girl. Don't ever forget that.'

But he knew what she meant about Maddy. When Ellen sang, it made you sing along, and smile with pleasure. But when *Maddy* sang, it was a haunting thing, a journey of the soul. She had that indefinable magic quality which only a very few performers possess.

~

It was late morning. The beds were made, the washing was blowing freely on the line, and the meat-pie for dinner was in the pantry, ready for reheating in the oven later in the afternoon.

'It's such a nice day,' Grandad suggested, 'why don't the two of you go into town, have a couple of hours to yourselves? The young lad's just been fed and I can take care of him; you've seen me change his nappy and rub his back. You could have a drink at a café – and what about that new dress-shop in Lytham? I heard the pair of you saying how much you'd like to pay a visit. Well, now's your chance.'

'But it's a half-hour bus-ride to Lytham,' Ellen protested half-heartedly.

'Then take the car, and you'll get there a bit quicker. I filled the tank up only last night, so there's no reason not to go. Besides, the pair of you haven't been out together for days. And don't worry about young Michael. He'll be fine with me.'

The girls were grateful for his offer.

'It's true,' Ellen told Maddy, 'we've not really been anywhere for days now, except for this morning when I went for a job at Woolworth's and was turned down, because,' in thin, nasal tones, she mimicked the manageress, '"I'm sorry, my dear, but we have so many applicants, we can pick and choose. And of course we must give priority to someone who's experienced".'

'You wouldn't have liked it anyway,' Maddy grinned. 'You know you can't stand being cooped up.'

'Yes, you're right. I couldn't stomach being stuck behind a counter for eight hours a day.'

'There's many as do.' Grandad had his say. 'Needs do when needs must.'

'Oh Grandad, I understand that. But you know what my feet are like, and I've worn high heels for so long, I couldn't do without them. But they're not ideal for standing on all day long.'

Maddy teased her, 'You're missing a lot though, Ellen. Think how many Nora Winterhouses you might get to serve?'

Ellen made a face. 'That settles it,' she declared. 'I think I'll look for a job as an usherette at the pictures. That way I'll be in the dark, and I can scowl to my heart's content.'

Grandad finished the conversation. 'You said you wouldn't go looking for work until the summer, so I don't see why you shouldn't stick to that plan. Unless o'course, you're all spent up?'

Ellen shook her head. 'Not yet,' she told him. 'Me and Maddy did our sums only the other day, and we're all right for a while yet.'

'There you are then.' Old Bob was pleased at that. 'Once you start work, there'll be no time for walking round the shops or strolling through the park. So make the best use of it while you can.'

~

A few moments later, Ellen and Maddy were away down the street in Grandad's Rover. 'I'll telephone you when we get there!' Maddy called through the open window. 'Meantime, if you need help before then, get Nora in from next door.'

'I'd rather walk around for a week with a bucket on my head!' he shouted back.

'I reckon he would an' all,' Ellen laughed.

Maddy knew he would be absolutely fine. Michael was a good baby. With his belly full and his bottom comfortable, he would probably sleep for the next three to four hours. 'All the same, if there's the slightest problem when we get there, will you bring me straight back?' she asked.

'Course I will,' Ellen replied, 'but we'll only be gone two hours – three at the most.' She gave a sigh. 'Oh Maddy, it's so good to be out on the open road. If it wasn't for you-know-who,

I'd be perfectly happy living as we are for the rest of my days. I wish they'd hanged him. Then we'd really be safe.'

Maddy was astonished. She had never heard Ellen talk like that. 'What's going to become of us?' she asked quietly. When the baby had arrived so unexpectedly, the girls' plans to move out and rent a place together had been put on hold. And now it seemed cruel to bring the subject up, as Grandad was in his element, with little Michael in the house.

'I don't know.' Ellen had often wondered the very same thing. 'Are you happy here, Maddy?'

Maddy nodded. 'Well, if I'm honest, I can't say I'm exactly "happy". It's more like . . . well, feeling secure. I don't mean to sound ungrateful.'

But Ellen agreed. 'I know what you mean,' she said, negotiating the junction. 'We're almost like prisoners, but we can't go back, not ever. London is finished, where we are concerned.'

'I have to!' Maddy had a sense of panic. 'One day, I *have* to go back . . . to make my peace with Alice.' She needed to stand over the place where they had laid her, and say all the things that were in her heart.

Now it was Ellen's turn to panic. 'Do you think that's wise?' she entreated. 'Raymond already told you – he took care of Alice. It would be dangerous for you to go back there. I mean, you can't know what Steve Drayton is up to, can you?'

Just the mention of his name sent shivers through Maddy.

For the remainder of the journey, both she and Ellen lapsed into deeper thoughts of what had transpired, back there in London.

~

'Here we are!' Excited and chatty once again, Ellen parked the car by the promenade.

'Look.' Pointing down the road, Maddy informed her,

'There's a phone booth. You get the parking ticket and I'll give Grandad a ring.'

Between the two of them they found enough coinage for the ticket machine so, leaving Ellen to do the business, Maddy ran the few yards to the phone booth.

A few minutes later she was back. 'Everything's fine,' she told Ellen. 'Michael is still fast asleep, and Grandad said we're not to fuss.' She took his gruff manly voice off to a T. '"I'll have you know, I am perfectly capable of looking after a scrap of humanity without being checked up on every few minutes!"'

'That's Grandad for you,' Ellen laughed. 'He's not about to be organised by some snip of a girl! And although it will kill him to do it, he *will* call on Nora if needs be – you mark my words. Anyway, we won't be all that long. Like as not, the little lad will still be fast asleep when we get back.'

Reassured, Maddy suggested they should make straight for a café. 'I fancy a mug of hot chocolate.' She licked her lips.

'You and your chocolate!' Ellen chuckled. 'It's a wonder you're not twice round as the gasworks.'

As it turned out, the café did not do hot chocolate. 'There's not enough profit in it,' said the owner, a surly man of weasel build. 'Pots of tea, coffee and thick bacon butties. That's where the money is.'

Needless to say, Ellen and Maddy decided to walk down to the bigger café, further along, where the middle-aged, bottle-blonde waitress told them. 'He'll not be there for long. He's a miserable, dirty old bugger. We've already poached the bulk of his customers.'

She was the sort of person who could turn her hand to anything. She took their order, made the hot chocolate, and served them each a freshly made cheese and onion toastie, which they ate with relish. 'I don't think I've ever enjoyed a mug of hot chocolate so much,' Maddy told her as they paid at the till.

'It's my own recipe,' the woman imparted in a whisper. 'The secret is to whisk the milk to a frenzy and get the air bubbles up – makes it nice and light. Then of course, there's my own special ingredient,' which she wasn't about to reveal, 'then a dash of nutmeg finishes it off a treat.'

Next stop was to give Grandad another call from the booth outside. 'How's it going?' Maddy asked. 'Is Michael still asleep?'

'No.'

'How long has he been awake? Is he crying? Maybe he needs his nappy changing!'

'Hey!' Grandad's stern voice cut her short. 'Enough of the panicking. Your baby son is lying here, kicking his legs and gurgling. Later, I might take him for a walk down the street. The fresh air will happen send him off again.'

When Maddy was about to make a suggestion, he pre-empted her. 'No, I won't forget to make sure he's covered up warm, and yes, if he needs his bottom changed I'm quite capable of doing that an' all. Now go and enjoy yourselves and stop fretting.'

A little more reassurance and Maddy went away satisfied. 'He's very special, your grandad,' she told Ellen as they walked along. 'Nothing is too much trouble for him.'

Ellen confided in her. 'It was wrong of me to desert him like I did,' she said, 'but you know what it's like. I wanted to see the big wide world, thought I'd find fame and fortune. And here I am, yes, with money in the bank, and yes, I've had my name on posters and I've seen the sights of London town.' She gave a sad little smile. 'I went away searching for my dream, when all along what I really needed was a simple, quiet life.'

She took a deep invigorating breath. 'But I'm back now, and I mean to stay.'

'Will you be content to stay in these parts for ever, though?' Maddy had seen for herself, how quickly and easily Ellen had fitted back into her hometown, like a foot in an old slipper.

For what seemed an age, Ellen lapsed into a brooding silence, before turning to Maddy with a deep, knowing smile. 'We all of us belong somewhere,' she murmured wisely. 'I belong here.' That was all. But it was from the heart. And in a way, Maddy envied her.

The shopping centre was designed round a small square, with seats and flowerbeds, and wide walkways where a body could pass without shuffling and pressing against other people.

'I think I'll pop in there.' Ellen stopped to look in the window of the new dress shop. There were dummies clothed in pretty dresses in the latest styles; shoes and high winter boots on shelves, and handbags of every shape, size and colour. And as she peered past the display she could see row upon row of striking outfits hanging on the rails.

'You go in,' Maddy suggested. 'I'll be over there.' Her figure wasn't quite back to normal yet, and she didn't want to waste money on clothes that wouldn't fit in a couple of months. Having spied a branch of Mothercare, she told Ellen, 'Look! There are loads of things I need in there.'

'All right then.' Ellen thought she might like to see inside that shop as well. 'I'll have a quick browse in here, then I'll follow on.'

While Ellen went in to find herself something pretty, Maddy walked around in Mothercare, filling her net basket with nappy lines, bibs and other baby paraphernalia. She also picked up three plastic feeding bottles, a box of steriliser tablets and half a dozen tins of formula. Michael had quickly graduated from the breast to the bottle. The health visitor said he simply wasn't getting enough to eat, and sure enough, when Maddy tried him with his first bottle of Cow & Gate formula, he had taken to it like a duck to water. At nearly two months old, he was growing plump and sturdy.

The big shop contained so many useful and so many wonderful things, Maddy didn't know which way to turn. As she seized a catalogue to take home, she was utterly absorbed in her shopping and had even forgotten to worry about Michael.

Putting all her purchases into a large pink shopping bag, Maddy made her way to the dress-shop, where she imagined that Ellen was trying on everything in sight. She was within yards of the shop, when she paused to glance at the display in Marchants. There was a particular pair of red boots that had caught her eye.

She did not notice the man who was lingering at the chemist's shop next door, pretending to scrutinise the window display while keeping a close eye on her.

Intent on reading the price, she was startled when the man came up beside her. 'Like those boots, do you?' Tall and willowy, with shoulder-length dark hair and piercing eyes, he had a sinister air about him.

Maddy merely smiled and made to walk on, when he laid his hand on her arm. 'I know you, don't I?'

'That's impossible.' Unnerved, Maddy had noticed his London accent. 'I've never seen you before.'

As she tried to pass him, he blocked her way, almost stopping her heart with his seemingly casual comment. 'You're a singer, aren't you? The Pink Lady Club – yes, that's it. Always top of the bill and rightly so.' He smiled knowingly. 'Last I heard, Steve had thrown you out in favour of somebody else.'

'No, you're wrong!' Desperately trying to sound calm and unruffled, Maddy was in turmoil. 'I've no idea what you're talking about!'

'Oh, I'm never wrong. I have an exceptional memory – and an eye for a pretty face.' Burrowing his eyes into hers, he said, 'So what are you doing so far away from London?'

'Let me pass – please. I have a friend waiting.'

He looked her up and down, taking in the simple, chainstore coat. 'Short of money, is that it?'

'Like I said, you've made a mistake. I'm not the person you thought.'

'All right, so we'll agree to differ. We'll pretend you're not Maddy Delaney, the Songbird of Soho. But that doesn't mean to say we can't have a little fun together, does it, eh?' He gave her a meaningful wink.

Instinct told Maddy to play his little game, After all, it was not so strange that someone should recognise her from the club. There must be thousands of people who had seen and heard her sing over the past three years. Besides, he seemed a nasty piece of work.

'I really must go now,' she said. With her heart racing and every limb trembling, she gave him her warmest smile. 'Nice meeting you though.'

Encouraged, he reached out; taking hold of her arm, he questioned her, 'Live round here now, do you?'

Inwardly shaking she answered politely. 'You've got me mixed up with someone else.' She thought it best to play his little game, and find out what he was *really* up to. 'Look, my husband is being transferred to a new post in Jersey. He's away at the moment, making arrangements for us to move there.' Maddy pointed to a small terrace of houses to the far right. 'That's where we live,' she lied convincingly. 'But like I said, it's only for another couple of weeks and then we'll be off.'

When he made no sign of making a move, Maddy took a gamble. 'You can call round later if you like,' she said, smiling suggestively. 'What with my husband being away, I get a bit lonely on my own, if you know what I mean.'

'So you do like a bit of fun after all, eh, sexy lady?'

'Well, who doesn't?' Maddy replied with a naughty grin. 'But, I've still got things to do. I should be home in about an hour though.'

His slow smile enveloped her. 'That's my girl. Now you're talking sense.' He glanced at his watch. 'Half three okay?'

'I look forward to it.'

As she walked away, trying not to run, he called her back. Turning, she put on a sweet smile when she was ready to scream.

'You didn't say which house?'

'The end one.' She pointed to the left of the row. 'By the garage.' Congratulating herself, she thought how by the time he knocked on that door, she and Ellen would be long gone.

He nodded; his lustful gaze following her back view as she walked away.

'I knew this was my lucky day,' he muttered smugly. 'Seems like it's Drayton's lucky day too.' He rubbed his hands together and crossed over to the corner pub, where he ordered a pint of beer and bided his time. Not for one minute did he suspect his quarry had got one over on him.

~

With four outfits over her arm, Ellen was on her way to the counter to pay when Maddy burst in. 'We have to get out of here,' she whispered frantically. '*He* sent him, I know he did!'

Ellen took hold of her and gave her a gentle shake. 'Maddy, calm down! You're not making any sense.' She paid the shop assistant and picked up her carrier bags.

Maddy waited impatiently, wringing her hands, glancing at the door and praying that the man had not followed her. 'Listen to me,' she hissed. 'That man . . . he knew me. He asked if I'd sung at the Pink Lady, he even knew me by name! We have to get away from here, Ellen! We have to go *now.*'

Realising this was serious, Ellen told the assistant, 'My friend here is feeling ill.' Keeping her cool, she asked, 'Is there a toilet we could use? I think she might be sick, and I wouldn't want her to spoil any of your beautiful clothes.'

That did the trick. In seconds, Ellen was hustling Maddy to the rear of the shop, and from there via the back door and onto the street, where they ran as fast as their legs would take them. In minutes, they were in the car and driving towards the outskirts of Lytham.

~

Having caught her breath, Ellen demanded that Maddy tell her everything. 'Word for word – what did this man say?'

Maddy breathlessly relayed the conversation. 'He knew everything – about me singing at the club, and that a new singer had taken my place. He didn't say anything about the shootings. He wanted to know if I had come on hard times, and asked did I need any money – did I want "a bit of fun", that kind of thing. But it was all a ploy. He was under orders, I'm sure of it.'

She took a deep breath, then continued, 'He asked me where I lived, started making advances. He wouldn't let me pass. I really thought he would shove me into a car and make off with me. Oh Ellen, I was terrified!'

'So, how did you manage to get away from him?' Ellen's eyes were huge and alarmed.

'I wanted to run, but I was afraid he'd come after me. Then I thought it might be best if I played along with him, so I told him I was lonely, because my husband was away. I said we lived in one of the terraced houses near the shops.'

Thinking of it now, made her skin crawl. 'I told him I had things to do and that I'd be back in an hour. We made arrangements for him to call round.'

'Could it have been that he just saw and recognised you?' Ellen asked. 'He may simply have been an old client thinking you were down on your luck, and trying to take advantage.'

Maddy shook her head. 'No. Knowing Steve Drayton, he's probably got men all over the country looking for me. Looking for *both* of us.'

Ellen had to concede the possibility. 'You could be right.'

'I am. I just know it.'

'But it doesn't make sense.'

'What do you mean?'

Ellen went over what Maddy had told her. 'If he *was* Drayton's man, why would he approach you in the first place? I mean, why didn't he just take a note of where he'd seen you, secretly follow you home, and report it back to Drayton?'

Maddy's heartbeat slowed down. 'Do you think he really was just a client who'd seen me singing at the club, and was coming on to me?' Oh, if only she could believe that, but every instinct in her body told her otherwise.

'I really don't know what to think,' Ellen sighed, 'although like I said, if he really *was* Drayton's man, he'd have been far craftier. On the other hand, he *could* have been sent to find you, and thought he could get his leg over for tuppence. After all, he's a man, and sometimes men can lose all sense of duty where a woman's concerned. Maybe he's wanted you for a long time and you were always out of reach. When he saw you today, his need of you was stronger than his fear of Drayton.'

Pulling up at the traffic-lights, she glanced at Maddy. 'You have to admit, it's possible.'

'Well, yes, when you put it like that.' Maddy was not altogether convinced. 'But even if that were true, it doesn't change the fact that one of the club-goers recognised me. What if it gets back? What if this man has links with him? If he thought he could get money out of it, what's to stop him from visiting him and asking if he's willing to pay for information regarding his old sweetheart?'

Ellen groaned. 'That is some imagination you have,' she said. But she didn't laugh, nor did she dismiss Maddy's fears.

Maddy first thoughts were for her baby. What would happen to Michael if *he* were to find her? She daren't even think of the consequences.

'I'm frightened,' she told Ellen in a choked voice. 'I thought we were safe. Now I'm not so sure.'

Choosing not to alarm Maddy any further, Ellen said nothing. But she fully understood her friend's fears. The past was catching up, and it was a dangerous thing – for Maddy and the child, more so than for herself.

There was no doubt about it. However much she might try to reassure Maddy, this was a frightening development, which needed some very serious thought.

~

The little man was sweating. His bleak surroundings were all too familiar. The stench of misery seemed to waft through the room, and there was a sense of hopelesness in the very walls of the prison. Behind him, the warder stood watching, ready for the slightest wrong move by either the prisoner or his wretched visitor.

The little man looked up, directly into the flat dark eyes of the burly warder. 'We're late today,' he said pleasantly, but his voice fell on deaf ears. He knew what it was like. Often the guards deliberately did not bring the prisoners out on time. It was as though they took sadistic enjoyment in making them sweat to the last minute.

The little man wanted to be out of there as soon as possible. Twelve years off and on he had lived behind prison walls, and the very thought of being locked in even as a visitor, made the sweat drip down his back like a running tap.

Turning again, he nervously smiled at the officer. As before, the other man made no response. Instead, he stared down on him through those shark-like eyes, his hard expression seemingly set in stone.

The little man twitched and focused on the door through which Drayton would arrive any minute.

The moment he had the thought, the door opened, and Drayton swaggered to the table where he pulled out the chair and sat down, his eyes riveted on little Danny. 'I take it you've got something for me?' Leaning forward he kept his voice low, so as not to be overheard.

Markedly jumpy, Danny glanced about.

'What the hell does that mean? You've either found her or you haven't.' Having recently tangled with the worst kind of enemy behind bars, Drayton was in no mood for games. 'Well?'

Not relishing the news he had to impart, Danny jogged Drayton's memory. 'Do you recall Jimmy Norman – the man who used to do a bit of running for you, at the club?'

Drayton wasn't listening. He was watching as the guards escorted in a huge mountain of a man. Physically daunting, with wide beefy shoulders and the neck of a bull, he seemed to dwarf the officers who flanked him.

Two days ago Brewster was sentenced to life. Powerful and merciless, his aim was to bring the other prisoners in Brixton under his control. However, he had not reckoned with Drayton – and there was already bad blood between them.

Now, when he sauntered by, the atmosphere in the room was dark with loathing.

'As I was saying . . .' Sensing trouble, the little man called Drayton's attention back. 'Jimmy Norman . . .'

'Dammit, man, get on with it!' With his eyes boring into the back of Brewster's head, Drayton looked fit to kill.

As quickly as he could, Danny told his story. 'It seems one of Jimmy's mates runs a gambling joint in Blackpool. Jimmy was up there – apparently the two of them are going into some venture or oth—' Seeing the look on Drayton's face, he began to gabble nervously. 'Bottom line is this. Jimmy was in Lytham when he spotted yer woman.'

Seeing how Drayton's face lit up, he swiftly explained, 'Sorry, boss, but you're not gonna like this. Y'see, Jimmy had no idea you were looking for her, so when he recognised her from the club, he just thought to make a play for her. She gave him an address, and later when he called there, the landlord said he didn't have no idea who this Maddy was. In fact, he threatened to make Jimmy pay for some other woman who had left the week before without paying the rent.'

'Stupid bastard!' Drayton pressed his clenched fists so hard against the table, the blood drained from his knuckles. 'So the little trollop fooled him, did she?'

'Seems like it, yes, but one good thing's come out of it. At least we've an idea where to be looking. I'm on to it, boss. You can count on me. North, south, east or west, trust me. There will be no stone left unturned.'

CHAPTER SIXTEEN

A WEEK HAD passed. A week of sleepless nights. And tonight was no different. Exhausted though she was, Maddy could not sleep.

Ever since the bad experience in Lytham, she could only suspect that all too soon, her whole world would come crashing in on her.

She could flee. She had done it before and if need be, she could do it again. As far as she knew, Ellen was in no danger from Drayton. But what about the baby? If Drayton wanted *her* out of the way, there would be no real reason why he should want to spare the child. He had never accepted it as being his, and never would. If anything, he probably hated the child even more than he hated her.

Sitting cross-legged on her bed, she swayed back and forth, going over everything in her mind. 'I have to leave,' she murmured. 'If I stay here, it could be disastrous for everybody. But if I leave, where will I go?'

Maddy knew it would be hard. She'd need to get as far away from here as possible. Find work. Make a home. And what of little Michael? Though her baby had come along in leaps and bounds and the doctors assured her his lungs were now as normal as those of any other baby, he had only this past week finished his hospital appointments. I don't want to leave him here with Ellen, she thought. She had an agonising choice to make. But then again, she couldn't put him in danger by dragging him from pillar to post. What to do? What to do?

Another sobering thought crossed her mind. If she left him behind, would she ever see him again? Climbing off the bed, she began pacing, searching for alternatives.

~

The night outside her window grew darker and thicker, and still she paced the floor. The darkness broke and the dawn crept over the horizon, and she was no nearer to some kind of solution.

After a while, she came to realise that, for the sake of those she loved above all others, she had no option but to take the only route left open to her.

She had to leave, and it had to be now, before full daylight came to change her mind.

It took but a few minutes to wash, brush her hair and get dressed. She kicked off her slippers and thrust her feet into the one pair of sturdy walking shoes she owned.

Going to the wardrobe, she took out an overnight bag and put in it only the most essential items: a hairbrush, toothpaste and toothbrush, underwear, warm tights, a clean skirt and blouse, and a big thick jumper.

She was already closing the bag when she remembered the club photographs. She climbed onto the chair and, reaching up to the top of the wardrobe, she retrieved the brown envelope; which she then slid into the bag.

She did not look at the photographs; she had no wish to. There were far more pressing things on her mind right now.

After putting on her winter coat, she stood awhile looking out of the window at the changing skies, the tears flowing down her face and her heart raw with pain. It was like her world had come to an end . . . again!

Going to the crib, she lifted her son into her arms and gently rocked him. 'You know how very much I love you, don't you?' she whispered. 'You know I would do anything for you.'

She kissed his eyelids and pressed her face to his, and when he stirred, she tucked him back into the cot. To gaze on that tiny face and know she might never see it again, was too much to bear.

In that awful, precious moment, she thought she had never felt so alone; not even when she was in that dark alley, with Alice and Jack lying so still on the ground.

Hardly able to see for the tears that blurred her vision, she padded downstairs to the kitchen, where she went to the dresser-drawer and, taking out a pen and paper, began to write:

My dearest friend Ellen,

Please don't think me a coward for leaving like this, but I honestly cannot see any other way to keep you and baby Michael safe from harm. I brought trouble here, and now I must take it away with me.

I think we both know that the man who stopped me in Lytham was sent by him, or will be reporting it back to him. And we both know that now I've been tracked down, Michael and I will never be safe. When he finds me – which he will – then he finds all of us, and I will have put you, Grandad and the baby in danger. I could never forgive myself for that.

It's me he's looking for, and because he is an evil man, who believes I betrayed him, he will not rest until he punishes me.

Oh Ellen, you have been a wonderful friend to me, and so has Grandad Bob, and I hope that what I'm about to do will repay your kindness. The only option for me is to go away and leave my baby in your care, until such a time when, God willing, I may come home and hold my son in my arms again.

He does not know whether I had the baby or not, so he won't be looking for him; though if I take Michael with me, I know for sure I would be putting his life at risk.

I know you will love him as I do, and I know you will care for him, and keep him safe. Tell him I'll be back as soon as I think it's safe.

I have no idea where I'm going, but rest assured I will contact you as soon as I can.

I love you like the sister I never had. Remember that always.

Please let Grandad know I am okay, or he'll worry and fret. You'll think of something to tell him, I'm sure. Give him my love.

God bless, and please try to understand. I am doing this because I don't know any other way to keep us all from harm.

If you think I'm wrong, then please forgive me.

Maddy
XX

Going back upstairs, and carefully slipping the note under Ellen's door, Maddy then returned to her own bedroom.

Gazing down on her sleeping son, she was tempted to change her mind. But her deeper instinct told her she had to make this sacrifice, or risk him being discovered. Circumstances had forced her to make a choice, when really there was no choice at all.

One last loving, lingering kiss, then with the tears burning her face, she collected her bag and walked away, leaving the bedroom door slightly open, so if he cried, Ellen was bound to hear.

Quickly and silently she went down the stairs and out the front door. She dared not look back, afraid she might change her mind.

Secure in the knowledge that she had done the right thing,

she started running, slowly at first, then faster and faster until she thought her lungs would burst.

The streets were eerily empty, her footsteps echoing against the flagstones like the patter of frantic fingers on a drumskin.

She didn't know which way to go; she followed no particular direction. There was no plan, but she had to keep running, away from the pain, and the child she had borne and whom she adored with every beat of her heart. And now the child was left behind, because of *him*.

Loathing flooded her soul. One day . . . One day, if there was any justice in Heaven, *he* would suffer. Like she was suffering now.

~

Emerging from Penny Street, she saw the National Express coach slow down at the traffic-lights. Quickly now, she ran out and put up her arms for the driver to let her in.

Astonished, he waited. The lights changed once, and then went back to red, and as she climbed on he told her gruffly, 'What the devil are you playing at? It's lucky for you there was no one behind me.'

'Where are you headed?' Breathless, she clambered on, as the door closed behind her.

'Last stop Bedford.' The lights changed and he moved forward.

'Bedford? Where's that?'

'What!' Making headway, he threw her an impatient glance. 'You're not telling me you've got on the wrong coach, are you?'

'No, no!' Maddy was quick to reassure him. 'Only my friend has just moved to Bedford. I'm paying a surprise visit, and I'm not sure where exactly it is, or how far?'

He laughed. 'You women,' he tutted. 'Absolutely hopeless!

You shouldn't be let out on your own – so disorganised it's a wonder you manage to get across the street without help.' He cast her another ironic glance. 'Bedford is in Bedfordshire – didn't your friend tell you that? It's a good six-hour trip. So, before we get there, I suggest you look in your bag and make sure you have her proper address.'

'Oh, I have, and once I get there, I'll have no trouble at all.'

As she struggled along to a seat, she heard him muttering, 'No trouble at all, eh? I wouldn't bet on it!'

There were four other passengers on the coach. 'Do you have a ticket?' That was the dumpling woman in front.

Maddy shook her head. 'I thought you paid on the coach.'

'Well, you can, and I expect the driver will take your fare when we make a stop. But it's not regular, and it's much easier if you get your ticket beforehand.' She bossily suggested Maddy should put her bag in the overhead locker. 'There are several pick-ups on the way, and you won't want folks stumbling over it, will you?'

'No, thank you.' Maddy dutifully slung it overhead onto the shelf.

'If you'd been on time at the coach station, the driver would have put it in the luggage compartment for you,' the woman fussed.

Maddy thanked her again, and a short time later when the dumpling fell asleep, she sorted out the money in her purse. As soon as I've found a place to stay, I must change my bank account, she thought. She needed to draw money out, but even more importantly, she had to erase all avenues by which she might be traced.

She thought about Ellen, and the shock she would get on waking, and her guilt was all-consuming. Yet, when she set it against having removed the threat from that cosy little house and everyone in it, the guilt seemed a worthwhile, albeit heavy price to pay.

Slumped in her seat, she buried her face in her hands and quietly sobbed. One man! One dark-minded man hellbent on destruction had done this to her. And in all her life she had never known such despair.

When the other passengers fell asleep, she was made to evaluate her circumstances. She felt strange – isolated, and swamped by the enormity of what she had done. She did not recognise who she was any more. What was she doing? Where was she going? How could she have left her child back there?

She shook herself mentally. The truth was, she had made herself a decoy. And how could she regret that?

To her mind, this was the only way she could help keep her precious boy out of Drayton's clutches. It was also the best way she might repay Ellen and Grandad Bob.

'Ellen.' She murmured the name with affection. 'I pray you will understand.'

~

Having fallen asleep with Maddy on her mind, Ellen woke with a start. For a moment she felt disorientated, but then the nagging worries that had kept her awake till gone midnight, came back to haunt her.

'It must have been Steve's man,' she murmured to herself. 'It was too much of a coincidence that he should suddenly bump into Maddy like that.'

Sliding out of bed, she made her way barefoot across the chilly lino. I didn't pay enough attention to what she was saying, Ellen thought. No wonder she was worried out of her mind.

When her foot trod hard on the piece of paper, she quickly snatched it up and unfolded it, her heart turning over as she skimmed through what Maddy had written.

I have no idea where I'm going . . .

I know you will love him as I do
And I know you will care for him,
and keep him safe . . .
I will contact you as soon as I can.

I love you like the sister I never had.
Remember that always.

'Oh, my God!' Dropping the note, she ran to Maddy's room and pushed the door wide open; the crumpled covers thrown aside and that awful sense of emptiness, told their own story. 'Oh, dear Lord! Maddy . . . what have you done!'

She hurried to the cot, where the baby was snuffling, fast asleep, oblivious to the drama that was taking place around him.

Running onto the landing and then down the stairs two at a time, Ellen checked every room. She even ran out into the street, glancing up and down, praying that Maddy was out here. Yet even as she looked, she knew deep down that her friend had gone. Maybe for ever. And who could blame her? 'Keep her safe lord', she mumbled, 'keep her safe!'

Maddy had written that note from the heart. She must have agonised for hours before she took such a hard decision. You tried to tell me, didn't you? Ellen thought. But I fobbed you off, hoping I was right and you were wrong. I should have realised how afraid for us you were. I should have talked it through – made plans. I was a fool to think it was a chance encounter. Oh Maddy, I'm so sorry . . . so very sorry.

Shivering, she came back into the house and closed the front door. As she made her way slowly up the stairs, her grandfather called out, 'Is that you, love?'

Swallowing hard, she tried to make her voice sound natural. 'Yes, Grandad.'

'Is everything all right, lass?'

'Everything's fine. I just went to the bathroom. Go back to sleep.'

'What time is it?'

'Time you stopped chattering, or you'll be fit for nothing in the morning.'

'Good night then, lass.'

'Good night, Grandad.'

Going into her own room, she cautiously switched on the main light and leaned against the wall, where she read and reread Maddy's every word.

Afterwards she walked round the room, the note clutched in her fist, her mind quickening with all manner of possibilities. Should she take little Michael and go after her? But where would she look? And how would she take best care of the baby? There must be a way, she thought. There *must* be a way of finding out where Maddy had gone.

She sat down, then she stood up, and now she was on the prowl again. And with each and every plan she imagined, there were a dozen reasons why they would never work. Maddy wants to keep us safe, she reasoned. That's why she took this drastic step. She knows if Drayton finds her, he'll find us, and the boy. Oh, dear God!

Thanks to Maddy's courage, Ellen's infatuation for Steve Drayton had come to an abrupt end when she became aware of his true nature. Thank God that evil man didn't know about little Michael. Oh, but if he ever did! That possibility did not bear thinking about, because he would instinctively know that the worst way to make Maddy suffer, would be to hurt her child.

In the end, commonsense prevailed, and Ellen had decided on her course of action. 'All right, Maddy. I'll do as you ask,' she promised. 'I'll take care of little Michael, and somehow, I'll cover your tracks here.'

She crept back into Maddy's room and gazed down on the

tiny boy. 'Your mammy said she would stay in touch,' she whispered, 'and I know she will. Meantime, you will have me and Grandad Bob to look after you.'

Reaching down, she stroked his silky hair. 'When the danger is over, your mammy will come back for you.' She thought of Maddy, of how loyal and loving she was, and how she had never asked to be put in such a frightening situation. 'I promise you, Michael, your mammy won't let us down. She loves you more than life itself, and she'll be back for you one day.'

She smiled tenderly at him. 'So we'll wait here, you and me,' she breathed. 'We'll do exactly as your mammy would want. We'll stay safe. And we'll wait.'

But there was another worry niggling at her now. What on earth could she tell Grandad? He was nobody's fool, so whatever story she cooked up, it would have to be convincing. She didn't want him suspecting anything untoward, and getting involved. She gave a nervous glance towards the door. What if he should ever be involved? Dear me no! That would never do.

So, while the young and the old slumbered on, Ellen laid back on Maddy's bed where, drawing the covers over herself against the early morning chill, she thought of a plan.

~

It was eight-thirty when Grandad finally came down. 'Good Lord!' Ruffling his red hair, he came into the kitchen and flopped down at the table. 'Have you seen the time?' He was incredulous. 'Half past eight! I can't ever recall sleeping till this time of the morning. Why didn't you wake me?'

'Because I'd already disturbed you once,' Ellen replied, placing a mug of freshly-brewed tea before him and putting some toast under the grill. 'And I expect that phone call disturbed you early on as well.'

He looked up, his brow furrowed with puzzlement. 'What phone call?'

Ellen reached into the cupboard for the marmalade; she dared not look into his face, or he might see how she was lying. 'It woke me an' all,' she said innocently. 'Half past six it was – frightened the life out of me. I'm surprised you didn't hear it.'

'Who in God's name was that, ringing here at that time of the morning? I hope you gave them an earful.'

'It was for Maddy.'

He took a long slow sip of his tea. 'Oh, aye?'

'It was her old aunt from Bournemouth.'

He frowned. 'An old aunt, eh? I don't rightly know why I should think it, but I were under the impression that Maddy didn't have no relatives?'

'Well, she hasn't – except for this old aunt in Bournemouth. They were very close when Maddy was young but I don't think they've seen each other in a long time, not since both her parents died.' She felt ashamed at lying to this darling old man. 'Maddy always kept an eye on her from a distance, if you know what I mean.'

He nodded. 'What, like birthdays and Christmas and that sort o' thing?'

Ellen was relieved that he seemed to understand. 'Yes, that's it,' she said, giving him a plate with two buttered slices of toast. 'Sometimes they talked on the phone, but that's all. The old aunt respected that Maddy had a life of her own, and Maddy respected her wish for independence.'

'Aye, well, I can understand that.' He spread some marmalade on his toast and bit into it. 'Sounds a bit like you and me, eh?' he mumbled. 'We've allus been here for each other in times of need, but we've never lived in each other's pocket, have we, lass?'

'That's exactly right, Grandad,' Ellen answered brightly. 'I hope you don't mind, but when Maddy asked if it was all right to give her aunt this number in case she needed to get in touch, I said yes. I'm sorry if I did wrong.'

'Well, o' course I don't mind.' He glanced about. 'Where's Maddy now?'

'She's gone.'

'Oh?' He grew anxious. 'Is everything all right, lass?'

'Not really, Grandad, no.'

'Then you'd best tell me all about it.' He put down his mug and sat up, his face wreathed with concern. He had a feeling that Ellen was nervous about something or another, and it wasn't altogether because she had given out his phone number. 'Come on, lass,' he urged. 'Out with it!'

Ellen gave her explanation. 'It's the old aunt I was just telling you about,' she said. 'Her neighbour heard a noise, ran round and let himself in, to find her unconscious at the foot of the stairs. He sent for an ambulance, and then he looked in her notebook for Maddy's number. He knew about Maddy, because the aunt often talked about her.' She had to be careful here, 'Anyway, he tracked her down.'

'And is she all right? Do they know what happened? Did she take a tumble down the stairs or what?' Though he was sorry for the old dear, his first thoughts were for Maddy.

'Apparently, she can't remember what happened, but she's really shaken up. She's covered in bruises and her arm's broken at the elbow. And now she's threatening to leave hospital and go home.' Ellen was amazed at how easily she could lie when necessary; though the bad feeling she had right now, was not pleasant. This was the second time she had told an outright lie to someone she loved, and she hoped it would be the last, although one lie always led to another.

'She's being very silly!' Grandad declared angrily, though to be honest, he would probably feel the very same if he was in her place. 'She needs to stay where she is and get proper treatment. Besides, she won't be able to manage at home, not with a broken arm she won't. And who knows what other damage she's done?'

He was admiring of Maddy. 'It's no wonder our Maddy took off at the drop of a hat. She's a grand lass.' He smiled. 'The pair of you make me right proud'. He set about making his toast.

Turning away, Ellen flushed pink with shame. If only he knew what lies I've told him, she thought, he wouldn't be feeling so proud of me then.

'The old aunt's not married then?' Grandad muttered through his toast and marmite.

'No.'

'Brothers, sisters?'

'Apparently not.'

'So, there are no children and no other folks to care for her?'

'No, Grandad. She lives completely on her own. Maddy is the only one she keeps in touch with.'

'I see. And Maddy's gone to take care of her for a while, is that it?'

'That's right, yes.'

'And what about the babby?'

'I told Maddy that I would take care of him – you and me together. If that's all right with you, Grandad?'

'I wouldn't have it any other way,' he declared soundly. 'In times like these we all have to do our bit.'

'Me and Maddy both thought it would not be right for her to take little Michael with her straight away. If she can persuade her aunt to stay in hospital, she'll come back for him, she said. She'll stay at her aunt's house with Michael, and visit the hospital every day if needs be.'

'Aye, lass, I understand all that. But even then it won't be easy. What if her aunt takes a wrong turn and they send for Maddy in the middle of the night? She'll have to wake the child and take him with her. On the other hand, if the old dear insists on coming home, Maddy will have her hands full taking care of them both.'

He tried to see it from Maddy's point of view. 'Yes, the pair of you did right in keeping the lad here with us. What's more, I don't think Maddy should come back for him, until her aunt is mending and settled. So, in my opinion, the sensible thing is for her to concentrate on the situation in hand, and let us get on with our bit at this end.'

'That's exactly what we thought,' Ellen said, relieved. 'And we mustn't forget that little Michael has only recently stopped his regular check-ups. He's still a bit wobbly after that bad start he had.'

'That settles it then.' His face beaming with a smile, Bob informed Ellen, 'When the lass calls, make sure you tell her that everything's all right and she's not to worry. The three of us will still be here, fine and dandy, when she gets back.'

'I will – and thank you, Grandad.'

Crossing the room, Ellen threw her arms round him. 'I knew we could count on you.' She had a nagging thought. 'What if the neighbours start asking where Maddy is? Especially Nosy Nora from next door. Lately, she's taken to drooling over little Michael every time Maddy takes him out.'

'We've got nowt to hide!' he retorted. 'So you just tell that interfering old biddy how it is! Knowing her, she'll have it round the street in no time, and if everybody knows the truth, there'll be no need for anybody to make up stories, will there?' He gave her a wink, then tapped the side of his nose in a conspiratorial fashion. 'Keep the enemy close. That's the way to win a war.'

'Shame on you, Grandad,' she chided. 'You're a canny old devil, that's what you are.'

'It's old age,' he grinned. 'You haven't got the strength to run, so you learn how to duck and dive.'

The sound of Michael crying for his breakfast, sent Ellen running up to fetch him.

'Give him to me while you get his bottle ready.' Grandad tickled the baby under the chin. 'See here now, little fella, yer mammy's gone away to look after your great-aunt.' He lowered his voice. 'Poor old thing, all alone like that. It wouldn't surprise me if she didn't throw herself down the stairs to get a bit of attention . . .'

'Grandad!' Ellen wagged a finger. 'That's not a very nice thing to say, is it?'

'Aye well, it were only a passing comment.' He paused, his voice falling to a whisper. 'Mind you, there's many a poor neglected soul who must think of it from time to time, especially when there's no one to care if they live or die.'

Sensing a sadness about him, Ellen went to hug him. 'Grandad?'

'Yes, lass?' The smile was back, and suddenly he was his chirpy old self again.

'What you just said . . .' The girl had to ask. 'Did *you* ever feel like that? Lonely enough to throw yourself downstairs?'

'Wherever did you get an idea like that!' He looked shocked, then burst out laughing. 'I wouldn't *dare* throw myself down the stairs. The weight of me bumping from step to step would bring the house down!'

In spite of herself, Ellen had to laugh.

As she walked back to the cooker, she turned to see him gently blowing bubbles into Michael's neck, the two of them chuckling, and felt a surge of sadness. She could not help but think about the way he had looked, when he talked about lonely old folks, and it struck her how hard it must have been for him, when she had stayed away all that time.

Loving him more than ever, she watched them a moment longer. 'Your mammy will miss you like thunder,' he was telling the child, 'but you're not to worry, 'cause she'll be back afore you can whistle dixie. Meanwhile, you've got me and our Ellen to contend with, yer poor little devil.' He sang a lullaby and afterwards brought the child to Ellen, who had his bottle warm and ready. 'He's all yours,' he said, and went away whistling, leaving Ellen both relieved and guilty, that he had taken her made-up story at face value.

'Come on, little one.' She cuddled the child onto her lap and put the teat near his mouth. He immediately lunged for it hungrily. By the look of Michael's rosy cheeks and fat little legs, he was thriving on the new feeding regime.

An hour later, with his belly full and his nappy changed, Ellen laid him in his pram downstairs, so she could keep an eye on him as she did some chores. 'Sleep tight,' she murmured tenderly. 'Your mammy's not here to tuck you in, but you'll never go short of love, I can promise you that.'

When the rain started pitter-pattering against the window, she looked up at the darkening skies with a sinking heart. 'Stay warm and safe, Maddy,' she whispered. 'And let me know where you are – as soon as you can.'

∼

One thing was certain.

She would not rest easy, until Maddy's voice was on the other end of that phone.

PART FOUR

~

Bedfordshire, 1979

Hideaway

CHAPTER SEVENTEEN

MADDY FELT INCREDIBLY lonely.

For six hours and nigh on two hundred miles, she had observed the changing winter landscape as she travelled further away from the home and the people she loved. Whenever the coach stopped to let passengers off, she was tempted to leave it and make her way back, as fast as she could, to Ellen and Michael, and that dear man who looked on her as another granddaughter.

The only thing that stopped her was the reason she had left, and it remained as pressing today as it was yesterday, and would be tomorrow. Steve Drayton's henchmen were still out there, looking for blood.

She glanced at her watch. Realising it was Michael's naptime, she closed her eyes and imagined him tucked up in his cot. She visualised Ellen leaning over him, whispering soft assurances into his ear and keeping an eye on him as he slumbered. Like dear Alice, Ellen had enriched Maddy's life. And she was immensely grateful for that.

Now as the driver pulled over and the last of the passengers had alighted, Maddy moved up to be nearer to him. 'How far to the terminus now?' she enquired.

'It's half an hour nearer than the last time you asked.'

'Sorry.'

'It's all right.' He glanced back at her. 'You seem a bit on edge, love.' Since she ran out of the coach in a panic, he had noticed how she fidgeted and looked about, as though waiting for someone to pounce on her.

Unsettled by his curiosity, Maddy chose not to answer. Instead, she asked, 'What's it like, Bedford?'

'It's an old market-town, set on a river, with bridges and cafés and a grand old market at its heart. There was a time when everyone knew everyone else, but like any other town, the population grows and times change; sometimes for the better, sometimes not.'

'So when did Bedford begin to change?'

'Ah, well now.' He thought back to when he was younger. 'I can tell you they had an influx of Italians in the fifties – looking for work in the brickyards, they were. They found work aplenty, so they stayed on and raised their families.' He made a quick calculation. 'There must be three if not four generations of Italians now, and as far as I know, they've been model citizens. And though they are proud of their Italian heritage, they've integrated naturally into the local community.'

'How do you know so much about Bedford?'

'Because that's where I grew up. My parents had a greengrocer shop, and my brother drives a cab there.' He thought about his rampant youth and the nostalgia was never far away. 'I met my first sweetheart there,' he confided, while keeping his eyes on the road. 'I spent my last couple of pounds hiring a row-boat to take her up the river, where I proposed.'

'Sounds lovely.' Maddy had visions of sunshine and romance.

'It was the most beautiful day,' he went on. 'We rowed right up the Great Ouse, then we pulled in, put up the oars and had a picnic on the grass bank.'

'Did you marry her?' Maddy was enthralled.

'I did,' he said dreamily. 'She said yes, and before she could change her mind, I had her down the aisle and wed.'

'So, no regrets then?' Maddy recalled her own dreams of walking down the aisle, dressed in white and giving her vows to the man who loved her. The reality had been so very different and now she feared her dreams might *never* come true.

'No regrets,' he answered. 'She was the best thing that ever happened to me. Over the next fourteen years, we had two sons and three daughters.' The smile slipped away. 'Sadly, my wife gave her last breath to my youngest daughter. It was a terrible blow. I've never wanted any woman since then. No one could ever come close to her. But I've got my family, and that's all I need.'

Realising that she had awakened painful memories, Maddy changed the subject. 'Do you think I'll be happy in Bedford?'

'Don't see why not,' he answered crisply. 'It's got everything you'd ever want in a town – shops to lose yourself in, colleges and libraries for sharpening your brain, oh, and that amazing river with its walks and parks.' And because she had intrigued him, he wanted to know, 'Are you moving to Bedford for good, or just visiting?'

'I'm not sure yet,' she answered cagily. 'It all depends on whether I can find work and lodgings.'

'If you want work, there are plenty of people who would take on a presentable girl like you. As for lodgings . . .'

Just then, the traffic-lights changed and he drew the coach to a halt. 'Good Lord!' Glancing down at his diesel tank, he gasped with horror, 'I'm on reserve. I'll need to take a detour and collect some fuel, or we'll end up pushing the damned thing.' Glancing at Maddy in the mirror, he informed her worriedly, 'I'm sorry, but it'll make us fifteen or twenty minutes late, I'm afraid.'

'That's all right,' she assured him. 'I'm in no hurry.'

It being too difficult to turn the coach around at the junction, the driver signalled left and followed the country lane. 'Nearest garage is a matter of ten minutes or so through the back lanes, but it's a bit bumpy, so it might be best if you return to your seat.'

Obeying him, Maddy sat back and enjoyed the beauty of the countryside. They passed two olde worlde pubs, and any number of quaint thatched cottages, and she remarked on how pretty it all was.

'We'll be going through the woods any minute now,' the driver said. 'You'll see a smattering of villages when we get out the other side. There's Woburn, owned by the Duke of Bedford, then there's Little Brickhill and Great Brickhill, and after that it's only a mile or so to the garage. Once we're back on the main road, it's a spit and a throw, and we'll be in Bedford town.'

True to his word, he arrived at the garage in no time. 'Do they sell newspapers?' Maddy had become paranoid about reading the papers, in search of news that might involve Steve Drayton. She was terrified that he might escape from Brixton Prison and come after her.

'They might,' he offered. 'Would you like me to fetch you one? It's the least I can do for nearly getting you stranded.'

Maddy graciously declined and followed him inside, and there on the counter was a small pile of *Daily Telegraphs*.

There was just one customer at the counter – a tall, good-looking man with wayward dark hair, wearing a long, somewhat grubby oilskin. Maddy calculated him to be in his mid-thirties.

'That'll be eight pounds, please, Brad,' said the bespectacled man behind the counter.

The man called Brad fished out eight pounds and handed it over. 'So, have you had any luck with my notice?' he asked.

'Nope!' Spectacles Man made a grimace. 'Seems to me how folks have lost the will to work. Either that, or there's too much work to go round and they're spoiled for choice. Would you like me to leave the notice in for another week?'

Brad looked disappointed. 'I'm surprised. I thought I might at least get one candidate,' he groaned.

'Well, *I'm* not surprised. Like I told you, I don't normally put notices up, but being as you're a long-time friend, I made an exception. Folks who call in here don't come looking for work, they come for fuel. It was a long shot, and I had hoped it might be of some use to you, but it looks like you'll have to take out an ad in the local paper. Meantime, we can leave the notice there. You never know, there might be that one person who sees it and takes an interest.'

'Okay, we'll leave it for another week,' Brad decided, 'and thanks for your help. I really do appreciate it.'

He lowered his voice to an intimate level. 'Since Tom and Joan moved to the coast, I'm absolutely desperate. I've got my hands full with the farming, there's a new barn going up and pipes being laid right down to the spinney . . . the top fields flooded twice last year, and ruined the seedlings. And on top of that, I've had one man off sick for a week, and my desk is piled high to the rafters with urgent letters and bills.'

He heaved a sigh. 'Sometimes you wonder if it's all worth it. Without Joan to keep on top of it, the house looks like a tip. So, yes, we'll do what you said . . . we'll leave the notice for another week. Meantime, I'll contact the *Bedfordshire Times* and organise an advert.'

'It's worth a try. Trouble is, you never know what kind of person you're getting. It's always best if you can recruit locally. That way, there's a chance you'll already know their background.'

'Right. Well, thanks anyway. So, we'll leave it a week, and see how we go.' He was about to turn away when he suddenly remembered, 'Oh! I forgot – I need to fill my can. They're late delivering my diesel, and I'm getting low. I daren't risk running out altogether.' Sorting through his loose change, he paid the extra amount.

As he turned away, he almost bumped into Maddy. 'Whoops!' he said with a sincere smile, before addressing the coach-driver, to apologise for the wait.

Moving forward to the counter, the coach-driver acknowledged his apology with a nod of the head. He paid for his fuel, and treated Maddy to her newspaper, which he promptly handed to her. 'You might as well go and find the cloakroom,' he suggested, 'while I finish up here.'

Stopping to look at the magazines on display near the door, Maddy overheard snatches of conversation between the driver and the man behind the counter. 'There goes a worried man,' the latter stated. 'As decent a bloke as you'll ever meet.'

Taking the driver's money, he chatted on, '. . . Name's Brad. He's a vet who also runs Brighill Farm, a couple of miles down the lane. Got a young son. His wife was killed in a road acident, couple of years ago. God knows how he's coping with every-thing he's got on *his* plate.'

'Oh, I know what that's like. Sounds like your man's got his troubles and no mistake,' the driver said kindly.

'You're right there – and now he's left with a little lad to care for. Life's a bitch as they say, and it's given him a few kicks, poor devil. It's been one bad thing after another. A hard-working, decent bloke like Brad? There's no way he deserves that.'

At this, Maddy left and hurried across the forecourt to where Brad was filling up the can. 'I'm really sorry I delayed you in there,' he said. His smile was open and honest. 'I had a bit of business to sort out, and I didn't realise there was anyone wait-ing behind me.' He paused, then said a little desperately, 'I don't suppose *you* know anyone who's looking for work and lodgings, do you?'

Before she could answer, he said, 'What's wrong with me?' and smacked his forehead. 'I take up your time in there, and then you can't even walk across the forecourt without me accost-

ing you. If I say sorry again, will you forgive me . . . please?'
He had a mischievous look on his face.

'Of course,' Maddy assured him. 'And no, I don't know
anyone who might be looking for work and lodgings.' Apart
from me, she thought, and the last thing I need is to take on
more troubles than I've already got.

'Ah, well. Thank you anyway.'

'I hope you find someone,' she said sympathetically.

'I'm sure I will.' He laughed. 'It's either that, or I throw
myself off a bridge.'

'That's not a clever thing to say,' Maddy chided. 'I understand you have a young son?'

He appeared shocked. 'How did you know that? Oh, I see
. . .' He glanced towards the garage. 'Sam's a fine friend, but
he does like to tittle-tattle.' He gave her a sheepish look. 'But
you're right, that was not a clever thing for me to say, and I
take it back. Is that all right?'

Maddy gave him a smile, which Brad thought was enchant-
ing. 'Like I say, I hope you find someone,' she said, and with
that, she left him filling up his can, and made her way to the
coach.

The driver was right behind her. 'Saw you chatting to the
man,' he said casually.

'No, he was chatting to me,' she said. 'He seems desperate
to find help.'

'So now you're thinking you should not set your heart on
Bedford, because here you have a home and work, all rolled
into one. Mind you, if he's a man on his own, you need to be
very careful.'

He started the engine and began pulling out.

Maddy took a sideways glance at the man called Brad, who
had replaced the cap on the can and was wiping his hands on
an old rag. He then threw the rag back into the bucket,
collected the can and started his way back to the Land Rover.

'STOP!' Grabbing her bag from the overhead shelf, she frantically yelled for the driver to pull over.

'Hey!' Drawing the coach to a halt, the man was astonished to see Maddy brush past him and start down the steps. 'What the devil are you playing at?'

'You made me think,' she told him. 'And you're right. That poor man needs someone to work for him, and I need the work and lodgings. It's ideal.'

'Don't be rash, love. You don't know anything about him.'

'And he doesn't know anything about me. I heard the man in the garage say he's a decent bloke, and he knows him, so I'm happy with that.' She told herself that no man could be as evil as the one from whom she was fleeing, an evil man who would take delight in doing away with her, and their son.

'If you were my daughter, there's no way I'd let you off this coach! And I thought you were going to stay with a friend?'

'But I'm *not* your daughter – I'm not anyone's daughter. Besides, I'm old enough to know how to take care of myself.' He opened the door and she clambered to the ground.

'What about Bedford?'

'There's time enough for that,' she said. 'And like you say, if this doesn't work out, Bedford is only a spit and a throw away. Thanks for all your kindness. And now I'm sorry, but I've got to dash. Bye-ee!'

Running across the forecourt, she called for Brad to, 'Hang on a minute!'

Turning round, he was astonished to see the pretty girl running towards him. Putting the can on the ground, he waited. 'Okay, what have I done now?' he asked.

'It seems you have what I'm looking for.'

'Dear me! And what might that be then?'

'I need work and lodgings, and you appear to have both.'

He studied her for a brief moment. 'Are you telling me you want to come and work at Brighill Farm?'

'Yes, I am.'

'But it's heavy stuff. It's a *man* I need more than anything.' He paused. 'You wouldn't happen to be a trained nursemaid, by any chance?' he enquired hopefully. 'I've got a young son – Robin. He's nearly eight.'

'No, but I'm used to children – with my smaller brothers and sisters, and all that.' She could feel herself blushing at the lie. 'And I can turn my hand to hard work if needs be. But I can't claim to do heavy labour. Like you rightly say, you need a man for that. But I'm keen, and I'm a quick learner, and I know my way round babies.' Her own darling son loomed large in her mind, making her heart dip. She prayed for the day when she could openly have him with her, 'Look here, Mr . . .'

'Brad . . . call me Brad, everyone does.'

'Well, Brad – and you can call me Sheelagh – Sheelagh Parson.' It was a combination of her middle name and her late mother's maiden name, so it wasn't too much of a lie, Maddy thought quickly. 'The truth is, I really need the work. Why don't you give me a trial, and if I'm not up to scratch, what have you got to lose?'

The man took another moment to study her; the long dark hair and slim figure, and that steely look in her chestnut-coloured eyes, then, 'Do you have references, Sheelagh?'

Looking him in the eye, she shook her head. 'No. Do *you*, Brad?'

She saw the smile growing on his face and when he laughed out loud, she laughed with him. 'You'll do,' he said. 'I'll give you a month's trial, okay?'

'Okay.'

As she clambered into his Land Rover, Maddy was knocked breathless by a huge hairy dog that leaped on her from behind.

'Down!' Brad gave the order and it leaped back into the boot. Then: 'Stay!' which it did.

'Are you all right?' he asked Maddy. She told him how she'd been taken by surprise, but that she wasn't hurt.

Brad apologised yet again, this time on behalf of the dog. 'His name's Donald. He's my sheepdog, and my best friend.'

Maddy was curious. 'Donald? That's a strange name for a dog.'

'It was either that or Duck,' he said wrily. 'When I first started training him to be a sheepdog, the daft capers he cut were nothing short of hilarious. They reminded me of Donald Duck. Hence the name.'

'He's beautiful.' Looking round, she observed his big black eyes and peculiar sticky-up ears, one white, one black.

'He's very special. Knows me better than I know myself,' Brad admitted. 'I expect you heard a snippet or two back there. These past two years, things have been pretty difficult.' He jerked a thumb at the dog. 'If it hadn't been for this fellow, I don't know what I'd have done.'

'It's good to have a friend through bad times,' Maddy said quietly.

'You sound as if you know a bit about it.' Something in her tone reflected a sense of hurt.

Maddy gave no response. Least said, least repeated, she thought. As for the man in the garage, she would not be too happy if a friend of hers was to break a confidence like that.

'Okay.' Brad understood, 'As long as you do your work, earn your keep and don't steal the family jewels, I'm happy to mind my own business.'

He gave a sigh, muttering under his breath, 'Roofs leaking, trenches to be dug out, acres of land that need turning over. Barns going up.' He started the engine, put his Land Rover into first gear and rolled his eyes in frustration. 'I need ten men to do the work, and here I am, taking on a slip of a girl who's got fewer muscles than my daft dog.'

'I heard that!' Maddy was trying not to laugh.

'You were meant to.'

'So, you don't want me after all?'

'Did I say that?'

'No.'

'The plan is, me and young Robin and Donald will give you a try, then if you're no good, you're out.' He glanced at the dog. 'Isn't that right, Don?'

Hearing his name, the dog sat up, cocked an ear, licked his master's face, slobbered on Maddy, then spreading himself flat on the floor, he dropped off to sleep.

Wiping off the slobber with the grubby rag Brad handed to her, Maddy giggled. 'You're right,' she said lightheartedly. 'Donald does suit him.'

As they drove away, the coach-driver watched, 'Women! They never listen,' he grumbled, 'still, that Brad seems a regular sort of a bloke. All we can do is hope she's made the right decision.'

~

After meandering past isolated farmhouses and lanes that were so narrow the sides of the vehicle sheared away the hedges, they arrived at what Maddy could only describe as something out of a painting. 'Wow! Is this your house?' At the end of a long untidy drive, the rambling cottage was immensely pretty, with its thatched roof and tiny windows. The porch was a smaller masterpiece, with stout wooden struts holding up the quaint little roof. Brad had left the lights on, and they lit up the surrounding dark, chilly landscape like a beacon.

'Like it, do you?' Brad was proud of his home, especially as he and his late wife Penny had lovingly brought it back from years of being derelict.

'It's adorable.' Maddy's enthusiasm was akin to his own.

'Well, thank you. But you wouldn't have said that if you'd

seen it some ten years back. It was just a heap of rubble and rotting timber, with the roof sagging into the downstairs rooms, and crumbling walls where the rain poured in.'

He described how hard it had been, bringing it back to its former glory. 'When we first saw it, Penny wasn't sure if she could live in it. But I fell in love with it straight off, so we went to the auction, and got it for a song. The surrounding forty acres of land were auctioned separately, and as my lifelong dream had been to start a veterinary farm, where animals might convalesce, I bought the lot.'

'And have you ever regretted it?' Maddy was thinking of the way his wife had given him a son, and then was sadly taken. In her deepest heart she was riddled with guilt at leaving her own son. She couldn't help but compare herself with his wife. But then, she told herself, there was a difference. His wife had no choice in it, while she had deliberately left Michael because her very presence had placed him in great danger. For that very reason, she must not regret leaving; only regret that she had ever set eyes on his father.

Brad answered her direct question. 'I could never regret living here,' he said. 'From the day they raised the roof and we were able to step inside, the cottage seemed to wrap itself around us, like a pair of loving arms.'

He gave a half-smile. 'It started out so well. Life was good.' Pausing, he went on, 'Then it was *not* so good. But the house was still there, constant, warm and comfortable.'

The smile broadened to fullness as he reached out backwards to ruffle the dog's shaggy coat. 'This scruffy fella might be daft as a brush, and at times he drives me mad with his scatty ways and bad manners. But he will never know how much I owe him.'

Maddy knew though.

She heard the tremor in Brad's voice and saw the love in his eyes, and she imagined how, after his wife got killed, the dog remained loyal; an ear to confide in, a constant and protective friend who gave his all, and asked nothing in return.

On arriving outside the cottage, Brad opened the rear door and Donald jumped out. Running straight to the water bowl, he lapped up the contents and promptly shook his head and spattered them all over.

He then sat on his haunches, wagging his tail and looking up at his master with a hopeful gleam in his eye. 'No, Donald.' Brad was firm. 'It's not your dinner-time. You can wait, like the rest of us.' Making a wide sweep of his arm, he told the dog, 'Get off and do your work. Check whether them damned foxes have had any of the sheep away. Go on! Get off with you!'

Ushering Maddy inside, Brad took her on a tour of the house.

As they went from room to room, Maddy thought she had never seen anything so delightful. Every room was different; Robin's bedroom had aeroplane curtains and the carpet was covered with Action Men, Lego and vehicles of all descriptions. Maddy nearly trod on a London bus as she backed out of the room, thinking it could do with a good clean.

'The lad's staying at his friend Dave's tonight,' said Brad, taking her back downstairs and into the office. This room was small and compact, fitted with shelves and cupboards and strewn with all manner of papers and files, and there was even a pile marked URGENT lying on the floor.

'As you can see, I'm in a complete mess,' Brad grinned. 'But I do have a system. I mark everything. *Very Urgent. Urgent, Can Wait* or *Dispose Of.*'

'And does it work?'

'No.' He spread out his hands in a gesture of helplessness. 'I don't get round to it, the piles get bigger, and then they send me threatening letters.'

'That's worrying, isn't it?'

'I know.' He chuckled. 'But in the end, it might work out in my favour.'

'How's that?'

'Well, if I don't pay they lock me up. And if I'm locked up, I can't work, and if I can't work I can't pay. So it'll be *them* that does the worrying. Not me.'

Maddy laughed out loud, she liked him. What with his wife dying and leaving him with a small child to care for, and then losing his loyal staff and trying to run a working farm and a vet business, he had taken a series of hard blows. Yet in the wake of all that, he could still smile and see the funny side of things.

'Right.' He led her through to the sitting room. 'This is where me and my scruffy dog put the world to rights,' he said. 'We have our dinner, cooked and ruined by me, then we flop down and moan at each other. Afterwards, we fall asleep and on the stroke of midnight, he slinks off to his bed in the kitchen, and I stagger upstairs.' His grin was infectious. 'Sad, isn't it?'

Maddy thought it was wonderful, and said so.

The central heating was on full blast. Every room in the house was warm, bright and inviting. Brad told her how all three bedrooms had panoramic views over the countryside, not that she could see them now, as it was pitch dark – while from the kitchen window, apparently, the long, meandering brook was clearly visible, dancing its way through the valley.

'It's the most beautiful place!' Maddy exclaimed. 'I'm not a country girl born and bred, but I can understand how you fell in love with it all.'

As though he had known her all his life, Brad confided his great ambition. 'I've been so busy just trying to survive, that things have gone wrong – but I will put them right,' he promised.

'I'm sure you will.' She had no doubts. 'Especially as you seem so passionate about it.'

'I am.' He clenched his fist. 'I must get the practices up and running again. When I was in my twenties, I went to veterinary college, got excellent grades and had a career all planned out. But then I went travelling across Europe, had an adventure or two, and somehow the time simply flew by. Then I met my wife. We saw this place, built up the practices, but when she died . . . I let them go to pot. And now here I am, with very little spare cash and spending all my time just trying to survive.'

'And was there never a time when you could use your veterinary skills?'

He went on, 'the thing is, you need money and a barrage of customers to make it as a vet. One day though, I'll clear the decks, pay the bills, and concentrate all my efforts on realising my dream. In fact I'm already laying the foundations, in a small way.'

'Well, that's good, isn't it?' Maddy admired his determination.

'It will be,' he said. 'Lately, I let it be known locally that I'm a qualified vet, so now I've got a smattering of customers . . . it doesn't pay though.'

'So, you do it for nothing?'

He winked at Maddy. 'Not exactly,' he said, 'Round here, we don't do too badly. Y'see, it's like this: we have our own special system. We barter.'

'How do you mean?'

'Well, I stitch a cut or two, and we get a cabbage or three, or I help a sheep through a difficult birth, and somebody makes us an apple-pie. For now, it's just a case of one neighbour helping another. Primarily I'm a farmer. I make money by growing crops, then I have my prime breeding flocks; in one season, I might get four hundred lambs, which I then sell on to the next stage.'

'And what does that mean?' Maddy was fascinated.

'It means I'm a softie,' Brad said with some embarrassment.

'I can't bring myself to fatten them up for the meat-market, so I simply wean them and sell them on, to somebody less squeamish than me, who does what a meat-farmer was born to do.'

He then picked up his coat and a torch, and asked Maddy to follow him outside. He guided her down the garden and through to the brook. Starlight sparkled on the water. 'What do you think of my bridge?' he wanted to know.

'What bridge?'

'Over there.'

Just then, she caught sight of it; made from rustic wood and twisted branches, it spanned the narrowest part of the brook.

'Oh, it's lovely!' Maddy was mesmerised. This entire area was unbelievably magical, with ancient trees dipping their branches into the water, and the valley, lush and velvet, going away in the distance.

In all her life, Maddy thought she had never seen anything quite so beautiful. It took her breath away, made her forget her cares.

Cupping her elbow with the crook of his hand, Brad led her to a peculiar clump in the ground, where he shone the torch downwards and drew aside the protective covering of newspaper. 'See there – isn't that amazing?'

'What am I looking at?' All Maddy could see was a remnant of newspaper and a mound of earth.

'Kneel down.' Squatting, he pointed and said, 'Now . . . can you see?'

Maddy knelt and peered at the ground and saw a plant.

'Look deeper!' Brad shone the torch right into the heart of the plant.

To her astonishment, Maddy saw a tiny, struggling, baby-green shoot coming right up through the middle. 'Oh, yes! Now I see it. What is it?'

Reaching down, Brad covered the shoot over and drew her

to her feet. 'It's a clematis,' he said reverently. 'A magnificent climber. When we first arrived here, it was clinging to the side of the house, the only thing left alive. It was midsummer, and it had festooned the outside wall with huge pink flowers; its winding tentacles had worked their way in through the open windows, and it was almost as though it had taken over. Oh, and the perfume from the flowers was simply amazing!'

'So, how did it get down here?'

'One day, we had to go into Bedford town centre to sort out bathrooms and such,' he explained. 'I left strict instructions with the builders that they were not to touch the climber, that it was to be kept safe, until I could deal with it. But when we got back, the foreman had gone to lunch and his young mate had ripped it out by the heart and chucked it on a bonfire he was building. It had lain in the sun for hours, so by the time I got to it, the sorry thing was dried to a crisp. There was little hope of it surviving. Anyway, I cut off the root, planted it, watered it, and hoped for the best.'

He pointed to the spot. 'For months it lay dormant out here, with no sigh of life, and I thought we'd lost it for sure. But the other day, I checked on it, and lo and behold, even though it's the wrong time of year, I found that new shoot. At first, I thought it might belong to another plant – a weed that had got in or something, but when I investigated further, it was definitely a shoot from the old root. It's like a miracle, Sheelagh – the first in a long, long time. So, with tender loving care, and a helping of luck, it might yet climb the house again.'

Maddy found it very easy to be in his company even though she found it strange being addressed as 'Sheelagh'. But it was imperative that she kept her identity a secret. 'I'm sure the plant will flourish', she told him.

Here was a big, able-bodied man, with work-soiled hands and an appetite for hard graft. And yet, somewhere in his make-up, he had this reservoir of tenderness and love . . . for his home, his son, his clown of a dog, and this ugly clump and its tiny newborn shoot, which against all odds, he had rescued from extinction.

'Come on then!' He was already moving her on. 'You're shivering. You've seen the house and the land, and now, you need to see your accommodation. Then we'll go back in and have some supper.'

Maddy had wondered where she was to sleep, but hadn't liked to ask. She had assumed that she'd be in one of the farm-house bedrooms, but Brad hadn't said anything, so she had bided her time.

The 'accommodation' turned out to be a small house standing a short distance from the main property. It had two bedrooms, a pretty, if tiny kitchen, and a fenced-off garden with a swing, and a lagoon of fruit-trees. 'This was my fore-man's house,' Brad explained. 'I think you'd better spend tonight in the spare room at the house, if that's all right, as I need to put the heating on for you and air the bedding.'

'Have you no staff at all now?' Maddy asked.

'Well yes, there's John. He keeps the machinery in tiptop condition. Then there's Liz, who comes in every morning to milk the cows and collect the eggs. Oh yes, then there's old Malcolm, who earns a bit of money, pottering about the gardens here. And of course, there's Timmo, the shepherd. I can work from dawn to dusk, and go for nights on end without sleep, but no man is able to tend three or four hundred sheep, with-out help of sorts.'

He took a moment to assess his situation. 'I still haven't replaced my foreman though. Tom was a good man. I'll be hard pressed to find one like him.' Bringing his gaze to bear on Maddy, he went on, 'His wife Joan took care of young Robin when he wasn't at school, and did all my paperwork. She also cooked, cleaned, and generally kept me sane.' He studied

Maddy's reaction. 'Do you think you could pick up where she left off, Sheelagh?'

'If she could manage the work,' Maddy said stoutly, 'then I don't see why it should be too much for me.'

Brad gave a long sigh of relief. 'You're a woman after my own heart.' He put the heating on in the small house, flicked on the fridge and gave her a grin. 'I hope you'll be very happy here. And now, let's go back to the warm and have a pot of tea.'

Back in the kitchen of the main house, Maddy followed Brad's every move as he put some sausages under the grill, chopped up some cold boiled potatoes to fry, and laid the table. Without asking, she fetched out other things they would need, and found the mugs, sugar and milk for the tea. The smallest of smiles drifted over her face as she thought how absolutely normal and genuinely friendly Brad was; unlike any other man she had known, apart from Jack. Unfortunately, living the life of a club-singer had not often afforded her the company of men like Brad.

They had tea, they enjoyed their meal, and they chatted further about farming and general topics, and now the conversation shifted to a more personal level. 'Do you have family, Sheelagh?' Brad asked.

Maddy thought of Ellen and Grandfather Bob, and of her own son, Michael, and her heart was wrenched with pain. 'No.' Her answer was quick and decisive. 'No family.' Even now she was afraid to confide in anyone; even this man, whom she instinctively trusted.

When she saw how taken aback he seemed by her curt answer, she quickly assured him, 'Sorry. It's just that my parents both died, and I am an only child. It's okay, though. It's not uncommon.'

He gave a long, sorry sigh. 'Forgive me. It was a clumsy question.'

Her smile put him at ease. 'Don't worry about it.'

He glanced at the bag she had brought with her. 'If you need to collect anything from your previous place, I'll take you there. Just say the word.'

Pointing to the holdall, she laughed, rather sadly. 'That's it. My whole life is in that bag.' Including my precious photos of little Michael and Ellen, she thought. And of myself, in another life. She sorely missed the singing; the crowds and the applause. It was as though she had dreamed it all, and now the dream was over.

He said not a word. Instead he looked long and hard at her, wondering what a personable young woman like Sheelagh Parson was doing travelling the country with just one bag, and such a desperate need for work and lodgings that she would go with a stranger, like himself.

'I'm glad we found each other,' he said quietly. 'I need someone like you, and you obviously need a roof over your head . . .' When it seemed she might reply, he stopped her with a gesture. 'No, Sheelagh. Don't say anything. Just remember, you have work, and a home here, for as long as you want.'

That said, his dark eyes smiled down mischievously. 'Mind you, if our Donald catches you slacking, he'll have you out on your ear before you know what time of day it is!'

CHAPTER EIGHTEEN

I T WAS TEN o'clock the next morning, and Maddy had nearly
finished cleaning the farmhouse kitchen. She had started
at eight, after an early breakfast with Brad, and now only had
the floor to wash. The place gleamed – it had been a pleasure to put this lovely room to rights. February sun streamed
in through the windows as she filled a metal pail with hot water
and began to rummage in the cupboard under the sink for
some Flash, a scrubbing brush and some J-cloths.

Just then, she heard a loud rat-tat at the front door, and as
Brad had left to go on his rounds of the farm, she wiped her
sweating face with the hem of the old pinnie she was wearing
and went to open it.

A tall woman stood there, with a hand on the shoulder of
two young boys. One, the image of Brad, looked surprised to
see her. 'Hello,' he said. 'Where's Dad?'

'He's in the yard,' Maddy told him, then added, 'Do come
in, everyone. My name is Sheelagh Parson, and I have come
to work for Mr Fielding. You must be Robin,' she said to the
lad, 'and this must be your friend Dave and his mother. How
do you do?'

The woman gave her a curious but not unfriendly glance,
introduced herself as Susan Wright, and walked inside with
the boys. An excited Donald came rushing in, barking and

jumping up at them, and the lads made a big fuss of him, much to the women's amusement.

Robin turned to Maddy and said, 'Sheelagh, next week I'll be eight! His cheeky freckled face, which had been thoroughly licked, was flushed with pride.

'Well!' Smiling, she said, 'I think that's wonderful. Are you having a party?'

'I don't know – I haven't asked my dad yet. I hope he remembers to get me a birthday cake.'

Maddy's heart went out to him. 'We'll have to see about that, won't we? And now, why don't I put the kettle on? Would you like a cup of tea, Mrs Wright?'

'Oh, call me Sue. And yes, I'd love a cup of tea. These two have fair worn me out this morning. We've already been swimming but it's made no difference to their energy. I'll be glad when half-term is over and they go back to school!'

The boys were making for the back door. 'Bye!' called Robin. 'Dave and me are going round the fields with Donald. Back soon!' On hearing his name, Donald was leaping up and down at the back door, yapping loudly and his tail going fifteen to the dozen.

'Just hark at that racket.' Sue was a woman in her early forties; she had the kind of smile that puts you at ease straight off. 'And those two will no doubt be up to all kinds of mischievous tricks.'

'Such as what?' asked Brad, coming in through the back scullery and taking off his boots. His ready smile betrayed a father's pleasure in the antics of his only son.   •

'You might ask!' Sue declared. 'One minute they're off climbing every tree in sight, and the next they're sat on the edge of the brook – with their feet in that freezing water and their trousers wet to the knees.' She rolled her eyes to heaven. 'They're like a couple of jack-in-the-boxes – I can't keep up with them.'

'Would a cup of tea help?' Brad asked, but the kettle was already coming to the boil.

'Sheelagh is already making us one,' Sue said, then added wickedly, 'I hope there's a chocolate digestive to go with it – although I know you keep them well-hidden.'

Brad made a startled face. 'Shame on you, Sue! When have I ever hidden away the chocolate biscuits?'

She gave Maddy an aside wink. 'Only every time you see me coming.'

'Well, they've all gone, so you're out of luck,' Brad said, then burst out laughing.

Coming to sit alongside Maddy, Susan quietly addressed her but kept an eye on him. 'He hides them in the oven. One of these days, he'll switch the oven on, forget they're there, and they'll melt all over the place. And serve him jolly well right!'

Maddy laughed out loud. 'I used to hide the biscuits too,' she admitted. 'My friend Jack would eat all the cream ones and leave us with the soggy ginger-nuts and boring plain ones.'

'Tell us about your friend, Jack.' Brad's inquisitive voice brought her up sharp.

She searched for a way out, but there was none. What in God's name had made her mention Jack? In one crazy, fleeting instant she had let her guard down.

Sensing her dilemma, Sue came to her rescue. 'I thought you were making the tea?' she chided Brad with a warning glance. 'My tongue feels like the back end of a saddle, and I'm sure Sheelagh here feels the same, after what she's done to this kitchen. I haven't seen it look like this since Joan went off to live by the sea. So, go on on with you! Chop! Chop! And *don't* forget the biscuits.'

Realising he had made a mistake in asking about Maddy's friends, Brad set about making the tea, clattering around in the kitchen. 'He didn't mean to pry,' She explained quietly.

'He's a man, that's all. And you know how they can put their big feet in it, even without trying.'

Brad poured the boiling water into a large tea-pot containing three tea-bags, then went to wash his hands in the small cloakroom.

Maddy felt amazingly comfortable in this homely woman's presence. Turning to her, she tried to explain. 'It's just that . . . well, Jack was like a brother to me. But that was another life – another time.' Yet never a day passed when she didn't see him lying there in the gutter. Alice too, and both of them gone forever.

Sue put her hand on Maddy's arm. 'Brad really didn't mean to intrude. But if he asks awkward questions again, just tell him to mind his own business.' She laughed. 'I tell him that all the time, and I'm still allowed through the front door.'

'He seems like a good man.'

'Oh, he is.' Her manner grew serious. 'Brad is a survivor. With what he's had to endure these past years, any weaker man would have put a gun to his head. But not him, oh no. He's like a mountain, always there, strong and enduring.'

She apologised, but, 'Can I ask . . . has he taken you on as his new housekeeper?'

Maddy explained, 'He hasn't exactly called me his housekeeper, but yes, he seems to think I might be able to do the work his foreman's wife did – Joan, wasn't it?'

'Ah, yes . . . Joan. She was a real treasure. She virtually ran his office, made sure the pair of them ate regularly, and kept this house spick and span.' She glanced discreetly at Maddy's slim figure and slight build. 'It's a job and a half. Joan was a big hulk of a woman . . . never stopped from morning to night.'

Maddy had noticed how she might be comparing her to Joan. 'I'm not big-built,' she admitted, 'but I'm strong, and I don't mind hard work.'

Sue said immediately, 'Aw, look, I wasn't making comparisons. I'm sure you'll handle it fine.' Lowering her voice, she winked at her. 'Just make sure you keep him in check. Joan told me he has a habit of walking in with half the field still clinging to his boots. Then one day he'll be in early, starving and ready to eat before you've had time to cook the meal, and the next, he'll arrive home long after the meal is ruined. He's unpredictable; aggravating, and at times he'll drive you crazy.' She finished with the promise, 'For all his many faults, he's loyal to his friends, and kind as the day's long.'

'He's already told me about his plans and such with the veterinary practices,' Maddy confided. 'He's so passionate about them, I really hope he can achieve what he's after.'

Lowering her voice, Susan was sympathetic, yet realistic. 'His work here is too demanding of his time and energy. And at the end of it, he earns just enough for his needs. Yet, night after night, you'll see him browsing over the other paperwork. You know, my husband runs a market gardening business, and he just falls asleep in front of the telly every night.' She threw up her hands and sighed, 'Men!'

'Here we are, ladies.' Brad arrived, drying his hands on a small towel, he poured out the tea. Going to a cupboard, he produced a packet of chocolate digestives and set them out on a pretty plate. 'I hope you two realise that these are the last of my supplies?'

'May your tongue drop out!' Sue wagged a finger at him. 'I bet you keep another stash hidden somewhere. I'm going to check that oven of yours!'

'Don't you dare!' Offering round the milk and sugar, Brad said, with a twinkle in his eye, 'All right – maybe I *do* keep a packet back for emergencies. But it's not for me . . . it's for young Rob. He gets right shirty if he doesn't have a biscuit with his nightcap.'

'No, I don't.' The boy came running through the door with

Dave and Donald on his heels. 'Them chocolate digestive things are yuk! I keep asking you to get some Jammie Dodgers, but you never remember!'

'Tuck in, everybody.' Brad stood up and fetched two more mugs for the boys and wisely chose not to get into an argument with his son. 'I've got some shortbread fingers too, somewhere.'

So they all sat down and chatted, and Maddy was surprised at how easily she seemed to fit in. The worry had not gone away; yet here, in this place, with these people, she felt protected and secure.

'So, are you taking on the job?' Brad asked.

'I've already warned her what a tyrant you are,' Susan chirped in.

Brad made a sad face and appealed to Maddy. 'I take it you won't be helping me out after all then?' Becoming serious, he added, 'I won't blame you if you think it's too much to take on.'

'Please stay, Sheelagh,' young Robin piped up, surprising Brad, and now he made an offer that surprised even Dave. 'If you stay, I'll let you go in my tree-house. My dad made it for me, and it's got a sofa and everything.'

Maddy smiled, a little tearfully. 'How can I refuse? Especially when I've been made to feel so welcome.'

Giving a loud whoop, Brad grabbed his son, and swung him up in the air. 'I built the blessed thing,' he chided, 'but you never offer to take *me* into your tree-house!'

'That's because you're too big, Dad. You'd break it!'

~

That evening, when Robin, worn out, was fast asleep in his bed, Brad and Maddy sealed the arrangement with a glass of Brad's homemade wine. 'Here's to you,' he said, raising his glass to hers, 'and here's to the future.'

Maddy echoed his words and drank, hoping with all her heart that things might improve for this kindly man.

They were not all that different, she and Brad.

He too, had come through a bad time when he had lost someone he had thought would be with him forever. But he had learned not to dwell on things he couldn't change. And even then, with his life and plans cruelly shattered, he had recovered the strength and belief, to hold on tight to his dreams.

Maddy thought him to be a remarkable man, a noble example to his young son, Robin.

~

Later that evening, under cover of a clear, moonlit sky, Maddy left her little house and wandered down to the brook. Seated on a fallen log, her thoughts drifted over the miles to Ellen and baby Michael, and she wondered if she would ever have peace of mind again.

She watched the water trickling over the pebbles, marvelling at how the moonlight caught its every turn, making the water seem like molten silver as it danced and twisted, and for one beautiful moment, her heart was at rest.

But it was just one, fleeting moment, when she foolishly let herself believe that everything would be all right. Then she remembered where she was, how achingly alone, and how far from her child she had travelled – and the hopelessness of the situation froze her heart. She thought of Steve Drayton, and her rage was all-consuming. *'I won't let you beat me!'* she muttered.

Fists clenched in anger, her tortured gaze searched the skies. 'Help me, Lord,' she pleaded, the tears rolling down her face. 'Help me to keep my baby safe. I need him so much. I want him with me, but I'm so afraid they'll find us.'

After a time, cold to the bone and wearied by the long tiring day in a strange environment, she set off back to the cottage.

~

Alerted by Donald's barking, Brad, standing by the bedroom window, saw her coming up through the spinney. He saw how she dragged her feet and how her head was hung low, and his heart went out to her.

His first thought was to go to her. From the first minute he had looked into her eyes . . . he cast his mind back to when he had literally bumped into her at the garage . . . he had known that she was running from something – or someone.

He kept his gaze on her, watchful, protective. 'You hide your troubles well,' he whispered. 'You talk and laugh as though in your world, all is well. Yet inside, you hurt so much. Like me, you make a brave face to the outside world. Yet inside, you need reassurance that it isn't too late; that somehow everything will come right.'

As she entered the garden, he stepped away from the curtains, though he kept a watchful eye until she was safely inside her cottage. Like a loyal sentinel, he stayed at the window. He saw the upstairs light go on, then he saw it go off, and when all was quiet, he returned to his bed.

~

Across the way, unaware that she had been watched, Maddy found it difficult to settle. She paced the floor, and occasionally she went to the window and looked out.

After a time she climbed into bed and fell asleep. But her sleep was fitful, and her nightmares, all too real.

~

Steve Drayton was none too pleased to hear that all his efforts had come to nought. 'I'm beginning to wonder what I'm paying you for.' The look he gave the little man left no room for imagination. 'Bloodhound! Huh! More like bloody useless if you ask me!' His cruel eyes bored right into the other man's soul. 'If I thought for one minute you were being paid by others to double-cross me, I swear . . .'

'No! You couldn't be more wrong.' Danny was in fear for his life. 'I know better than to cross you. We'll find her, I can assure you of that. Besides, I'm still inside the time-frame you set me.'

'Why haven't you found her, then? What's the delay?'

'Look, all I can say is, I've got the very best of men out there looking. Somehow or another, she must have discovered you'd put the word out on her, and gave us the slip. There's no other explanation for it. She's obviously gone into hiding and, for the time being, she's managing to stay one step ahead of us.'

He quickly explained the situation. 'We scoured every square inch of the Blackpool area, in a radius of forty miles. We've tried the rental companies and B&Bs; we've kept a twenty-four-hour watch on the clubs and gaming houses up there, and still there's no sign of her.' Putting up his hands in a gesture of defeat, he fell back in his chair. 'I don't mind telling you, guv, I thought it would be a hard and fast case; to be accomplished well within the time and me away to my next assignment. But I swear . . . it's like she's vanished off the face of the earth.'

Drayton wasn't listening. Instead he was deep in thought, casting his mind back to that last big fight between himself and Maddy.

'Danny Boy?'

'Yes, guv?'

'Did you try the local hospitals?'

'Can't say I thought o' that. Why? Are you thinking she might have tried to top herself?'

Drayton's face creased into a wicked grin. 'Nah. I'm thinking she might have had a kid. According to her, she was up the duff. She claimed it was *mine*, silly tart. You can get rid o' the brat, an' all. Two for the price of one, like.'

The little man was horrified. 'I've done some things in my time, but I've never done for a kid, no sir. And I'm not gonna start now,' he said.

'Is that so?' Drayton said softly. 'In that case, you might as well hang up your gloves here and now. And I'll make sure to let everyone know how you'll only do a job if it suits your conscience. You've every right to make a stand if that's how you see it. But you have no right being in this business if you let yourself become squeamish.'

'I'm *not* squeamish, and you know it!'

'If I let the word out, Danny, it could finish you off altogether. Is that what you want?'

''Course not. It's taken me years to get back in.' The hired killer looked indignant.

'Then do the job, and do it well. Afterwards, I'll make sure everybody knows how they can always rely on you. That you haven't lost your touch . . . that you're still as good as you ever were.'

Danny felt physically sick. 'How do you know she didn't get rid of the kid when you two split up? She might've had an abortion – gone to one o' them Harley Street clinics.'

Drayton gave a snigger. 'No way. I know her better than that. She would no more get rid of that kid, than I could walk out that door without being tackled to the ground and handcuffed.'

Leaning forward, Danny whispered, 'About the kid – are you *really* saying you want me to . . .' Disturbed by the very thought of murdering a child, he glanced nervously at the patrolling officer.

'Look,' Drayton snapped, 'the kid isn't mine, all right? She

276

was carrying on with some other man and when she got caught out, tried to use it to snare me into marrying her.'

Danny would have said something in return, but Drayton gave him *that* look, so he remained silent and listened.

'Sharpen your ears, Danny Boy. I need you to hear what I'm saying.' His voice inaudible to others, he instructed, 'I want the bitch found, and soon. I want her *hurt bad* before you finish her off. And if the kid happens to be with her, then you know what to do . . . don't you?'

When the little man fell silent, he glowered. 'Cat got your tongue?'

'I know what to do, yes.'

'And is that a problem for you?'

'No, not a problem at all.' Though his stomach turned over at the very idea.

'Then you'd best get on with it, hadn't you?'

Danny nodded. In his haste to put space between him and Drayton, he felt a pang of sympathy for Maddy. 'Jeeze! You can't blame the woman for keeping her head down,' he muttered. 'Not with that crazy bastard on her tail.'

All the same, because he knew no other trade, and because he desperately needed to earn the trust of others, he would do the job he was being paid for.

Above all else, his reputation – and his livelihood – depended on it.

~

Behind him, Drayton seemed to have met his match, in the bulky form of prisoner Armstrong.

While Drayton was searched, Armstrong was kept waiting a short distance away, under the eagle eye of the second officer.

It was when Drayton and Armstrong were ushered to the outer door and Armstrong turned to look at him, that Drayton felt the full weight of the other man's loathing.

The feeling was mutual, and of this Drayton left the other man in no doubt.

So far, they had each managed to stay on the right side of commonsense.

But the brooding atmosphere intensifying between them, kept all the other inmates at bay.

CHAPTER NINETEEN

'Ellen!' poking his head in through the open kitchen window, Bob shouted for his granddaughter. Abba's new hit, 'Chiquitita', was blaring out on Radio I, and Ellen was warbling along to it. '*Ellen!* The phone's ringing! I can't go in, because I'm up to my neck in it.' With new spring flowers scattered all over the bench, he had part-emptied the flower barrel and was now in the middle of refilling it with fresh soil. 'ELLEN!' he bawled. The phone was insistent, and still no sign of her.

'All right! I'm on my way, don't panic.' With the child in her arms, she ran to the radio, turned it off and snatched up the phone in the hall. 'Hello?' A pause, then, 'Oh Maddy – how are you? Is everything all right?'

There was a time, not so long ago, when if she heard Maddy's voice, a smile would light up her face. But not today. In fact, not for these past few weeks. Since she had grown ever closer to baby Michael, the idea of Maddy claiming him back was devastating.

'I'm fine. And how are you and Grandad Bob?'

'We're both well. In fact, Grandad's outside in the back garden at the moment, pulling out the winter plants and replacing them with summer ones, and making one hell of a mess in the process!'

'Well, give him my love,' Maddy said, and then, her voice full of yearning, she asked, 'So, how's my baby?' Maddy wanted to know everything. 'Is that bothersome tooth through yet? Has his hair thickened up? Oh, and what about—'

'Hey! Hang on – give me a chance and I'll tell you,' Ellen laughed. 'Michael is absolutely thriving. His tooth is just about through, with the one next to it beginning to show. So as you can imagine, it's sleepless nights for everyone. His cheeks are red, and he's dribbling so much I have to keep changing his bibs. And he's chewing on everything in sight. He's doing so well with his feeding, Maddy. We've got him on mashed-up vegetables and gravy and bananas and stewed apple. He eats every scrap.'

'I miss him so much.' Maddy tried hard not to let it show, but the tremor in her voice told it all. 'I want to come back. I want to see him, to hold him in my arms.' The tears broke through. 'Oh Ellen, I don't know if I can stay away any more. I'm missing everything: his first tooth, cuddling him and feeding him, hearing his little baby noises. Even the sleepless nights. How long will it be before he starts crawling, then taking his first step?' She burst out sobbing. 'Have I made a big mistake in thinking it was better for me to leave and keep you all safe? Every day seems like a lifetime away from him . . . from all of you.'

Hearing the sobs on the phone, the child in Ellen's arms began to wriggle and whimper. 'Just a minute,' Ellen told Maddy. Putting the baby on the floor, propped up between her feet, she gave him a rusk to suck and picked up the receiver again.

Lowering her voice, Ellen tried to calm her. 'Take it easy, love. Think what you're saying. You were not wrong in going away. You *have* kept us safe in doing that, and what happened a fortnight ago makes that crystal clear. You know exactly what I'm talking about: why would the hospital ring up and ask permission to give out our address? Apparently, somebody was asking after you and Michael. That somebody was out to find you by any means. So don't even think about coming back just yet.'

There was a long, painful pause, during which Maddy realised that Ellen was talking sense. 'You did what we agreed, didn't you?' she asked in a trembling voice. 'You told them they were not to give out the address under any circumstances?'

'Of course! I already told you. I said I was moving to Scotland the very next day, anyway, just to put them off the scent. And like I said, they assured me they would do as I asked – me being you, of course.'

'And you've heard nothing since?'

'Not a word. But it doesn't mean to say they won't try another way to find you. So, for now, Maddy, you must stay where you are. Promise me you won't think about coming back – not until we're sure they're not watching the place.'

Maddy took a moment to answer. Then: 'Ellen, I've been thinking about something. In fact, it's been on my mind a lot lately.'

'Go on then, tell me.'

'Well, I've been wondering – what if you came here? Bring little Michael, and the three of us could spend a few days together.'

'Maddy! Are you crazy?'

'I don't think so. I mean, they don't know where I am, do they? You could travel at night . . . Oh please, Ellen! I miss you and Michael so much. I look at the photographs you send, and I see how he's growing, and I can't bear it.' The main worry she had, was, 'If he doesn't see me soon, he won't know who I am. And that scares me.'

'Listen to me, Maddy,' Ellen began. 'I didn't tell you this before, because I didn't want you to worry.' She was amazed at how easily the awful lie came to her mind. 'The last time me and Grandad took Michael out, I couldn't shake off the feeling that we were being watched.'

Having begun the lie, she elaborated, 'I can't explain it, and as far as I know, we were not followed. But it's worrying all the same. They obviously know you had Steve Drayton's child. And I dare say they'll keep scouring the area to find you.'

'Why didn't you tell me this before?' This was the last thing Maddy wanted. 'Thankfully, they're obviously looking for *me*, not you, and hopefully the ones who are looking will not know you by sight. But you should have told me. I need you to tell me every little thing that happens. I don't want to be kept in the dark.'

Her ploy had worked. Ellen felt desperately ashamed, but she couldn't risk losing 'her' baby. 'So now you can see why I don't think it would be a good idea for us to travel down to see you. And the reason I didn't tell you was because I didn't want to frighten you. But, like you just said, I'm probably not on his list, and hopefully, they won't know me by sight. So, as long as I keep a low profile and we all stay away from each other, we should all be safe.'

She added a sweetener. 'We will come and see you one day, I promise. But not yet.' Before Maddy could comment any further, she skilfully changed the subject. 'What about you, Maddy? How's it going?'

Still uneasy after Ellen's warning, Maddy told her that, 'It's going okay. This is such a lovely place, and my boss, Brad, is kind and generous, as are the neighbours, especially Sue, who is the mother of Dave, Robin's best friend.'

'So you're keeping busy then?'

'I'm working every minute I can. It helps keep me sane. I'm earning decent money, which I can put away, because the cottage is rent free. The only real money I spend is what I send you and Michael, so my savings are building up really well.'

Anticipating Ellen's next question, she added, 'I haven't opened a bank account, because I don't want to use my real name So, I put the cash safely away, where I can find it quickly if I need to.'

'This Sue sounds like a nice person.'

'She is – they all are. Even so, the loneliness is awful. It's not so bad during the day, but when my work is done and I go back to the cottage, I shut the door behind me and I'm so alone. I can't stop thinking about you all back home. I want to be with my baby; I need to see you and Grandad. The truth is, even though Brad is a lovely man, and a dear friend, I can't help but feel isolated.'

They chatted on, with Maddy asking a myriad questions about life at number 8 Ackerman Street, and even about Nosy Nora next door.

'Oh, and Raymond rang again.' Ellen was always cautious when mentioning Raymond. 'He asked again where you were exactly, but I told him he should send all his messages through me.'

'Did he understand why? Did you tell him that the fewer people who know, the better?'

'Yes, and he fully understood.'

'And did you give him my love, like I said?'

'I did, and he sends his back. Also, he says you're not to come back here, until such a time as Drayton might stop looking.'

'Oh.' Maddy was surprised. 'Does Raymond really think he will stop looking, one day?'

'Well, he reckons that if they search long enough and still don't find you, Drayton just might turn his mind to other matters. Besides, it's bound to be costing him an arm and a leg paying for these people to track you down.'

Maddy fell silent, her mind going back over that night and the words he had uttered as he was taken away. She muttered them now: *'Keep looking over your shoulder . . . wherever you go, I'll find you.'*

'Maddy?' Ellen's voice echoed down the receiver. 'Maddy, are you still there?'

'I'm here. Sorry, I was just thinking.'

'About what?'

'About what Raymond said . . . that *he* might call a halt because it's costing him money.' There was no doubt in Maddy's mind; 'Raymond is wrong. The cost of tracking me down won't bother a man like *him*. It's a matter of principle, as far as *he's* concerned.'

'But surely he can't keep a contract out on you forever?'

Maddy enlightened her. 'If he has to, yes. Especially when he's so sure I blew the whistle on him. That is something he *can't* let go. Believe me, Ellen, however much it costs him, and however long it takes, he won't stop until he finds me. I *know* him. Alice knew him, too. His enemies know him even better, and they would tell you the same. He is a man feared by many people, and for good reason. He's never been known to issue a threat, and not see it through. It's a pride thing – a show of power to keep the troops in order. No, Ellen, trust me. That bastard will never let it rest.'

There was a moment of silence at each end, as the two of them contemplated Maddy's foreboding words.

In a quiet, shaking voice, Ellen broke the silence. 'Maddy, from what you've just told me, you must realise, you can *never* come back here. We have to find another way. We have to try and outwit both him, and his cronies. Let them scour this area all they like but it's only a matter of time before they realise you're not here any more. That's when they might look else-where – so when their guard is down, we'll make our move. We'll keep them foxed if we can.'

'All right, Ellen.' Maddy gave a deep, heartbroken sigh. 'Meantime, please . . . be careful. Look, I'd better go. I'm in the phone box on the village green, and there's someone wait-ing to use it.'

They said their goodbyes and for a long time, Ellen remained by the phone as the baby gurgled at her feet. It made her heart sore to think that Maddy might one day take him away from her.

The more she thought on it, the more panic-stricken she became.

With all the tenderness of a mother, she gathered the sleepy baby into her arms and began to quietly rock him, removing his bib and wiping his sticky hands with it. 'Your other mammy wants you back,' she murmured, lovingly stroking his face with the tip of her finger. 'She wants to take you away from me. But we can't have that, can we? Especially when it was her who put you in danger, when she got on the wrong side of *him* – that monster, your daddy. And now he wants to kill her *and* you! But I won't let him. I'll keep you safe . . . like I always do.'

The look of love she gave him was all-enveloping. 'She went away – and now she thinks she has a right to reclaim you. And that's a shame, because she can't have you. *You're mine now, my own little boy.*

Chucking his chin, she made him smile, that curiously wonky smile that babies make. 'You see, she gave up all rights to you when she went out the door. So now, it's only fair that you belong to me. You're *my* baby . . . not hers! *I'm* your mammy now, and that's the way it should be.' She kissed the top of his downy head, and his little nose.

Grandad Bob opened the kitchen door and called through: 'Was that Maddy on the phone?'

'No.' In her misguided belief that she had a right to keep the child, Ellen was becoming an accomplished liar. 'It was just a wrong number.'

'Oh dear. So that makes a fortnight since we heard from her. Do you think everything's all right wi' the lass?'

'Perhaps she finds it hard to get to a phone.' Ellen did not want to raise his suspicions, though she was not averse to letting him believe that Maddy had started to shift away from her son. 'Mind you, if it were me, I'd move heaven and earth to find out how my son was.'

'Oh, I don't think it's anything to do with her not wanting to ask after him.' He was shaken by Ellen's comment. 'Happen her aunt has taken a turn for the worst and she doesn't want to worry us.' His voice fell to a mumble. 'All the same, I can't understand why we haven't heard from her in almost two weeks, when prior to that, she was calling every other day.'

Ellen was secretly disappointed that her grandfather had dismissed her comment as unbelievable. 'Never mind how fond he is of her now,' she told the child, carrying him upstairs for a nappy change and a sleep, 'at least the seed is set. The more I work on him, the sooner he'll come to believe that you've been well and truly deserted.'

She felt for Maddy, and she meant her no real harm. But after caring for that small being for several months now, she had long seen him as her sole responsibility.

The deep love and commitment she felt for Maddy's child had crept up on her, until now it was an obsession. Almost without realising it, Ellen had forgotten the delicate role which Maddy had entrusted to her. Now, at whatever cost, she would lie, cheat, fight tooth and nail, to keep him with her.

She was not able to realise how the taking of something that was never yours, could be a dangerous thing.

CHAPTER TWENTY

AFTER THE CONVERSATION with Ellen, Maddy felt empty and afraid. I don't know how much longer I can go on like this, she thought. She couldn't relax, couldn't sleep and now, with that disturbing phone call from the hospital playing on her mind, she was at her wit's end. 'I hope Ellen really has settled it once and for all,' she told herself worriedly. 'But I should have realised. *He* knew I was expecting his child. After his man saw me, it was inevitable that they would check all the local maternity units.'

There were consolations though. Firstly, she did not have Michael with her when she was seen in Lytham, and secondly, Ellen had dealt wisely with the query from the hospital.

So, with luck, *he* had discovered nothing about his son – although, knowing his cruel and vengeful nature, it was likely that he had given the order for both her and her child to be punished. And it was that which haunted her.

The thought followed her as she worked through the day – and later, when she went to the barn to tidy up and sweep the earthen floor. The thought of her son being murdered because of her, was too shocking to contemplate. That alone was her prime reason for leaving little Michael. It was hard – at times unbearable. But in the light of *that man*'s determination, and Ellen's recent warnings, she was given no choice.

'Penny for them?'

Momentarily startled, Maddy swung round. 'Oh, Brad!' She visibly relaxed. 'I didn't hear you come in.'

'That's because you were deep in thought, as usual,' he remarked with a half-smile. 'I called you as soon as I came through the door, but you were miles away, in a world of your own.'

'Sorry.' For his own sake, she hoped he would not become too curious. She bent her head to stroke Donald, who had lolloped in behind his master.

The half-smile became an expression of concern. 'Something's worrying you, isn't it, Sheelagh?'

Maddy shook her head, but made no reply.

He observed her for a moment, before offering encouragingly, 'I do want to help. You know that, don't you?' Approaching closer, he placed his hands on her shoulders. 'I've known since that first day – you're in some kind of trouble, aren't you?'

When again she shook her head, there was something in her eyes, a kind of silent plea, that made him determined to help. 'You don't trust me – is that it?'

'No! I mean yes, of course I trust you. But honestly, there's nothing—'

He placed a finger gently over her lips. Then, without removing it he told her quietly. 'You mean a lot to me, Sheelagh, and it hurts to see you upset. We both know there's something playing on your mind. Tell me what it is, and I give you my word, it won't go any further.'

Maddy had never felt closer to him than she did right now. Dangerously close. 'Why do you want to help?' she asked, fighting tears. 'You don't even know me. You don't know who I am, or where I come from. I could be a criminal, for all you know.'

The smile began in his eyes, then the corners of his mouth were stretching upwards, and now he was laughing out loud, making Donald erupt into excited barking. 'Let me see now,' he chuckled. 'Have you robbed a bank? No? Oh, then are you perhaps an international spy on government work – yes, that's it! It's all top secret and you can't divulge it to anyone.'

When he saw the answering smile creep over her face, he nervously peeped into the corners of the barn. 'Ssh! You'd best not confide in me . . . there might be somebody listening. The walls have ears.'

Maddy laughed too. 'Don't be silly!'

When he fell silent, she looked up at him, all manner of questions in her mind; tugging at her heart.

One brief second became another, then a minute, and still he was gazing on her, and she gazing back, her heart turning somersaults. She wanted to run, to stay, to reach up and twine her arms round his neck, but most of all to run. But he kept her there; the look of love in his strong, dark eyes.

'I'm sorry.' Afraid, she drew away. 'I have to go.'

'No, please . . . stay here with me.' He held out his hand and it was all she could do to turn away. But turn away she did, and then she was out of the barn and back to her cottage, running away from him, away from the feelings that were urging her to go back, to be with him.

'What's wrong with me?' Rushing in through the door, she slammed it shut and lay against it, panting and afraid. 'What do I want from him? What does he want from me?' She began pacing up and down, her emotions in turmoil.

All evening she thought about Brad. She recalled the powerful sensations that had surged through her when he was near. 'I'll have to leave this place,' she said out loud, as she lay in bed contemplating the future. 'I don't want to get involved with another man.' Her feelings were still too raw, and the fear of being found never really went away.

~

After a restless night, she woke at first light and, clambering out of bed, decided to have a hot shower, get dressed in some warm clothes and go back to the barn to finish the work she had started. Afterwards, she would have to decide whether to go, or whether to stay. And yet she was so content here, with him – with Brad. She knew now that she had fallen in love with him. But because of her circumstances, she could not afford the luxury of loving any man, and so she must harden her heart.

With that in mind, she donned her wellingtons and overall and returned to the barn, where everything was exactly as she had left it.

A moment later, she was reaching up to place a fork in its special place on a nail, when two strong arms reached over the top of her and did it for her.

'I couldn't sleep either,' Brad whispered in her ear. 'Every time I closed my eyes, you came to haunt me.' Placing his large gentle hands on her shoulders, he turned her round to face him. 'You're in my dreams, driving me crazy,' he murmured. 'I want you every minute of every day and night. Somehow, you've gotten into my blood, and there's not a thing I can do about it.' Wrapping her to his heart, he asked, 'Say you love me too, Sheelagh . . . for I know you do.'

Maddy shook her head. 'No!' The fear was stronger than her feelings for him. 'You're wrong! I don't love you.'

'Ssh!' He placed his finger over her lips. 'I don't believe you.'

Maddy would have pulled away, but some deep stirring of emotion kept her there, draining all resistance, and with his arms like steel bands around her body, she was lost.

'I need you with me, my darling.' So shocking; such wonderful words. 'I think I've loved you from the first moment I saw you.'

Maddy could say nothing, but when she now pressed closer to him, he knew his love was returned.

With immense tenderness, he reached out to cup her face in the fullness of his palms. Leaning, his mouth was so close to hers she could feel the warmth of his breath against her lips. When he kissed her, it was long and full, awakening every sensual part of her body. In the shadowy warmth of the barn, he threw his coat on some bales of hay, drew her down and began peeling off her clothes, one by one – and it seemed the most natural thing in the world.

Naked now, each being shy as the very young on a first date, they touched each other, exploring, learning every curve. He, tender in every way, and she, safe in his arms.

There was no need for words, because they had already been said, over the past weeks and days, with every glance, every accidental touch, every sweet, lingering smile. The love that bound them had crept up without them knowing, and now, the fulfilling of it was a wondrous, magical thing. There was no hurry, no frantic interaction; just a deep, emotional learning together. An experience that neither would ever forget, or regret.

When the love-making was over, they stayed content in each other's arms, deeply awakened by the closeness they had shared.

'Sheelagh?' Rolling towards her, Brad tilted her face to his.

'Yes?' Maddy thought her heart would burst with happiness.

'How did I survive before you came along?'

There was no answer to that, except a fleeting kiss of reassurance and the hurried whisper, 'We'd best go, before someone finds us here.'

'Would you mind that so much?'

'I think so, yes.'

'In that case . . .' Clambering up, he took her hand and drew her to him. 'Let's go.'

~

Under the early morning sky, he walked her back to her cottage.

At the door, he leaned forward and placed the flat of his hands either side of her so she was trapped as he whispered in her ear, 'I wonder if you know how much I love you?'

She felt ridiculously shy. 'I know.' How could she not?

Clasping her to him he confided, 'I've never loved any other woman since Penny died. But now that you have come into my life, I feel so happy. I hardly dare leave you, in case you fly away, like a butterfly in the breeze.'

Maddy gave a brief, fleeting smile, but her heart sank at all the lies and complications. Why, he didn't even know her real name. 'Are you sure, Brad?' she asked timidly.

'Absolutely sure, my love, and as soon as we can arrange it, I want you to be my wife. Oh, my lovely girl, this will be the beginning of a new life for us all – you, me, and Robin.'

And little Michael, Maddy thought. But there was time enough for him to find out about her son, and her past. Meantime, she had issues to deal with, and with his next words, Brad touched on that.

'I want you to put your troubles on me,' he said, as though he could read her mind. 'Whatever they are and however difficult, we'll deal with them together.'

As Maddy watched him walk away back to the farmhouse, she thought how she would hate to burden him with her problems. They were, after all, of her making . . . not his.

Ellen was right, she thought. If it was even remotely possible, they must find a way of outwitting their pursuers.

Not for the first time, she thought of going to the police. But the belief that somehow or another, Drayton would manage to squirm or pay his way out of it, had prevented her from doing so. In fact, if she were to bring in the police, it could well alienate this good, kind man who genuinely loved her, and whom she desperately wanted to be a part of her future – and Michael's.

With that thought came the obvious one: I must tell him I have a son, she mused. If Brad is serious about marriage, and I'm sure he is, then I must be totally honest with him where Michael is concerned. Oh, dear Lord! Supposing he didn't want to take on another man's child, never mind the child of a convicted murderer, currently banged up in Brixton Prison!

The more she thought about it, the more unsettled Maddy became. How would Brad take such a revelation? And what would he think of her, for having been the mistress of such a man, and of having a child out of wedlock?

That night, she agonised over the problem into the early hours of the morning. Then, after a few snatches of sleep, she crept down to the kitchen and drank endless cups of coffee, waiting to ring Ellen and tell her of this development, wondering what she might say – whether she would be pleased for her, or concerned. After all, Ellen did not know Brad, so she might be naturally suspicious.

At six-thirty, she ran down to the callbox and telephoned the house in Ackerman Street; fortunately, she didn't get Grandad Bob. She hated lying to him, pretending she was with her aunt; all of these lies had to end – and soon. It was no way to live, for any of them.

Ellen had been fast asleep. 'Good grief, Maddy! Whatever's the matter?' Yawning and groaning, Ellen asked her what she was doing, ringing up at that time of the morning? The baby had been awake, fretting with his teeth, and she was exhausted.

Maddy launched into a long explanation, about how Brad had proposed to her

'So, you see how it is,' she said. 'I'm over the moon at the thought of being Brad's wife, but I'm in such a predicament. If we do marry, I'll be more than happy to take on Brad's young son, Robin, and Brad knows that. But at the same time, he will have to take on Michael. Yet I'm afraid to tell him about

293

Michael, and I'm afraid *not* to.' She gazed out at the chilly village green through the murky panes of the red kiosk.

Wide awake now, and on the alert, Ellen spoke her mind. 'It's all a bit quick, isn't it? Are you sure he's not just after what he can get, and then it's "on your bike and thank you very much"?'

Maddy could not be more sure. 'I think I've loved him all along and never let myself believe it – or that he loved me. But he does, and oh Ellen, I'm so happy.' She paused, looking for a suitable solution. 'I've thought and thought, and there is no other way. He simply has to know that I've got a son. If and when he meets Michael, I'm sure he'll love him so much that nothing else will matter.'

Ellen was frantic. This news was the last thing she could have imagined.

'Ellen?' Maddy wondered at the silence. She put more coins in. 'Look, I know this is all out of the blue, and I know it won't be easy. But I do so want you to be happy for me.'

The other girl collected herself and managed to say, 'So what are you going to do next? And where do I come in?'

Maddy took a deep breath. 'Well, either I take a calculated risk, and come up to Blackpool to get Michael or you bring him down here – or even meet me halfway, if you'd rather?'

Ellen was not best pleased. 'So, you're throwing caution to the winds just for a man, eh, even after I told you about the call from the hospital, and the suspicions I have that we're being watched. You're honestly telling me that, after all this time of running and hiding, you'd put your son at risk by taking him halfway across the country? Well, I won't be a part of it,' she said peevishly. 'Seems to me, you're not thinking straight.'

She needed to change Maddy's mind. 'Your man should also know that Michael's father, your ex-boss and sweetheart, is a convicted murderer. And you'll need to tell him all that *before* he meets Michael. No matter how you say it, Maddy, he's not going to like it, not one bit. In fact, that could spell the end of your relationship. Who would want to get mixed up with the ex-girlfriend of Steve Drayton, eh?'

Maddy was astonished at Ellen's almost violent reaction. She put it down to having woken her out of a deep sleep. 'I thought you might be pleased that I've found a man I truly love, and who loves me,' she said, abashed. 'I thought you wanted the same as I did – for me and Michael to have a proper home, not just foisting ourselves on you and Grandad Bob.'

Cursing herself for not feigning a degree of sympathy, and maybe even having risked arousing Maddy's suspicions, Ellen apologised. 'I'm a bit cranky this morning,' she said quietly. These days, lying had become second nature: 'I've been up with the baby most of the night.'

'Well, there you are.' Maddy understood. 'That only goes to prove what I'm saying – that you've done so much for Michael and me, and it's time I took the burden off your hands.'

'And how do you expect to do that?' Ellen asked worriedly. 'Even if you take Michael from me, nothing's changed. The fact that you want to get married doesn't mean the danger has gone away. It doesn't mean that Drayton won't want you and Michael off the face of the earth! So tell me, how will you be any safer than you were before?'

Maddy shovelled in some more 20p coins, admitting, 'You're right, I'll admit I may not have fully thought it through. But Brad has already guessed that I'm hiding a secret; he's told me that whatever it is, he'll help me. And he will, I know it.'

Ellen forced herself to stay calm, but the fear of losing Michael was all she could think of. 'Look, Maddy, this new man of yours might mean well, but the poor bloke doesn't know what he's taking on.'

'I promise you, Ellen, I've already thought of that, and even if it all goes wrong, I've decided I still want Michael with me.

I just can't go on without him. So, this is how I see it. I either come and get him, or you can bring him to me. Stay awhile, if you like, or stay for good. There's room enough, and it would be great to have you near. You're my one and only friend, Ellen. And I do miss you so.' She would never forget how Ellen had stood by her through the worst time in her life.

Ellen remained silent while Maddy finished explaining. 'The choice is yours,' she said. 'Either way, I need my son here when I tell Brad the truth. I know in my heart, that he won't turn us away. He loves me and I love him, and he *will* help us. Somehow or other, Brad will find a way.' She had to believe that. 'So, do you think you can bring him here?' she asked now. 'Or do you want me to come and fetch him? I'll be careful. I'll travel at night, stay indoors during the day, then travel on the night coach back to here.'

'No!' Ellen almost lost control, but there was too much at stake to risk everything now, so she took a deep breath and went on in a quiet tone, 'No, Maddy. The danger is still here for you – for all of us. Look, don't worry. I'll bring him to you. I'll travel like you suggested. That way, we might just get away with it.'

As they made their plans, for Ellen to travel down in two days' time, Maddy was beside herself with joy. The prospect of holding her baby in her arms again, and seeing Ellen, was something wonderful, though she knew the risks were real. With her heart in her mouth, she said, 'Be very careful. Please?'

'I will. Maddy, you know you can trust me.' And that was the biggest lie of all.

Maddy had always trusted Ellen, who she regarded as being like a sister, 'All right. But you must take every precaution . . . keep a wary eye out.'

A few moments later, having arranged to make the journey over the weekend when there would be more people about, Maddy replaced the phone.

For what seemed an age Ellen paced up and down, thinking, making her own plans, determined that come what may, she would not give Michael up, 'You're not having him!' She glanced at the phone, 'I can't give him up. Not to *you* . . . not to anyone.' Her loyalty to Maddy meant nothing compared to her love for the child.

～

Being Tuesday, Grandad Bob had gone into town to place his weekly bet. At five-thirty he returned home to find Ellen sitting at the kitchen table in subdued mood. 'All right, sweetheart?' He went to the sink and filled the kettle. 'Fancy a brew?'

Ellen shook her head, 'No thanks, Grandad.'

'Well, I'm gasping. It were that hot and crowded in the bookies, I were sure I'd pass out.' He went over and looked at Michael, lying asleep in his pram, then made his tea and brought it to the table. 'You're a bit quiet, lass. What's up?'

'Just thinking.'

'Well, whatever it is you're thinking, I'd stop it and think o' summat else, 'cause it seems to be mekkin' yer miserable.' Bending his head to see her better, he asked, 'A trouble shared is a trouble halved. Did yer know that?'

'I'm not troubled, Grandad.'

She had been. But not any more, because now she knew what she must do; although when contemplating the shocking consequences, she did not feel good about it. Yet she comforted herself with the belief that it was Maddy herself who had forced her into it.

～

It was visiting time at Brixton Prison. Drayton's man, Danny, had something to report, and he was not looking forward to it.

When the door opened and Drayton strode forward, dark and scowling as ever, the little man noticed the bruised swelling on his cheekbone. He was curious but would not dare ask, so he waited as Drayton threw himself moodily into the chair. 'Well?' His flat, staring eyes fell on Danny, sending a shiver through his spine. 'What have you got for me? Something useful, I hope.'

Finding it hard to keep his gaze from that raw, angry swelling on Drayton's face, Danny forced himself to concentrate on the matter in hand. 'It's not good,' he began gabbling. 'I tried every which way to talk that nurse round, but she was having none of it.'

'I might have known it. Useless, the lot of you!' Taking a breath that doubled the size of his chest, Drayton leaned forward. 'Did you make up to her like I said – flattery . . . money? Did you offer her whatever she wanted?'

'I swear, I did all that. But she's one of them rare women who can't be swayed by fancy promises. Would you credit it, she actually believes in marriage? Dotes on her husband, so I believe.'

For too long a moment, Drayton stared at him, the tips of his fingers drumming on the table.

'Lord knows, I tried. I followed her like a puppy after its master, offering all sorts of inducements. But she threatened to report me if I didn't leave her alone, so I backed off. You can see how it was.'

'So, is she the *only* woman who works behind the desk at the maternity unit?' Exasperated, Drayton momentarily closed his eyes. 'I'm surrounded by damned fools!'

'The other women were too official – they'd have you thrown out, soon as look at you. But there's a young fella, recently taken on from what I can gather. He's one of the porters, forever flitting in and out behind the main reception desk. As he's going out with one of the nurses, I reckoned he might be my best bet, so I got friendly with him – told him my mother was in for regular treatment with her arthritis. The thing is, I'm making headway with him.'

Pleased with himself, he gave a nervous little grin. 'I've already found out that he owes money, and that his girl is pushing him to get wed. So it's only a matter of time before he's desperate enough to get me the address we're after.'

Drayton momentarily lost concentration. He had other problems behind these prison walls, without having to tell idiots like Danny Boy what to do. 'I don't give a bugger who you talk to, or chat up, or even go to bed with.' In a dark, impatient mood, he seemed to bounce on the chair, his big outstretched hands nervously twitching. 'I want this done – and quick. Do whatever you have to do. Whatever it takes. Just get that address.'

He lounged back in his chair, as though letting Danny dwell on his instructions. Then he leaned forward, bent his head like a venomous snake and hissed out a final warning. 'I won't have that bitch getting the better of me. The next time you come here, you'd best be telling me that you've done what you were sent to do. Or so help me, it'll be *your* neck on the line.'

From the way he kept glancing about and twitching, it seemed to Danny like Drayton was on drugs or something. 'Are you all right, guv?'

For a moment, the other man gave no reply. Instead he stared at Danny as though he was having difficulty concentrating. 'Tell me, Danny Boy, have I given you a job that's too big to handle? Is that it?'

'No, boss. I've said I'll find her and I will. I'm this far,' he pinched his fingers together, 'from finding out where she went after leaving the hospital. We're also covering other avenues besides the hospital. I've got the men on their toes, and because she had the baby in Blackburn, and Jimmy sighted her in

299

Lytham, it follows that she would live in the area, though I accept the possibility that she's long gone from there.'

'Don't assume the obvious. She's a cunning bitch.' Had he once loved her? Drayton thought drowsily. For a second, sweet music – the sound of his Songbird singing onstage – filled his memory, as well as a vision of her seductive beauty, and her smile . . . The moment lingered, and caught inside it, he recalled the sensation of happiness. But then it faded, being quickly replaced by a black wave of fury.

'Look, boss, she's bound to make a false move soon,' Danny whined. 'We're closing in, I can promise you that. It hasn't been easy. Up to now, she's either been very clever, or damned lucky.'

'Lucky, eh? Well, you listen to me, Danny Boy. I'm stuck here in this damned hell-hole, having to rely on scum such as you. You say she's been lucky. Well, *you* won't be so lucky if the next time you come here, you haven't done the job I'm paying you for.' He smiled that wicked, unstable smile. 'I hope you're getting my gist . . . Danny Boy?'

When Danny opened his mouth to answer, Drayton got up, sauntered over to the officer on duty, and without a backward glance, gestured to be taken out.

Behind him, Danny lost no time in getting outside to the fresh air, where he stood a moment, reflecting on Drayton's increasingly odd demeanour. 'Mad!' He scurried off down the street. 'Mad as a bleeding hatter!'

There was no doubt in hs mind. Drayton had made a direct and chilling threat to him. 'If it's the last thing I do, I'll get this job done,' he muttered. 'He wants the girl and he wants the kid. Like he said, I'd better get the job done – and soon!'

CHAPTER TWENTY-ONE

THE DAY FOLLOWING Maddy's phone call, Ellen had finalised her plans, right down to the last detail.

And now, on this Thursday morning, and still in her dressing-gown, she bade cheerio to her grandfather, who was leaving for a day at the races with his old friend Jasper. 'You enjoy yourselves,' she told them. 'I'll see you when you get back, Grandad.'

'I'm not sure I'm looking forward to it,' he confided when Jasper went to play pat-a-cake with Michael. 'I had a real bad night with me left knee, and to be honest, I'd rather go straight back to bed.'

'Aw, you'll love it.' Ellen wanted him out of the way. 'You and Jasper haven't been out together for months, not since he had his hip operation. But look at him – he's raring to go now, aren't you, Jasper, and once you're there, you'll have a wonderful time. So go on,' she said, handing him the bag of sandwiches and a flask, 'take this. There's enough in there to keep the pair of you going all day long.' And then some, she hoped.

After the two men had gone off in Grandad's Rover, she carried Michael upstairs and put him in the playpen amongst a collection of his favourite toys. She then quickly rooted through her wardrobe. After some deliberation, she put on a burgundy-coloured jumper and a pair of blue Levis, together with a short green anorak which she had last worn the night before she left for the bright lights of London town.

The garments still fitted her. In fact, if anything, they were a little loose, though that might work to her advantage, she thought. She then located a long-time favourite, a denim baseball cap, together with her sunglasses, and put both items in her coat pocket.

Next, she filled a large overnight bag with clean underwear, a couple of other jumpers and tops, two more pairs of jeans and a second pair of shoes. She then squashed in a pile of Michael's freshly ironed garments, and a number of spare nappies and other necessities. Then, after pushing the lot down as far as she could, she zipped up the bag and set it aside, next to a carrier-bag crammed with their toiletries.

She then got Michael dressed and ready, and carried him downstairs, where she strapped him in his pushchair with a biscuit to keep him quiet. She had a freshly-made bottle of baby food, two rusks, a banana and two jars of Cow & Gate meals for later.

'Now, where does he put it?' Standing in the kitchen, chewing on her fingers, she tried to remember where her grandfather kept his 'rainy-day' money. He had always been adamant; 'You need to keep a bit o' ready cash for emergencies. After all, banks don't open on a weekend, do they?'

Suddenly it came to her. 'Aha!' She distinctly recalled him mentioning something about . . . Hurrying to the hallway, she opened the understairs cupboard and stooping low, switched on the light. Peering into every shadowy corner, she could see nothing that might be a savings box, or biscuit tin.

Disappointed, she felt in every corner, cleared the shelves and tidied them up again, and still there was nothing. 'I wonder . . .' Scrutinising the old brown lino on the floor, she spotted a loose section and lifted it up. One of the wooden planks beneath was clearly shaped to form a lid.

Hooking her finger under the edge, she prised the board up, and there, nestled in the darkness, was an old baccy-tin. Inside, Ellen found a slim bundle of ten-pound notes; sitting cross-legged on the floor, she hurriedly counted them. 'Two hundred pounds!' She sat there, feeling guilty and small, and for the moment unable to bring herself to take the money from her old grandad.

However, when Michael started crying, she came out of the spell. If only she didn't have to do this, but her money had run out. She couldn't resist treating the baby to expensive outfits, and hadn't earned a penny for six long months, and so her savings had dwindled. The rent money from the house in Bethnal Green was spent almost as soon as it landed in her account.

She would pay her beloved Grandad Bob back as soon as she could, the girl vowed.

The baccy-tin was stuffed back into its hidey-hole, and everything was replaced as before.

Tucking Michael's dummy into his mouth she left the baby and, running up the stairs two at a time, she collected the overnight bag and checked around to make sure she had not forgotten anything.

Satisfied, she returned downstairs and, after squashing the bag into the shelf beneath the pushchair, she went to the drawer and took out a writing-pad and pen. It was time to tell some more lies.

Dear Grandad

A letter just arrived from Maddy. She wants me and Michael to go to her straight away. Her aunt is home, and it seems she's back on her feet again.

The thing is, she wants to be on her own now. Maddy has been offered a job at the local garden centre, and has found a cottage to rent.

She loves the area, and thinks Michael and I would love it too. She asked me to tell you that she's really grateful for letting her stay with you, and that she'll come and see you every so often.

She sends her love,

I'm so excited, Grandad. She's sent me the coach-tickets, which she bought at the other end, so the baby and I have to go now, before you get back, because the coach leaves in half an hour. I'm sorry that it's all so last-minute. I think her letter was held up in the post.

Anyway, you're not to worry, it's for the best. I'll give you a ring when we're settled.

She signed it with a kiss and left the note propped in front of the kettle, where he was bound to see it. Then she crossed the hall to the telephone table, where she picked up the address book and searched for a certain page; when it was found she tore it out by the roots.

The first note had been an outright deception.

The second was a betrayal of friendship and trust, borne out of coveting one person, and envying another.

She held the pen above the fresh sheet of paper for a brief moment, before disguising her handwriting to set down the words:

> *A message for Steve Drayton.*
> *He will find Maddy Delaney*
> *at the following address:*

To be certain she had it exactly right, she consulted the torn page of the address book. Satisfied she knew it by heart, she then carefully folded the paper, thrust it into her pocket, and recommenced writing:

SONGBIRD

The Cottage
Brighill Farm
Little Brickhill
Buckinghamshire

She added a PS at the bottom –

THE CHILD WAS PUT UP FOR ADOPTION.

Closing the front door behind her, Ellen dropped the key through the letter-box, and said, 'Goodbye, Grandad.' She did not expect to be back this way again. Marching the pushchair smartly down the path, she waved to Nosy Nora weeding in the front garden, but did not stop to chat.

Within the hour, she had taken a taxi to Lytham and was walking down the main road front, her eyes peeled for a sight of the man who had accosted Maddy that day. Okay, it had been weeks ago now, but Steve Drayton would be very thorough, Ellen knew that from her dealings, with other 'low-lifes in Soho. He'd be bound to have kept someone on watch in this area.

Maddy's description of the man was imprinted on her mind: 'Tall, willowy and sallow-looking, with thick shoulder-length hair. He had piercing eyes and a trampish look about him.' For days afterwards, Maddy had spoken of him in a fearful voice.

Up and down, backwards and forwards, across the street and down the alleyways; for two hours, Ellen covered as much ground as was possible. But there was no sign of any such man. It was fortunate that Michael was having his morning nap.

Weary and thirsty, she made her way to the café where she and Maddy had drunk hot chocolate.

'Well, hello, you.' The homely middle-aged woman recognised her instantly. 'Where's your friend – I never did catch her name. Sally, wasn't it – or was it Molly? Yes, that was it –

Molly. Yes, I remember now. She loved my hot chocolate, that lass did.'

Ellen smiled encouragingly. 'Molly had to go and see a sick aunt,' she said. 'I thought, being as it was a nice day, I'd take my son for a walk.'

'Aw, the little darling.' Peeping at Michael, she tickled him under the chin. 'You're a handsome little fella an' no mistake.' Looking up at Ellen she asked, 'What's his name?'

'Robert.' Her grandfather's name came into her mind. And it was Michael's middle name.

'Nice name – suits him. But I hope you realise, folks will call him Bob for short. They always do.'

'I don't mind. Bob is a good name for a man. I'll have a pot of tea and some toast, please.' Then Ellen settled herself at the table by the window, from where she could clearly see the length of the street.

A short time later, when she had shared her toast with the baby and was on her second pot of tea, Ellen was none too pleased to see how the café was beginning to fill up.

When a young couple took the table right alongside, blocking her clear view of the street, she gulped down her tea and took her handbag over to the counter. 'I'd best be going,' she told the woman. 'How much do I owe you?'

'That'll be one pound fifty to you, dear. Drop in again, next time you're round here, and bring the babby and your pal. I'd rather have customers like you in here any day than them hoity-toits.' She glanced at a couple of well-dressed women in the far corner. 'Come in here with their airs and graces – never a tip or a thank you.'

Ellen grinned, and bade her cheerio. Just as she was about to manoeuvre the pushchair over the step, she looked up – and there, large as life, standing on the far side of the street, his sharp eyes watching every passer-by, was the man himself. However, he was completely unaware of her presence. Now, much to her horror, he suddenly turned down a side street. It's him! she thought. It's that man! There was no doubt in her mind. She set off after him, pushing the heavy buggy as fast as she could.

Just around the corner, the man had stopped to light up a cigarette. He had his back to her. Ellen took the opportunity to pull her hair up under the cap, and, hunching her shoulders to disguise herself as best she could, she sauntered up alongside him. As she went quickly by, she deliberately dropped the folded paper in front of him. That done, she looked around and began running as fast as she could back up to the main road, while yelling to a non-existent friend, 'Janette! Wait for me, dammit!'

Behind her, she could hear him calling her. 'Hey! This fell out of your pocket!'

Hurrying round the corner, she hid against the wall, then peered back, to see him staring at the folded paper. Then slowly, he opened it out and read it. When he looked up, she could see how excited he was.

Quickly now, she pushed the sleeping Michael into the corner shop beside her and bought some crisps and a magazine. She was exhilarated. He had Maddy's address: he had seen it, and knew the note was meant for him. But thankfully, he did not know who had delivered it, and that was fine. Just fine!

Congratulating herself, she paid the shopkeeper a pound to phone and order a taxi, and then she and Michael were on their way to a new life.

~

From Blackpool station, the pair travelled to Euston, and from there to Waterloo and Southampton, and the ferry-port.

By evening time, they were boarding the ferry to the Isle of

Wight. Standing on deck with the baby wrapped snugly in her arms, Ellen watched as the lights of the mainland shore receded in the dark-blue night.

Ellen had so wanted to change Michael's name, but felt as though in changing it, she might be doing him an injustice. 'Michael,' she kept repeating it. 'Michael Drew: it has a certain ring about it. And if over the years people call you Mick, that's all right too.'

She decided it didn't matter that he had been named by Maddy, because he was his own little character now, and besides, his mother had not seen him grow and flourish like she had. Maddy didn't know him; she had surrendered her right to him the minute she left. 'You're my responsibility now, darling,' Ellen whispered, and glanced up as though talking to some unseen being. 'That's right, isn't it? Michael is *my* son, now and forever.'

Not far away, a woman and her husband had been watching her. 'She's a strange one,' the woman commented now. 'She's holding the child so tight to her, that it can hardly breathe. It's like she's afraid someone might snatch it away.'

'Stop staring, Nancy!' Her husband drew her away. 'The poor woman's probably afraid he might fall into the water.'

'Then why has she come out here, tell me that?' There was something about Ellen that made her curious. 'I saw her inside and she was just as strange then . . . nervously looking about, as though someone might be after taking her child.'

Persuading her away, her husband light-heartedly chided, 'Honestly, Nancy! As always, your imagination is working overtime. The poor girl's probably had a bad experience or something. Either way, it's none of our business.'

Oblivious to the lookers-on, Ellen felt happier than she had done in a long time.

Smiling into the little one's sleeping face, she snuggled him even closer to her. 'I'll work hard to make a life for the two of us,' she promised, 'and don't you worry: nobody will ever find us where we're going.'

She thought of Maddy. And her grandfather. And for just the briefest moment, wondered if she would be lonely without them.

Then she saw the baby's eyes open, as he gazed up at her, trusting her unquestioningly, like a child does. And her heart soared. 'We don't need them,' she told him. 'We'll always have each other.'

Then, deciding it was too chilly out here on deck, she took Michael inside, still pressing him to her, as though she would never let him go.

~

Back in Blackpool, Bob had come home from his outing full of the joys of spring and in possession of two packets of fish and chips for him and Ellen, only to find the note propped up against the kettle.

'By!' he muttered. While he understood that Ellen needed to get to Maddy, he was deeply hurt at the manner of her going. 'Well, I never! What was so urgent that she couldn't have waited till I got back!'

He dumped the soggy bags from the chippie on the table, his appetite gone. What with Maddy's sudden disappearance, now Ellen's, he didn't know whether he was coming or going.

Going slowly upstairs, he wandered through the rooms, and where there had been Ellen and the baby, there was now the most awful silence.

Standing by the door he felt incredibly lonely, wondering if he would ever see them again. It might have been better if Ellen had never come back at all, he thought, because this time, what with Maddy and the baby and all, he'd miss them more than ever.

Half an hour later, he was still there, sitting on the bed, reliving all the pleasant times they'd enjoyed. 'By! That little lad did enjoy the beach, didn't he, eh? Squealed every time he saw a wave come in, and when we took him for a trip to the Pleasure Beach in his pushchair, the look on his little face was pure magic.'

It was that particular memory that broke the old chap's resolve, because now he could not hold back his emotions. He laughed and cried, but after a time he began to deal with the knowledge that he was on his own again. 'You'll manage all right, Bob,' he told himself sternly. 'You've done it before, and you can do it again.' All the same, it was a painful thing.

Surprised to hear the phone ringing, he went down the stairs two at a time. That'll be our Ellen, he thought, and his heart lifted. She'll be full of apologies, same as always.

Snatching up the phone, he said straightaway, 'Why didn't you wait, pet? I can tell you it were a bit of a shock finding that—' He was cut short when a strange voice asked to speak with Ellen.

'Who is that?' he asked.

'Oh, I'm sorry. It's a friend of hers . . . Raymond.'

'Oh yes, I've heard her speak about you. But Ellen's not here, I'm afraid. She's gone away.'

There was a brief silence, before Raymond asked, 'Do you know where she's gone?'

'She's gone to see her friend, Maddy. I've no idea how long she'll be away. She's always been a bit of a gypsy, has our Ellen – teks off at the drop of a hat, and sometimes you won't clap eyes on her for years.'

'I see.' Another brief pause. 'I don't suppose you've got a telephone number or an address where I can reach her, have you?'

'Yes, I think so. My granddaughter did write something down. Hang on a minute and I'll get it for you.'

Going to the telephone table, he picked up the address book and opened it, astonished to see that the very page with Maddy's contact number and address on it had been torn out. Now, why would she do that? Why didn't she just copy it down? He thought it an odd thing to do, tearing out the page like that.

Returning to the phone he told Raymond, 'I'm sorry, but she seems to have taken the address and phone number with her.'

'And have you no other way of contacting her?'

''Fraid not, no. But she left me a note to say she'd be in touch as soon as she got settled. When she does, I'll tell her you rang, and I've no doubt she'll get back to you.'

'Thank you. I'd appreciate that.'

The conversation was ended, leaving Bob even more confused by his granddaughter's action. 'She must have been in a terrible hurry to rip out the page like that,' he muttered irritably. 'Seems she hadn't even got the time it would take to jot down the information.'

He shook his head in frustration. 'That lass is a mystery to me. I never have been able to fathom her. Too much like her mother, that one!'

~

It was nearly midnight when Ellen disembarked at East Cowes. After travelling all day, with a heavy baby, an even heavier bag, and a push-chair, she was exhausted, but keeping going on pure adrenaline. Fortunately, a kindly steward from the ferry helped her find a taxi, recommending a good boarding house along the coast at Ryde, eight miles away.

'It's called Seaview House,' he told her. 'I've used it many a time myself when family visit. The landlady there loves kids, so you'll be fine. She has fourteen grandchildren herself, scattered all over the island. Off you go, love – I'll phone her if you like, let her know you're on your way. She's a nightbird, so she'll still be up. What name shall I say? Mrs Drew? I'll do that right away. Have a lovely holiday, won't you. See you on the return trip!' And off he went to make the call, after giving the taxi driver the full details.

Ellen was a bit anxious about whether there would be vacancies at Seaview House, and she confided this in the taxi driver, who told her: 'It should be fine, love. The season hasn't really got going properly yet.' This comforted the young woman, as she began to rehearse the story she would tell.

Ryde seemed like a beautiful place, from what Ellen could see in the back seat of the taxi in the middle of the night. Her senses quickened with jubilation. She had really done it! Got away and covered her tracks.

~

Mrs Simpson was a friendly, barrel-shaped woman wearing a large green dressing-gown and with a cigarette between her fingers. She helped Ellen out of the taxi and into her little office off the main hall of the hotel. Ellen had her story ready.

'I'll need a room for at least a month,' she told Mrs Simpson. 'I've just gone through a nasty divorce. The house was sold, everything is gone. But I did secure a decent settlement. So now, I'm here to have a little holiday and to decide a future for my baby and myself.'

'Divorces are sad things.' The large woman spoke from experience. 'One of my own daughters has just spilt from her husband and it's heartbreaking for the children. You do right to take a breather. All I need is for you to let me know what you decide, just so's I can organise my bookings. But there's no hurry. Take your time, and enjoy the island. And now let me show you and the young feller-me-lad to your room. It's a nice big one, with a cot and its own bathroom, so you should be in your element. I can let you have it at a special weekly off-season rate, too!'

'Oh, thank you,' Ellen said gratefully, following the land-lady's broad rear up to the first landing.

'There's a kettle in your room and I'll bring you up some leftover sandwiches from supper. Just let me know if the baby needs anything.' Flinging open the door of No. 3, she ushered Ellen inside. It was perfect.

A month should be plenty of time to work out our future, Ellen thought tiredly. By then, her little note should have done its work, and the dust would have settled.

She fully realised that the note she had delivered so callously, was like a signed death warrant. But that was exactly what she wanted because with Maddy alive, her chances of hanging on to Michael were slim to none.

Now, she simply wanted Maddy out of the way for good. After all, Maddy had caused her own problems, whereas the baby had done nothing wrong.

With that in mind, and the child secure with her, she hardened her heart to her friend the Songbird's fate.

Not for one moment, did she give any regard to the possibility that, one day, Michael might discover the terrible thing she had done to his mother.

CHAPTER TWENTY-TWO

MADDY HAD KISSED young Robin goodbye and sat him down in front of children's TV with a tray of Marmite sandwiches, and a Cadbury's choc roll, next to a big mug of milk.

'I'll be back in half an hour,' she told him. 'I'm just popping home to have a bath. Be a good boy, eh?'

Maddy was just opening her front door when she caught sight of Brad. Dressed in thigh-length fishing leathers, and carrying his keep-net and basket, she didn't need to ask him where he was off to.

He hurried over and hugged her. 'After a day cleaning out clogged-up ditches, I had a hankering to sit by a cool river and catch a plump fish,' he told her. 'So I just threw on my galoshes, and grabbed my fishing gear. I hope you don't mind keeping an eye on the boy while I'm gone. I'll have a long hot bath when I get back.' Stretching out, he stroked her face. 'You're amazing, my darling Sheelagh. It doesn't matter how tired you are, or how grubby and covered in straw, you always manage to look beautiful.'

Maddy had always been aware that she was no real beauty, although she used to scrub up well at the Pink Lady. But now she thought of her face, devoid of make-up, with her hair all unkempt, and knew she looked like something the cat had dragged in. 'Beautiful?' she laughed. 'I don't think so.'

He strolled with her to the cottage. 'Are you sure you and Rob don't want to come fishing with me?'

Maddy declined graciously. 'No, because he's settled and I want my bath, but thanks all the same. I'll see you later though, won't I? You said we would spend a cosy evening in together – me, you and Robin. That's still all right, isn't it?'

His full-on kiss told her it was more than all right.

'I want you to stay the night,' he whispered in her ear, making her blush. 'I'll only be gone for an hour or so,' he went on. 'Oh, and apparently, Sue has made us one of her famous steak pies. She'll be here any minute, so there's no need to rush your bath. Young Dave will keep Robin amused.'

'Oh, that's wonderful!' Maddy replied, 'how about if I cook a few roast potatoes and a fresh cabbage to go with it?'

'Sounds good to me.' Whistling for Donald, who came rushing out of the house as if his tail was on fire, then slithered to a comic halt in front of him, Brad told Maddy, 'I'll see you later then.' Another kiss, and he was striding away with Donald running and leaping at his heels.

As she watched him go, Maddy marvelled at how easy she and Brad were with each other. Yes, their love was wonderfully passionate at times. But there was more to a true relationship than sexual excitement, and she and Brad seemed to have found it – a deep and lasting commitment which, God willing, would carry them right through their lives together. She knew that tonight, she would have to reveal to him the truth of who she really was – the Songbird, the Pink Lady, ex-lover of a London thug and mother of a darling six-month-old baby boy. But she felt sure that Brad would take all of this in his stride. At least, she fervently hoped so, for Ellen must already be packing for the journey tomorrow.

In spite of the many setbacks she had endured, Maddy counted herself among the lucky ones. She and Brad had found each other, and that was amazing. The very thought of becoming his wife was what made her days joyous – that, and the prospect of having her son with her again.

Whenever she closed her eyes she could see his face so clearly, that tiny, baby face with those trusting eyes. But he was months older than when she last saw him, and she couldn't help but wonder if he would remember her. Yet she could not let herself think like that. All she wanted was to love him, and watch over him, as a mother should.

~

Once inside the cottage, Maddy locked the door and went upstairs for a bath. She lay in the hot soapy water, thinking and worrying, about Ellen, and Michael, and the consequences of confessing to Brad this evening. Dressed and back downstairs, she glanced at the wall clock. Ellen had said she would let her know what time she and Michael would arrive at the station in Bedford. A small, niggling worry began to gnaw at her.

What if she had somehow put them in danger? What if Drayton's men were watching Ellen, and followed her here?

She grew so concerned that she abruptly leaped to her feet deciding, I have to tell Ellen not to come! She needs to stay put and keep on her toes, until we think of some other way.

Try as she might, Maddy could not rid herself of a sense of danger. She didn't know what it meant, or why she should suddenly feel this way, especially after she and Ellen had talked it through. All she knew was that Ellen and Michael must abort the journey.

A few minutes later, having donned her boots and long cardigan, she glanced towards the main house and saw Sue's car parked there, so she knew Robin was all right. Brad wouldn't be back for a while, so she herself wouldn't be needed just yet.

Since this was a highly confidential phone call, Maddy could not use Brad's home phone. She preferred to use the callbox on the village green.

The walk to the telephone booth usually took ten minutes, depending on country traffic using the narrow lanes. This evening though, the lanes seemed busier than ever, with cars and lorries, a cart piled high with logs, a horse and rider, and a group of ramblers who stopped her to ask the way.

'Got to make a detour,' Maddy muttered, 'or it'll be midnight before I get to talk with her.'

Cutting off to the right, she ran across the field and down the steep incline, before veering off up the bank towards the outer rim of the village. The telephone booth was situated at the bottom of Pound Hill.

It was not the easiest nor the shortest route, but except for the lanes, it was the only one she knew.

~

By the time she got to the red kiosk, the evening was already closing in. Delving into her jeans pocket, she found the necessary coins, and slotted them into the machine; the smaller ones instantly rolled out and she was about to run up to the pub and ask for change, but on a second try, the coins clicked in.

Anxiously, she dialled the number and waited; it rang and rang, and went on ringing, and still there was no reply. 'That's odd!' Maddy recalled how Grandad sometimes went out to play dominoes of an evening with his pals. But Ellen should be there, babysitting Michael. 'Come on, Ellen, where are you?' she muttered frantically.

Impatient, she began hopping from one foot to the other. 'Ellen, it's me. Answer the phone!' she prayed. She let it ring for a few minutes, then, wondering if she had misdialled, she replaced the receiver, picked up her coins and started all over again.

When there was still no answer, she began to think all manner of worrying things, then tried to calm herself. There was bound to be an explanation. Then she had another, more disturbing thought. Oh no! Don't say you've already left to come here . . . Oh please, please, still be there. But she obviously wasn't, and Maddy was beside herself.

Maybe Ellen was next door with Nosy Nora? Yes, that was it! She'd have gone next door. Sometimes the old dear would get herself into a pickle. Either one of her light-bulbs had blown and she couldn't reach to put another one in, or her cooker had gone on the blink, and Grandad and Ellen had to sort it out.

Frustrated, yet trying hard to convince herself that all was well, Maddy dropped the coins back into her pocket. Knowing Nora, Ellen could be round there for an hour and more, especially if their neighbour started on about her youth, and all the escapades she got up to then.

Maddy hung about for a while, before trying yet again, without success. Glancing at her watch, she realised it was time to go round to Brad's farmhouse. Maybe she could use Brad's phone after all. He had offered before, but the last thing she wanted was for him to get the gist of her conversations with Ellen.

This time she had little choice. I'll just have to make certain I'm not overheard, she decided.

~

The car was silent and smooth as it cruised the narrow lanes near Brighill Farm. Inside, the two men kept watch, intent on their mission. 'Pull over!' The driver was a bony-faced man with thick fair hair and baby-blue eyes; softly-spoken, he could

JOSEPHINE COX

have been mistaken for a true gentleman. But behind the polished veneer, he was a cold-hearted villain with an insatiable appetite for money and power.

The passenger was hard-faced and hard-cored; possessed of a cold heart and vengeful nature. 'What's wrong, boss?'

'Check that address again – and don't put the light on. There's a small reading-torch in the glove compartment. Cover it with your hand, we don't want it showing.'

Quickly locating the torch, the man in the passenger seat bent his head to examine the address. 'Brighill Lane – yes, this is it, gov. We're on the right track.'

'And have you committed her description to memory, like I said?'

The other man softly laughed. 'Oh yeah. Right down to her pretty brown eyes.'

'So now, we're looking for Brighill Cottage. Check it!'

The address was swiftly checked and confirmed, and so the car quietly glided further down the lane; both men with their eyes peeled for Maddy Delaney's hiding-place.

～

Disappointed and deeply apprehensive about Ellen and baby Michael, Maddy trudged home. It was almost dark now, and very lightly spattering with rain. With nothing to keep her dry should the rain come down harder, she quickened her step across the fields.

She was now back on the road, and halfway along the lane, *as she walked under the light of the street lamp, they saw her*, from where they were parked in the shadows on the opposite side of the lane.

'Seems like our luck's in,' the driver said. 'Get out and slip across the other side of the lane before she gets too close. Quick, man! And remember – don't let her see you! And don't make a move until I give you the nod. I need to make certain it's her. If it is, for Chrissake make sure you gag her before she starts screaming and shouting. The last thing we need is one of the neighbours raising the alarm!'

While Maddy was still passing in the light of the lamp, he shoved the other man out. 'Stay hidden . . . be ready!' He kept his gaze intent in the rearview mirror, watching Maddy as she drew closer, and the more he could see of her, the more he knew it was Drayton's woman; the distinctive sexy walk, the slim, boyish figure and that long rich hair. 'Saw you in the club many a time,' he growled, 'but you never had time for a nobody like me, did you, eh? Bitch!'

Satisfied that the other man had slipped unseen to the other side of the lane, he gestured for him to stay back.

The car was so cleverly hidden that Maddy did not even see it until she was almost opposite it. When she hesitated, the driver quickly gave the nod, and it was too late. Taken completely by surprise, Maddy was grabbed from the rear, her arms pinned tight behind her back and a piece of coarse rag rammed into her mouth. Knocked off balance, she was then shoved forward, her head pushed down to her chest and the rag so far into her mouth that she found it difficult to breathe.

And no matter how she kicked and fought, she was no match for her abductor's brute strength.

Roughly manhandled into the back of the car, her attacker threw her to the floor and, pinning her there with his feet, he pulled her arms tight behind her back until she feared they would snap out of their sockets. The pain was excruciating. She was unable to move or make a sound, except for a gurgling, muffled noise that went unheard by her abductors.

Wheels spinning over the tarmac, the driver was away in a matter of minutes, and the entire incident was executed so swiftly that no one ever knew they had been there.

Bruised and battered, fearing for her very life, Maddy was totally disorientated. Yet she was conscious enough to realise that Drayton had tracked her down at last, and that she was at his mercy.

All she could think of was Ellen, and the baby, and though she feared for her own life, her prayers were offered for them.

She could hear the driver talking to her; in a distant kind of way she recognised his voice, but didn't know where from. 'You should have known better than to think you could do the dirty on a man like Drayton and get away with it.' His voice was soft, and refined. 'You above all people should know, he *never* lets go. Especially when some silly spiteful bitch goes out of her way to shop him to the police. Well, you'll pay now, make no mistake about it.'

There was a pause, during which he seemed to take pleasure in making her suffer. 'First though, before Danny Boy tells Drayton the good news, he'll need a few answers. I mean, he can't report back with only half a tale, can he? Drayton wouldn't like that. Y'see, he's all wound up about the kid. Wants to know where it is, and who's got it.'

He gave a velvety laugh. 'It's no use you holding out, or thinking you can lie your way out of it, because then you'll be treated real bad, until you'll have no option but to satisfy Drayton's curiosity. After all, he has a right to know the kid's whereabouts – him being the child's father and all.'

For good measure, the man in the back stamped his foot into the back of her neck, at the same time growling a warning for her not to get too clever!

Racked with pain, unable to move or breathe easily, Maddy was almost choked when a sudden gush of blood spurted from her nose to trickle, warm and sticky across her neck. She fought to keep her senses, but the pain was too great.

The last words she heard were from the driver: 'Easy, matey, we don't want to be delivering a corpse, or the two of us will likely get the same treatment!'

Desperate to have her off his hands, the driver put his foot down and sped out of Brighill. He went at great speed through the Brickhill villages, then onto Woburn and out of Aspley Guise. Once he was through Husborne Crawley, the motorway was only minutes away. 'The M1 is just ahead,' he called excitedly. 'Another hour before we dump her into Danny's custody . . . and I for one won't be sorry to be rid of the bitch.'

They had travelled a good distance along the M1 when it happened. Maddy had opened her eyes; she could feel the thrust of a powerful engine driving them along, and knew that they were going dangerously fast. She told herself that either they would all be killed before they got her to this 'Danny' they talked of, or she would be handed over and murdered when they were done with her. Killed on the road, or murdered by one of Drayton's henchmen. Either way she would be a goner, and Michael would be left without his mammy.

She decided she would pretend to be unconscious, and that somehow, if the chance arose, she would make a break for it.

She glanced up. In the flickering light from the motorway lamps, she saw that her captor must have realised that she was unconscious, because he was not paying her any attention. Instead, he was yelling at the driver to, 'Slow down, you damned lunatic, or you'll kill us all!'

Having been held up behind two juggernauts and a car hogging the fast lane for several miles, the driver was losing his temper; one minute he was surging forward, and the next he was shaking his fist and shouting obscenities at every driver who got in his way.

Seeing his chance to get out from behind the juggernaut, he swerved out in front of a coach, shot past at speed and almost clipped the car in front as he tried frantically to get back in.

As a result, he was forced to slow down, and allow the coach to pull in front; and all the while there were car horns honking and people shouting through open windows at him, 'Bloody fool . . . shouldn't be on the road!'

The man in the back was leaning over the driver's seat, telling him to, 'Use your head, man! Run alongside, until we can get out of here!'

For the moment, because he was now jammed in, he could do no other, than to run at the same aggravatingly slow speed as the car in front. 'Bugger this. We'll never get there at this rate!' Thumping his fist on the dashboard, the driver was manic. 'I'm coming off at the next slip road,' he shouted. 'We'll make time by cutting across. We'll get back on the motorway at the next junction.'

~

Maddy marked the moment and she took it.

At the place where the slip road ran off, she felt the car brake violently and skew off to the left. When they got to the junction at the top, the car slowed right down, in order for the driver to check the road signs. 'It's right – go right!' the man in the back was telling him.

So, while her captor was still intent on watching the road ahead, she mustered all the strength she could. When the driver revved the engine and started forward, she sensed it was now or never; she reached up, threw open the door and scrambled out, knowing that whatever happened after that, she had nothing to lose.

As the air whooshed all around her, both men were yelling; there was the sound of screeching brakes, then she felt her body thud to the ground and catapult into the air. As though in slow motion, she hit the ground, bounced several times, and now she was rolling uncontrollably down a grassy embankment and into a muddy ditch. When she actually heard the sickening sound of her bones breaking, Maddy was convinced that by the time she stopped, she would be cut to ribbons.

Then all went black, and she knew no more.

~

Maddy survived, but she was badly hurt.

Afterwards, she learned that she had crashed through the fencing at the side of the slip road, before rolling into the ditch below, where she remained undiscovered for hours.

While she lay there, Maddy imagined she heard the voices of her captors, and in her deepest senses, she experienced the feeling of being shaken and moved about. And yet she was told that when she was found, there was no one in sight, no one searching for her – and no reports of a young woman of her description going missing.

~

The farmer's wife was an amateur photographer, who liked to photograph local wildlife at night, in their own habitat. This was what she had been doing when she came across Maddy's seemingly lifeless body, lying crumpled in the ditch, doused in her own blood. At first she thought Maddy was beyond help. She ran back to the farm and together she and her husband managed to lift Maddy out of the ditch and on to a makeshift stretcher, before carrying her back to their home and phoning for an ambulance.

Now, after two weeks in intensive care, following several operations, she was awake to the world.

Maddy opened her eyes, to look into the concerned face of the doctor leaning over her. 'Ah! Awake again? Good girl,' he said. Throwing back the bedcover, he ran his hands over her legs, stroking and tapping and asking if she could manage to move her toes. 'Gently now.'

When Maddy managed to move not only her toes, but to raise her legs as well, he grinned like the Cheshire Cat. 'Excellent! Wonderful!'

He explained that she had been discovered in the field near the motorway. 'You're a very fortunate woman to have been found,' he told her. 'If you'd lain there for much longer, I'm certain you would not be here today. It was a very cold night, and you had lost a lot of blood. Can you remember anything about the accident? The police will want to interview you, when you're feeling a little better.'

Maddy's head was all over the place as she tried to remember. She recalled being in the villains' car and making a break for it. Then after that, nothing!

Now, agitated, as she tried to move, the pain in her chest was crippling. 'Where is this place?' She looked about, realising this was a hospital, but she had no idea where.

'You're in Bedford General Hospital,' the doctor advised her. 'When they brought you in, you were in bad shape. You had many abrasions! A dislocated shoulder plus a broken ankle, two broken toes, a fractured rib and . . .' placing his fingers beneath her left hand, he raised it to where she could see how, in the region where her thumb had been, there was a large dressing. 'I'm sorry, but every sinew and bone in your thumb was smashed beyond repair.'

Maddy let the words sink in. She looked at her hand, swollen with dark bruises and meandering cuts, and she was in no doubt.

He confirmed what she was thinking. 'I'm sorry. We had no choice but to amputate the thumb.'

Maddy closed her eyes. She thought of Ellen and Michael; she relived that moment in the car when she had jumped knowing full well that she might be killed. But she had had no choice. And now, at least, she had managed to outwit Drayton yet again. And her son was safe. A bittersweet joy filled her heart. *At least her darling son was safe!*

She had lost a thumb, yes. But it was a small price to pay.

There was something else. On waking, Maddy had quickly realised that one side of her face was swathed in dressings; now, as she raised her fingers to touch them, she asked, 'My face – what happened to my face?' Of all the injuries he had mentioned, the doctor had said nothing about her face, and the idea of being scarred was the most fearful.

The doctor was non-committal. He called a nurse over, and asked her to stand by while he undid the bandages. 'We had some repair work to do on the side of your neck and face, which was where you took the brunt of your injuries,' he told Maddy. 'It's time to take off the bandages, so we can see how it's all healing.'

Her heart beating fast, Maddy sat very still while the bandages came off. It seemed to take forever. She wondered how bad it was. Had the side of her face been sheered when she careered across the concrete? Did it get damaged when she crashed through the undergrowth and into the ditch? Suddenly she could recall every heart-stopping minute – every twist and turn as she rolled faster and faster, even the dull thump as she hit the ditch and fell inside the muddy green tomb.

The last strip of dressing fell into the basin. 'Mmm,' the doctor kept saying. 'Mmm.'

Asking the nurse to bring a mirror, he turned his attention to Maddy, who was by now holding her breath, afraid to ask. Afraid to know the truth.

He did not mince his words. 'Your left ear was almost detached by the impact,' he informed her quietly. Seeing the look on her face, he said quickly, 'The ear is fine now, and your hearing should not be impaired; indeed, from our conversation so far, I'm delighted to note that it appears not to be affected at all. As for the scarring, well . . . all I can tell you is that we've done the very best we can. The scars will be angry for a while, but in time they will fade, I can promise you that.'

When the nurse returned with the hand-held mirror, the doctor took it from her and held it out to Maddy. 'The first sight may alarm you, but like I say, the scars *will* fade in time.'

For a long, nervous moment, Maddy clutched the mirror to her chest, afraid to look, afraid of what she would see. Then, finally, knowing she must, she held the mirror up.

Horrified at the sight reflected there, she gave a cry, dropped the mirror and sobbed as though her heart would break.

Both nurse and doctor thought it best to let her cry it out. Then, after a moment, the nurse collected the mirror and pressed it into her hand. 'Look again,' she urged Maddy. 'You have to look and see what a wonderful job the surgeons have done. They sewed your ear back on, and repaired all of the other damage. And yes, there are scars, and there will *always* be faint marks. But they can be disguised, with special make-up, skilfully applied; your hair will grow back where we trimmed it away, and in time the traces of your accident will hardly be noticed.

'Please, look again,' she repeated, 'and remember what I said.'

So Maddy looked again, and she remembered what the nurse had told her, but her heart dropped like a stone at the sight of her neck and face. Yes, the ear was sewn back on, and though the skin was raw, it seemed as normal as it ever did, except for the marks all around . . . deep, meandering, red gashes of skin that spread from the front of her ear into the side of her face and down to her neck. The front of her face was bruised and you could see the line of fine cuts that were fast healing. But the damage to the side of her face and neck was a great shock.

Maddy told herself that, considering how she might have been killed, the awful sight of her face and neck did not matter. But it did. *It did!*

Silently, she cursed the man who had caused this to happen. But once more, the over-riding thought was for Ellen and the baby. As long as they were safe, she kept telling herself, she could live with this disfigurement.

∼

The man she had cursed was already celebrating the news that his instructions to do away with Maddy had finally been executed. 'Are you absolutely certain?' he demanded.

Danny assured him, 'The Songbird is no more!' Grinning from ear to ear, he boasted, 'She won't ever trouble you again, boss. Oh, I'll admit things got a bit out of hand, and she got hurt bad in the process. But you said to make her squeal – to tell us where the kid is, and that's what we tried to do. The trouble was, she weren't anywhere near as tough as you think, because she croaked too soon.'

'So now you're saying, we're not likely to find out where the brat is?' Drayton frowned.

'Sorry, boss. But if you need the information that bad, we can start over, see if we can't find out who negotiated the adoption?'

Drayton considered that for a moment, then he shrugged carelessly.

'Nah, don't bother,' he told Danny. 'Let the little bastard get off scot-free. To tell you the truth, I've got more important things on my mind right now.' Glancing behind him, he seemed unusually nervous.

Danny took that to mean he had been causing trouble and there was some kind of a backlash. He wasn't surprised.

Steve Drayton had been at the top of the tree for too long.

It followed that some bolder, younger villain would be waiting in the wings, ready to take over.

Either way, it was not Danny Boy's problem. 'So, you'll arrange for me to be paid then?' he asked.

'Have you ever known me to welch on a deal?'

'No.' Danny knew that Drayton usually paid up in matters of this kind.

'Right then. You sit tight and you'll get your money in due course.'

With that, Danny left, satisfied on all counts.

When Drayton's woman jumped from that car, she had saved them the job of killing her. The description his men gave him, of her lying dead in the ditch, was not a pretty one.

But hey! What did Danny Boy care? He would have his payment, and his reputation was revived. He went away whistling.

CHAPTER TWENTY-THREE

IT WAS EARLY in July of that eventful year of 1979, that Maddy was allowed to leave Bedford Hospital. She was almost whole in body, but far from whole in mind and spirit. The accident and its aftermath had knocked the stuffing out of her, and she felt more disorientated than ever before in her life. She had lost her home, her child, her lover, her career, and most importantly, her identity. She didn't even look like herself any more.

The Songbird, she thought dully, would never sing again.

~

The young nurse Cathy, who had looked after Maddy during her stay in the ward, helped her pack her things and put her medication in a safe place. The Lady Almoner had ensured that Maddy left hospital fully equipped with clothes, shoes and all the other things she needed, for her torn and bloody clothes had been thrown away when she was admitted. Of course, there had been a police investigation into the accident, but they had come up with a complete blank – Maddy saying that she had accepted a lift from a couple in a red car, but had fallen out of it as the back door was not properly closed, due to her own carelessness, and that possibly the driver had not gone to the police for fear that she had died

331

and he might be arrested for manslaughter. The police unwillingly accepted this story, sensing that there was more to it than she was telling, but they were adamant that the driver was guilty for not reporting the accident, which could have led to her dying undiscovered in the ditch.

Fortunately, Maddy was so ill at the time of their questioning that they did not pressurise her. She had given them the Blackpool address – not that they would use it – and her name as Sheelagh Mulligan – using dear Alice's surname – in a feeble burst of self-protection, so that those thugs could not ring the hospitals and find out that she was still alive . . .

In the complete absence of any visitors, Nurse Cathy had become something of a friend. Maddy had accounted for the lack of visitors by saying that her grandad was too old to make the journey from Blackpool.

Now, as she handed Maddy her toiletries bag to push down the side of the holdall she had been given, Cathy asked, 'Will you be all right, dear?'

'Yes – I think so.' But Maddy had no idea where she would end up. All she knew was that she had to get out of here, find lodgings of sorts, and contact Ellen as soon as possible. For now though, it was a milestone too far. She was still very weak.

'I can help, if only you'd let me.' The young nurse was no fool. She suspected that Maddy was a loner, with no roots or family. Using her recovery as an excuse, Maddy had confided very little about herself to anyone.

Lost in gloomy thoughts, Maddy did not hear and thus gave no answer. For endless weeks, this bed and this ward had been her home. Now, she had no idea where she could go – for Blackpool was closed to her, as was Brighill. Her mind went to Brad, and her eyes smarted with unshed tears.

In the depths of despair, she sat on the edge of her bed, her head hanging on her chest and her heart brimming with regrets. Her arms ached to hold her child. Where she had once been filled with optimism, now she was devoid of any ambitions or sense of joy. In fact, she felt like a completely different person – as though Maddy Delaney had been dragged into that car, and someone else had woken in that ditch.

It was a frightening, lonely feeling. So lonely, that for the first time in many months, she began to weep as if her heart would break.

Filled with compassion, Nurse Cathy drew the curtains round the bed, sat down and slid her arm about Maddy's shoulders. 'Let it out,' she advised. 'My mother always says if you're feeling bad, it's better out than in.'

And so Maddy cried and clung to her, and when at last she was quieter, Cathy asked, very gently, 'Where will you go?'

Maddy shook her head and sobbed, 'I don't know.'

The nurse bent her head to look into Maddy's face. 'Please . . . won't you let me help? I know where you can get lodgings *and* wages to help you along, until you sort yourself out. It's not charity,' she added hastily. 'It's hard work, but it's regular, and it's there for as long as you need it.'

This time, Maddy glanced up. 'Where?'

'In this very hospital. They've been in desperate need of general help for a while now, in the kitchens and on the ward floors. The hospital owns a number of houses; some of them are nurses' homes, and some are kept for other employees.'

She gave Maddy a cheeky wink. 'I happen to know they have a vacant property on North Park Street, which would suit you just fine. It's within a short bus ride of the hospital, or a twenty-minute walk on a good day. The shops are just round the corner.'

Sensing that Maddy was interested, she went on, 'You can explain about your accident, so initially, you'll be given light and easy duties.' She gave Maddy a friendly nudge. 'So, do you want to give it a try? I know it's not glamorous, but who cares? It's a job. If you don't like it, you don't have to take it.'

Maddy decided to go for it.

That very afternoon, after Nurse Cathy finished her shift, she took Maddy down to meet the kitchen manager, a small beady-eyed woman called Miss Atkins, with a tiny little mouth and sticky-out feet.

There followed a brief interview, then a brisk walk round the main kitchens, which Maddy would be helping to clean. She was told, 'Because there is a lot of foot-traffic during the day, the kitchens are best cleaned at nights. Does that pose a problem for you?'

'No, it's not a problem for me.' In fact, it was ideal.

'Good! Of course, the work is hard . . . that's why we currently have vacancies. I'll give you a month's trial, starting the day after tomorrow. If you knuckle down and work well, we'll get on all right. But if I need to reprimand you more than twice, you'll be out on your ear.'

Nurse Cathy had already explained about Maddy's terrible accident. 'I have no wish to throw you in at the deep end,' Miss Atkins said, less briskly. 'You can start with the smaller tasks, then as you get stronger, you can take on some of the more demanding jobs.' She actually smiled. 'Don't worry, dear. I have no intention of working you into the ground. Don't want to see you back here as a patient!'

~

The next thing was to arrange somewhere for Maddy to live. The nurse enquired at the staff office about the house on North Park Street, and after a bit of a tussle, and more paper-work and hanging about, they were given the key.

'The house has been unoccupied for two months,' the Personnel Manager told them, closing the big green filing-cabinet drawer. 'It will need cleaning and opening up to let the cobwebs blow away.' The man gave no apology. 'There's no doubt it will be damp and univiting. But that's the way it is, Sheelagh,' she told Maddy. 'I'm afraid.'

Thanking her lucky stars for being given a roof over her head, Maddy signed the contract there and then.

Cathy, the nurse, said she would accompany Maddy to the house, but that first, they must go and have a sustaining meal in the staff canteen. Maddy was happy to do this, as she was feeling very wobbly by now.

~

With its stone mullions and deep Georgian windows, the house had once been a proud dwelling. When they opened the door however, the stench of damp hit the two women like a wall. 'Phew!' Cathy led the way, carrying Maddy's bag. 'I'd best give you a hand to get rid of this smell.'

They went from room to room, and each one was the same – damp and dingy, and filled with second-hand furniture that had seen better days.

'We'll soon have it ship-shape and Bristol fashion,' said Cathy, and they did.

An hour later, with the windows having been thrown open to let the bad air out and the fresh summer air in, Maddy could see its potential. Not that she cared about such things any more. This house was a roof over her head, that was all. For now, she needed nothing more, except to be left in peace, allowed to hide from the world and not be a bother to anyone.

Under the sink they found cleaning materials and a round plastic bowl, and out in the yard Maddy located a bucket with its handle missing. But, 'It will do the job,' she claimed.

So, the two of them got stuck in, and the old house began to look like a home. 'You need bread and milk,' Cathy noted as they cleaned out the cupboards 'and food of sorts.'

'I saw a little shop down the road,' Maddy recalled. 'I'll go and get a few things, and sort myself out tomorrow.' When she realised she had not even a penny, the shame enveloped her. 'I'm sure they'll let me have a tab or something, until I get my first week's wages.'

Cathy would not even hear of it. 'You rinse that rusty old kettle out,' she said, 'while I go and get a few things to start you off.'

By the time she returned, with eggs and milk and bread, and a few treats like chocolate biscuits and a box of cornflakes for morning, Maddy had not only scrubbed and boiled the kettle twice over, but she had also found a pair of clean sheets in the airing-cupboard. 'I've shaken up the mattress,' she told Cathy, 'and I've shaken and aired the blanket, so at least I've got a bed to sleep on tonight.'

Cathy had an idea. 'Why don't you come back with me to the nurses' home, just for tonight?'

'I thought nurses weren't allowed to bring anyone in?' Maddy asked.

'I'll smuggle you in, if I have to.'

Maddy thanked her, but said, 'No, it's all right. I don't want to get anyone into trouble. Besides, now that I've got a bed and food – for which I shall pay you back when I get my first pay-packet, I'll be fine here. Besides, I've got to get used to it, haven't I?'

The truth was, Maddy had lost all faith. She did not intend being beholden, or close to anyone, ever again. Whenever she felt good, and came to believe life was giving her a fair chance at happiness, something always knocked her down again.

They ate their biscuits and drank their tea out of chipped cups, but that was okay, because between them, they had secured Maddy a home, and a job, and for that she was immensely grateful.

'How about I call round after work tomorrow,' Cathy offered as she was leaving, 'if that's all right with you?'

Maddy lowered her gaze. The nurse had been so good to her, but, 'I'd rather you didn't,' she told her. 'Just now, I need to be left alone to sort myself out . . . *please?*'

Cathy nodded. She fully understood. She had seen Maddy come into the hospital, broken in body and spirit, and dangerously close to losing her life. She had seen how the surgeon had carved into the side of her face to mend the damage, and saw the stricken look in Maddy's eyes as she stared at herself in the mirror. And she knew that, even in her wildest dreams, she could never imagine the physical and mental trauma that this quiet and scared young woman had gone through, and would still have to go through, before she was a whole person again – if ever.

Moreover, she wondered what had happened to her, in the moments before she went into the ditch? Something bad, Cathy was certain. Something that she had never spoken of – *to anyone.*

~

They said their fond goodbyes, and afterwards, Maddy walked across the room to the fireplace, where she carefully lifted down the old cracked mirror and stood it on the chair. Then, removing the scarf from around her head, she looked deep into the mirror, shocked at the woman who stared back at her.

For a long time, she examined her face, the shorn hair that had flowed long and thick. The thick tramlines of scarring around her ear and down her neck, and tears filled her eyes until she could see no more.

She looked away. But the image was etched into her mind for all time. There would never come a day, she thought bitterly, when she might glance into a mirror and see the same Maddy she had always known. She might never have been conventionally pretty, but she had sometimes felt attractive – and sexy. Brad had loved the way she used to look. The person in the mirror was not Maddy. She was a sad and lonely stranger; someone she did not know, or want to know.

'They say it will get better and that I will hardly notice the scars,' she murmured bitterly, 'but they're *wrong*. In my mind I'll see them every minute of every day, and I'll know over and over, how they came about.' She was more bitter than she had ever been in her life. 'But I can hide from the world and it's cruelty. And I will!'

Her resolve hardening, she lugged the mirror out to the yard, and then fetched the old sheets from the bed upstairs. Laying them out, she sandwiched the mirror in between them. Now, with part of a broken paving-slab from the yard, she smashed the mirror to pieces, sobbing wildly as the glass shattered and leapt underneath the sheets.

That done, she grabbed the corners of the sheeting and dragged the remains to the corner of the yard. For a moment she gazed down on the misshapen bundle. 'Like me,' she whispered and shuddered. 'Broken. Just like me.'

~

Returning to the front room, she sat on the old rocking chair, closed her eyes and, for the first time in months, sang to herself. She chose the song made famous by Marlene Dictrich – 'Falling in Love Again' – and sang the bittersweet words with all of her heart. In her mind's eye, she saw herself onstage at the club, looking glorious in a flowing deep-pink gown, with her hair falling loose about her shoulders, and her new man standing at the foot of the stage, looking up at her.

She gazed down at him, as she crooned the words 'Love's always been my game', and suddenly he was not smiling. Instead, he had the look of murder in his eyes, and the fear was like a physical presence. With a jolt she sat up in the chair and opened her eyes, staring about, searching for Drayton in every dark corner.

When she realised he was not there, she took in every dirty patch on the rug, every stain on the wall and the window panes, so filthy that you could hardly see through them.

The contrast between the magic of what she had been, and the sad reality of what she had become, was like a death-blow. Somewhere along the way, Maddy Delaney, the singer, lover and mother, had been swallowed up whole.

She curled up into the chair, like an injured animal licking its wounds. Deep in the back of her tortured mind, she feared that the Maddy she had known would never be found again.

She began laughing, a hard, angry kind of laugh that shook her whole body. When she started, she couldn't seem to stop. And then she was dancing madly, twirling in a frenzy around the room, laughing and dancing . . . then crying as though her heart would burst.

~

When, many years later she looked back, Maddy truly believed that this had been the turning moment, when she had slipped into madness.

PART FIVE

~

Bedford Town, 1996

Sacrifices

CHAPTER TWENTY-FOUR

F OR A LONG time, Maddy stayed in her private madness, though now it had mellowed to silence, and simple self-loathing.

Over the years, she had slipped deeper into seclusion. Locked in her memories of a life gone away, she chose the existence of a hermit; hiding herself away in the darkness, not knowing or caring what was going on around her.

During the day she would lock her doors and windows and stay inside, even when the sun was shining, as it was today.

When evening fell, she would pull on her old coat, cover her now long undisciplined hair and partly hiding her face with a long dark scarf. Then she would hurry through the back ways to her work at the hospital.

Miss Atkins considered Maddy to be one of her best workers, and made sure she got every perk going. In truth, she found it difficult to recruit people prepared to work regular nights, and so the woman known as Sheelagh Mulligan was a valued member of staff.

Maddy knew that her strange, furtive appearance made people wary of her but she barely noticed them giving her strange looks. As far as she was concerned, she kept herself clean, did her work properly and minded her own business.

Every Friday morning, just before her shift ended, the

manageress would come down with her wages, and Maddy would hurry home, stopping at the shop before it got busy, to buy enough groceries to last her a full week.

Along with a week away each year in a secluded hotel by the sea in South Devon, that was her life pattern. And she wanted nothing more.

On this particular morning, she sat with her cup of tea and slice of toast, and while she ate, she listened to the radio. Madonna was singing 'Don't Cry for Me, Argentina' – a song Maddy loved for its haunting quality. For some reason, today the music was making her tired. And she was so *very* tired. She was approaching fifty now, too old to be doing the heavy cleaning work.

Afterwards, she could never remember how it happened, but when she stood up to clear the table, it was as though a cloud filled her vision. She gasped, gripped the table as faintness overwhelmed her and the years rolled back. She couldn't see, then she was falling . . . bouncing across the concrete road, before rolling down the bank and crashing from a great height, into the ditch . . .

Next door, Betsy was getting her books ready for college, when she heard the almighty crash. 'Dave!' she screamed. 'Someone . . . anyone!' She had run halfway up the stairs when Dave rushed out of his room in his T-shirt and boxers.

'What's all the noise about?' Robin asked sleepily, emerging from Betsy's room. 'What's going on?'

Since their heart-to-heart talk some months ago, when Darren was being so poisonous, the couple had become much closer and were now boyfriend/girlfriend and passionate lovers. Robin spent as much time as he could in Bedford, as it was harder for Betsy to stay with him in his tiny room in the hospital in London.

'Something's happened,' Betsy said worriedly. 'I heard a loud crash from next door. I think she might be hurt.'

In a matter of minutes, all three of them were hammering on Maddy's front door. Unconscious now, she didn't hear them.

Unable to get in through the front, Robin climbed over the locked back gate to look through the window; he saw her there, awkwardly spreadeagled on the floor, with the table tipped over and the mess all around. Shouting for the others to call an ambulance, he smashed a small pane in the back door, reached inside to unlock it and hurried through to check on their eccentric neighbour. She was breathing, but had a sweaty pallor and it was obvious that she was in a bad way.

~

It took only a matter of minutes for the ambulance to arrive, during which they had righted the table, cleared away the mess, and made Maddy as comfortable as possible.

As she sat beside her, holding her hand and tenderly talking to her, Betsy was shocked to see how Maddy's long, greying hair had fallen to one side, revealing the mass of scar tissue all around her left ear. 'What happened to you?' she tenderly moved the hair over the scar, with tears in her eyes. She murmured softly 'Is this what made you the way you are?'

While the ambulancemen prepared Maddy for travelling, Betsy and Robin waited outside.

'Are you sure you want to go with her?' Robin was concerned to see Betsy so upset.

'Yes, I'd like to be with her,' Betsy answered sincerely. 'I don't think she has anyone else.'

345

'Then I'm coming with you.'

'I hope it's safe to leave the back door like this. We'll have to replace the glass and . . .' she looked about. 'I'd like to clean this place up – make it brighter for her to come home to.'

Robin reminded her of how, that very evening, his father was making the trip into town to meet her. 'If you like, I can ring my dad and postpone it to another time?' he suggested.

Betsy told him she didn't want that. 'I've heard so much about your dad, I'm really looking forward to meeting him,' she said, with a cheeky little grin. 'Especially now we've decided to get engaged.'

'He can be difficult,' Robin warned.

'So can I,' she replied, and knowing how feisty she could be, the young man suspected that Betsy and his father would get on like a house on fire.

~

At the hospital, while the doctor examined Maddy, Betsy and Robin were asked to fill out a form with the patient's details. 'We don't know anything,' they said, 'only that she lives next door and works at night – or at least, that's what we think.' They could give no more details than that, but they promised to find out, if they could.

Meantime, when the doctor called a nurse to undress the patient, it was the very same one who had tended Maddy some seventeen years ago. On seeing the scars, Cathy recognised her immediately; though she was deeply shocked at the way her former patient had deteriorated.

Interrupting the doctor, she explained how, 'This lady was a patient here about seventeen years ago, when I was young and newly qualified. Apparently she was involved in a terrible accident, though they never found out exactly what happened.' She recalled how many times she had tried to keep in contact, but that Maddy had been so unresponsive that she eventually gave up trying.

'Her name is Sheelagh Mulligan, and she works here at the hospital,' she informed him. 'She does the night-shift, cleaning the kitchens and so on.'

With the examination over, the young doctor ordered that Maddy should be treated for iron deficiency. 'I'm not surprised she keeled over,' he told Betsy and Robin. 'She's badly anaemic. Added to which, she appears to be underfed – *wasting away*, more to the point.'

'But will she be all right?' Betsy was concerned.

'She will if she takes care of herself,' he replied brusquely. 'I shall recommend that she stays in for forty-eight hours, until we see how she is.'

While Maddy slept, Betsy suggested that she and Robin should go back and start putting the house in order for her. 'And we'll need to get the window mended,' she reminded him.

He agreed, whole-heartedly.

A short time later, having made sure that Maddy was still asleep and mending, they returned to the house. 'I ought to find a nightie for her, and some clean clothes,' Betsy said. As an afterthought she suggested, 'If needs be, I'll go to town and buy something.'

Their first task was to blitz the house, which they did, hoovering and dusting in every nook and cranny. 'I'm not sure we ought to be doing this,' Robin said worriedly. 'Our neighbour is a very private person. She might take offence at us going through her house.'

Betsy was more pragmatic. 'According to what the doctor said, she's as weak as a kitten, not taking care of herself and probably not eating properly. She might well be cross at first, but if we do a good job, she'll realise we were only trying to help.'

They did not stop until the rugs were dust-free and fluffy; the kitchen was given a good scrub and even the windows were thoroughly cleaned. Then while Betsy carried on upstairs, Robin measured for the broken window and went out to get some glass cut and a bag of putty.

When he got back, he found his girlfriend standing upstairs by the open wardrobe door; her attention taken by something inside. 'Did you find a nightgown?' he asked, crossing the room to her.

Betsy told him she hadn't yet, but, 'Look at this!' She gestured to the inside of the wardrobe.

Robin took a look, and there, pinned all over the inside of the wardrobe door, were a myriad of photographs; each and every one of the same young woman. Heavily made up for the stage, here she was wearing a long, tight-fitting pink dress; there she was clothed all in black and looking absolutely stunning. In each of the photographs, she was onstage, sometimes jokingly posing, other times serious as she sang into the mike, or leaned down to talk with clients.

To Robin, she seemed strangely familiar, but he assumed he must have seen her on TV, or written about in the papers. Not for one moment did he connect her with his past, when he was a lonely little boy who had recently lost his mother . . .

'So, who is it?' He was suddenly very curious. 'And why has she got these pictures all hidden away like this?'

Betsy had a theory. 'Do you remember, a few weeks ago, when we heard that amazing voice coming through the wall, singing to our music?'

He couldn't believe what she was implying. 'Yes, I remember,' he said, 'but you're surely not suggesting that whoever was singing was *her*?' Incredulous, he pointed to the pictures. 'Are you saying these are photos of *her*? Our poor little shabby neighbour?' He shook his head. 'Never! Not in a million years.' But even as he said it, a door was opening in his mind, taking him back to a place and a time when a loving young woman called Sheelagh had brought music and warmth to his life, and to his father's. And then she had vanished, taking her songs and her smile with her, never to be seen again.

'Look at her!' Betsy grew excited. 'That slim figure, that long dark hair – and in the shop that day, you said you saw her eyes – "amazing eyes", that's what you said. "Dark as night"!'

She opened the door wide. 'Look again.'

'I *am* looking! And I still say you're imagining things.'

But he was agitated; deeply moved. He studied the lovely woman in the pictures, relaxed and glamorous, and as he tried to relate her to the sad, neglected woman lying in the hospital bed, he saw a caption: *The Pink Lady Cabaret Bar, Old Compton Street, Soho, 1976; Maddy Delaney, the Songbird, singing the blues* . . .

There was a mystery here, something linked to himself and his father, and Robin was determined to find out what it was.

~

It was early evening, and Brad was ready to leave Brighill Farm to drive into Bedford. 'It would be so good if I could change his mind,' he told Sue Wright, who was now employed by him as a secretary and jill-of-all-trades. 'A man needs his son alongside him. Besides, who will I leave all this to, if he doesn't want it?'

'You can't make the boy do what he doesn't want to do,' she chided, for the hundredth time. Her Dave had been a late starter, and she was simply thrilled that he was knuckling under and studying Physics at the uni. No way would she have tried to persuade *him* to give it up. 'Just as you had a dream of starting your chain of veterinary clinics, so young Robin has a dream of becoming a fine doctor.'

Brad felt ashamed. 'I know,' he admitted. 'And I know it's selfish of me to try and undermine him.'

'Then don't.' Sue always spoke her mind. 'Look.' She pointed to the clock over the cooker. 'You've still time to have a cuppa and a slice of that apple pie.' Her other four sons were all married or living away, and she hadn't got out of the habit of baking for a large family.

Brad gave a sigh, then with a shrug of his broad shoulders, he relented. 'Oh, go on then. Get the kettle on, you big bully! I'll run up to the office and collect that brochure I want to show Robin.'

A moment later, studying the new, shiny reprint of his clinic brochures, he sat with Sue at the table. 'Do you ever miss the old days?' she asked him suddenly. 'You know, when our lads were best friends at school? Life seemed a lot more simple than.'

When Brad made no comment, she looked him in the eye. 'You still miss that Sheelagh, don't you?'

He gave a little smile. 'Does it show that much?'

'All the time,' she said. 'And if I'm honest, I still miss her too. She was such good company, always smiling and helpful; she was a special person. I can't believe she was only here for such a short time. But how cruel of her, to disappear like that, leaving you and the boy so worried and upset! We've *never* found out what happened, have we?' Sue shivered. It had been a mystery as total as the vanishing of the *Marie Celeste*. Sheelagh's clothes and few possessions had been left behind . . . Sue sometimes secretly wondered if the poor young woman had died – or some such inexplicable thing.

Encouraged by Sue's comments, Brad opened his heart. 'You know how much I loved Penny,' he started. 'When I lost her, I thought the world had come to an end. I could never see myself with anyone else.'

He leaned back in his chair, his thoughts returning to the lonely years before Sheelagh had arrived in his life. 'Then Sheelagh came along, and wham! Almost without me realising it, she crept into my heart. She gave me hope for the future.'

'Why do you think you never found her?'

He shrugged his shoulders. 'I did my best – enquired at all the hospitals, and put notices up, and ads in the papers, but she just vanished without a trace. Someone said they'd seen her making calls from the phone-box in the village, so perhaps she had a private life I knew nothing about. She may even have used a false name. I suppose after I asked her to marry me, she took fright and scarpered which, if I'm honest, was probably for the best. She obviously didn't feel the same way about me as I did about her. She went, and I had no right to stop her.'

He gave a weary smile. 'It was Sheelagh who made me pull myself together,' he confided. 'She really wanted me to succeed. She told me I must never let go of my dreams.'

'And after she'd gone, you never did.'

He lapsed into silence for a moment, before saying softly, 'I wish she was here now, to share it with me.'

'Well, for what it's worth, I still think you should have gone after her with more determination – searched the four corners of the earth if you had to! After all, what did you have to lose?'

'Maybe you're right, Sue. Maybe I should have made more of an effort to find her. But she obviously didn't want me to find her, or she would never have gone off like that in the first place, without so much as a goodbye.' That was the part that really hurt. Remembering what it had done to his young son, he felt angry, too.

Grabbing his coat, he threw it on and thanked her for the tea and apple-pie. 'I'll see you tomorrow.'

'Yes, and I'd better get back home to my husband. He'll be wanting his supper. Pass on my love to Robin then, and don't forget to give him the benefit of doubt, both as far as his career is concerned, and the girl he's chosen to be with. Try not to be too critical.'

He laughed. 'Critical? Who – me? Shame on you, Sue. When have I ever been critical?'

Sue remained at the window, watching Brad until he was out of sight. Next to her was Roxy, the red-setter bitch who had replaced the much-loved Donald when his big doggy heart had given out, years ago. 'You're a proud, unhappy man,' she said to the tail-lights of Brad's car. 'You should have gone after her.'

~

It was just after six p.m. when Brad arrived at North Park Road.

When he knocked on the door, it was Dave who answered it.

'Hi, there, Mr Fielding. They're next door, Rob and Betsy,' Dave informed him. 'Our neighbour collapsed and was taken to hospital. Rob and Betsy have been clearing up for her. I think you'll find your son replacing a window he broke in the back door when getting into the house.'

He sniggered. 'It's his second attempt – the first one didn't fit properly. I don't suppose he took the right measurements, but then again, he's not all that hot at taking measurements – unless it's of a girl's vital statistics.'

Choosing to ignore Dave's light-hearted banter, Brad clapped him on the shoulder and set off down the path. 'Okay, thanks. I'd best go and find him then. See you later, Dave. Your mum's looking forward to having you at home next weekend. I think she's planning to fatten you up, so I wouldn't bother to eat till then, if I were you.' Chuckling to himself, he went round the back of next door, and found his son struggling to get the window-pane to fit.

'Oh, Dad!' Robin's face lit up on seeing Brad. 'I didn't think you'd be here for at least another hour.'

'Got my work done early,' Brad winked. 'Thought I'd

catch you unawares.' He rolled up his sleeves, and together the two of them had the pane fitted and sealed in record time.

'Thanks, Dad. I had the blessed thing in once, only it wouldn't fit properly.'

'So, where's your girl? Young Dave told me she was round here with you.'

'Betsy's upstairs, putting the net curtains back up. She's washed and dried them – got a ton of dirt out of them.'

Brad found her as Robin had said, climbing down from a ladder, and looking flushed and rather dishevelled.

'Ah! And you're Betsy, are you?' Brad said. He thought her to be an attractive young woman.

He went to shake hands, but when she kissed him on the cheek, he was taken aback. 'Does your young lady greet all your friends like this?' he chuckled as Robin walked in the door.

'No. Only my dad – I hope?' He gave her a mock severe glance, before introducing them properly.

Brad was interested in the woman who had collapsed and was now in hospital. He wanted to know if she was all right.

Betsy told him how their mate Darren had called her the 'Shadow-Thing' because, 'You hardly ever see her during the day, and when she's out at night, she scurries about, hiding her face and avoiding any eye-contact.'

'She peeks at us from behind the curtains,' Robin offered. 'Betsy feels sorry for her and, to tell you the truth, so do I.'

Brad was sympathetic. 'Poor thing. Sounds to me like she's had a rough deal in life. Otherwise, why would she hide away like that?'

His son told him how Betsy had a theory that she had been a famous singer, fallen on hard times.

Brad smiled. 'And what makes you think that, young lady?'

Betsy herself could not altogether explain it, apart from the evidence of the photos but, 'The woman in hospital has let herself get into a pitiful state, but even through the layers of clothes and the way she hides under that long scarf, she has a look about her . . . There's something really special about her, I can just sense it. It's as though she's in mourning or something . . . but,' she shrugged, 'Oh, I don't know. It's just that I feel she's so sad!'

Growing excited, she grabbed him by the hand. 'Look, Mr Fielding – here.' She took him to the wardrobe. 'I know we shouldn't be snooping like this, and Robin thinks I'm mad, but I think *this* is who she really is.'

When she threw open the doors, Brad stepped forward and as he looked on Maddy's face, he felt the blood drain from his own face. 'Oh, my God!' He couldn't breathe. 'It's Sheelagh! ROBIN, look – don't you recognise her? It's really her!'

When he spun round to look at his son, his voice broke and he was in pieces, laughing and crying all at the same time. 'My God, son! That's Sheelagh, that's who she must have been before she came to us. Didn't you know? Couldn't you tell?'

'It can't be.' White and shaking, the young man came to see. And when he looked closer, he knew it must be her. 'I thought she was f-familiar,' he stammered. 'But wearing those clothes, that stage . . . I didn't connect her with us.' He looked now, and he could see Sheelagh there, smiling and lovely as he remembered her from a boy. How could he be expected to equate this glamorous woman, with the sorry being who lived here?

He saw the joy in his father's eyes and his heart went out to him. 'She's not the same, Dad,' he warned. 'The Sheelagh we knew is vastly different.'

But Brad wasn't listening. He was running down the stairs two at a time. 'Where is she?' he was shouting. 'Which hospital did she go to?'

SONGBIRD

~

Nurse Cathy had finished making Maddy comfortable, after a savoury supper, followed by a shower and shampoo. 'There!' With her long hair combed out and twisted into a plait, and her face glowing, Maddy was sitting up, feeling a whole lot better.

'You look like a different woman,' her old friend was telling her. 'With your hair done in that pretty style, we can get a good look at you. You don't want to hide yourself, dear – not with those cheekbones and those eyes.'

Having grown quite plump, and having acquired a few grey hairs of her own, she leaned forward to smile into Maddy's face. 'I bet you feel much stronger now that you've had a little nap and some decent food. With the iron treatment, you'll be back on your feet in no time at all.'

Maddy merely nodded. 'Thank you, Cathy.' She had been silent for so many years, she had forgotten how to converse.

On hearing the doors swing open at the other end of the ward, Maddy glanced up. She recognised the girl, and the young man, as her student neighbours. But who was that with them? That big, broad-shouldered man with the greying hair, almost running up the ward . . . was he making for her? For one wonderful moment, she thought it was Brad.

But this man couldn't be Brad, could he? This man was older, slightly heavier. And yet . . . A strange sensation came over her. She tried to swallow, but the lump in her throat got in the way. And now he was in front of her, and he was crying. *Brad was crying!* And try as she might, she couldn't even open her mouth to speak.

Suddenly he reached out and she was in his arms, and all the sorrow and trials of these long years simply melted away in the warmth of his love. 'Oh, my darling! I've watched for you every day,' he sobbed, and there was desperation in his voice. 'You went away, and you never came back. Oh Sheelagh, why did you never come back to us? We missed you so much.' He laughed tearfully. 'Donald missed you too!'

Then he held her at arm's length, reaching up to wipe away her tears; he looked long and hard at her; into those melting brown eyes that had stolen his heart, and the face he had cherished in his dreams. And he could hardly believe that she was here, in his arms. He pressed her close to him.

'I love you,' he whispered. 'I've loved you since that first day at the garage, and I've loved you every minute since!'

'And I've loved you' she whispered brokenly. Hold me.' With both arms she clung to him, as though someone might come and drag her away. 'Brad, please . . . *never let me go.*'

~

Watching this amazing, tender scene, the young couple were made to wonder at the pain these two had suffered apart; and they were deeply moved, so much so that for a long time they stood and watched, holding hands, and loving each other all the more.

Gradually, loath to intrude, Robin came forward. 'Hello, Sheelagh,' he said shyly, a little boy again and asking for a birthday cake.

Maddy looked up, her eyes alight with recognition. 'Hello, Robin.' She hugged this fine young man, then held out her hand to Betsy, who came to sit beside her. 'I've seen you two,' she said softly. 'I've watched you from my window, not knowing who you were. But I know, like me and Brad . . . you two belong together.'

~

At her desk, Nurse Cathy too, had witnessed this tender reunion. 'You'll be all right now, my mystery lady,' she whispered. 'Now that you have your family about you.' Checking her watch, she went about her work, leaving them to catch up on all those wasted years.

Maddy pushed her hair back to show Brad the scars. 'What scars?' he said, feigning ignorance. 'I can't see any scars.' All he could see were those wonderful dark eyes, and the beloved face of his darling Sheelagh.

Beyond that, nothing else mattered.

Maddy smiled. There were still many things to deal with, confessions to embark on, and people to see – especially her own beloved son, Michael. But she was not afraid any more.

Nothing in the world could be worse than the hurt and pain of what she had already endured.

CHAPTER TWENTY-FIVE

WITH ELLEN AND MICHAEL strong in her thoughts, Maddy spent a few wonderful weeks recuperating with Brad, telling him the true story of her life, revealing that she was not Sheelagh Parson but Maddy Delaney – the Songbird. Eventually, it was time for her and Brad to travel north, to Blackpool, in order for her to start putting the past to rest and laying down a future based on truth and unconditional love.

When Nora saw the couple knocking on Bob's door, she came out, walking awkwardly with her stick to ask, 'Are you looking for Mr and Mrs Clark? They've gone out for the day.'

'Hello, Nora.' Smiling broadly, Maddy opened her arms to embrace the old lady.

With poor eyesight, it took Nora a moment before she recognised Maddy, and on seeing who it was, she was beside herself with excitement. 'Is that really you, young Maddy? How wonderful! I never thought I would see you again.'

When the greetings and introductions were over, she welcomed the couple into her house, where in a serious tone she addressed Maddy. 'I'm so very glad you've come. I didn't know where to find you . . . or Ellen.' She paused, looking flustered and awkward. 'Oh my dear, I'm so sorry.'

She sat them down, and made a pot of tea. 'Your son isn't with you then?' she asked, looking about. 'Oh, I suppose he's grown up now, isn't he? My! How time does fly. I remember when he was a weeny little thing.' She hoisted herself up and stomped painfully over to the sideboard.

'Here, you'd best have these.' Collecting a bundle of documents from the drawer, the plump little woman put them on the table in front of Maddy.

She appeared nervous, and Maddy guessed that there was bad news to come. And why wouldn't there be, when nearly twenty years had passed? Nothing stayed the same; nothing was forever. She braced herself.

'These are Bob's belongings,' Nora began. 'It was a year ago, lass. I'm afraid he had another stroke, and this time they could do nothing to help him. He died in the ambulance. He had an earlier one – soon after Ellen left, it was. Oh, but he did fret over her, especially when she never contacted him after that.'

While Maddy was taking in the shocking news – both of Grandad Bob's death and of Ellen's disappearance – the old woman went on, 'I suppose by rights these are Ellen's, but as she isn't here and you're the next nearest thing he had to a living relative.'

She pushed them towards Maddy. 'These are private documents – letters and such. I had to deal with his estate, along with the solicitor, as he asked me to after the first stroke, should anything happen. But I haven't opened any o' these.' She was adamant. 'The official things I had to deal with – but the letters are personal things, d'you see?'

Maddy could not begin to cope with the news that her son had vanished all those years ago, with Ellen. A cold horror clutched at her. True, in her period of madness, she had not written, or given her new address in Bedford town, but she had pictured her boy growing up here, loved and nurtured by those two good people. It was another blow, another sorry illusion.

Putting her fears aside for a moment, she told Nora how sad she was not to have seen Grandad Bob for so long, but that there had been a lot of trouble in her life, and she had been unable to travel. The old woman could see from the threads of grey in her hair and the marks of suffering on her face that this was true.

Maddy felt Brad's hand over hers, and she spoke calmly again. 'It must have been so hard for you, Nora,' she said. 'Thank you for your kindness to him, when we both let him down so badly.'

'Well, like I said, he had that first do just days after Ellen had gone. It got so he was having difficulty looking after himself, so in the end I persuaded him to move in here – as a lodger, you understand?'

In other circumstances, Maddy would have grinned at the thought of what Grandad Bob would have had to say about this. So Nosy Nora had got him in the end!

Number 8 Ackerman Street had been sold, and Grandad had turned most of his pension over to Nora, to pay for his keep. The £15,000 he had received for the house had gone into his bank account, and was still with the solicitor, while they attempted to find the beneficiaries.

The old lady leaned forward and lowered her voice confidentially.

'Just before his second stroke, you see, love, he asked for the solicitor to come and see him. Must have felt it coming on, I reckon. That was when he changed his will: he left half his money to you, and the other half to Ellen. He made me a token gift of his Rover, and do you know, I learned to drive an' all! I even took him out in it a few times, although he was as nervous as a kitten.' She chuckled.

While Brad tactfully took Nora off to the kitchen to make another pot of tea, Maddy slowly opened the letters, one by one, praying for news of her son.

It was a good thing that she was fitter in mind and body then she had been in many years, for the revelations contained in this bundle of papers were about to turn Maddy Delaney's life upside down. Again.

~

There was a letter to Grandad Bob from Ellen, dated a year ago, just before he had had his second stroke. The address was Ryde, in the Isle of Wight. As Maddy held the paper with shaking hands, she read Ellen's message of love and contrition to her grandfather, trying to explain why she had done the terrible things she did – of abducting Maddy's child and of deserting her beloved grandfather, stealing from him and lying to him. Michael had grown up bonny and bright, she wrote, and now she needed to make her peace with her grandfather, and also with her dear friend Maddy, whom she had never forgotten. She loved them both, and craved their forgiveness.

Please will you tell Maddy that her son is a fine boy of seventeen now, she wrote, *and that I love him like my own flesh and blood.*

While Maddy was trying to come to terms with all the emotions that arose when she read these words, she opened the next letter, and her heart nearly stopped with the shock of what it contained.

The letter, which was dated eighteen months ago, was addressed to Ellen. Grandad Bob had not opened it, and Maddy imagined that his health had prevented him from making contact with his granddaughter. For Bob Maitland, it had all happened too late.

The letter was from Raymond, the gentle giant from the Pink Lady club, and Maddy read it with amazement and disbelief, followed by a painful kind of joy.

SONGBIRD

Dear Ellen,

I have finally plucked up the courage to get hold of you, after all these years. I need to tell you what's on my mind.

The thing is, Alice says it might be time now to tell Maddy the truth, since her tormentor was put out of his misery by another 'good for nothing' at the prison some time ago. It was bound to happen, and I for one have no regrets about the demise of Steve Drayton. May he rot in hell, that's what I say!

Anyway, Ellen, please get in touch. Alice would like Maddy's address. She needs to break the news gently, so it won't come as such a shock. But I'm sure Maddy will understand how we only made her believe that Alice had been killed, to keep her from coming back and putting herself and the baby in danger.

I hope she can forgive us, but I know it will be hard, and maybe too much to ask.

So many years have passed and no doubt many things have occurred, but I hope this letter reaches you, my dear. It's time to put the past to rights. None of us are getting any younger, and we don't know how much time we have left.

Lots of love – hope all is well with Maddy and yourself, and the boy.

Waiting to hear from you,

Raymond and Alice
XX

The news that Alice was alive more than compensated Maddy for the riveting shock she felt, at learning how the three people she loved had betrayed her.

She tried to think of Michael as he was now. Where had she been while he was growing up? For a long time she had been trapped in another place, in limbo, unaware of the world around her. The years had flown by, and she hadn't even noticed. The most important thing in her life was to see her beloved son again, to hold him close, against her heart, where he belonged.

The news of Steve Drayton having been murdered lifted her spirits and made her utter a prayer of thanks. For too long she had remained in her own prison – one of fear. And today was the date of her release.

So justice had prevailed, and the evil punishments *he* had dished out to others over the years, had come back to haunt him.

As Raymond so rightly said, *May he rot in hell.*

~

Before they left, Maddy told Nora that she wanted no part of Grandad Bob's money, and that she would instruct the solicitor to make it over to Nora, at the first opportunity.

The old lady could hardly believe it. 'I need a new three-piece suite,' she confided with embarrassment. 'I've had this one for thirty years; it sinks, you know, when you sit on it. And I could do with a new set of teeth!'

Both Brad and Maddy had quietly noticed these things, but thoughtfully kept the revelation to themselves!

Maddy was hopeful that the money would more than replace Nora's sagging three-piece suite. In fact, she wouldn't be at all surprised if Nora wasn't able to get a whole new houseful of furniture, a new car *and* go on a well-deserved holiday into the bargain.

As for herself, in the years when she worked night-shift at the hospital, she had saved most of her wages, using only a small portion for her own modest needs. So she had plenty of cash.

~

On their way out of Blackpool, Maddy and Brad stopped and bought a bunch of carnations, which they took to the small churchyard where Bob Maitland had been buried. his grave, Maddy felt the sense of a life-chapter closing. 'Thank you for being a good friend when I needed one,' she told him, blew him a kiss, and said her goodbyes.

Though she would write to Nora and make sure she was all right, Maddy knew that she would never come this way again.

~

Maddy wondered if Brad needed to go back home before they set off on the second leg of their journey, to Southampton and the Isle of Wight. 'I need to be wherever you are,' he told her lovingly.

Sue and her family were taking care of things, along with the other staff at Brighill Farm, and the veterinary practices all had their own teams running them, so the 'Fielding empire' as Maddy called it, could manage without him for a few days, Brad said. Although he wasn't sure about Roxy, who was just as silly a four-legged creature as dear old Donald had been.

'Are you sure you're up to making this trip, sweetheart?' Brad asked, as they settled themselves in the café-lounge on the ferry. He had watched Maddy slowly recover over the past weeks, and though she was truly well now, he was worried that the unsettling batch of news Nora had passed on, might prove to be too much for her.

Maddy put his mind at rest. 'I've been out of it for so long,' she reminded him. 'I won't rest, until all the pieces are back together.'

'I can't wait to meet your son.' Brad had been told everything, and to his dying day he would regret not being there when she most needed him.

As they drove off the ferry, Maddy noticed a garage and

shop at the end of the street. 'If you pull over, I'll go and get a map,' she suggested to Brad. 'We need to find the way to Ryde. It can't be too hard, as the island isn't very big.'

Brad did as she asked, and drew in and parked.

As Maddy came out with her map, she was almost knocked flying by a burly figure of a man. 'Sorry, missus. Born clumsy, that's me,' he apologised. He was a cheery sort. 'Ah! Bought yourself a map then?' he enquired. He pointed to it. 'You could 'ave saved your money and asked me,' he said. 'There's not a place or a road on this island that I don't know about.'

Maddy showed him the address. 'I know the place well,' he informed her proudly. 'Intending to stay there, are you?'

Maddy shook her head. 'I'm looking for my friend. She moved here a while back.' She took her leave, anxious for them to be on their way, now that they were so close to her son. Wishing him well, she made her way back to the car.

Brad was just pulling out when he reached over to squeeze Maddy's hand. 'Somebody up there must be watching over you,' he said warmly.

Maddy was certain of it. 'I know that.' She leaned over to kiss him. 'Because we found each other again.' She loved him so much it frightened her.

~

When they reached the address on Ellen's letter, they found a tidy little bungalow with a garden full of flowers. Shaking like a leaf, Maddy knocked at the door, but there was no reply.

The lady next door was busy clipping her front hedge. She gestured to Maddy, who went over to her, and saw that her garden was overflowing with gnomes.

'Is it Mrs Drew you want, love? You'll not find her in at this time o' day. She's at work.'

She told Maddy exactly where to find Ellen. 'Down on the

esplanade, there's a café called The Beach Place. You'll find her there most days. She works from seven of a morning right through till six at night, sometimes. It's no wonder she had a bad spell in hospital a few months back – run right down, she was. But she was soon up and on her feet, and now that the boss is retiring, she's made him an offer.'

She rolled her eyes to heaven. 'God knows what makes her want to be in debt like that. But in a few years, she'll be able to sit back and let others do the hard graft.'

A born gossip, the neighbour gave Maddy a true picture of what life was like for Ellen, and Maddy could not help but feel compassionate. 'She came here long ago, as a divorcée, she told me, and she doesn't appear to be interested in meeting anyone else. Her only real joy in life is that lad of hers. She worships the ground he walks on! As for young Michael, he would do anything for his mum. Every day after sixth-form college, he's down there, helping her out, and in the morning he does a paper round to earn his pocket money. Ah, but there'll come a day when his mother's debt is paid and he'll be looking to build up a business of his own. The lad is ambitious enough, that's for sure.'

Having thanked her, Maddy and Brad strolled down the steep road towards the café. Maddy felt as though her heart would burst with the tension.

Staying far enough away to get the lie of the land, she soon spotted her old friend Ellen. She was thinner than Maddy remembered, and slightly stooped from all the bending and carrying. She seemed well enough though, tanned and pretty, chatting to the customers and taking their orders. But there was a terrible fatigue about her.

Suddenly, a tall young man appeared. He was wearing a school blazer and carrying a bag full of books.

'Look, Brad!' Breathless with emotion, she drew his attention to the young man. 'My head tells me not to leap to conclusions, but my heart tells me this is my son, lost to me all those years ago.' There was an odd mingling of pride and awe in her voice which now shook with emotion.

Brad could make no response. He felt like an intruder, at the scene of this drama, yet unable to tear himself away. With his immediate concern for Maddy, he gazed down on Ellen and the teenager, and he was deeply touched by the affection that flowed between them; just like the bond between a mother and her son.

Maddy saw it too. She saw how Ellen's face lit up at the sight of this young man; the coveted baby who had been stolen all those years ago. Her heart was sore when she saw how he hugged his 'mother' and chatted to her, each of them so content in the other's company. There was no denying it. Ellen had seemed like a woman at the end of a long road, tired and weary, going about her work like a robot. Yet, when the boy appeared, it was as though she had suddenly come alive.

A great feeling of longing came over Maddy. She wanted to run and hold her son, and tell him who she was, and how desperately she had missed him. But then she watched them a while longer, these two; Ellen, who had no other love than that for the boy, she had cared for from the beginning as if he was her own. And the young man, so easy in Ellen's company; to all intents and purposes, she was his mother. It was painfully obvious to Maddy that he loved her deeply, in that very special way that a boy can love his mother.

The one thing that stood out in Maddy's mind, more than anything else, was *how very much like his father he looked.* She prayed it was only in appearance and not in nature.

~

Suddenly, all the pent-up emotions broke loose and, turning away, she began to cry. When Brad's comforting arm slid around her shoulders, she thought how fortunate she was to have such a good man, hopefully for the rest of her life.

Maddy had come here for one purpose and one purpose only. And that was to claim her son.

Now though, she was torn. She had seen the love these two had for each other. Her heart was like a lead weight inside her. Turning to Brad, she asked brokenly, 'Will you wait for me, please?'

Having witnessed it all, he understood and nodded, and so she went from him, and as he watched her walk away, he saw a lonely, forlorn soul, and his heart reached out to her. Sadly, there was nothing he could do. This was for Maddy to decide.

She did not look back. Instead, she kept on walking. She climbed down the steps and wandered onto the beach, lost in her thoughts and filled with memories of happier times with herself and Ellen, and the child that was conceived with a monster, who had long wanted her dead.

With her gaze fixed to the horizon, she wended her way out across the beach and on towards the sea; and from the shore-line, Brad watched, desperate to go to her, yet knowing he must not.

∼

As the gentle waves slapped over her shoes, at her feet, Maddy turned it all over in her mind; Ellen and the boy, and the way they had grown together, built and shared a life together. And while even through her illness, she had kept her son in her deepest heart, it was painfully obvious to Maddy that Ellen had wiped all traces of his real mother from Michael's mind. To all intents and purposes he was now Ellen's child, and he loved her, as she loved him. So now, if she was to take him away from the woman he knew as his mother, how would he react? And what would become of Ellen?

'Would Michael hate me, if I came between them now, after all these years?' Maddy stared up at the shifting skies, and hoped that some almighty power would guide her. But she felt nothing, except confusion and doubt.

'And if I left him here and walked away, how would I feel afterwards?' she murmured. 'Could I live with the knowledge that I had abandoned my own son yet again and worse . . . to a woman who had stolen him from me? More than that, can I ever forgive her?' Another thought occurred to her. 'If I took him now, and he was desperately unhappy . . . the damage I had done might be irreversible. If I destroyed his peace of mind, could I ever forgive myself?'

A sense of ontrage shook her. 'But it isn't my fault! *She* was the one who did wrong!'

Raising her face to heaven, she called out in anger, almost as though justifying herself to some unseen person, 'ELLEN BETRAYED ME. SHE BETRAYED US BOTH. SHE STOLE MY SON!'

But then she thought of *he* who was at the heart of all the pain, revenge and fear . . . and knew that the blame needed to be apportioned elsewhere.

～

From the shore, Brad had seen her stop and raise her arms, and though the wind carried her voice away, he realised she was grappling with herself as to what must be decided. 'Do what you think is right, my darling,' he murmured. 'That's all you can do.'

～

Far off, Maddy paced up and down for what seemed an age. Then, when the air struck colder and the skies took on a frown, she made her way back, and as she came towards him, Brad saw the look of resolution in her face.

'It's time now,' she said softly. 'It's time for us to go.' Her sad smile touched him deeply.

'Are you sure?' he whispered.

She merely nodded, and he understood. 'You really are a remarkable woman,' he told her.

What she did next was also remarkable.

She went across the street to the newsagents, to buy paper and an envelope, and right there, leaning on the promenade wall, she penned a letter to Ellen:

My dearest Ellen,

I came to take my son away from you, but I now realise that he left me long ago. He's your son now. And if the day ever comes when he discovers the truth, tell him now, I could not have loved him more than you have done.

When he's older, and a chance discovery might tell him of his past, please . . . show him this letter.

I so want to forgive you, but for now, you must be content with the knowledge that I leave my son in your hands, and you in his. Giving him up to you is so hard that I cannot contemplate forgiveness.

In time, I pray I will come to feel compassion towards you, and the forgiveness will surely follow.

Until then, be happy with this wonderful boy, and guide him well through his life. Sometimes I may be watching from a distance, and at other times, I will be far away. But I will think of you both always.

God bless, and be content.

She added a P.S.

You need to contact Nora. There is good news and bad. But in the end, the good may help you build a secure life for you – and our Michael.

Though you hurt me, Ellen, I can't help but love you both with all my heart.

Maddy
xx

She crossed the road and, unseen, she entered the café, went straight to the counter and left the envelope, simply addressed to Ellen. On the way out, she was shocked to the core when Michael smiled on her. Yes, he had the look of Steve Drayton, but the kind, chestnut-brown eyes told her he was not his father's son at all.

He was her son. And he always would be.

~

As Maddy and Brad walked back to their car, Ellen saw the envelope and, thinking it was a tip, she was about to thrust it into her apron pocket when she caught sight of the handwriting. It was familiar. Her heart gave a strange leap in her chest. She opened the envelope and read the letter. Then *'Maddy!'* She ran out to the road and looked up and down, calling MADDY . . . Maddy!' There was no sign of her old friend.

Returning to the café, she read and reread the letter, and when Michael came to ask what she was looking at, she quickly folded it up and put it in her handbag. 'It's a tip,' she told him, adding softly, 'the most wonderful and generous I'm ever likely to get.'

She looked again up the road, hardly able to speak for the lump straddling her throat. 'Thank you, Maddy,' she whispered. 'From the bottom of my heart.'

As the tears ran down her face, she quickly turned away. After all, she would not want Michael asking difficult questions, would she?

~

A week later, after Maddy's preliminary letter to Raymond, Brad took her to meet with him.

Waiting in the hotel foyer, in the little Cambridgeshire village, Maddy was like a bag of nerves. What would she say? How would she greet her old friend Alice, and had she forgiven her and Raymond for what they had done?

She didn't know. She could not tell.

Yet when Raymond walked in the door, accompanied by Alice, it was as though the years fell away, and they were back there in the Pink Lady, laughing and talking, with Alice telling her she was 'too skinny by half'.

When the two women saw each other, their eyes were moist with emotion. For a seemingly endless moment, they looked at each other each with tears rolling down their faces, soaking in the love and regrets, and slowly the emptiness that had been between them was no more.

Now Alice was close, her arms opened wide to take Maddy into her embrace.

Maddy stood up, hardly able to see for the tears that swam across her vision.

Then Alice held her fast. And the long, aching years were as nothing.

'You're too skinny by half!' Alice complained. And Maddy laughed out loud.

She had her life back.

More than that, she had Brad.

And her joy was complete.